Yambo Ouologuem

Yambo Ouologuem

Postcolonial Writer, Islamic Militant

edited by
Christopher Wise

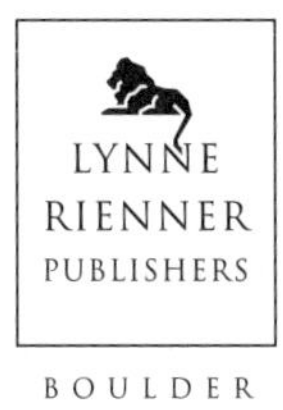

BOULDER
LONDON

Published in the United States of America in 1999 by
Lynne Rienner Publishers, Inc.
1800 30th Street, Boulder, Colorado 80301

and in the United Kingdom by
Lynne Rienner Publishers, Inc.
3 Henrietta Street, Covent Garden, London WC2E 8LU

Library of Congress Cataloging-in-Publication Data
Yambo Ouologuem : postcolonial writer, Islamic militant / edited by
Christopher Wise.
p. cm.
Includes bibliographical references and index.
ISBN 0-89410-861-1 (hardcover : alk. paper)
1. Ouologuem, Yambo, 1940– —Criticism and interpretation.
2. Islam in literature. 3. Ouologuem, Yambo, 1940– —Interviews.
I. Wise, Christopher, 1961–
PQ3989.2.08Z98 1999
843—dc21 98-46339
CIP

British Cataloguing in Publication Data
A Cataloguing in Publication record for this book
is available from the British Library.

Printed and bound in the United States of America

The paper used in this publication meets the requirements of the American National Standard for Permanence of Paper for Printed Library Materials Z39.48-1984.

5 4 3 2 1

This book is dedicated to three people:
Georg M. Gugelberger,
Mountaga Tall, and
al-Hajj Sékou Tall

Contents

PART 2 DECOLONIZING WRITING? OR, *PISSE-COPIE* AESTHETICS RECONSIDERED

PART 3 HISTORICAL RECONSIDERATIONS: ISLAMIC-SAHELIAN INFLUENCES IN OUOLOGUEM'S WRITINGS

PART 4 INTERVIEWS: YAMBO OUOLOGUEM TODAY

Acknowledgments

Many people assisted in bringing this volume to fruition, especially the latter portions, where my indebtedness will be obvious. Nonetheless, I would like to acknowledge here the contributions of the following people: Georg M. Gugelberger, Donald Herdeck, and Pierrette Frickey, for their encouragement and support when this book was only an idea; Nancy Farmer, librarian at the State University of West Georgia, who did a lot of digging for me, far beyond the call of duty; Thomas Hale, Sandra Barkan, and Bernth Lindfors, for their suggestions and lively e-mail exchanges; at Western Washington University (WWU), John Purdy, for negotiating the leave of absence that allowed me to go to Burkina Faso, and Peter J. Elich, for giving the green light; Geri Walker and Moheb Ghali, for their financial support through WWU's Bureau of Faculty Research; Cora Agatucci, Bonnie Barthold, and Bill Lyne, for serving as readers; Jean Hay for many helpful editorial suggestions; Ann Martin, Linda Rhoad, and the Fulbright-Hays Scholarship Program; USIS–Ouagadougou and the American Embassy–Ouagadougou, especially Virgil and Diane Bodeen and Sharon Wilkerson; at the Université de Ouagadougou, Sanou Salaka, Joseph Paré, Jean Zida, Michel Tinguiri, and many others too numerous to mention here; Utë Fendler and Jean-Claude Naba, for their valued friendship and support, without which this project would have been greatly diminished; Nicole Vincileoni, who put me on the right track; James Wade, for unswerving commitment to this project; my father, Robert L. Wise, for looking after things in Georgia; Moumounie Kiema, for goat delivery, Twareg tea, and a hundred other services; Habibou Sinaré, for chasing Ayesha out of my office. Finally, I would like to thank Judi, Zachary, Zoë, Ayesha, and Michael, who made it all worthwhile.

Christopher Wise

Nagaba was the founder of Bandiagara. A great hunter, he once killed an elephant in the forest where the village was later built. He cut off a piece of the animal's flesh and put it in his knapsack before resuming the hunt. Along the road, Nagaba came upon another hunter who told him, "I hope you brought a big eating bowl [*bandiara*]. Not far from here, there's so much meat, you won't know what to do with it." From that day forward, *bandiara*—"the big eating bowl"—became *Bandiagara*.

—al-Hajj Sékou Tall

1

Introduction: A Voice from Bandiagara

Christopher Wise

Readers unfamiliar with the Malian author Yambo Ouologuem will immediately be struck by the wildly divergent responses to his writings that are recorded in these pages. From the earliest days of *Bound to Violence*'s appearance in the late 1960s, Ouologuem's importance as a writer has been heatedly debated by critics across the globe. Is Ouologuem a fraud, a *mere* plagiarist? An apologist for the French? An anti-Gaullist? Is he the African Marquis de Sade, an immoral pornographer and misogynist? Is he a fierce critic of Islam, or is he its staunchest defender? Does Ouologuem deliberately "deconstruct" Western literature, or is he the hapless victim of an irresponsible publisher? Is he a charlatan or a great genius? A madman or saint? Perhaps no other author of the twentieth century has generated as much deep critical disagreement as Yambo Ouologuem. The articles gathered in this volume may indeed leave one wondering if any number of Ouologuem's cannot be constructed to fit the arbitrary needs of the critic, or if the fissures in Ouologuem's thought are greater than the unity that many critics claim for him. Despite the absence of any real consensus, one thing seems clear: Yambo Ouologuem remains one of the most intriguing African writers of this century.

In 1940, Yambo Amadou was born the son of Boukary Yambo Ouologuem and Aïssata Umar (*née* Karambé)[1] at the Ouologuem family residence in Bandiagara, Mali, capital of the Toucouleur Empire of al-Hajj Umar Tall and the administrative center of the *pays Dogon*. The history of Tall's jihad in nineteenth-century West Africa has been well documented by both African and Western historians.[2] Originally from northern Senegal, Tall brought into Mali his own version of Tidjaniya Islam, which he had learned from Sheikh Mohammed al-Ghâli, caliph of the Tidjaniya in

Makkah. Al-Hajj Umar Tall's Tidjaniya faith, which differed from previous Tidjaniya brotherhoods in West Africa, stressed the importance of Islam as a *total* way of life, an all-encompassing belief system affecting every aspect of one's daily existence. Though Tall himself was a Toucouleur (or "sedentary Peul"), his Tidjaniya Empire was based in the heart of the *pays Dogon* among Yambo Ouologuem's immediate ancestors, all of whom were prominent members of the Dogon aristocracy. The Dogon, who had resisted Islam for centuries prior to the founding of the Toucouleur Empire, were nonetheless unable to resist al-Hajj Umar Tall's militant call to conversion. The extent to which Ouologuem's own family cooperated with Tall, employing Islam to their own material advantage, would be a question that would later haunt the young author of *Bound to Violence*.[3]

In Ouologuem's early years, he would have undoubtedly been shaped by the profoundly religious belief system of the Umarian Tidjaniya, his birth coinciding exactly with the death of Cerno Bokar Salif Tall, the renowned "sage of Bandiagara";[4] however, he could not have escaped feelings of alienation from his fellow Dogon, in part due to his family's close ties to the Toucouleur ruling caste of Bandiagara. The ancestral privileges accorded to Ouologuem would include access to the top educational institutions in both Mali and France, as well as eventual inheritance of extensive landholdings throughout the *pays Dogon*. Given the great poverty of his fellow Dogon, as well as the Talls' historical complicity with the French colonial administration (both in the case of al-Hajj Umar Tall and King Aguibou Tall[5]), the contradictory alliances behind Yambo Ouologuem's early identity could only have complicated his perspective on Islam and French colonialism. If we may not doubt the great religious integrity of the Umarian Tidjaniya (both Toucouleur and high-caste Dogon), we may equally be certain that political pressures during the era of French colonialism left few local leaders with unsoiled hands. Another well-known Bandiagara author (and former close colleague of Yambo Ouologuem) has left us with an amazing portrait of the complex relations that formed between French colonizers and local Muslim leaders: Amadou Hampâté Bâ's portrait of Wangrin in his novel *L'Étrange destin de Wangrin* (1975) shows us how both ends were often played against the other in colonial Mali. In this light, Ouologuem's earlier character Saif ben Isaac al-Heit may well be seen as a Wangrinlike trickster and manipulative survivor. It is easy to imagine the impatience of the young Ouologuem with the "hypocrisies" of previous generations, the lifestyles of those caught between the demands of faith and necessity.

What must be emphasized, however, is the relatively *small* impact of French colonization in Bandiagara and the outlying regions of the *pays Dogon*: that is, the writings of Yambo Ouologuem are best construed in terms of the Islamic-Sahelian culture of northern Mali, as it has been shaped by the Dogon, Bozo, Toucouleur, Macina Peul, and other ethnic groups of that region. Not unlike the Concord of the "American Renaissance," the Bandiagara of notable figures like Cerno Bokar Tall, Amadou Hampaté Bâ, Yambo Ouologuem, and others will no doubt stand as one of the most remarkable intellectual communities in recent history. The original voice of Yambo Ouologuem, a voice that first disarmed in its self-confident *indifference* to the West, emerges from within this specific cultural context. In this sense, the real scandal of Ouologuem's "unknown" voice resides not so much in the audacity of its self-preoccupations (and even less so in its alleged inauthenticity), but in the West's historical ignorance of the cultural traditions that have produced it.

Perhaps one of the most revealing cases in point is Ouologuem's critique of African American Islam in the late 1960s, a critique that was widely misunderstood in the politically charged environment of that era. In a series of interviews and public lectures in the United States, Ouologuem categorically rejected any attempt to define oneself by virtue of one's status as oppressed, what he referred to as "the attitude of the slave" (Watkins 34). His remarks in this instance were aimed directly at African Americans, especially those seeking their "roots" in Islam. "Those who want to find their roots," he stated, "should not define themselves in reference to the outside enemy—the white—since the enemy can be black also" (Kuehl 313). Not unlike the Frantz Fanon of *Black Skin, White Masks* (1952), Ouologuem questioned the very existence of the "black man," the "Negro," even the "Afro-American," all terms which he argued are "symptoms of the attitude of the slave," for they originate in the misdirected need "to define oneself by reference to another rather than to one's self" (Interview 135). In his *Lettre à la France nègre* (1969), a book sardonically dedicated to "the victims of anti-racism everywhere," Ouologuem put it this way: "Properly speaking, there is no 'black problem,' only human problems" (10). In contrast to the African American, he implied, the African defines himself not in reference to any outside enemy but rather in reference to his status as an individual within a distinct community: "Universality begins with individuality," he insisted. "It is when you are yourself that other people recognize themselves through your own humanity. If you belong to nothing, you are an artificial man" (Kuehl 314).

On an even blunter note, Ouologuem maintained that "it was a mistake for black Americans to attempt to get back to their African roots through Islamic civilization" (Watkins 34). During the brief period when he lived in the United States, he was especially critical of attempts by African American scholars to connect Africans with ancient Egyptian civilizations. Instead of studying Egypt, he argued, blacks in the United States should be studying traditional African societies, how "*they* were great [but] not in connection with any other [civilization]" (Kuehl 313). In perhaps his most pointed remarks, Ouologuem stated:

> Many mistakes have been made inside and out of Africa about the Arabs. Many people thought the Arabs were a mirror image of African civilization. Look at the phenomenon of Cassius Clay [who] . . . thought that the best way to find his roots—which is to say, with Africa—was to go through Arabian civilization. But that's a mistake. If he had read the Qur'an—the Holy Scriptures—he would have found in it a code defining the status of slaves, for the slave trade is inherent in Islam. It is as if a Jew—because he didn't know his own history—referred to Hitler in order to discover his own identity. (Kuehl 312)

If such comments seem aggressively hyperbolic, they may appear in an altogether different light when considered from the vantage point of the Islamic Sahel. In Mauritania, for instance, which borders Western Mali and which remains central to Ouologuem's concerns, blacks have historically been victims of the most outrageous forms of racism imaginable, largely at the hands of Arab and Berber Muslims. However expedient it may have been for American Muslims like Malcolm X to emphasize the "color-blind" nature of Islam, the fact remains that race relations throughout the Islamic Sahel have seldom been worse.[6] In truth, the nonracist and utopian form of Islam that is celebrated in the latter, more "highly evolved" Malcolm X is routinely overdramatized by the U.S. media, not to mention by the Islamic Republic of Iran, Spike Lee, Inc., and many others—all of whom have profited by emphasizing the "color-blind" nature of Islam, or by reducing the crises and complexities of history into malleable sound bites for provoking certain types of behavior. In *The Satanic Verses*, Salman Rushdie shows how this happened in Iran through his caricature of Malcolm X (appropriately renamed Bilal X), an unreal creation of the Imam (210–211).[7] In *Bound to Violence*, Ouologuem opts for a more homeopathic cure for our forgetfulness, brutally compressing images of human suffering that overwhelm in their singularity: the cure for violence is violence itself, he seems to imply, or at least rubbing our noses in it. But we are not to doubt for an instant the historicity of these images.

In recent years, the most dramatic instance of Arab racism toward the black population in Mauritania occurred between the months of October 1990 and March 1991, when some 500 black political prisoners were executed by the Mauritanian government, an incident that received almost no media attention outside West Africa. In a hearing before a U.S. congressional subcommittee, Holly Burkhalter of Human Rights Watch reported as follows:

> Executions, torture, forcible expulsion, and destruction of black villages are but the most visible sign of government oppression against Mauritania's black ethnic groups. Repression against the community occurs at all levels; indeed, it is fair to say that the Mauritanian government practices undeclared apartheid and severely discriminates on the basis of race.

> Even the heinous abuse of slavery continues, despite its formal abolition in 1980. . . . There are tens of thousands of black slaves in Mauritania who remain the property of their master, subject[ed] entirely to his will, working long hours for no remuneration, with no access to education and no freedom to marry or to associate freely with other blacks. They escape servitude not by exercising their "legal" rights but mainly through escape. We have received testimony of terrible torture visited upon slaves who attempt to escape or otherwise infringe their master's law . . . The ferocity of such torture is clearly meant to serve as a message to other slaves about the fate of those who challenge their master's authority or attempt to flee. (U.S. Congress 30)

Although such descriptions may seem shocking in Europe and North America, they would surprise few in Senegal, Mauritania, and Mali, where it is widely known that blacks continue to be illegally enslaved by Beydane (or "white Moor") Muslims.[8] As scholars like Germaine Dieterlen, John Hunwick, Thomas Hale, and others have pointed out, Dogon identity has itself been profoundly affected by Arab Islamic incursions into West Africa, which continue to influence black-Arab relations throughout the Sahel.[9] The Yambo Ouologuem of the 1990s, who angrily insists that "the worst enemies for blacks right now are racist Arabs," merely reiterates one of the more unsavory themes of *Bound to Violence*, published some thirty years ago. The "novelty" of such a theme, of course, depends upon the relative ignorance of the reading audience. It only needs adding here that the price for such ignorance is steadily rising.

In the case of Ouologuem, however, who is presently seeking a more active role in Mauritanian politics, the plight of the black population there has perhaps never been far from his concerns.[10] In fact, Ouologuem's interest in Mauritania may date back to his days as a promising college student in Mali, before his departure for France. During this period, Ouologuem and his father Boukary Ouologuem were personally visited by Sékou Touré, who was then president of Guinea. According to Ouologuem, Touré and Boukary Ouologuem discussed the possiblity of Yambo's eventual assumption of a major role in Mauritanian politics, possibly even the presidency. Ouologuem's concern for Mauritania, as well as for human rights violations against the Hal-Pulaar population at the hands of the Beydane government, may date from this interview.[11] In this light, *Bound to Violence* may be described as a meditation upon historical crises that have little to do with France or with the Occident in general—except insofar as it behooves the international community to bring an end to Beydane "apartheid." Ouologuem's recent appeal to African Americans to join him in this fight merely revisits themes integral to his goals as a young author.

In the meantime, postcolonial theorists in the North American academy remain under the spell of an increasingly hypostatic politics of *différance*, purely academic politics that deny the possibility of knowledge predicated on identity: precisely the terra firma of Yambo Ouologuem. "Whatever the political necessity for holding the position . . . " Gayatri Chakravorty Spivak has stated, "knowledge is made possible and is sustained by irreducible difference, not identity" (254). But what if knowledge of self or community is not, after all, sustained by *irreducible* difference, as Spivak suggests?[12] In other words, postcolonial theory's greatest strength, its deconstruction of what Zhang Longxi has called "the myth of the Other,"[13] may equally turn out to be its greatest weakness: its politically expedient denial of the alterity of the other. Christopher Miller makes this point in his reading of Ouologuem in *Theories of Africans* (1990): "Ouologuem's 'theory' of Africans is a vision of the African holocaust, Africans being led in bondage toward a new world, a reminder that any link can be a link in a chain of enslavement" (24).[14] From such a perspective, the current consensus that it is not really possible "to maintain a cultural and political position 'outside' the Occident from which, in security, to attack it" (Clifford 11), may seem oddly counterproductive if not defeatist. It is certain, in any event, that such an argument would seem presumptuous on the streets of Bandiagara.

Much has been made in the West of plagiarism controversies regarding *Bound to Violence*, so much in fact that I hesitate to further exaggerate their significance by replaying them here. Nevertheless, it is at least curious that so much critical interest has been generated by the essentially legal question of *Bound to Violence*'s status as literary property. For obvious reasons, such preoccupations tend to concern Ouologuem's Euro-American readers far more so than his African ones, who prefer to remember him for his purgative attack on Senghorian négritude. In fact, the latest flurry of critical interest in Ouologuem in North America has centered on his alleged "theft" of European literary sources in an effort to aggressively "deconstruct" Western writing practices. During a recent RÉLIS conference, where I gave a paper on the critical reception of *Bound to Violence* in the United States, such arguments tended to provoke indulgent smiles from my African colleagues, many of whom wagged their fingers at me about the "antics" of American critics.[15] For most of my colleagues, the idea that Ouologuem may have deliberately "stolen" from authors like Graham Greene, André Schwarz-Bart, and Guy de Maupassant seemed to have relatively little bearing in ascertaining his significance as an African writer today.

A far more likely scenario is that Ouologuem told the truth in this matter from the earliest days of the controversy: that is, the original publishers of *Le Devoir de violence* made numerous unauthorized changes in his manuscript, deleting references to European sources while leaving references to the *Tarîkh el-Fettach*, the *Tarîkh es-Soudan*, and other "unknown" African sources intact.[16] In other words, Yambo Ouologuem may have suffered a grave disservice at the hands of his publishers, a disservice that has had long and painful repercussions for him. In fact, it is significant that, although Ouologuem's brief response to plagiarism charges has been analyzed in some detail by his detractors, the written response of his publisher has escaped close scrutiny altogether.

In his brief defense against plagiarism charges, entitled "Polémique: Le Devoir de violence," Ouologuem stated that his editors had revised his manuscript by removing citations from Greene and Schwarz-Bart.[17] In his "In Defense of Yambo Ouologuem," Kaye Whiteman testifies to having actually seen the manuscript in question, including handwritten lines by Ouologuem such as "Here ends *The Last of the Just*." During my recent visit with Ouologuem in Sévaré-Mopti, Mali, he told me that both the manuscript of *Le Devoir de violence* and its English translation went to press without his full prior knowledge or consent. In other words, the novel's final "cut" (or its final published form), in which references to European texts had been deleted, was never authorized by Ouologuem himself. This means that no fully authorized text of this novel has ever been printed. Given the fact that Ouologuem now disavows his French-language writings, it seems unlikely that there will ever be such a version.

Responding to erroneous statements made by Eric Sellin, publisher Paul Flamand wrote to the editors of *Research in African Literatures*, especially to defend himself against the allegation that Éditions du Seuil had commissioned Ouologuem to write *Le Devoir de violence*.[18] Flamand demonstrates that this was not the case; however, Ouologuem himself never made such a claim, only Sellin did. In this letter, Flamand says nothing at all about whether or not unauthorized editorial changes had been made to Ouologuem's manuscript by Éditions du Seuil. In fact, Flamand makes clear that Éditions du Seuil was fully cognizant of the fact that Ouologuem had made use of Schwarz-Bart, which is why they bothered to contact Schwarz-Bart about this matter in the first place. It is likely that Éditions du Seuil was aware of Ouologuem's use of Schwarz-Bart because this was made plain in the manuscript that Ouologuem had submitted to them. If this were not the case, at the very least Éditions du Seuil would have been guilty of gross negligence in approving publication of Ouologuem's book after "detecting" evidence of such "blatant plagiarism" and then not bothering to question the likelihood of further instances in the manuscript. Flamand's letter only exonerates Éditions du Seuil from charges made by Eric Sellin, which were largely irrelevant (as well as "inadvertently tendentious," to quote Sellin).[19]

Far more hostile is the response of someone named "B. P." in an article ironically entitled "Le Devoir de vérité." As a matter of fact, it is unclear whether or not B. P. actually edited Ouologuem's manuscript or was in any way associated with Éditions du Seuil. However, B. P.'s article in *Le Figaro littéraíre,* which is strategically wedged between the response of the author (mentioned above) and the response of Graham Greene's literary agent, Marie Schébéko, clearly illustrates the dishonesty of the French literary establishment in responding to this situation. B. P. lists a few brief points in his or her response to Ouologuem's defense, none of which address Ouologuem's claim that his publishers had made unauthorized revisions in his manuscript. For example, B. P. states as follows:

> Yambo Ouologuem defends himself from plagiarism charges by claiming that the [missing] quotation marks may be found in his own [handwritten] manuscript. The trouble is that they are absent from the book which, need we say, only critics and the public have access to. (1)

Of course B. P. is correct, but such a statement merely begs the question: Did the editors of *Le Devoir de violence* remove references to other works without Ouologuem's consent? If so, why? Furthermore, why did his editors not request necessary revisions from Ouologuem if they were truly concerned about plagiarism? Given the unusual nature of Ouologuem's borrowings, would it have been possible for Ouologuem to revise his novel accordingly? Such complications may have led the novel's editors to conclude that simply deleting references to Greene, Maupassant, and others offered the easiest solution to the creative problems his manuscript posed.

Later, B. P. deliberately misreads Ouologuem to the point of absurdity. In his statement, Ouologuem had implied that Graham Greene should have responded to this crisis by coming to his aid (much like Schwarz-Bart had at an earlier date); instead, Greene sided with the publisher of *Le Devoir de violence,* who took the liberty of pleading "guilty" on Ouologuem's behalf—without even bothering to consult him. "It is significant," Ouologuem stated, "that this publisher should plead guilty in my name without even questioning me, and that, without the slightest claim by Mr. Graham Greene, he [my publisher] should withdraw my book from sale throughout the entire world." B. P. responds as follows:

> To write that Graham Greene made no claim is false. It was at the request of the great British novelist that Mme Schébéko, the director of the Clairouin agency which represents Greene in France, made contact with Paul Flamand. (1)

However, Ouologuem does not state that Greene never complained about the alleged "plagiarism" of his novel, *It's a Battlefield.* What Ouologuem states is that Greene, as a fellow author, should have taken the initiative to intervene on Ouologuem's behalf, preventing the unnecessary removal of the novel from the bookstores. B. P.'s final remarks are simply insulting:

> When Yambo Ouologuem borrows from himself, his thought is obscure and his prose entangled. It would not occur to Graham Greene to plagiarize him. Nor to anybody else. (1)

The omissions, evasions, and arrogance that characterize these responses may provide insight into why Ouologuem remains bitter towards the French literary establishment today. As an African student in a foreign capital, only twenty-eight at the time his novel was published, Ouologuem's situation cannot inspire envy: the full weight of an embarrassed intellectual community was exerted against him. As I have tried to suggest here, some of those involved may have had a vested interest in obscuring their own role in producing a "plagiarized" text, specifically through altering Ouologuem's original manuscript.

Aside from this question, there can be no doubt that intensive and harmful scrutiny was brought to bear upon Ouologuem in ways unthinkable in cases when European artists have freely borrowed from African sources. For instance, few art historians speak of "plagiarism" or "theft" when discussing the paintings of Pablo Picasso, Georges Braques, or Amedeo Modigliani. Yet Ouologuem has been subject to a series of highly refined attacks on his character for nearly thirty years, more recently by those who congratulate him for his "cleverness" in deliberately "stealing" from European writers.[20] More importantly, prolonged discussion of Ouologuem's "plagiarism" of European sources has diverted attention away from urgent historical questions many would prefer to ignore: a fact that is probably not incidental to the proliferation of a particular kind of critical discourse on him.

Ouologuem's decision to return to Mali and wash his hands of writing in French was an incalculable loss to world literature. The fact that he has refused to state his own case, skeptical of the utility of such a gesture, is indicative of the contempt he now feels for French culture at large. What this refusal must restore to him is his own dignity, something he obviously prefers to the praise of foreign intellectuals.

The critical reception of Yambo Ouologuem forms one of the most interesting chapters in the history of African literature. In *Yambo Ouologuem: Postcolonial Writer, Islamic Militant,* the reader will find only a few of the most significant responses to Ouologuem's writings over the last three decades. In organizing this book, my original goal had been to offer a chronological and comprehensive sampling of this material, primarily in an effort to shed light upon an eclipsed historical dimension in Ouologuem criticism. Unfortunately, this goal had to be abandoned when it became apparent that two volumes would be needed to fully document the many controversies that have raged over Ouologuem's writings, especially in France and North America. As a compromise, it seemed wiser to locate Ouologuem's reception more squarely within the context of African concerns, sweeping aside the concerns of European critics about the alleged illegality (or "inauthenticity") of *Le Devoir de violence*.

Part 1 of this book therefore focuses upon a few representative responses to Ouologuem's writings from African critics. As mentioned previously, Ouologuem is often credited with delivering the final death-blow to Senghorian négritude, with clearing the way for a more honest literature divested of the sickly longing for a false African past. For some, *Bound to Violence* signaled an entirely new direction in African letters, a fiercely courageous, postindependence literature. For others, Ouologuem's "untimely" portrait of Africa may have revealed far too much, bringing to light horrors that most preferred to forget. In Chapter 2, Wole Soyinka, who has been criticized by Chinweizu (among others) for too quickly negating the oppositional potential inherent in négritude, finds much to appreciate in Ouologuem's refreshing lack of sentimentality; however, he remains uneasy about the "intensity of contempt for the victims" exhibited throughout *Bound to Violence*. In Chapter 3, J. Mbeloko ya Mpiku, who is no fonder of négritude than Soyinka, is even more troubled by Ouologuem's shocking depiction of the *négraille*, or "niggertrash," which for him seems yet another unhelpful mystification, malleable to Western misreadings. Tunde Fatude, who offers his own Marxist reading of Ouologuem in Chapter 4, goes even further than Soyinka or Mpiku by suggesting that Ouologuem might well be "on the side of the exploiting ruling classes."

If all of these readings are later contested, they nonetheless demonstrate a certain malaise among Ouologuem's African readers from all sides of the political spectrum. Whereas early European and North American readers celebrated the historical "honesty" of *Bound to Violence*, African critics wondered if Ouologuem was merely "self-hating" (Soyinka), an apologist for the oppressors—French *and* African. "[N]o African critic who loves his people and is proud of them," Mpiku states, "can agree with Ouologuem's view that the black man's predicament today is the result of an ontological flaw, an innate collective proclivity to slavery and spoliation." Whatever else may be said about *Bound to Violence*, there can be no dismissing the novel's chilly reception across Africa, the wide-ranging suspicion toward the novel that has by no means diminished thirty years later.

In Chapter 5, Chris Dunton explores yet another difficult aspect of *Bound to Violence* for African audiences: its frank depiction of homosexuality. In fact, it may not be an exaggeration to suggest that this dimension of Ouologuem's writing may be even more disturbing for many African readers than his views on history. It would be inaccurate to state that Dunton's essay is representative of the "African" reaction to this question, which may be better described in terms of a resounding silence; or, perhaps, Cheikh Hamidou Kane's opinion best encapsulates the perspectives of many:

> Ouologuem has a concept of love which is atrocious; homosexuality which does not exist in our culture; all that is vice, incest, animality, and so many things that belong to white people or exist in the white man's mind. He gives all these traits to African characters. This is false. (Phanuel Akubueze Egejuru 18)

Dunton sensitively probes this question, but there is clearly need for further discussion about Ouologuem's deployment of such themes. In regard to the Lambert-Kassoumi episode, what has perhaps not been emphasized enough is the metaphorical nature of this relation, an image of the respective positions occupied by the colonizer and colonized under European imperialism. This metaphor is made explicit by Ouologuem in *Lettre à la France nègre*.

In a widely discussed article on Ouologuem, revised for publication here as Chapter 6, Kwame Anthony Appiah concludes the first part of this book by locating *Bound to Violence* in the context of wider debates on postmodernity and postcoloniality. Unlike previous African critics of Ouologuem, however, Appiah finds in *Bound to Violence* an ethically motivated concern for those who have suffered the devastating effects of nation building following decolonization. Perhaps more than any other recent essay on Ouologuem, Appiah's remarks have contributed the most toward a rethinking of Ouologuem's significance as a "postcolonial" writer, both in Africa and across the globe.

Part 2 focuses upon Euro-American debates surrounding Ouologuem's controversial method of composition, a question that has enjoyed renewed attention in the aftermath of poststructuralism's ascendancy within the North American academy. Eric Sellin, who was himself instrumental in shaping the early reception of Ouologuem, in Chapter 7 offers a historical overview of plagiarism controversies from his unique perspective as a key participant. Later critics such as Christine Chaulet-Achour (Chapter 8) and Christopher L. Miller (Chapter 9) will complicate Sellin's ethical dismissal of Ouologuem as "plagiarist," demonstrating the architectural complexity inherent within *Bound to Violence*'s construction.

Similarly, in the first extended critical consideration of *Lettre à la France nègre*, Caroline A. Mohsen argues in Chapter 10 that plagiarism controversies totally eclipsed this brilliant early work, rendering it unable to get a fair hearing in France or elsewhere. In a carefully crafted examination of *Lettre à la France Nègre,* Mohsen shows how Ouologuem uses irony and paradox to "institute himself violently as an agent of change." In Chapter 11, Ann Elizabeth Willey focuses upon both *Lettre à la France Nègre* and Ouologuem's pornographic novel *Les milles et une bibles du sexe*, published under the pseudonym of Utto Rodolph. In response to poststructuralist critics like Miller, Willey argues that critical attention to Ouologuem's deliberately subversive narrative strategies has elided the way in which women are silenced in Ouologuem's texts, their oppression taken for granted or "naturalized." "Objectifying women to make the point that Europe objectifies Africa," Willey states, "writes women out of the picture."

In Part 3 of *Yambo Ouologuem: Postcolonial Writer, Islamic Militant*, the reader will find detailed studies of Islamic-Sahelian influences that inform Ouologuem's writings, which contest the early critical consensus that his writings lack "authenticity." Thomas A. Hale's extensive study in Chapter 12 of oral and written sources that inform *Bound to Violence* shows the remarkable range of African traditions from which Ouologuem draws. In Chapter 13, I focus upon elements of Ouologuem's writings that may be clarified with reference to quranic hermeneutics and Sufism, especially to challenge the view that *Bound to Violence* offers a strictly negative critique of Islam. What emerges from these two essays is a more complex portrait of Yambo Ouologuem as a *Sahelian* author, deeply rooted within the concerns of his own community and its troubled history.

Finally, I include materials collected during my recent year in residency at the Université de Ouagadougou in which I was able to make two separate trips to northern Mali to meet with Ouologuem. Part 4 will update the reader on Ouologuem's doings following his withdrawal to Mali in the early-1970s. Though Ouologuem has refused to discuss his writings in French, he remains an active member of the Tidjaniya community in Sévaré-Mopti and Bandiagara, collaborating in writing projects with Amadou Hampâté Bâ before Bâ's recent death and working for educational reform in both Mali and Mauritania. Above all, he seeks to bring an end to the racial oppression of black Muslims throughout the Sahel, especially at the hands of Arab Muslims.

NOTES

1. Throughout northern Mali and elsewhere in the Sahel, it is customary to give the family name first.

2. See, for instance, David Robinson, *The Holy War of Umar Tal* (1985), B. O. Oloruntimehin, *The Segu Tukulor Empire* (1972), and Brad Martin, *Muslim Brotherhoods in 19th-Century Africa* (1976).

3. See Linda Kuehl, "Yambo Ouologuem on Violence, Truth, and Black History," p. 312.

4. See Amadou Hampaté Bâ, *Vie et enseignement de Tierno Bokar: Le sage de Bandiagara* (1980) or Louis Brenner, *West African Sufi: The Religious Heritage and Spiritual Search of Cerno Bokar Salif Tal* (1984).

5. Not unlike Ouologuem's Saif, al-Hajj Umar alternated in his relationship with the French between antagonism and collaboration, depending upon the need of the moment. As David Robinson points out, "It is ironic that the image of an intransigent Umar, largely generated by the French, has been retained and belabored by modern Senegalese nationalists anxious to portray the Fulbe leader as a hero of resistance to European conquest" (1985: 40; also see 5). In the case of al-Hajj Umar's son Aguibou Tall, however, the relation was obviously more collaborative, and subordinate (Abun-Nasr 143; Robinson 1985: 27–31). Also, see Yves Saint-Martin, "Un fils d'El Hadj Omar: Aguibou, roi du Dinguiray et du Macina (1843?–1907?)."

6. See George Breitman, *The Last Year of Malcolm X: The Evolution of a Revolutionary.*

7. Also see Mehdi Abedi and Michael M. J. Fischer, *Debating Muslims,* p. 433.

8. The British Anti-Slavery Society estimated in 1981 that there were a minimum of 100,000 total slaves in Mauritania, with an additional 300,000 part-slaves and ex-slaves (U.S. Congress 30).

9. See Germaine Dieterlen, *Le Titre d'honneur des Arou: Dogon, Mali,* p. 9; John O. Hunwick, *Shari'a in Songhay: The Replies of al-Maghili to the Questions of Askia al-Hajj Muhammad,* p. 123; and Thomas Hale, *Scribe, Griot, and Novelist* p. 142.

10. Ouologuem was apparently offered a position as Minister of Education in Mauritania by former President Moctar Oul Dada. This offer may have been retracted at a later date. See my "In Search of Yambo Ouologuem."

11. The details of this meeting were reported to me by James Wade, the Liberian chauffeur who accompanied me during my second meeting with Ouologuem, at Ouologuem's house in Sévaré-Mopti, Mali, on February 20, 1997.

12. It might well be asked, can the transcendental signifier of "irreducible difference" honestly be construed in nonidenitarian terms?

13. See Zhang Longxi, *The Tao and the Logos: Literary Hermeneutics, East and West,* p. xvii.

14. Miller nonetheless goes too far in this assertion: "Ouologuem's response to false images of cultural identity is to undermine the notion of identity itself, to construct a universe in which all bonds of unity are bonds of enslavement, including the bond between Ouologuem's writing and the European texts that he plagiarized" (1990: 21).

15. "Yambo Ouologuem dans le postmoderne: Les débats littéraires sur *Le Devoir de violence* depuis 1985," Vè colloque international de littérature, Réseau d'Études Littératures Sahéliennes, Université de Ouagadougou, Burkina Faso, November 21, 1996.

16. See K. W. (Kaye Whiteman), "In Defence of Yambo Ouologuem."

17. Yambo Ouologuem, "Polémique: Le Devoir de violence," *Figaro littéraire*, June 10, 1972.

18. Paul Flamand, "Letter to the Editor," *Research in African Literatures*, Vol. 2, No. 2 (1971): 116.

19. See Sellin's reply *Research in African Literatures*, Vol. 2, No. 2 (1971): 116–120.

20. See "Something *New* Out of Africa?" Though such arguments are now bolstered by reference to poststructuralist theory, the seeds of this critique were already present in the earliest, most slanderous accounts of this controversy. The anonymous writer of this piece asks, "Is Ouologuem on to something: a style of literary imperialism intended as revenge for the much-chronicled sins of territorial imperialists?" (525).

Part 1

Swabbing the Deck: African Responses to Ouologuem

2

Remarks on Yambo Ouologuem's *Le Devoir de violence*

Wole Soyinka

Iconoclasm by itself may embody a social vision, and the question is certainly raised by Ouologuem's uncompromising work, *Bound to Violence*.

But first, a problem which cannot be honestly ignored. The charges of plagiarism in Ouologuem's work appear to be well substantiated; it would be futile to deny this. The literary question remains, however, whether or not we are confronted with an original contribution to literature, in spite of the borrowings. The *drama* of the novel is original; this, I believe, has not been disputed. The stylistic "griot" propulsive energy and the creative vision are unquestionably Ouologuem's. It has been claimed that the thematic structure has been borrowed also from a previous Prix Renaudot winner; by this I mean the disposition of theme into the transmitting media of events, place and temporal relations. I have not read the other work so this question is one which I cannot resolve. There are also moral and philosophical questions. The former can be resolved quite simply: it would have been preferable if Yambo Ouologuem had acknowledged his sources. The philosophical aspect concerns the principle of ownership of the written word. This was the line which I rather expected Ouologuem to adopt in his response to the charges, not from any interest in the results but in anticipation of a debate which, given the French penchant for speculative philosophy, would certainly have resulted in obscuring the original issues

---

This chapter was previously published in *Myth, Literature, and the African World* (Cambridge: Cambridge University Press, 1976). Reprinted with permission of the author.

and left Ouologuem's readers to carry on regarding his work as literature, until given evidence to the contrary. Which is precisely what I propose to do.

The charge of plagiarism was, however, not the only reaction produced by the work. It is not surprising, given the nature of the political alliances which dominate the world at present, to find that the intelligentsia of the black world are in ideological disagreement over the question whether enforced cultural and political exocentricity, as a retarding factor in the authentic history and development of Black Africa, should be recognized as appertaining only to the European world. The existence of the school of thought which thinks *not* is our present concern, nor is its expression among African writers and intellectuals as new as is commonly supposed. Yambo Ouologuem unquestionably triggered off the critical alarm in the opposing school, but what he has done with his fictional re-creation of history is no more nor less than a Cheikh Anta Diop or Chancellor Williams has done for decades in their several essays on African civilization. The researches and findings of Diop, Williams, Frobenius and other historians and ethno-scientists made *Le Devoir de violence* inevitable and salutary—Ouologuem's savage satire on Sh(F)robeniusology notwithstanding. The outcry of sections of black American militancy over this aspect of the book is simply misguided.

Le Devoir de violence (I shall use the original in preference to the English version of the title) marks a studied repudiation of historic blinkers. It re-writes the chapter of Arab-Islamic colonization of Black Africa, but moves beyond history and fiction to raise questions of the very structure of racial heritage. Accepted history is held against an exhumed reality; the resulting dialectic can only lead to a reassessment of contemporary society and its cultural equipment for racial advance. This intellectual dimension of the writing places it amongst the literature of prognostic inquiry, in spite of the negative approach. The question is implicitly assertive: if "Negro art (and culture, history) found a patent of nobility in the folklore of mercantile intellectualism," what constituted the authentic nobility of Negro art? The tapestry of repudiation comes alive before our eyes, as if a light is played upon it, activating shadow after shadow with its blood-red illumination. A neutral, tight-lipped humor fitfully relieves the oppression, varying from the mordant and sardonic to cosmic belly-laughs; great passages of history are set in motion by a public split in the trousers of the great. The Bible, the Quran, the historic solemnity of the griot are reduced to the histrionics of wanton boys masquerading as humans. Ouologuem leaps frenetically from the cliché "café au lait" joke to the sadistic guffaw with the lofty indifference of a ringmaster manipulating his whirl of freaks at the touch of a foot-pedal, halting long enough to treat his audience to a little perversion act, then moving on to the next exhibit. Is there a touch of self-hate in Ouologuem's "dispassionate" recital? The intensity of contempt for the victims is clearly intended to reflect the alienation of the torturers from the concept of the victims as human, to reflect their religious-imperial justification for acts of barbarism, yet beneath this device lurks, one suspects, the discomfort of the author himself. The epithets are spat through gritted teeth; the antidote for victim-identification appears to be a deflective masochism—Ouologuem has been accused of an alienation technique; the opposite seems truer—such a level of inventive degradation suggests that Ouologuem is practicing some form of literary magic for the purpose of self-inoculation.

Ouologuem has also carried the devaluation technique (through proximity and non-differentiation) to its conceivable limits. The method is invariably iconoclastic; nothing survives in it, not even love or (to keep our demands modest in a work of this nature) mutual physical attraction. Kassoumi's love for Tambira (both serfs) is not permitted to remain long in the natural order of things. Custom dictates that he resort to the burning of "nail parings, three eyelashes, seven head hairs, seven pubic hairs etc., etc." to sprinkle on the bride's nuptial viands; while for himself crushed lion-penises, cocks' testicles and goat sperm provide the fare. The obscenity of the seigneur's right of the first night prolongs the reductive cynicism of the event (the novel's first *human* event) by its own ceremonial burnings of "incense, sublimate of camphor, aloes, Indian musk and amber" in a mockery of defloration. Slave and master are made to undergo these humiliations with complete equanimity; the law of the absurd and the obscene, narratively imposed until now, becomes fully sublimated in the first human realist portraiture. This is the first moment that the semblance of an individuated character (and contact) has emerged from the tapestry, but its function is merely to confirm and reinforce the pattern of the established norm; from here on, further human delineation will immerse each product of Nakem's history in the gory degradation of its past, and most deeply, our would-be central character, fruit of the obscene rites of the union of serfs—Raymond Spartacus Kassoumi.

In preparation for the summative European pilgrimage of the young Kassoumi, art, religion and cultural concepts are brought together in contemporary time for a final iconoclastic collision, elaborating Ouologuem's cynical observation noted earlier in the midst of mayhem: "the blessed union of knowledge and morality is fragile." Kassoumi's quest for knowledge (and liberation) is foredoomed; he will neither escape his Nakem past nor its present transposition to the "Shrobeniusology" of distant Europe. The avenues of possible salvation through religion are firmly closed, even to the extent of assailing their modern defenders with that most lethal weapon, parody. For instance, the metempsychotic delirium of the wife-murderer Sankolo reads suspiciously like a sex-orgiastic parody of Hamidou Kane's transcendentalist apologia for Islamic spirituality. Recourse to an indigenous metaphysics, a "cosmological religiosity" or "inner landscape" has become impossible, because it is deprived of identity by the intellectual conmanship of Europe's anthropologists. The pathway in that direction is clotted up with the superficial debris of intellectual excavations. The Shrobenius invasion of Nakem is stretched to represent the tradition of falsification, coupled with a leveling down of the Aryan myth, the symbolic blonde beast brought to rut in the degenerate earth of black Nakem, naturally enough in the context of the highest quest conceivable to German civilization—the quest for *Kultur*! But even as the concepts of Aryan self-reversal are mouthed, ostensibly to compensate for the long heresy of Eurocentric belittlement of black Africa, they are brought flatly down within sordid motivation—entrepreneurial greed and opportunism even in the service of Kultur! The idea that the revolutionary potential of Nakem's serfdom will approach this source for intellectual sustenance compounds the sham. Study for young Kassoumi has become a "fanatical cult," the "instrument of his liberation." But the quality of all possible knowledge is falsified in advance; worse, the foundation of his elevation, his mother's sordid sacrifice, hangs over any eventual achievement like a miasma. Ouologuem excels himself: not only does the mother prostitute herself to the sorcerer for her sons' success; she is subsequently raped by Saif's two gorillas, then murdered (or commits suicide) in the slaves' latrine, up to the neck in excrement. Kassoumi's father lovingly sucks the worms from her nostrils!

How ironic that the novel's only episode of consciously rendered affectionate relationship should be homosexual, and yet how appropriate to Ouologuem's misanthropic vision! It raises questions, certainly. The tender narrative of Raymond Spartacus's affair with the Strausbourgois, Lambert, is such a drastic departure from the rest of the narrative, containing so little of the earlier brutality or cynical undermining, that it reads like a heightened James Baldwin. It is not only tender; it is *sympathetic* and sincere despite the occasions when the author, recalled to himself, appears to feel obliged to liken Kassoumi's love to that of a whipped dog, or, acknowledges in Lambert an "obscure desire to get even, to avenge himself, to wound his nigger." Such insertions are both rare and even self-conscious, betraying a suspicious desire to complicate, to keep some level of dialectic tension going at all costs by exploiting the racial context. The mercenary calculation of Raymond Spartacus at the start is made ambivalent even in the very first night of copulation. Nothing wrong with that, but what we encounter is not lust, in keeping with Nakem's history of pederasty, sodomy, sexual sadism, etc., but tenderness. Yet nothing till now has suggested Kassoumi's homosexual leanings. The morning request for payment for his services sounds pathetic rather than commercial, and of course he soon graduates to the status of a kept "mistress" in what is clearly no longer a commercial arrangement but one of love. Long after Spartacus has ceased to need Lambert financially, the affair is continued by both. The significance of this episode is certainly elusive, since its treatment removes it from the pale of suggestive criticism or subjective contempt either of European decadence or of the individuals. Such solemn cadences, extolling the anal salvation of the lonely in the inhuman and indifferent society of Europe, belong to the fictional prose of Baldwin and Genêt, and cannot be integrated into the mold of iconoclastic literature. Neither, incidentally, can the Victorian melodrama of brother-beds-sister-in-brothel fable. This reads at first like an attempted parody, but it then becomes the instrument of crucial revelations of homeland for Spartacus (and a further confirmation of his whipped character). The extension of the melodrama into the neurotic reality of the milieu—the razor blade in the bidet soap which ends Kadidia's life a bare week later—only mildly restores the earlier consistency, being a predictable extension of the violent destiny of the Nakemians. But then, a short while later, the incongruously tender homosexual interlude!

If there is any doubt that *Le Devoir de violence* owes much in its conception to a desire to counter the Islamic apologia of Hamidou Kane, the duplication of the hero's pilgrimage to Europe dispels much of it and the final duet of the Bishop and the Saif, a confrontation in the idiom of grim political exegesis, which corresponds to Hamidou Kane's mystic exegesis of death, removes the last of it. But the reaches of *Le Devoir de violence* are far wider; the work does not specifically address itself to the Islamic myth. It is a fiercely partisan book on behalf of an immense historic vacuum, the vacuum this time being Ouologuem's creation, not Stoddard's. And the charge of (unlocated) racism, is departicularised by the author's uniform manipulation of the rhetorical style of the legendary heroes and their associative civilizations: Judaic, medieval, Arab-Islamic, Christian-European. The neat juxtaposition of incongruous prayers and pietistic lore with events of cunning, duplicity and barbarism may seem an obvious literary device but, since the characters themselves appear perfectly at home in this tradition of florid diplomacy (French, Arabic, and so on) the author's organizing hand is hardly felt. Statesmanship and strategies are snared and rendered indistinguishable from the mere rhodomontade of the discourse of duplicity, a medieval variant of Newspeak. A culture which has claimed indigenous antiquity in such parts of Africa as have submitted to its undeniable attractions is confidently proven to be imperialistic; worse, it is demonstrated to be essentially hostile and negative to the indigenous culture. As a purely sociological event, such a work was bound to create violent passions. Re-interpretations of history or contemporary reality for the purpose of racial self-retrieval do generate extremes of emotion, most of all among claimants to intellectual objectivity. Ouologuem's verdict is a painful one—a sanguinary account of the principal rival to the Christian mission in Africa cannot be anything but provocative. Ouologuem pronounces the Muslim incursion into black Africa to be corrupt, vicious, decadent, elitist and insensitive. At the least such a work functions as a wide swab in the deck-cleaning operation for the commencement of racial retrieval. The thoroughness of its approach—total and uncompromising rejection—can only lead to the question already posed: what was the authentic genius of the African world before the destructive alien intrusion? And the question can today be confidently asked, backed as it is by findings from the labor of ethno-scientists. Stoddard's thesis is predictably exposed as fallacious; the alternative candidate for stuffing up the cultural black hole of the continent is yet another rubble-maker of cultural edifices.

It is true that Ouologuem takes no interest in presenting to the reader the values destroyed in this process. The positive does not engage his re-creative attention, and what glimpse we can obtain of the indigenous reality is presented within the undifferentiated context of the oppressed and the oppressor, the feudal overlord and slave—undifferentiated, that is, from the later political relations of Arab and European colonialism. Ouologuem speaks indeed of a "black colonialism." The premise for this expression is suspect, and it has affected Ouologuem's concepts of the pre-colonial reality of African society. A social condition in which Semites (though black and pre-Islamic) are overlords and negro-Africans the slaves still leaves the basic curiosity about black historic reality unsatisfied.

3

From One Mystification to Another: "Négritude" and "Négraille" in *Le Devoir de violence*

J. Mbelolo ya Mpiku

At the time of its announcement, the Prix Renaudot 1968 made front-page news in most French papers. It would not have done so had not the prize winner, Yambo Ouologuem, been black. That gave the event another dimension, and the prize-winning book, *Le Devoir de violence*,[1] went on to elicit extravagant comments. The author himself was hailed as "an exceptional being who no doubt, like Léopold Sédar Senghor, was one of the rare intellectuals of international stature presented to the world by Black Africa."[2] Disappointment came, however, when Ouologuem published his second book, *Lettre à la France nègre*, a pamphlet in every way inferior to his novel.

The riot of journalistic praise for *Le Devoir de violence* was followed by serious articles in specialized reviews, which rightly stressed the originality of Ouologuem's work and attempted to place it within the context of African literature in French.[3] Our own study takes that new critical and historical perspective into account.

The Négritude Writers

It needs to be stressed that, some years ago, "African literature in French" was almost synonymous with "the poetry of négritude," at least in the

This chapter was previously published in *Review of National Literatures*, Vol. 2, No. 2 (Fall 1971). Reprinted with permission of *Review of National Literatures*. Translated by Hena Maes-Jelinek.

public's mind. This can no doubt be accounted for by the artistic success of the négritude group and by the mediocrity of French African writing before they appeared on the literary scene. The first generation of French African writers emerged between 1920 and 1935, when a few authors such as Ahmadou Mapate Diagne (b. ca. 1895), an elementary school teacher, and Bakary Diallo (b. 1892), a Fulani shepherd educated in the army, produced a small number of literary works of little value. They obviously took for granted the policy of assimilation imposed by the French as a solution to African problems and sanctioned the idea that black people were inferior to whites.

The next generation of writers rejected and severely condemned assimilation, at least theoretically. They denounced it as simply another racist consequence of colonialism, with all its evils. Rejection of assimilation was, indeed, to be the first self-imposed task of the négritude movement led by the well-known triad Damas-Césaire-Senghor in the years 1933 to 1935. The word "négritude" as originally defined by Léopold Sédar Senghor (b. 1906) embraces "all the cultural values of the Black world."[4] Senghor, moreover, makes a distinction between the *négritude of origins*, that is, the African values of the precolonial era, and *present-day négritude,* or "the Negro-African people as an efficient instrument of liberation."

The original négritude writers sought initially to define, assess, and develop precolonial African values in order to contribute to what Senghor calls "the civilization of the universal." To do this it was first necessary, as Walter A. E. Skurnik has pointed out, for the négritude writers to recover their own identity:

> The formative phase of "negritude," that of the search for dignity, was rooted in the destruction of an ideal: absorption by French civilization. Along with other Africans being educated in France, Senghor had been taught that, as an African, his mind was a "tabula rasa." Hence he was, at first, ready and willing to be impregnated by French civilization. As Senghor later expressed it: "Our ambition was to become carbon copies of the colonizers: 'Black-skinned Frenchmen.'" Africans were expected to be "soft wax in the fingers of the white God" and to seek salvation in the haven of French culture.[5]

In the historical context of the 1930s and 1940s the reaction of the négritude writers was quite justified: they were addressing themselves primarily to a Western audience in order to remodel the latter's view of Africa and of the Negro. But the method used by Senghor and his Caribbean friends was questionable. When describing their cultural values, they called upon history and ethnography more often than upon their own experience. They drew inspiration for their own works from the findings of European anthropologists, notably the German Leo Frobenius and the Frenchman Maurice Delafosse.[6] This purely intellectual process, which was their "return to the origins, their revaluation of the African past," obviously has a mythical character in the romantic sense of the word. However, racism and assimilation were a genuine part of the négritude poets' experience and contributed fruitfully to their literary output. The Caribbean writers, for instance, protested forcefully against their twofold alienation: the uprooting by which slavery cut them off from their African homeland and the French assimilation that made them cultural hybrids.

Whereas Léon Damas (b. 1912) and Aimé Césaire (b.1913) protested against their inhuman condition, Senghor, from his very first collection of poems, *Chants d'ombre* (1945), conjured up an idyllic picture of Africa. To the image of a barbaric, uncivilized Africa created by the colonizer, he opposed, as if by way of compensation, an ideal Africa of his own making. If Senghor's image of Africa is understandable in its historical context, it is undoubtedly fictitious in various respects, such as the excessive faith in the ancestral tradition, its exclusive presentation of the positive side of precolonial African society, and a kind of messianism that heralds a "universal civilization."

The most valuable achievement of négritude lay in the birth and growth, both in quality and volume, of Negro literature in the Caribbean and in Africa.[7] The idealization of the African past was a source of inspiration mainly to poets. It left its mark on only a few novels, the first of which was *L'Enfant noir* (1953) by the Guinean writer Camara Laye (b. 1928), who describes the bucolic Africa of his childhood. Laye's vision of Africa, like that of most négritude poets, arises from his escape into the past. He relies on his own memories to recreate an Africa that is no longer real but to which he remains deeply attached. This approach is fundamentally different from that of artists writing in English, who, instead of turning to the past, try to render their immediate experience. As early as 1963, Gerald Moore appropriately pointed out that essential difference:

> We should expect a reduction of the mystique of Africa (which was to some extent a carryover from Caribbean poets who had never seen it), and a greater trend towards realism, towards the detailed observation of modern Africa and the direct recording of experience. And these are precisely the qualities which we find already in the work of men like Peters of Sierra Leone or Soyinka, Clark, and Okara of Nigeria. To them, Africa is the living environment in which they have grown.[8]

As far as Negro writing in French is concerned, this trend of realistic observation first took shape in the Caribbean, particularly in Haiti, for historical reasons. Indeed, although Haiti has been independent since 1804, many Haitian intellectuals insist that their country is not free because it is still ruled dictatorially by a privileged class. In their writings, social, economic, and political problems are defined with a realism still unknown in French-speaking Africa. This appears in the works of Jacques Roumain (b. 1907), Jacques Stephen (b. 1922), and Jean Brière (b. 1909), all of whom criticize the political exploitation indulged in by black men. But besides the idealizing approach a realistic trend had also developed in French African writing, first apparent in *Karim* (1935) by the Senegalese writer Ousmane Socé (b. 1911). Though a disciple of Senghor, Socé in *Karim* deals with urban life in Senegal. Another Senegalese, Abdoulaye Sadji (1910–1961), author of *Nini, mulatresse du Senegal* (1947) and of *Maimouna* (1953), illustrates the same trend.

After those early attempts, realism in French African writing gained sudden impetus with the Cameroonian writers Mongo Beti (b. 1932) and Ferdinand Oyono (b. 1929), and with the Senegalese writer Sembene Ousmane (b. 1923). Their fiction is committed to anticolonialism, but their satire, mainly directed against their colonizers, does not spare the African either. This criticism of African society stands in contradiction to the négritude outlook because it applies not only to those Africans who naively support colonialism but also to traditions that thwart individual development at the same time that they impede economic and political progress. Among those traditions presented as most harmful are some religious and magical beliefs, superstitions, polygamy, and parental authoritarianism. As Gerald Moore has shown, their criticism of African society brings those novelists nearer to their Nigerian fellow-writers. . . . [9]

The growth of French African literature coincided with the political awakening of the African countries; it reached its climax in 1960 when most of those countries became independent. After that date, African writing in French was marked by a decline of négritude, the last echoes of which are heard in *L'Aventure ambigue* by the Senegalese writer Cheikh Hamidou Kane (b. 1928). In spite of its promising start, the literary activity of French-speaking Africa dwindled almost to extinction. After 1960 the African literary scene was clearly dominated by English writing, mainly from Nigeria, where the trend of realistic observation has been asserting itself since 1953. Since the 1950s, writers such as Cyprian Ekwensi (b. 1921), Chinua Achebe (b. 1930), Wole Soyinka (b. 1934), John Pepper Clark (b. 1935), and Gabriel Okara (b. 1921) have been casting critical eyes on the modern society of their country and denouncing the corruption that prevails in Africa.

The analysis and criticism of the situation following independence first found its way into French African writing after 1966, with the publication of Camara Laye's *Dramouss*. That novel, which in its first part takes up again the theme of *L'Enfant noir*, presents at the end a critical picture of the political situation in Guinea after independence. It prepared the way for *Le Devoir de violence,* which belongs to the same trend of social and political criticism also illustrated in Côte d'Ivoire novels, *Violent était le vent* (1966), by Charles Nokan (b. 1937), and *Les Soleils des indépendances* (1968), by Ahmadou Kourouma (b. ca. 1927).

LE DEVOIR DE VIOLENCE: THE PLOT

In *Le Devoir de violence,* Ouologuem tells the "bloody history" of the niggertrash (*négraille*) of Africa, epitomized in the chronicle of an imaginary West African empire called Nakem. The empire was founded centuries ago by a foreign immigrant, "the Black Jew Abraham al-Heit, issued from the marriage of a Negro with an Oriental Jewess." Abraham al-Heit comes to Nakem with a gang of adventurers. Internecine wars, he finds, have left the people divided into a number of small tribes ruled by Muslim overlords. A shrewd and calculating man, he gathers into an army all the discontented among the Nakem tribes: escaped slaves, rebellious peasants, and ordinary poor people. He defeats the feudal lords, lays down the foundations of the Nakem empire, and takes the title of Saif. After his death in 1498, his descendants strengthen the Saif dynasty by resorting to crime, murder, forced labor, and the slave trade, which remain current practice for centuries, reaching a climax at the end of the nineteenth century under the rule of Saif ben Isaac al-Heit, the last representative of the dynasty. The first part of the novel, entitled "The Legend of the Giants," ends with his accession to the throne.

The second part, "The Ecstasy and the Agony," starts with the arrival of French colonizers in Nakem. Saif ben Isaac El Heit puts up some military resistance but is soon defeated. He succeeds, however, in retaining his authority by signing a peace treaty with the French in 1900. Six months later he agrees to send his younger son, Madoubo, on an official visit to France. The young man receives from the French government and people all the honors due to a head of state and comes back to Nakem with numerous presents. Thus is the "cooperation" between France and Nakem consolidated.

The third part of the narrative, entitled "The Night of the Giants," deals mainly with the black slaves, with the fate of the *négraille* during the colonial period. Schools are opened by missionaries and education becomes compulsory, but to protect the ruling aristocracy from cultural assimilation, the Saif makes sure that only the sons of slaves are sent to school. To perpetuate his power he raises asps, using them to dispose of colonial agents, settlers, unfaithful servants, and prying slaves—in short, all those who might thwart his influence. At the same time, he makes a show of being on friendly terms with the French, who, incidentally, make him a knight of the Légion d'honneur in 1902. He takes advantage of the gullibility of the whites: for instance, when ethnologist Fritz Shrobenius comes to Nakem, the Saif makes large profits by selling him counterfeit masks. As soon as World War I breaks out, he provides France with native infantry, thus earning the title of "Savior of France in Nakem" and a new decoration: the Saif is made a high officer in the Légion d'honneur. Meanwhile, the *négraille* live in utter destitution. One man only is concerned with their plight: Bishop Henry, who nurses the sick, helps the peasants, and converts the people.

After World War I, life reverts to normal. In 1920, the first pupils at the missionary school receive their lower certificates, among them Raymond Spartacus Kassoumi, son of one of the Saif's serfs. Whereas his brothers become clerks in the colonial administration, in 1924 Raymond receives a scholarship enabling him to study in France.

While in Paris, Raymond hears of his family's misfortunes from his sister Kadidia, whom he meets by chance in a brothel: his father has been sold, his fiancée has been killed by the Saif, and his brothers have been drugged and are now insane. Shortly afterward Kadidia dies, the victim of a sadist. Raymond falls into moral degradation but after many trials eventually graduates as an architect. He marries a Frenchwoman and settles in Strasbourg, where he is overtaken by World War II. Enrolled in the French army, he fights on the Rhine and in Italy. He and his wife are reunited in 1945. Meanwhile, the political situation in Nakem has changed. Raymond returns to his country to find an electoral campaign in full swing. But the Saif, who has seen through the plans of the French to manipulate the elections to their own advantage, forestalls his enemies. To outwit both the French and the *négraille,* he presents Raymond as the sole candidate and has him elected deputy of Nakem. The novel ends with a tête-à-tête between the Saif and Bishop Henry, who unmasks the sovereign. Instead of slyly killing the Bishop, however, the Saif eventually throws his asp into the fire and goes on playing chess with his guest.

THE NÉGRAILLE

Though the plot of *Le Devoir de violence* deals with the history of Nakem and its rulers, its real protagonist is the *négraille*. It is therefore necessary to define this term, which Ouologuem may have borrowed from Césaire's *Cahier d'un retour au pays natal* (1939). To Ouologuem the *négraille* are the African masses in their genuine condition, that is, in their original primitive state. They are the "population baptized in suffering" as opposed to the ruling classes. The *négraille* are petrified in their magico-religious, fetishistic beliefs. That is why they have been easily kept in that state of primitiveness, first, by their puny Islamized chiefs, then by the Saifs, and finally by French cultural imperialism. Those beliefs explain the continuity of their fate from the thirteenth century to the period of independence.

The original primitiveness of the *négraille* shows, on the one hand, in their complete lack of moral insight and cultural values and, on the other hand, in their strong inclination for anthropophagy, crime, rape, sexual frenzy, and endless tribal warfare. Ultimately, this primitiveness is to Ouologuem the very essence of Africa:

> Cruel peoples whose speech is a kind of croaking—fierce killers, men of the jungle, living in a state of bestiality, mating with the first woman they find, tall in stature and horrible to look upon, hairy men with abnormally long nails, the Zulus, Jaga, and Masai feed on human flesh and go naked, armed with the shields, darts, and daggers. Savage in their customs and daily lives, they know no faith nor law nor king. (13–14)

According to Ouologuem, this original primitiveness makes the *négraille* incapable of reaching political consciousness, which might drive them to revolt or even revolution. As Ouologuem sees it, sub-Saharan Africa's *négraille* are characterized by a state of debasement that in a way is ontological. They are doomed to remain at the mercy of alien powers: the tyranny of the Saifs, Islam, French imperialism, and Christianity. Of these, Christianity alone will be beneficent to the *négraille.*

In the first part of the novel, "The Legend of the Giants," Ouologuem shows how Islam serves as a convenient alibi for the tyranny of the Saifs, who encourage "the religious discipline enforced by the five daily prayers recommended by Islam" and transform religion into pedagogical training in the service of the whole mystification. Ouologuem conveys his negative vision of Islam through his ironical use of ritual Muslim formulas interspersed in the narrative. . . .

In the second part of the novel, Ouologuem shows that the *négraille,* in addition to being oppressed by Muslim rulers, are also made to suffer under French imperialism. The meeting between the European colonizers and Nakem falls in with the general temper of the story and is also marked with violence. After turning the *négraille* into fanatics, Saif ben Isaac El Heit makes use of their religious feeling to encourage their resistance to the French. He resorts to razzias, looting, and all sorts of exactions to recruit soldiers, but so do the French. The *négraille,* thus forced to serve two masters and twice enslaved, fall into unprecedented degradation, yet they are so naive as to think they have been "saved" by the French when the latter win a military victory over the Saif. Their delusion is proportionate to their ignorance: "The Empire was pacified, broken up into several zones which the Whites divided. Saved from slavery, the niggertrash welcomed the white man with joy, hoping he would make them forget the mighty Saif's meticulously organized cruelty" (31).

Only to save face and to retain effective power over Nakem had the Saif signed a peace treaty with France. The journey of his son Madoubo to France brings together the two vilest sources of oppression imposed on the *négraille*. In light of this rapprochement, the title of the second part, "The Ecstasy and the Agony," acquires its full meaning.

While carrying on with his imaginative exploration of the *négraille* in the third part of the novel, "The Night of the Giants," Ouologuem also presents a cruelly ironic criticism of négritude in its two aspects, the *négritude of origins* and the *négritude of assimilation*. I have already mentioned the enthusiastic reception initially given by the négritude writers to the work of the German ethnologist Leo Frobenius, who at the beginning of the twentieth century initiated the reassessment of African culture. In the novel, the German scholar is easily identified as Fritz Shrobenius, whom Ouologuem describes, however, as a mere "dealer and ideology-maker" and as a shrewd profiteer. Since he cannot find his way into Nakem society, Shrobenius spends his time filming hippopotamuses and caimans. As an ethnologist, he merely collects the false data given him by fake informants and by Saif ben Isaac himself. . . .

In France, a poet, Guillaume Apollinaire, rather than an ethnologist, had first responded to the religious symbolism of Negro life and art. In the novel, Ouologuem ascribes this discovery to Vandame, a French governor in Nakem, who is indebted to the African witch doctor, Sankolo, who has been banished by the Saif. To win Vandame's confidence, Sankolo fabricates "a mixture of pure, symbolic, and religious art." Vandame, fascinated by this interpretation, eagerly passes on Sankolo's freakish theory to the inquisitive visitors, tourists, sociologists, and ethnologists who come flocking to Nakem. Always on the lookout for profits, the Saif exploits the white people's interest in this kind of art: he orders masks hastily carved after the ancient models and lets them be sold as antique works of art. Hence "Negro art [that] was forging its patent of nobility from the antics of mercantilist spirituality" (95) becomes nothing more than a commodity produced to order to be consumed by foreigners eager for exoticism.

But the brunt of Ouologuem's bitter satire falls on German ethnologists. In Europe, where he has won a high reputation and "une haute chaire sobonicale," Shrobenius, a composite satirical portrait of the European forerunners of négritude, becomes a speculator in Negro art. . . . A branch of ethnology, which Ouologuem calls "Shrobeniusology," is founded on inaccuracies, as is a school of Africanists "clinging to the clouds of a magico-religious, cosmological and mythical symbolism." Consequently, if we are to take Ouologuem's word for it, the revaluation of Negro art and by implication of African culture in general is only the expression of a certain "Afrolatry." It follows that the *négritude of origins* is pure fantasy with no bearing on reality. The satire is aimed at both Europeans and Africans.

Ouologuem also satirizes the *négritude of assimilation*, that is, the Negro's desire to break free of his primitiveness by assimilating to Western culture. This aspiration is personified in Raymond-Spartacus Kassoumi, or rather, in his old father, the serf who had hoped to "save" his children by sending them to the missionary school. Ouologuem renders with ironic pathos old Kassoumi's conversation with Bishop Henry . . . (124). Old Kassoumi believes that the French school will rescue his children from slavery and will make them important men in the black community. His eldest son, Raymond, is the main victim of this cultural assimilation. The old man's urgent advice to him is reported with equal irony: "And you, Raymond, the first-born, become so brilliant and good that the mere sight of you will change the black night within us into bright day—may your success gleam like a sword and be more penetrating than an arrow" (131).

Raymond hopes that, through his assimilation into French culture, he can save the *négraille* from destitution. But he is soon undeceived: instead of commanding respect as he thought he would, he becomes an object of mockery for his schoolmates because he is the best pupil in the class; he is despised by the higher-caste boys. When he has obtained his elementary certificate, Raymond is once again subjected to the Saif's authority. He leads the idle life of a courtier; his knowledge is of no avail. He becomes the symbol of a half-educated elite, whose members labor under the delusion that they have risen to the highest offices but who are mere servants of the Muslim potentate.

Throughout his life Raymond will be a symbol of the perpetual slavery that is the fate of the *négraille*. The cultural and psychological trauma he suffers, which originated in Nakem, is aggravated in France. To ingratiate himself with the whites, Raymond despises his own society; he thus loses his own identity and contributes nothing to Europe, from which he borrows indiscriminately. He becomes a mere verbalist, a typical alienated, decultured, African intellectual . . . (137).

In his determination to adjust to the white world, Raymond worships learning for its own sake. Having failed in his first examinations, he loses his scholarship but refuses to go back to Nakem. When he at last gets his degree, together with the ridiculous title "Black pearl of French culture," he believes he is clever enough to frustrate the Saif's intrigues. He marries a Frenchwoman and receives French citizenship. He believes he has risen to eminence, but he is greatly mistaken. Back in Nakem, he becomes, as noted earlier, a mere instrument of the Saif's policy; the Saif has him elected as a deputy to exert closer control over him. The "weapon of his emancipation," which he thought he was creating by studying, by steeping himself in white culture, proves inefficient against the Saif. Raymond is thus incapable of saving his people and remains a real *négraillon,* that is to say, a permanent slave.

By the end of the third part, the *négraille* have been shown to be the very opposite of what négritude stands for: a "stupefied and fanatical" people, "simple-minded and credulous," conspicuous for their "imbecile vocation" for servitude; they are obviously doomed to endless slavery and debasement, from which even their initiation into modern civilization cannot redeem them.

Only in the last part of the novel, entitled "Love," does a hope of salvation, rather clumsily embodied in Bishop Henry, appear in this gloomy, contemptuous book. The bishop is the only uncorrupted character. The values he represents are unknown in the institutional church, itself contaminated by the will to power; they are the values of genuine Christianity, whose most eloquent manifestation is love. Henry is the only efficient defender of the *négraille,* who, without his help, could never rid themselves of their tyrant. A clever, courageous, and strong man, Henry lets the Saif understand that he knows the Saif's secret and compels ben Isaac to renounce his evil power. That is the significance of the novel's close. When the Saif is formally exposed, he throws his asp into the fire, and the long-awaited dawn is at last ready to break in Nakem.

In the conflict that brings them face to face, Bishop Henry and the Saif represent opposite values, an opposition given concrete form in the game of chess at the close of the novel. Much has been said about the "enigmatic" or "mysterious" ending of *Le Devoir de violence*, but there is no real mystery; the symbols used in this part of the novel are clear enough. The Saif loses his power, and his defeat is conveyed symbolically: the asp hidden in the flute represents the secret apparatus he has devised to maintain his tyrannical power. The bishop's victory symbolizes the triumph of Christian love over tyranny and the evil designs of the temporal powers. In other words, the death of the asp implies the end of absolute Muslim rule and the rise of the better values upheld by the Western world, a world alien to the *négraille*. In Ouologuem's view there is nothing in the *négraille* that might be credible; they deserve only contempt. Salvation can only come from outside. The novel ends with the bishop and the Saif "speaking the same language for the first time," the language of love as it is taught by the Christian religion.

Unfortunately, from an artistic standpoint, this last section, deliberately offered as a positive conclusion, comes as an anticlimax when compared with the rest of the novel. It is unconvincing; one is tempted to see it as a kind of deus ex machina, as if after describing so many scenes of violence, eroticism, horror, and barbarism, the author had suddenly decided to give his work a hopeful ending.

THE HISTORICAL THEME

The undeniable originality of *Le Devoir de violence* as a novel has been described by Albert Gérard:

> Escaping out of the French distinction of the literary genres as well as of the African tradition of the linear novel centered on one single character, it is first of all a vast historical fresco, or rather pseudo-historical, which gradually is focused on an anti-hero and ends as a novel of the classical model. That is because Ouologuem's subject-matter is the black community as well as the African individual.[10]

Indeed, the "historical" theme of *Le Devoir de violence* is what makes it different from other African novels in French; it fits in with the oral tradition whose best interpreters are West African griots. By placing the *négraille* at the center of his chronicle, the author relates the odyssey of a whole people who endured the same fate for centuries. Saif himself is more of a symbol than a real person: because of his hateful activity, his presence hangs threateningly over each Nakem family; he is the very embodiment of tyranny.

The most striking feature of the novel is its style, the originality of which can only be compared with that of Amos Tutuola (b. 1920) or perhaps Okot p'Bitek, both writing in English. Although preserving the spontaneity of the oral tradition, Ouologuem's chronicle of oppression and debasement, of horror and violence, is told in a truly epic yet also sarcastic manner: the many parentheses, full of exclamations and quranic formulas, give the sentences a broken, sinuous syntax that does not mar the novel's unity of tone. Unfortunately, those qualities are practically absent from the last part of the book, where the narrative rhythm becomes slow and heavy and the tone pedantic.

The unique significance of *Le Devoir de violence* for the history of French African writing lies in the image it offers of the black continent, an image as far removed from the romanticism of négritude as from the anti-colonial realism of the novelists. The work is clearly intended to offer the Western reader an alternative picture, less complacent, less imbued with anti-European rancor, presented as more faithful to the reality of Africa. This has not escaped the attention of Hena Maes-Jelinek in her sensitive review of the novel. After recalling that, in Ouologuem's view, "colonialism was only an episode in the long and cruel history of Africa," she goes on to observe:

> The author explodes one by one all the taboos that hide from the world *the true image of Africa*: Religion-Fetishist, Muslim, Christian—Negro Art, African Civilization, Ethnology. . . . Ouologuem does not accuse; he de-mystifies by painting his own poignant vision of Africa.[11]

Undoubtedly, Ouologuem as a novelist is entitled to "his own vision," and it is even his duty as an artist to present it as a "true image." But, by the same token, it is this African's critic privilege and duty to voice his doubts about the truth of this image, in the same way as it is his right to question the methods and assumptions of the négritude writers. For Ouologuem, too, borrows from European scholars such theories as may suit his purpose. One of these is the notion that the Saifs are of Jewish origin. As Jacques Lanotte perceptively points out:

> Following up Delafosse's thesis which argues that the Peuls are emigrated Jews from Cyrenaique, Ouologuem gives a cruelly ironical significance to the expression "negro king": Saif himself, the almighty tyrant, would be seen by the universal consciousness as a slave because he is a Jew. Thus the true significance of that bloody feudal system reveals itself to us in a startlingly new light.[12]

By deliberately selecting from the African past only those elements that may debase it, Ouologuem created a myth different from but as dangerous as the one he was seeking to destroy. In his assumption that the essence of Africa does indeed lie in its original primitiveness, he achieved a real tour de force by heaping up scenes that would not have been out of place in such films as *Ya bon Banania* and *Mata-Mata,* which until recently were a source of facile mirth for a certain European public. I have insisted enough on the savage and barbaric character of the *négraille*. It is worth noting that such ethical values as motherly love or the sense of solidarity and the social harmony inherent in the clan system, as well as such cultural values as dance and music, are all absent from Ouologuem's Africa. The legendary modesty of Muslim society is completely ignored. Ouologuem's image of sub-Saharan Africa is one of total permissiveness and generalized promiscuity. Do we have here "the true image of Africa"? The African reader does not hesitate to answer in the negative: Ouologuem's Africa is a myth born of what he himself called in his *Lettre à la France nègre*, "la gymnastique opératoire de l'écriture."

This myth is all there is in the "historical" theme that is Ouologuem's main concern in *Le Devoir de violence*. His interpretation of the colonial period and of the whole historical development of West Africa is, to say the least, disconcerting. He seems to believe that European colonization in no way modified the old social and political structures set up by the Muslim rulers. More than that, he insists that those African leaders used French colonizers as mere tools for the benefit of their own colonialism:

> But to Nakem the colonial powers came too late, for with the help of the local notables a colonial overlord had established himself long since, and that colonial overlord was none other than Saif. All unsuspecting, the

> European conquerors played into his hands. Call it technical assistance. At that early date! (24)

Ouologuem's vision stands in contradiction to African reality. As everyone knows, European colonizers were using black chiefs everywhere in Africa to help them establish their own administration. Decorated by the French in a spirit of derision, those notables assisted the colonizers in levying taxes, recruiting infantry, and instituting the forced labor system. Colonization was a procedure for the economic expansion of the European powers, who therefore did not object to the traditional chiefs retaining an exclusively moral authority over their clans. On the contrary, they exploited this ascendancy to ensure the efficiency of their administrative and commercial activities. The black notables, who lost forever the economic control of their country, no longer wielded real power; they merely entertained the illusion that the colonizers, for whom they were a convenient instrument, acknowledged their authority. It was they who were serving the European colonizers.

As Yves Benot's comments clearly show, not all Western critics were taken in by Ouologuem's picture of Africa:

> Everything is by no means false in this disconcerting picture; for the precolonial social structures have not all been destroyed at one blow by the new masters, but have rather been conserved, or strengthened, often enough in their more oppressive aspects. But it was only to the extent that the colonizer gained more profits in such a system, the oppression of which helped and strengthened the colonial domination, collaborating toward the exploitation of the land by the European imperialist powers. Those among the chiefs and notables who did not give in were beaten and crushed by the colonizers who did so to preserve their interests, whether in the case of Alpha Yaya in Guinea, or the Achanti's king in the Gold Coast, or many others. And it is here that Ouologuem denies the reality of history or would make it read completely in reverse.[13]

More specifically, Ouologuem offers a highly personal interpretation of the French educational system in Africa: the Saif ordains that "only the sons of servile condition should be subjected to education by the French, compelled to attend mass and be baptized by the missionaries" (60). But in reality, to secure the cooperation of the traditional chiefs, the French colonial administration created the so-called *Écoles d'otages* [School of Hostages] generally reserved for the sons of African notables, so as to simultaneously control their parents and train their sons for public office in the colonial administration.

The most glaring illustration of Ouologuem's distorted presentation of history is no doubt Raymond-Spartacus Kassoumi's election as a deputy. When the Union Française was created, a number of Black students living in France were hurried back to the colonies to be elected as deputies. Sent out to deceive the African masses, they were the mere pawns of the colonial power. In Nakem, however, it is the French who are duped by the Saif. Ouologuem has conveniently downgraded European colonization into a mere historical incident that had no serious impact on African society. When confronted with historical truth, Ouologuem's Africa is seen to be but an abstract composition bearing no resemblance to reality.

This inverted interpretation of history seems to have been dictated by Ouologuem's wish to create an authentic African literature, for he considers that the works written before independence could not have been genuinely African:

> I do not call the literature of the Colonial times African literature. In my opinion it is more anti-Colonial literature; I see it as being mostly an answer to the situation raised by the presence of the White instead of being deeply rooted in Africa as such. So it is perhaps after Independence that one should expect an explosion of African literature.[14]

There is thus little doubt that Ouologuem's urge to create a truly African literature—free from the anticolonial complex as from the romanticism of négritude and shaped by the most recent Western narrative techniques—made him choose a deliberately different approach from that of his predecessors. Yves Benot rightly points out that various non-African literary ingredients went into the making of *Le Devoir de violence*:

> As has been made evident, this African novel has all the ingredients of the English black novel of the 1800s, that is, of a certain type of popular serial: a string of murders—all perfect crimes—poison, witchcraft, drugs, eroticism, and pederasty; not to mention the edifying sequence of the bondsman's son who rises to become a deputy. We have here an impressive anthology. A stylistic anthology also; a cursory reading evokes the musty odors of the assorted rejects of Kateb Yacine, Sartre, Gatti, and even Godard (the dialogue between the prostitute and Bice Parain)—not to mention the distorted echo of the négraille of Césaire's *Cahier d'un retour au pays natal*, and many others, no doubt. As a result, the novel seems cloaked with a certain stylistic ostentation which can easily surprise and actually fascinate. From this point of view, it is a greenhouse product, wholly artificial. (Sankolo's account of his adventure as a mort-vivant, who is drugged and sold is a passage of virtuosity which owes a great deal to Paris and hardly anything, it seems, to Africa.)[15]

The literary influences that have entered into the service of Ouologuem's aesthetic purpose do not of themselves explain his approach to his subject. Political motives, namely, the bitter disappointment experienced by many African intellectuals since the end of colonial domination, must also be taken into account. During the struggle for independence, enthusiasm was at its highest; everyone aspired to a better world with plentiful opportunities for individual development. But those great expectations were ill-founded: the greater part of independent Sub-Saharan Africa has since swayed between anarchy and dictatorship; its history is already ridden by civil wars and military coups, and its politics is too often the product of clan nepotism and shameful corruption.

As early as the 1950s, the disillusionment of idealistic intellectuals was openly expressed in the novels of Cyprian Ekwensi, since joined by other Nigerians such as Chinua Achebe and Wole Soyinka and by Ayi Kwei Armah from Ghana. It is no doubt an indication of their growing maturity as intellectuals and citizens that writers from French-speaking Africa, among whom Camara Laye, Charles Nokan, and Ahmadou Kourouma are most notable, should at last criticize modern African society. Thanks to *Le Devoir de violence*, Yambo Ouologuem holds a prominent position in that group. However, no African critic who loves his people and is proud of them can agree with Ouologuem's view that the black man's predicament today is the result of an ontological flaw, an innate collective proclivity to slavery and spoliation or an inveterate inability to work out adequate solutions for his own problems. Clearly, between the utopian lyrical exaltation of négritude and the contemptuous denunciation of the *négraille,* the African novel in French has still to find the middle course of a nonmythical assessment of African reality.

Notes

1. Yambo Ouologuem, *Le Devoir de violence* (Paris: Éditions du Seuil, 1968). Quotations are from Ralph Manheim's translation, *Bound to Violence* (New York, 1971).

2. *Le Monde*, November 19, 1968.

3. See, among others, Albert Gérard, "Littérature francophone d'Afrique: Le temps de la releve," *Revue Nouvelle*, Vol. 49 (1969), 198–204; Jacques Lanotte, "Un Renaudot africain: *Le Devoir de violence*," *Culture et Développement*, Vol. 1 (1969), 670–676; Sully Faik, "Yambo Ouologuem: *Le Devoir de violence*, Prix Renaudot 1968," *Congo-Afrique*, Vol. 9, No. 32 (1969), 91–101; Hena Maes-Jelinek, "Yambo Ouologuem," *African Literature Today*, Vol. 164 (1970), 54–55; and Yves Benot, "*Le Devoir de violence* de Yambo Ouologuem est-il un chef-d'oeuvre ou une mystification?" *La Pensée*, No. 149 (February, 1970), 127–131.

4. Léopold Sédar Senghor, "Rapport sur la doctrine et la propagande du parti," quoted by Lylian Kersteloot, *Les Écrivains noirs de langue française: Naissance d'une littérature* (Brussels: Editions de l'Université de Bruxelles, 1963), p. 110.

5. Walter A. E. Skurnik, "Léopold Sédar Senghor and African Socialism," *Journal of Modern African Studies*, Vol. 3 (1965), 349–450.

6. Frobenius's *Kulturgeschichte Afrikas* (Paris: Gallimard, 1933) was available in French translation as *Historie de la civilisation africaine* as early as 1937 (reprint, 1952). See also Maurice Delafosse, *Les Noirs de l'Afrique* (Paris: Payot,

1922), *Civilisation négro-africaine* (Paris: Librairie Stock, 1925), *Les Nègres* (Paris: Editions Rieder, 1927), and *L'Ame nègre* (Paris: Payot, 1922).

7. For more information about négritude, see especially, besides Lylian Kesteloot's book already mentioned in note 4, Albert Gérard, "Historical Origins and Literary Destiny of Négritude," *Diogenes*, No. 48 (1964), 14–38; and two excellent articles by Abiola Irele: "Négritude and Black Cultural Nationalism" and "Négritude Literature and Ideology," *Journal of Modern African Studies*, Vol. 4 (1965), 321–348 and 499–526.

8. Gerald Moore, "Towards Realism in French African Writing," *Journal of Modern African Studies*, Vol. 1 (1963): 61–73.

9. Ibid.

10. Gérard, "Littérature francophone d'Afrique," 198–204.

11. Maes-Jelinek, "Yambo Ouologuem," 54–55. Italics are mine.

12. Lanotte, "Un Renaudot africain," 670–676.

13. Benot, "*Le Devoir de violence* de Yambo Ouologuem," 127–131.

14. "Interview: Yambo Ouologuem." *Cultural Events in Africa*, No. 61 (1969): 2.

15. Benot, "*Le Devoir de violence* de Yambo Ouologuem," 127–131.

4

Images of Working People in Two African Novels: Ouologuem and Iyayi

Tunde Fatunde

1

This essay aims to examine the images of working people in two African novels, *Violence* by Festus Iyayi of Nigeria[1] and *Le Devoir de violence* (*Bound to Violence*) by Yambo Ouologuem of Mali.

Frantz Fanon's definition of violence is two-fold: physical harm and mental harm. This definition may be applied to neo-colonial as well as to colonial Africa.[2] Physical violence was, of course, the indispensable spine of the colonial order. It was necessary to make colonized peoples yield to the imperialist economic ambitions of the colonizing capitalists. In fact, the antagonistic relation between colonized and colonizer makes all colonial societies tend towards the police state. On the other hand, in a neo-colonial situation, the presence of physical violence is apparently attenuated and diffused. But still in this diffuse form it continues as the indispensable instrument of the local comprador bourgeoisie in its collaboration with the foreign capitalist in extracting more surplus value from African working people.

Mental violence in both the colonial and the neo-colonial situation cannot be divorced from physical violence. Religion and sexuality, for example, are parts of the superstructure molded by the neo-colonial ruling

---

This chapter was previously published in Georg M. Gugelberger, ed., *Marxism and African Literature* (Trenton, N.J.: African World Press, 1985). Reprinted with permission of Georg M. Gugelberger.

class as effective weapons to exert mental violence on African working people. Certain class values embodied in religion and sexual relations serve to maintain the exploitative social relations of production. According to Fanon:

> The church in the colonies is the white people's church, the foreigner's church. She does not call the natives to God's ways but to the ways of the white man, of the master, of the oppressor. And as we know, in this matter many are called but few chosen. (32)

The Arab Islamic religion plays a central and oppressive role in *Le Devoir de violence* by Ouologuem. This is in keeping with Fanon, who regards European Christian religion and Arab Islamic religion as convenient partners in the naked colonization of African people (104–105). His materialist and revolutionary position could not condemn one religion and excuse another.

Sexuality also occupies a crucial position in Fanon's theory of mental violence. In colonial and neo-colonial societies, patriarchal values predominate, and women are the victims of these values, suffering from sexual discrimination and exploitation, especially when they are working class women. Their social situation is worst when they live in feudal societies that have undergone foreign domination. Consequently, Fanon recommends that post-colonial revolutionary Africa:

> . . . must guard against the danger of perpetuating the feudal tradition which holds sacred the superiority of the masculine element over the feminine. Women will have exactly the same place as men, not in the clauses of the constitution but in the life of every day. (163)

The use of violence by the exploiting and ruling social classes calls forth the redeeming violence of the "damned." Fanon justifies, dialectically, the use of violence as an instrument of liberation, because the only language the colonialists understand is "the language of pure force" (45). Amilcar Cabral realized in practice this Fanonist theory of violence, demonstrating historically in Guinea-Bissau that a mass-based working people's violence can totally neutralize that of the exploiting ruling class. The violence of liberation is never violence for violence's sake, but a physically and spiritually redeeming counter-violence. It is difficult therefore to accept Jack Woddis' critique of Fanon's theory of liberating violence. He accuses Fanon of making "a mystique of violence."[3] But violence must be broadly conceived as meaning economic, political, and ideological as well as military struggle between the "damned" and the exploiter. In liberating themselves by counter-violence from all kinds of alienating mental and physical violence imposed by the colonial and neo-colonial exploiters, the "damned" would also be working towards the dis-alienation *of the exploiters* (228). Fanon's concept of violence is thus dialectical.

2

The fundamental image of African working people in *Violence* and *Le Devoir de violence* is identical: the workers are the producers of all social wealth.

In Ouologuem's novel, for over seven centuries the slaves and peasants have been forced to provide their labor power in order to guarantee and sustain the survival of the feudal Nankem Kingdom (80). In most cases, they were slaves for three different masters: the feudal aristocracy of Saif, who controls a diminishing kingdom, Arab Moslem slave dealers, and European Christian colonizers. The people are made to work in order to provide surplus-value for one local and two foreign masters at the same time. Yambo Ouologuem divides this imposed historical burden of the working people into two important epochs. For most of the seven centuries of feudal and colonial order, the working people were subjugated as mere chattel slaves. Only the last small fraction of this period is the neo-colonial epoch in which slaves have now been converted into peasants. This transformation should not, however, be considered as an emancipation, for the essential character of exploitative social relations of production remains intact.

In *Violence*, by Festus Iyayi, the working people, represented by Idemudia and others who gather at the Iyaso Motor Park, are constantly looking for work. Here again, people are forced to sell their labor power to the local bourgeoisie in order to survive. In most cases they are employed merely on a daily basis, so there is no job security. Since the surplus-value created is to be shared between the local and the foreign masters, Idemudia and his comrades are grossly exploited as manual laborers in off-loading cement bags and as workers with building contractors.

An implicit critique of patriarchal and sexist values is to be found in both novels. For example, Saif has a so-called divine right to mate first with the proposed wife of any of his subjects. And in *Violence* the comprador bourgeoisie uses women to gain contracts. One should note the "proletarian" revulsion manifest by Idemudia and Adisa when they are asked, on different occasions, to satisfy the sexual needs of members of the comprador class. Saif, the feudal king of Nakem, never excludes women when he wants to sell off some of his subjects as slaves. The reason for this mixed-sex chattel slavery is simple: the reproduction of slaves can only be guaranteed by taking along both males and females. In [*Violence*], Adisa, the wife of Idemudia, unwillingly submits herself to sexual humiliation in order to procure the money necessary for her husband's hospital bill. And thus the working people have to undertake often inhuman tasks to regain crumbs of the surplus-value which they themselves created. Idemudia and his comrades even have to sell some pints of their blood in order to live.

The feudal court of Saif has never suffered any material privation. On the contrary, it has enjoyed abundant material wealth and absorbs a large part of the surplus value in order to present itself as "divine," "natural," and "normal." Ouologuem has successfully depicted the manner in which some pre-colonial and colonial African feudal lords lived on the sweat and blood of the African working people. The social situation of the twentieth century neo-colony shown in *Violence* is strikingly similar. Obofun, a highly placed bourgeois civil servant, and his wife, Queen, squander a great deal of cash on expensive cars. They certainly do not present the image of the thrifty and hard-working bourgeoisie which is interested in saving capital in order to move from the position of hoteliers and rentiers to that of manufacturers and industrialists.[4]

The organized violence of the state is portrayed in both novels. The feudal lords of Nakem Kingdom make abundant use of the apparatus of coercion against the working people, both under Arab and European administrations. In Iyayi's work, Idemudia and his co-workers are threatened with state violence if they press on with their case for an increase in their daily wages. Queen, the business woman, feels very comfortable in her handling of the workers' demands because her personal connections with some highly placed civil servants guarantee police protection if ever a protest should arise.

The Saif ruling family of Nakem kingdom makes "creative" use of religion. For example, Saif combines traditional religion and Islam because this is useful for subduing the working people. In the mosques and Islamic schools, Saif is presented as a divine ruler, and at the same time the presence of Arab slave traders is legitimized as a "god-sent" partnership in the task of purifying souls. With the advent of European slave-traders and colonizers, Christianity is said to have philanthropic and civilizing aims and thus helps to foist another colonial master on Africa. One is reminded that Christian benediction was given to African soldiers who were recruited to fight both the First and Second World Wars of international capitalism.

Both Arab Islam and European Christianity had devastating effects on African traditional religions. Even the cultural and artistic artifacts of Nakem Kingdom were stolen with the open complicity of both religions. In one case a Bishop of the Catholic Church stole accomplished artifacts under the pretense that these artistic works were pagan and must be destroyed.

3

The image of working people in *Violence* and in *Le Devoir de violence* is the same in some respects and different in others. It is the same in so far as one immediately grasps the ongoing antagonistic relation between the working people and the exploiting ruling classes. In *Le Devoir de violence*, violence pervades the social relations of production between the feudal Islamicized ruling family of Nakem Kingdom and the "damned" under their domination. Also, one hardly perceives any sharp delineation between direct violence, religion, and sexuality as instruments of the ruling class. Their synthesis and employment at times reaches the point of pathological sadism. The vivid framing of these bloody and brutal images clearly asserts the historical falsity of Senghorian négritude, a neo-colonial ideology which presents the African past as peaceful, pastoral and devoid of class struggle. *Violence* also demonstrates both the pervasiveness of violence in an exploiting economic structure and its fusion with ideological instruments.

A fundamental difference in the framing of images by Ouologuem and Iyayi revolves around the character of the working people. In *Le Devoir de violence* working people are presented as passive and dormant victims for over seven centuries; apparently there was not a single occasion when the people protested their living conditions. They did not struggle to liberate themselves; rather they prayed piously and appealed to the ruling classes for their liberation. Consequently, we see occasional periods of "liberation" of the working people by the feudal lords in Ouologuem's presentation.

In *Violence*, however, the working people are presented as individuals who believe in struggling for their liberation—as fully conscious human beings who are prepared to face their problems with courage. At the same time, they are not presented as infallible heroes but also have their human weaknesses. Idemudia, for example, is tempted to propose sex to Queen even though he realizes that this might adversely affect the ongoing struggle between Queen, the contractor, and Idemudia's own labor union.

Yambo Ouologuem presents the working people as an amorphous mass belonging to a single social class in society. Of course he is correct to show vividly how this class was oppressed by the feudal lords of Nakem in alliance with Arab and European slave traders who came under the umbrella of a so-called civilizing mission, but he gives us the impression that the working people are lacking in any spirit of rebellion to that oppression. They refuse even to attempt to cut the parasitic sucker binding them to the local and foreign exploiters. And thus in *Le Devoir de violence* there appears the eternal omnipotence of African lords and foreign colonizers.

In Festus Iyayi's novel a balanced picture is given, both of the working people and of the exploiters. Neither social class is infallible. They both show a degree of human failing and human strength, although it is abundantly clear that Iyayi is on the side of the working people. As a radical writer he is not complacent towards the plight of those who have only their labor to sell. But he does not legitimize Idemudia's attempt at beating his wife; neither does he approve of the (understandable) "sexual methods" of Adisa, who searches for money to pay off Idemudia's hospital bill.

Certainly the creative role of labor is emphasized in Iyayi's work. Working people are essentially responsible for humanizing the natural surroundings of mankind:

> Not far off were the houses which sweat and labor had already erected. Life there was ablaze where labor had left its positive mark, the labor of hundreds of thousands of workers, working in the intense sunlight or in the biting cold or in the blinding rain, piling the blocks higher and higher and wiping the salt and sweat from their eyes and their foreheads with the backs of their hands and all underpaid, treated no better than slaves. (Iyayi 255–6)

Unlike Ouologuem, the working people in *Violence* are not presented as an amorphous and faceless thing lacking in its own goals. Instead, they are seen as indispensable agents of human progress. Iyayi emphatically rejects the presentation of a situation in which "slave traders took all the credit for the achievements of the slaves" (256). Here again is the difference between Iyayi and Ouologuem. The latter apparently gives all the social credit to slave traders and bourgeois colonizers; while Iyayi rehabilitates the image of working people as the primary historical force, and one to be politically reckoned with in society. . . .

Violence is accordingly viewed differently by the two novelists. In *Le Devoir de violence* it is regarded as an abstract, a-historical and philosophical phenomenon. In this universe there cannot be *class* violence. This might have been the outlook of a colonial Catholic bishop. In this novel, in fact, the dominant views of members of the exploiting classes are given aesthetic preference.

In a colonial and neo-colonial situation one cannot but give empirical credence to a Fanonist view of violence. This school of thought regards violence as inextricably bound to counter-violence. But in *Le Devoir de violence* it is a force used only by exploiters against the exploited. In this bourgeois presentation of violence, working people did not come up even with a spontaneous response.

A deeper look at the philosophical position of Festus Iyayi on violence reveals the following points: Violence is a historical phenomenon. It has a class basis. Surplus value is forcibly extracted and expropriated from the working people by the owners of the means of production. Consequently, Idemudia feels that violence

> . . . consisted not of physical brutal assault but a slow and gradual debasement of himself, his pride as a man. (Iyayi 251)

Despite the constant presence of class violence pitted against the working people, the latter are portrayed as determined to overcome it within historical limits. At work, in hospitals and at home, the working people face violence of one form or another with courage and resistance.

In both *Le Devoir de violence* and *Violence,* history and religion are dialectically interwoven. But once more, the views of the two writers on this issue are diametrically opposed. Saif and the colonial Catholic bishop could be regarded as Yambo Ouologuem's mouthpieces as regards history and religion. The history of mankind, according to them, is shaped and determined by an extra-terrestrial being. Man wanders aimlessly in the early desert and is innately full of faults; and these faults cannot be rectified because man is permanently sick and degenerate. Thus it is not possible to resolve the problem of human misery. One has to submit without question, for redemption can only come after death. Religion teaches that Salvation is not possible in any human society and that the history of humanity is finite, whereas God's (or Allah's) kingdom is a-historical and eternal. Therefore, while on earth, man should undergo preparation for eventual acceptance in God's kingdom.

Thus man is always condemned to recommence from the beginning, and any struggle by the working people to free itself from the pedagogy of the oppressor is futile. As everything is predestined by God, exploitation is natural. Therefore, one has the impression that the working people are powerless human beings who should not put into question the status quo. It may be tempting from all this to adduce that Yambo Ouologuem is on the side of the exploiting ruling classes, local and foreign, because, as Trotsky said:

> All the social illusions which mankind has raved about in religion, poetry, morals or philosophy served only the purpose of deceiving and blinding the oppressed.[5]

On the other hand, history and religion are considered by Festus Iyayi as the entire handiwork of man. His philosophical emphasis is on human labor. Man became what we know of him today as a result of labor. This is all the more reason why working people must be given their rightful place in human history. Iyayi's presentation of the truck-pushers is a good illustration of his materialist conception of history. According to him, these two truck-pushers did not think of the church. Their truck was their church and their labor was their God. Unlike Yambo Ouologuem, the author of *Violence* does not give credence to any metaphysical school of thought which posits that the destiny of man is in the hands of an extra-terrestrial being. He asserts, for example, that the two children of a beggar, stretching out their hands at the doorstep of a church, " . . . were the children of the world, not created by God" (Iyayi 228).

Thus we may conclude that *Le Devoir de violence* is uneven. The feudal class and the foreign colonizers are given too much prominence. The working people only come in as a negligible and almost superfluous element in the novel. This is a serious and unacceptable amputation of historical reality. In *Le Devoir de violence*, mankind must always submit itself to the exclusive destiny proposed by God; but we assert that art should be able to portray the potential of man to struggle against all obstacles.

Festus Iyayi's concept of art tallies with that of Fanon. In his novel, he sees the working people as people always in the process of asserting their existence through struggle. They face the future with determination. At the same time, a balanced view is given of the members of the neo-colonial comprador class. They are also portrayed as human beings, but as human beings debasing themselves and others in their efforts to appropriate the surplus-value created by the working people. On the whole, Iyayi's concept of art is progressive and Fanonist because he recognizes that

> This art needs a new self-consciousness. It is above all incompatible with mysticism, whether it be frank or whether it masquerades as romanticism, because . . . collective man must become the sole master, and . . . the limits of his power are determined by his knowledge of natural forces and by his capacity to use them. (Trotsky 15)

NOTES

1. Festus Iyayi, *Violence*. London: Longman, Drumbeat, 1979.
2. Frantz Fanon, *The Wretched of the Earth*. London: Penguin, 1967. I am using the French edition, *Les Damnés de la terre*. Paris: Maspero, 1973.
3. Jack Woddis, *New Theories of Revolution*. New York: International Publishers, 1972.
4. Fanon predicted the historical inability of the African bourgeoisie to industrialize given its dependence on the foreign bourgeoisie, its role as commercial intermediary and its wasteful spending. Some radical African writers like Ousmane, Beti, Armah, Ngugi and Iyayi confirm Fanon's prediction.
5. Leon Trotsky, *Literature and Revolution*. New York: Monthly Review Press, 1974: 88.

5

The Representation of Homosexuality in Ouologuem's *Le Devoir de violence*

Chris Dunton

The following excerpt from an article published in 1989[1] discusses some aspects of Ouologuem's treatment of sexuality and of the representation of sexuality in *Bound to Violence*: in particular his treatment of the homosexual relationship between Raymond Kassoumi and his white patron Lambert.

To place *Bound to Violence* in context in this respect, it should be pointed out that in the great majority of texts by black writers from sub-Saharan Africa in which the subject is introduced, homosexual activity is stigmatized as being unnatural, an import from the West (or the Arab world), symptomatic at one level or another of exploitation. This applies to "high art" novels, popular fiction, drama, poetry in English and French, the work of the Hausa poets of northern Nigeria, the autobiographies of black South Africans. There are dozens of examples, a fair sample of which are documented by Daniel Vignal (1983)[2] and myself (1989). In the latter article, I summarized the general orientation of these texts as follows:

> Almost invariably, if the engagement of the West with the African continent is generally identified as being exploitative, then homosexual activity is seen as being a particularly repugnant aspect of this. In a number of different contexts—the colonial situation; the neo-colonial state ruled through collusion with Western advisers; the prison system under apartheid;

Portions of this chapter were previously published as part of "'Wheyting Be Dat?' The Treatment of Homsexuality in African Literature," *Research in African Literatures,* Vol. 20, No. 3. Reprinted with permission of *Research in African Literatures.*

> the situation of the African student living in the West—homosexual activity is identified with exploitation, being enabled by money or power relations, and understood to be all the more disturbing because alien to African society. (1971: 424)

It is true that a small number of other texts offer a less pejorative treatment of homosexual activity, even one that may appear sympathetic. In most of these cases, however, homosexual activity can hardly be said to be adopted as a subject-matter *in its own right,* rather there is a more-or-less overt binding of the subject to the text's wider thematic concerns, a function that requires the subject to be co-opted for some ulterior service, to be processed or specialized. In common with Ama Ata Aidoo's *Our Sister Killjoy*, Wole Soyinka's *The Interpreters*, Yulissa Amadu Maddy's *No Past, No Present, No Future*, Rebecca Njau's *Ripples in the Pool,* and Thomas Mpoyi-Buatu's *La Re-production*, Ouologuem's *Bound to Violence* appears to be one such novel.

In the first chapter of *Bound to Violence*, Ouologuem's strategy is similar to that of Ayi Kwei Armah in *Two Thousand Seasons*: accounts of homosexual orientation/activity are employed at several points to strengthen—to make more repugnant—images of violence and oppression. Ouologuem identifies homosexual activity as one of the vices of the autocratic Saifs, pederasts whose deaths are as ironically fitting as those of Armah's "predators" (16). Later, however, Ouologuem introduces a more extensive homosexual episode, the impact of which is far more ambiguous.

Ouologuem charts the metamorphosis of Raymond Kassoumi from son of a serf in the French colony of Nakem to student in Paris, a project initiated by the father ("intent on steeping his children in white culture," p. 124) and eagerly adopted by Raymond, for whom study becomes "the instrument of his emancipation" (125). Ouologuem describes the political relationships that overdetermine son's and father's aspirations, noting that Saif sees an educated, Westernized Raymond as "an instrument of his own future policy" in accommodating the French colonial authority (135). He shows how the adoption of a cosmopolitan personality alienates Raymond from his own society to such an extent that, as a student in Paris, divorced from the realities of life in Nakem, he is no longer able to determine how dominant an influence is "the white man" in him (137).

Then comes the crisis, provoked by Raymond's unwitting incest with his sister, by the news that his father has been sold into slavery, and by the death of his sister a few days later. Failing his exams, sinking into poverty, he makes incessant visits to a cafe, to drink, smoke, and find company in order "to forget himself" (149). While he is in the cafe, he is approached by Lambert, a wealthy homosexual.

Ouologuem's account of this episode proceeds in three fairly distinct stages. When Raymond realizes Lambert wants to pick him up, his first reaction is a realistic assessment of his own situation—"what can you hope for if you're a nigger?"—and a recognition that if he goes with the man he will be paid and that, after all, he has to live (152). Then there is a shift in consciousness as a deeper disturbance strikes him, signaling his realization that the relationship might have more to offer him than his keep. Lambert might constitute, at least temporarily, a paradoxically free context in which he can satisfy his previously unfulfilled capacity for tenderness.

Acknowledging that he is about to submit to Lambert, Raymond sees his action neither as pragmatic nor as an act of self-consciously apprehended degradation (as with Kanaan, the central character in Saidou Boukoum's novel *Chaîne*[2]), but as a kind of apotheosis, a realization of his brotherhood with "the world's unhappiness in the face of its gigantic hunger for self-destruction." Lambert's seduction speech, which now follows, imposes an idealist interpretation on their meeting ("'I've been looking for you for a long time, in every boy I've ever encountered'") and then—superrealistically—makes a direct appeal to Raymond's desolation:

> Don't be afraid. I know what it is to be without a woman, what it is to believe in a woman, to belong to a woman and not to possess her, to suffer long silences, not to be a man with a woman, and then, instead of love, to know the silent cry of a thirst together. (152–153)

As the two leave, then, and walk to Lambert's flat, their apprehension of the significance of the union is identical, with both absorbed in "a dream of peace and solitude" (153).

Ouologuem's description of their lovemaking does nothing to disrupt this sense of harmony. It differs markedly not only from any other passage in this novel but from nearly every other evocation of homosexual activity in African literature. The one element emphasized is tenderness: a regard for the other shared by both men. This, too, is an extremely reticent passage in its physical detailing: there are no references to the couple's sexual organs—a conspicuous silence in a book in which genitals generally have attributed to them the vivid particularity of independent characters. In place of this, there is an emphasis on sensuousness, which brings into relief the couple's absorption in each other, and an emphasis on the escape from self that Raymond achieves through their lovemaking (155).

In the following pages, however, the episode enters its third and final stage as Raymond achieves a full realization of the relevance of his middle name, Spartacus. Now, for the first time, he sees clearly the history of his continent; further, without dismissing the magnitude of the impact it has had on him, he identifies the relationship between himself and Lambert as the product of a history of exploitation and alienation. Recognizing now "the problem of his body and his skin, the body and money of his partner" (157), he realizes that he is enmeshed in a historical-cultural crisis from which he is unable to extricate himself.

In this episode, then, Ouologuem seems to make use of a homosexual affair as a way of exploring Raymond's alienations. At the same time, the treatment of the subject appears more thoughtful than in novels where homosexual activity is simply identified as a particularly disagreeable aspect of Western exploitation.

Yet to leave it at that would be disingenuous. In this novel the homosexual episode eludes accurate assessment unless it is seen in the contexts of Ouologuem's larger strategy—and it remains elusive even then. *Bound to Violence* consistently challenges false and falsifying representations of history—this being perhaps its primary aim. A great deal of the commentary that the novel has attracted turns on its apparent denigration of African culture. Yet, although that is hardly an imaginary problem, Ouologuem's primary targets are, in fact, the ideological formations through which that culture has been (mis)represented.

The novel comments explicitly on this process of falsification: noting the inaccessibility of fact; caught between the conflicting accounts of griots, chroniclers, and elders; satirizing the mania of the Africanist Shrobenius for construing indigenous philosophies "which had lost all living reality," a habit of mind Ouologuem identifies, angrily, as having been passed on to Africans themselves (87). Ouologuem exposes the process by which fact is consciously, deliberately transmuted according to the needs of competing ideologies. Thus, the legend of Saif ben Isaac al-Heit becomes a vital component in "black romanticism" and in African nationalist thinking; whether the legend is "truth or invention" is hardly relevant (8). *Bound to Violence* constitutes an attack on falsifying representations—on racism, obviously, but also on any mode of representation that rarifies, rationalizes, and sentimentalizes the history of the continent.

But literature, too, is, at one level, representation—a fact that Ouologuem insists on foregrounding throughout the novel. As Eric Sellin comments, there is here "an intentional fragmentation of structure . . . which . . . constantly reminds us that we are dealing with a fiction, an extension of the mind . . . of a creator" (1976: 142).[3] It also vitally reminds the readers of *their* minds and of their capacity—like that of the serfs of Nakem—for accepting falsifying representations.

As Robert McDonald comments, Ouologuem's treatment of the episode of Raymond and Lambert is "strikingly sympathetic and sensitive"; there is a poetic lyricism here that isolates the episode from its context—so that, like many other parts of the novel, it reads as a discrete entity: hence McDonald's speculation the passage may be an imitation of an episode in some American gay novel (67–68).[4]

If the Raymond-Lambert episode strikes a discord with its surrounding material because of its tenderness, other episodes describing sexual relationships are equally obtrusive: a passage on the courtship of Raymond's parents has its tenderness disrupted by the ludicrously exaggerated account of the husband's ritual observances on the marriage eve (49), and the account of the lovemaking of Sonia and Madoubo has its mild eroticism deflated by the German girl's asking—"on the brink of ecstasy"—whether the background music is "functional" (89–90).

A more elaborate episode is the seduction of Awa by Chevalier, for which Ouologuem first employs his borrowings from Graham Greene's *It's a Battlefield* (54–56) and then an imitation of the kind of early-twentieth-century pornography that used to be printed in France for illegal import into English-speaking countries (56). This episode (an apparently gratuitous extension from the plot, Awa having been sent by Saif to spy on Chevalier) and Ouologuem's blatant imitation of period pornography seem to emphasize his view of the political dispensation of a colonial state. History is exposed as farce, suggesting that it *deserves* to be represented in this way. This attitude is later supported when a passage on Raymond's feelings about his imminent election to the French National Assembly—a sensitive issue in the context of the political developments of the late 1940s—is suddenly interrupted by a long paragraph describing his wife's treating him to a session of oral sex (168).

The absurd dislocations and distortions that Ouologuem's text performs may well be intended to alert the reader to the nature of representation, to suggest, especially, that the ideology of colonialism and neocolonialism depends upon a ruthless misrepresentation of real (and especially material) relationships. This seems, however, not to be Ouologuem's entire subject, since a large part of the novel suggests a concern with the proper way to present sex in serious fiction—and a scathing disregard for the conventions to which the majority of African literary texts subscribe. Here again Ouologuem seems to identify a history of misrepresentation: in this instance, society's convention-bound falsification of the status of sexual relationships. The episode of Raymond and Lambert may play another function, apart from allowing Ouologuem to develop ideas about the condition of alienation among an African elite. Deliberately offending a conventional sensibility by projecting a homosexual relationship as tender and mutually satisfying, his episode may be meant to reflect on the role of sex in the way we articulate the priorities and the ordering of society. When Ouologuem describes the first night of Raymond and Lambert's affair as the "apogee of the natural order of love" (155), the critical focus is set firmly on the word "natural": the whole novel, after all, questions whether ideology bears such a natural relationship to fact as it claims, that is, whether ideology derives organically from fact, unmediated by any process of selection, distortion, or exclusion. Further, one specific aspect of the novel—its account of sexual relationships—questions whether the official history of sexuality (which includes its representation in literary texts) really corresponds so very closely to our actual sexual orientation, desire, and performance—that is, to the real order of sexuality in our lives. Ouologuem's text in this respect links to Roland Barthes's work on signification and could be seen, even, as providing an African novelist's anticipation of work on the history of sexuality and its ideology by Michel Foucault.[5]

In the end, however, it is difficult to determine precisely what Ouologuem's intention is. One problem in this novel—or one distinctive feature, since Ouologuem's challenge may lie just here—is that there is no still point in the text, no acknowledgment signaling immutable fact, only the counter-pointing of competing false rationalizations. For example, although the novel's stylistic dislocations and imitations are obvious enough, much of its quotation and plagiarism might have gone unnoticed were it not for the diligence of some early readers. What kind of novel would it then be? Or, for that matter, what kind would it be if, as Ouologuem himself has suggested, the novel was intended to be printed with an apparatus of quotation marks and references surrounding its borrowings?[6] That doubt refers us again to the problem of representation. Ouologuem's intention seems to be to warn us against the process of falsification, to counsel, as does his Bishop Henry, "'Keep your eye on the other man's play . . . You must learn to know it and to know yourself in it'" (177). The difficulty is that Ouologuem's procedures are, variously, both so blatant and so covert—as if he has participated in Henry's admission, "'I want to play as if they did not see me playing'" (177)—As if he wished both to proclaim (from the rooftops) and to dissolve the notion of difference, of other. The novel leaves wide open the question of what is the relevance of recognizing Ouologuem's borrowings for what they are—representations of representations. I am leaving this question unanswered; it provokes some doubt as to what is the relevance of relevance.

NOTES

1. Daniel Vignal, "L'homophilie dans le roman négro-africain d'expression anglaise et française," *Peuples Noirs, Peuples Africains,* Vol. 33 (May-June 1983): 63–81.

2. Saidou Boukoum is a Guinean novelist. Published in 1974, six years after *Bound to Violence*, *Chaîne* is—like the Ouologuem novel—highly audacious in its construction of narrative and characterization in a way that contradicts "normal" expectations of African fictional discourse on sexuality.

3. Eric Sellin, "The Unknown Voice of Yambo Ouologuem," *Yale French Studies,* Vol. 53 (1976): 137–162.

4. Robert McDonald, "*Bound to Violence*: A Case of Plagiarism," *Transition,* Vol. 41 (1972): 64–68.

5. Under this reading, *Bound to Violence* is a work that might have appealed to Roland Barthes:

> The 'healthy' sign for Barthes is one which draws attention to its own arbitrariness—which does not try to palm itself off as 'natural' but which, in the very moment of conveying a meaning communicates something of its own relative, artificial status as well. . . . Signs which pass themselves off as natural, which offer themselves as the only conceivable way of viewing the world, are by that token authoritarian and ideological. It is one of the functions of ideology to 'naturalize' social reality, to make it seem as innocent and unchangeable as Nature itself. (Terry Eagleton, *Literary Theory*, Oxford: Blackwell, 1983)

6. See K. W. (Kaye Whiteman), "In Defence of Yambo Ouologuem," *West Africa*, No. 2875, July 21, 1972: 939–941.

6

Yambo Ouologuem and the Meaning of Postcoloniality

Kwame Anthony Appiah

Tu t'appelais Bimbircokak
Et tout était bien ainsi
Tu es devenu Victor-Emile-Louis-Henri-Joseph
Ce qui
Autant qu'il m'en souvienne
Ne rappelle point ta parenté avec
Roqueffelère . . . [1]

—Yambo Ouologuem

All aspects of contemporary African cultural life—including music and some sculpture and painting, even some writings with which the West is largely not familiar—have been influenced, often powerfully, by the transition of African societies *through* colonialism, but they are not all in the relevant sense *post*colonial. Many areas of contemporary African cultural life—what has come to be theorized as popular culture, in particular—are not concerned with transcending—with going beyond—coloniality. Indeed, it might be said to be a mark of popular culture that its borrowings from international cultural forms are remarkably insensitive to—not so much dismissive of as blind to—the issue of neo-colonialism, or "cultural imperialism." This does not mean that theories of postmodernism are irrelevant to these forms of culture: the internationalization of the market and the

This chapter was previously published in different form in *In My Father's House: Africa in the Philosophy of Culture* (New York: Oxford University Press, 1992). Reprinted with permission of the author.

commodification of artworks are both central to them. But it *does* mean that these artworks are not understood by their producers or their consumers in terms of a postmodern*ism*: there is no antecedent practice whose claim to exclusivity of vision is rejected through these artworks. What is called "syncretism" here is made possible by the international exchange of commodities but is not a consequence of a space-clearing gesture.

Postcolonial intellectuals in Africa are almost entirely dependent for their support on two institutions: the African university, an institution whose intellectual life is overwhelmingly constituted as Western, and the Euro-American publisher and reader. (Even when these writers seek to escape the West, as Ngugi wa Thiong'o did in attempting to construct a Kikuyu peasant drama, their theories of their situation are irreducibly informed by their Euro-American formation. Ngugi's conception of the writer's potential in politics is essentially that of the avant-garde, of left modernism.)

Now this double dependence on the university and the Euro-American publisher means that the first generation of modern African novels—the generation of Chinua Achebe's *Things Fall Apart* and Camara Laye's *L'Enfant Noir*—were written in the context of notions of politics and culture dominant in the French and British university and publishing worlds in the 1950s and 1960s. This does not mean that they were *like* novels written in Western Europe at that time, for part of what was held to be obvious both by these writers and by the high culture of Europe of the day was that new literatures in new nations should be anticolonial and nationalist. These early novels seem to belong to the world of eighteenth- and nineteenth-century literary nationalism; they are theorized as the imaginative recreation of a common cultural past that is crafted into a shared tradition by the writer; they are in the tradition of Sir Walter Scott, whose *Minstrelsy of the Scottish Border* was intended, as he said in the preface, to "contribute somewhat to the history of my native country; the peculiar features of whose manners and character are daily melting and dissolving into those of her sister and ally." The novels of this first stage are thus realist legitimations of nationalism: they authorize a "return to traditions" while at the same time recognizing the demands of a Weberian rationalized modernity. . . . From the late 1960s on, these celebratory novels of the first stage become rarer: Achebe, for example, moved from the creation of a usable past in *Things Fall Apart* to a cynical indictment of politics in the modern sphere in *A Man of the People*. But I want to focus on a francophone novel of the late 1960s, a novel that thematizes in an extremely powerful way many of the questions I have been asking about art and modernity: I mean, of course, Yambo Ouologuem's *Le Devoir de violence*. This novel, like many of the second stage, represents a challenge to the novels of the first stage, it identifies the realist novel as part of the tactic of nationalist legitimation, and thus it is (if I may begin a catalogue of its ways of being *post*-this and that) *postrealist.*

Now postmodernism is, of course, postrealist also. But Ouologuem's postrealism is surely motivated quite differently from that of such postmodern writers as, say, Thomas Pynchon. Realism naturalizes: the originary "African novel" of Chinua Achebe (*Things Fall Apart*) and of Camara Laye (*L'Enfant noir*) is "realist." So Ouologuem is against it, rejects—indeed, assaults—the conventions of realism. He seeks to delegitimate the forms of the realist African novel, in part, surely, because what it sought to naturalize was a nationalism that, by 1968, had plainly failed. The national bourgeoisie that took on the baton of rationalization, industrialization, and bureaucratization in the name of nationalism turned out to be a kleptocracy. Their enthusiasm for nativism was a rationalization of their urge to keep the national bourgeoisies of other nations—and particularly the powerful industrialized nations—out of their way. As Jonathan Ngaté has observed, "*Le Devoir de violence* . . . deal[s] with a world in which *the efficacy* of the call to the Ancestors as well as the Ancestors themselves is seriously called into question."[2] That the novel is in this way postrealist allows its author to borrow the techniques of modernism, which, as we learned from Fredric Jameson, are often also the techniques of postmodernism. (It is helpful to remember at this point how Yambo Ouologuem is described on the back of the Éditions du Seuil first edition: "Né en 1940 au Mali. Admissible à l'École normale supérieure. Licencié ès Lettres. Licencié en Philosophie. Diplômé d'études supérieures d'Anglais. Prépare une thèse de doctorat de Sociologie." Borrowing from European modernism is hardly going to be difficult for someone so qualified—to be a Normalien is indeed, in Christopher Miller's charming formulation, "roughly equivalent to being baptized by Bossuet."[3])

Miller's discussion—in *Blank Darkness*—of *Le Devoir de violence* focuses usefully on theoretical questions of intertextuality raised by the novel's persistent massaging of one text after another into the surface of its own body. The book contains, for example, a translation of a passage from Graham Greene's 1934 novel *It's a Battlefield* (translated and improved, according to some readers) and borrowings from Guy de Maupassant's *Boule de Suif* (hardly an unfamiliar work for francophone readers; if this latter is a theft, it is the adventurous theft of the kleptomaniac, who dares us to catch him at it).

And the book's first sentence artfully establishes the oral mode—by then an inevitable convention of African narration—with words that Ngaté rightly describes as having the "concision and the striking beauty and power of a proverb"[4] . . . and mocks us in this moment because the sentence echoes the beginning of André Schwarz-Bart's decidedly un-African

1959 holocaust novel *Le Dernier des justes*; an echo that more substantial later borrowings confirm.[5]

> *Nos yeux* boivent l'éclat du soleil, et, vaincus, s'étonnent de pleurer. Maschallah! oua bismillah! . . . Un récit de l'aventure sanglante de la négraille—honte aux hommes de rien!—*tiendrait aisément dans* la première moitié de ce *siècle; mais la véritable histoire* des Nègres *commence* beaucoup plus *tôt*, avec les Säifs, en l'an 1202 de notre ère, dans l'Empire africain de Nakem. . . . [6]
>
> *Nos yeux* reçoivent la lumière d'étoiles mortes. Une biographie de mon ami Ernie *tiendrait aisément dans* le deuxième quart du xxe *siècle; mais la véritable histoire* d'Ernie Lévy *commence* très *tôt*, ver l'an mille de notre ère, dans la vieille cité anglicane de York. Plus précisément: le 11 mars 1185.[7]

The reader who is properly prepared will expect an African holocaust; and these echoes are surely meant to render ironic the status of the rulers of Nakem as descendants of Abraham al-Heit, "le Juif noir."[8]

The book begins, then, with a sick joke against nativism at the unwary reader's expense, and the assault on realism is—here is my second signpost—postnativist; this book is a murderous antidote to a nostalgia for *Roots*. As Wole Soyinka has said in a justly well-respected reading, "The Bible, the Koran, the historic solemnity of the griot are reduced to the histrionics of wanton boys masquerading as humans."[9] It is tempting to read the attack on history here as a repudiation not of roots but of Islam, as Soyinka does when he goes on to say:

> A culture which has claimed indigenous antiquity in such parts of Africa as have submitted to its undeniable attractions is confidently proven to be imperialistic; worse, it is demonstrated to be essentially hostile to the indigenous culture. . . . Ouologuem pronounces the Muslim incursion into black Africa to be corrupt, vicious, decadent, elitist and insensitive. At the least such a work functions as a wide swab in the deck-clearing operation for the commencement of racial retrieval.[10]

But it seems to me much clearer to see national history as what is being repudiated, to see the text as postcolonially postnationalist as well as anti- (and thus, of course, post-) nativist. (Indeed, Soyinka's reading here seems to be driven by his own equally representative tendency to read Africa as race and place into everything.[11]) Raymond Spartacus Kassoumi—who is, if anyone is, the hero of this novel—is, after all, a son of the soil, but his political prospects by the end of the narrative are less than uplifting. More than this, the novel explicitly thematizes, in the anthropologist Fritz Shrobenius—an obvious echo of the name of the German Africanist Leo Frobenius, whose work is cited by Léopold Sédar Senghor—the mechanism by which the new elite has come to invent its traditions through the "science" of ethnography:

> Saïf fabula et l'interprète traduisit, Madoubo répéta en français, raffinant les subtilités qui faisaient le bonheur de Shrobénius, écrevisse humaine frappée de la manie tâtonnante de vouloir ressusciter, sous couleur d'autonomie culturelle, un univers africain qui ne correspondait à plus rien de vivant; . . . il voulait trouver un sens métaphysique à tout . . . Il considérait que la vie africaine était art pur . . . [12]

At the start we have been told that "there are few written accounts and the versions of the elders diverge from those of the griots, which differ from those of the chroniclers."[13] Now we are warned off the supposedly scientific discourse of the ethnographers.[14]

Because this is a novel that seeks to delegitimate not only the form of realism but the content of nationalism, it will to that extent seem to us misleadingly to be postmodern. *Mis*leadingly, because what we have here is not postmodern*ism* but *postmodernization,* not an aesthetics but a politics, in the most literal sense of the term. After colonialism, the modernizers said, comes rationality; that is the possibility the novel rules out. Ouologuem's novel is typical of this second stage in that it is not written by someone who is comfortable with and accepted by the new elite, the national bourgeoisie. Far from being a celebration of the nation, then, the novels of the second stage—the postcolonial stage—are novels of delegitimation, rejecting the Western imperium, it is true, but also rejecting the nationalist project of the postcolonial national bourgeoisie. And, so it seems to me, the basis for that project of delegitimation is very much not the postmodernist one; rather, it is grounded in an appeal to an ethical universal. Indeed, it is based, as intellectual responses to oppression in Africa largely are based, in an appeal to a certain simple respect for human suffering, a fundamental revolt against the endless misery of the last thirty years. Ouologuem is hardly likely to make common cause with a relativism that might allow that the horrifying new-old Africa of exploitation is to be understood—legitimated—in its own local terms.

Africa's postcolonial novelists—novelists anxious to escape neocolonialism—are no longer committed to the nation, and in this they will seem, as I have suggested, misleadingly postmodern. But what they have chosen instead of the nation is not an older traditionalism but Africa—the continent and its people. This is clear enough, I think, in *Le Devoir de violence*; at the end of the novel Ouologuem writes:

> Souvent il est vrai, l'âme veut rêver l'écho sans passé du bonheur. Mais, jeté dans le monde, l'on peut s'empêcher de songer que Saïf, pleuré trois millions de fois, renaît sans cesse a l'Histoire, sous les cendres chaudes de plus de trente Républiques africaines.[15]

If we are to identify with anyone, *in fine*, it is with *la négraille*—the "niggertrash," who have no nationality. For these purposes one republic is as good—which is to say as bad—as any other. . . .

If there is a lesson in Ouologuem's cultural bricolage, it is surely that we are all already contaminated by each other, that there is no longer a fully autochthonous pure-African culture awaiting salvage by our artists (just as there is, of course, no American culture without African roots). And there is a clear sense in some postcolonial writing that the postulation of a unitary Africa over against a monolithic West—the binarism of Self and Other—is the last of the shibboleths of the modernizers that we must learn to live without.

Already in *Le Devoir de violence*, in Ouologuem's withering critique of "Shrobeniusology," there were the beginnings of this postcolonial critique of what we might call "alteritism," the construction and celebration of oneself as Other. Ouologuem writes: "Voilà l'art nègre baptisé 'esthétique' et marchandé—oye!—dans l'univers imaginaire des 'échanges vivifiants!'"[16]

And then, after describing the fantasmatic elaboration of some interpretative mumbo-jumbo "invented by Saïf," he announces that "Negro art created its patent of nobility from the folklore of mercantile spirituality, hey, hey, hey."[17] Shrobenius, the anthropologist, as apologist for "his" people, a European audience that laps up this exoticized Other; African traders and producers of African art, who understand the necessity to maintain the "mysteries" that construct their product as "exotic"; traditional and contemporary elites who require a sentimentalized past to authorize their present power: all are exposed in their complex and multiple mutual complicities.

> "Témoin: la splendeur de son art, la grandeur des empires du Moyen Age constituait le visage vrai de l'Afrique, sage, belle, riche, ordonnée, non violente et puissante tout autant qu'humaniste—berceau même de la civilisation égyptienne."
>
> Salivant ainsi, Shrobénius, de retour au bercail, en tira un double profit: d'une part, il mystifia son pays, qui, enchanté, le jucha sur une haute chair sorbonicale, et, d'autre part, il exploita la sentimentalité négrillarde—par trop heureuse de s'entendre dire par un Blanc que "l'afrique était ventre du monde et berceau de civilisation."
>
> La négraille offrit par tonnes, conséquemment et gratis, masques et trésors artistiques aux acolytes de la "shrobéniusologie."[18]

A little later, Ouologuem articulates more precisely the interconnections of Africanist mystifications with tourism and the production, packaging, and marketing of African artworks.

> Une école africaniste ainsi accrochée aux nues du symbolisme magico-religieux, cosmologique et mythique, était née: tant et si bien que durant

> trois ans, des hommes—et quels hommes!: des fantoches, des aventuriers, des apprentis banquiers, des politiciens, des voyageurs, des conspirateurs, des chercheurs—"scientifiques," dit-on, en vérité sentinelles asservies, montant la garde devant le monument "shrobéniusologique" du pseudo-symbolisme nègre, accoururent au Nakem.
>
> Déjà, l'acquisition des masques anciens était devenue problématique depuis que Shrobénius et les missionnaires connurent le bonheur d'en acquérir en quantité. Saïf donc—et la pratique est courante de nos jours encore—fit enterrer des quintaux de masques hâtivement executés à la ressemblance des originaux, les engloutissant dans des mares, marais, étangs, marécages, lacs, limons—quitte à les exhumer quelque temps après, les vendant aux curieux et profanes à prix d'or. Ils étaient, ces masques, vieux de trois ans, *chargés* disait-on, *du poids de quatre siècles de civilisation.*[19]

Ouologuem here forcefully exposes the way in which an ideology of disinterested aesthetic value—the "baptism" of "Negro art" as "aesthetic"—meshes with the international commodification of African expressive culture, a commodification that requires the manufacture of Otherness. Shrobenius, "ce marchand-confectionneur d'idéologie" (this marketer-manufacturer of ideologies), the ethnographer allied with Saif—image of the "traditional" African ruling caste—has invented an Africa that is a body over against Europe, the juridical institution, and Ouologuem is urging us vigorously to refuse to be thus Other.[20]

NOTES

1. You were called Bimbircokak
And all was well that way
You have become Victor-Emile-Louis-Henri-Joseph
Which
So far as I recall
Does not reflect your kinship with
Rockefeller . . .

Yambo Ouologuem, "A Mon Mari," *Presence Africaine,* Vol. 57 (1966): 95.

2. Jonathan Ngaté, *Francophone African Fiction: Reading a Literary Tradition* (Trenton, N.J.: Africa World Press, 1988), p. 59.

3. Christopher Miller, *Blank Darkness: Africanist Discourse in French* (Chicago: University of Chicago Press, 1985), p. 218.

4. Ngaté, *Francophone African Fiction,* p. 64.

5. Ngaté's focus on this initial sentence follows Aliko Songolo, "The Writer, the Audience and the Critic's Responsibility: The Case of *Bound to Violence,*" in *Artist and Audience: African Literature as a Shared Experience,* Richard Priebe and Thomas A. Hale (eds.) (Washington, D.C.: Three Continents Press, 1979), pp. 126–140. Cited by Ngaté, *Francophone African Fiction,* p. 64.

6. "Our eyes drink the flash of the sun, and, conquered, surprise themselves by weeping. Maschallah! oua bismillah! . . . An account of the bloody adventure of

the niggertrash—dishonor to the men of nothing—*could easily begin in the* first half of this *century; but the true history of* the Blacks *begins* very much *earlier,* with the Saifs, in the year 1202 of our era, in the African kingdom of Nakem. . . . " Yambo Ouologuem, *Le Devoir de violence* (Paris: Editions du Seuil, 1968), p. 9. (Translation mine.)

7. *Our eyes* receive the light of dead stars. A biography of my friend Ernie *could easily begin in the* second quarter of the 20th *century; but the true history of* Ernie Lévy *begins* much *earlier*, in the old Anglican city of York. More precisely: on the 11 March 1185." André Schwartz-Bart, *Le Dernier Des Justes* (Paris: Editions du Seuil, 1959), p. 11. Emphasis added to indicate similarities between the two books. (Translation mine.)

8. Ouologuem, *Le Devoir de violence,* p. 12.

9. Wole Soyinka, *Myth, Literature and the African World* (Cambridge: Cambridge University Press, 1976) p. 100.

10. Ibid., p. 105.

11. I discuss this aspect of Soyinka's writing in Chapter 4 of my book *In My Father's House: Africa in the Philosophy of Culture* (New York and Oxford: Oxford University Press, 1992).

12. Ouologuem, *Le Devoir de violence,* p. 102:

> Saif made up stories and the interpreter translated, Madoubo repeated in French, refining on the subtleties to the delight of Shrobenius, that human crayfish afflicted with a groping mania for resuscitating an African universe—cultural autonomy, he called it, which had lost all living reality; . . . he was determined to find metaphysical meaning in everything. . . . African life, he held, was pure art. . . . Yambo Ouologuem, *Bound to Violence,* trans. by Ralph Mannheim (London: Heinemann Educational Books, 1968), p. 87.

13. Ouologuem, *Bound to Violence,* p. 6.

14. Here we have the literary thematization of the Foucauldian *Invention of Africa* (Chicago: University of Chicago Press, 1988) that is the theme of Valentin Mudimbe's important recent intervention.

15. Ouologuem, *Le Devoir de violence,* p. 207: "Often, it is true, the soul desires to dream the echo of happiness, an echo that has no past. But projected into the world, one cannot help recalling that Saïf, mourned three million times, is forever reborn to history beneath the hot ashes of more than thirty African republics." Ouologuem, *Bound to Violence,* pp. 181–182.

16. Ouologuem, *Le Devoir de violence,* p. 94: "Henceforth Negro art was baptized 'aesthetic' and hawked in the imaginary universe of 'vitalizing exchanges.'"

17. "L'art nègre se forgeait ses lettres de noblesse au folklore de la spritualité mercantiliste, oye oye oye. . . . " Ouologuem, *Le Devoir de violence,* p. 110.

18. Ouologuem, *Le Devoir de violence,* p. 111:

> Witness the splendor of its art—the true face of Africa is the grandiose empires of the Middle Ages, a society marked by wisdom, beauty, prosperity, order, nonviolence, and humanism, and it is here that we must seek the true cradle of Egyptian civilisation.
>
> Thus drooling, Shrobenius derived a twofold benefit on his return home: on the one hand, he mystified the people of his own country who in their enthusiasm raised him to a lofty Sorbonnical chair, while on the other hand he exploited the sentimentality of the coons, only too pleased to hear from the mouth of a white man that Africa was "the womb of the world and the cradle of civilization."

In consequence the niggertrash donated masks and art treasures by the ton to the acolytes of "Shrobeniusology." Ouologuem, *Bound to Violence,* pp. 94–95.

19. Ouologuem, *Le Devoir de violence,* p. 112:

An Africanist school harnessed to the vapors of magico-religious, cosmological, and mythical symbolism had been born: with the result that for three years men flocked to Nakem—and what men!—middlemen, adventurers, apprentice bankers, politicians, salesmen, conspirators—supposedly "scientists," but in reality enslaved sentries mounting guard before the "Shrobeniusological" monument of Negro pseudosymbolism.

Already it had become more than difficult to procure old masks, for Shrobenius and the missionaries had had the good fortune to snap them all up. And so Saif—and the practice is still current—had slapdash copies buried by the hundredweight, or sunk into ponds, lakes, marshes, and mud holes, to be exhumed later on and sold at exorbitant prices to unsuspecting curio hunters. These three-year-old masks were said to be charged with the weight of four centuries of civilization. Ouologuem, *Bound to Violence,* pp. 95–96.

20. Ouologuem, *Le Devoir de violence,* p. 111.

Part 2

Decolonizing Writing? Or, *Pisse-Copie* Aesthetics Reconsidered

7

The Unknown Voice of Yambo Ouologuem

Eric Sellin

Un témoignage et une voix inconnus.

—*Le Monde*

In 1968 Éditions du Seuil, which has over the years published an impressive list of works in French by African and Maghrebine authors, brought out a first novel, *Le Devoir de violence*, by Yambo Ouologuem.[1] Ouologuem was born in Mali in 1940 and is reportedly descended from the kings of the ancient Mali Empire. He went to Paris in the early 1960s to study at the École Normale Supérieure and took degrees in literature, philosophy, and English.

I shall not attempt to summarize *Le Devoir de violence* in any detail. Through historical flashbacks and accounts of the modern adventures of the family protagonist Raymond Spartacus Kassoumi, the book recounts the chronicle of an area of central West Africa, the fictitious kingdom of Nakem (perhaps an anagram of Kanem), from about 1200 to modern times. Written in a checkerboard of styles, and consisting of a sequence of violent acts, erotic deeds, and unexpected turns of events, *Le Devoir de violence* provides engrossing reading. Not surprisingly, the translation rights to this novel with its sure-fire formula of sex and violence were snapped up at the Frankfurt Book Fair by leading publishers in Britain, Germany, Italy, and the United States. The British and American publishers' plans included a

---

This chapter was previously published in *Yale French Studies*, Vol. 53 (1976). Reprinted with permission of *Yale French Studies*.

large distribution in paperback. When the novel was awarded a coveted literary prize, its success story seemed to be an author's dream come true. At the time, no one knew that it was soon to turn into a nightmare for publisher and author alike.

Up till now, my publications regarding Yambo Ouologuem's *Le Devoir de violence* have told the story of my elation and subsequent deflation at encountering this fascinating work and then seeing its presumed authenticity eroded by a number of discoveries of literary dependency. In this essay I should like to summarize the scandal in which I and others became involved: but I should also like to develop some thoughts on the relative attitudes in Africa and Europe regarding imitation and plagiarism. I shall no doubt fail to be definitive in both areas since in the first one we find ourselves brought down to the impasse of a writer's word against his publisher's and, in the second, we are bound to the use of speculation and generalization.

In the August 24, 1968 number of its biweekly literary supplement, *Le Monde* carried the following brief announcement in its regular "Vient de paraître" column:

> Yambo Ouologuem. *Le Devoir de violence*. This half-historical, half-fictional novel about the penetration of the Whites into Africa, viewed from the African side, is the first work of a young Malian, accepted as a candidate in the École Normale Supérieure, who has his *licence* in literature and in philosophy. An unknown voice and testimony. (Le Seuil, 207 pp., 15 F.)[2]

Most of the books thus launched have few repercussions and no one could predict the enormous success this book was about to enjoy, nor the subsequent critical and ethical storm which was to sweep it off the store shelves.

As the weeks and months passed, *Le Devoir de violence* met with unqualified enthusiasm from most reviewers, and its fame—and ultimately its notoriety—was assured when the judges of the Prix Renaudot awarded it the Prize in the first week of October. On October 12, the literary supplement of *Le Monde* printed two brief articles dealing with Ouologuem's book. Critics were later to react viscerally to what they considered a betrayal, and the intensity of their reaction may be explained in part by the converse intensity of the initial enthusiasm, typified by these reviews. When we now consider the compositional methods utilized by Ouologuem in writing *Le Devoir de violence* and which he openly advocates in an essay in his *Lettre à la France nègre*, the retrospective perusal of the first critical acclaim becomes ironic, almost comic. But I do not feel that we have experienced a response growing out of hurt pride, such as the reaction which drove critics to destroy Thomas Chatterton and van Meegeren after their respective forgeries had become known. In the case of *Le Devoir de violence*, we are not dealing with a forgery à la Brother Rowley or à la Vermeer but with a reliance on other writers' imaginative powers and a mechanical creative process which the author and the book itself (including the cover "blurb") had at first led critics to take for a genuine impulse emanating from an individual talent and lending expression to the historico-ethnic heartbeat of a misunderstood continent. It is all well and good to eschew critical standards as outmoded devices and to maintain that art is solely in the eye of the beholder, but the fact remains that a number of critics had felt that Ouologuem had enriched literature, not merely exploited or perpetuated it.

The two articles in *Le Monde* are representative of the critical reaction which greeted this first novel, especially in Europe and America. The reviews stress Ouologuem's unique and independent imagination and the authenticity of his role as a mouthpiece for the African ontology. In the first of the two *Le Monde* pieces on *Le Devoir de violence*, Matthieu Galey praises Ouologuem for the way in which he has dug deeply into his past to lend strength to his characters:

> The principal merit of the first book by Yambo Ouologuem, born in Mali twenty-eight years ago, is the fact that it is a novel, a real novel. Surely, he, too, devotes some thirty pages in the beginning of his work to the evocation of a distant Nakem empire which must be the novelistic transposition of an historical reality. But this harkening back to legend, through the vehicle of his ancestors, introduces the most astonishing, or rather one of the most astonishing characters of *Le Devoir de violence*: Saïf ben Isaac El Heit.[3]

In the second article in *Le Monde*, Philippe Decraene spoke for most readers when he extolled the powerful rhetoric, the individuality, the freshness of material, and the authentic "Africanness" of Ouologuem's work. There is a certain unwitting humor in these early reviews, for—shades of Cocteau's beloved use of accidental truths in the rhetoric of *La Machine infernale* and in the final sentences of *Thomas l'imposteur*[4]—the apprised reader recognizes that Ouologuem did, indeed, "borrow" or "assume" the "most direct means" in telling his tale. Decraene presumably did not know the precise nature of the means at the time that he praised Ouologuem's rhetoric in the following terms: "Abhorring rhetorical devices, rebelling against every compromise, he always adopts the path which appears to him most direct."[5] Decraene admired—and which reader would not?—the way in which the young writer's vision apparently sprang from the profound reservoir of African tradition: "Six years living in France, long months of teaching at the Charenton *lycée* and at the little seminary at Conflans, the preparation of a Diplôme d'Études Supérieures in English—successfully completed—followed by preparation for the Agrégation de Lettres, have in no way altered the authentically African view of things which he has retained" (Ibid.). Decraene again is unwittingly ironic when he states that "For Ouologuem, 'decolonization has not yet been achieved.' That is the main reason he refuses to consider himself in the same light as other Malian authors" (Ibid.). According to Decraene, four years of work on *Le Devoir de violence* had left Ouologuem undaunted, the Malian having just completed a "Lettre ouverte à la France nègre," for which he was seeking a publisher.

Critics throughout the world expressed a similar reaction to *Le Devoir de violence*. The only reservations came from some Africans who felt that the novel didn't ring true, but did not state why. Some felt that there were certain things a real African simply would not say; others wished to discredit Ouologuem for having laid a portion of the blame for the slave trade at the doorstep of conniving Black chieftains. Typical of this dismay is the reaction of the Zaïrese critic Mbelolo ya Mpiku who categorically states that "Ouologuem's vision stands in contradiction to African reality."[6] His uneasiness becomes quite personal by the end of his article when he rejects Ouologuem's assessment of Black history: "However, no African critic who loves his people and is proud of them can agree with Ouologuem's view that the black man's predicament today is the result of an ontological flaw, an innate collective proclivity to slavery and spoliation, or an inveterate inability to work out adequate solutions for his own problems" (Ibid., 145).

When *Bound to Violence* appeared in its American edition, *Time* and *Newsweek* both gave it considerable coverage and praise. Nor can I claim immunity. Several passages of a brief comment published in the *French Review* bear witness to my initial enthusiasm for the book and give an inkling, by contrast, of how disappointed I was to become when it later became evident that Ouologuem was not all that I thought him to be:

> These general characteristics and the rich and intricate history of West Africa from 1200 to today form the backdrop to, and at times the very stuff of, Yambo Ouologuem's brilliant first novel, *Le Devoir de violence*. The author makes exciting and enlightening use of the splendor of the ancient empires and the subsequent sweep of history without his work degenerating into florid exoticism.[7]

I glibly attributed irregularities of structure and style to a willed disruption of narrative in the tradition of the *noveau roman* and went on to stress the rôle Ouologuem's unique vision played in this creation: "Ouologuem tempers his naturally effusive prose with (1) strangely effective moments of crudity and brutality (2), digressions in a flat, controlled style, and (3) an intentional fragmentation of structure which, in keeping with the rationale of the *nouveau roman,* constantly reminds us that we are dealing with a fiction, an extension of the mind, the will, and the typewriter of a creator." (Ibid.) Upon rereading this review, I am struck by the emphasis on expressions and words like "strangely effective," "controlled," "intentional," "extension of the mind," and "creator." As though this were not ironic enough, I concluded my review on the following hopeful note:

> The first offering of this young writer (born in Mali in 1940) greatly enriches Francophone African literature and is well-deserving of its receipt of the Prix Renaudot. I shall eagerly await further works by this man. (Ibid.)

There are reports that Ouologuem has written at least one other novel under a pseudonym, but it was, as a matter of fact, the wished-for next book published under Ouologuem's own name which began to cause many critics to have some nagging doubts, not because of the contents *per se* but because of its flimsiness of diction and weakness of structure. One critic, not yet aware of the full importance of foreign sources in the composition of *Le Devoir de violence*, put it bluntly but accurately when he exclaimed that "Disappointment came, however, when Ouologuem published his second book, *Lettre à la France nègre*, a pamphlet in every way inferior to his novel" (Mpiku, 124). The only way, in fact, that it is superior to *Le Devoir de violence* is in its authenticity, for there is no reason to think that this work is not fully the product of Ouologuem's own talents and abilities! Critics found it difficult to reconcile the novel and the book of essays. The discrepancy was disappointing, and it was so great that it could not simply be attributed to the "sophomore jinx" which has temporarily blighted many a career. A year or so after the publication of Ouologuem's first novel, disquieting charges of borrowings, extensive imitation, and outright plagiarism began to circulate as rumors and then in a series of articles which in turn drew two reactions: on the one hand, a number of people wrote to the authors and editors of these articles supplying further examples of stylistic indebtedness; and, on the other, some critics sought to minimize the significance of plagiarism in general and to defend Ouologuem in particular.

At the "Colloque sur les littératures canadienne et africaine d'expression française" held at the University of Vermont in June, 1971, I demonstrated the similarity between certain passages in André Schwarz-Bart's *Le Dernier des Justes* (Paris: Éditions du Seuil, 1959), and Ouologuem's *Le Devoir de violence*. There were audible gasps from the audience. Afterwards, one young African who contributed a good bit to the conference as a conspicuous Devil's advocate at a number of the sessions complained: "Why are you White people and Europeans always doing this to us? Whenever we come up with something good in Africa, you say that we couldn't have done it by ourselves." The fact is, many authentic good things have come out of Africa and this novel appeared to be one of the finest, whence my great disappointment. Subsequent research and correspondence has revealed that some people were aware of the similarity to Schwarz-Bart's novel even when *Le Devoir de violence* was in manuscript. According to Paul Flamand, the publisher of Éditions du Seuil, the manuscript was received just like any other unsolicited manuscript and turned over to an editor, François-Régis Bastide, who noticed similarities to the general structure of *Le Dernier des Justes* but did not realize how closely certain passages resemble the earlier work until after publication, when the resemblance was noticed by the Schwarz-Bart editor at Seuil. Schwarz-Bart was immediately contacted and he reassured the publishers that he was not in the least offended but rather flattered by the use to which his work had been put by Ouologuem:

> The use made of *Le Dernier des Justes* in no way annoys me. . . . I have always thought of my books as apple-trees, pleased when someone eats some of my apples, and pleased if one is now and then picked in order to be planted in a different soil. I am especially touched, even overwhelmed, to think that a Black writer should have relied on *Le Dernier des Justes* in creating a book like *Le Devoir de violence*. Thus Mr. Ouologuem is not indebted to me, but rather I to him.[8]

Nor did M. Flamand and his staff at Éditions du Seuil have knowledge of the other more direct borrowings which later came to light: "It was only after publication that Ouologuem published at Nalis his *Lettre à la France nègre* and that he sent it to us. . . . But how could we have suspected, in the manuscript, those 'borrowings' which the author made, almost verbatim, from other works?"[9]

Any young writer has been influenced by other writers and will attempt to emulate what he admires, either consciously or unconsciously. He will, as in the case of such fine writers as Christopher Okigbo, John Pepper Clark, Léopold Sédar Senghor, and others, write "in the style of" Pound, Yeats, Eliot, Perse, Claudel, or someone else, without his effort being anything more than apprenticeship derivation or the result of a spontaneous kinship. Certain reviewers seemed to sense such echoes of other literatures in *Le Devoir de violence*; and perhaps one might assume their existence in a first novel. My very first reaction upon completing *Le Devoir de violence* was a fleeting thought that perhaps its author had been impressed by Kateb Yacine's amazing novel, *Nedjma* (Seuil, 1956), and had wanted to do something along those lines for the Black African novel. Rather than condemn him for this, I admired him for apparently having the vision to undertake a similar blend of the "retour aux sources" and the culture shock inherent in the vicissitudes of rapidly marching modern history. Such "remous" or echoes of foreign literatures reached other critics, as well. Consider, for example, the comment of Yves Benot:

> We have here an impressive anthology. A stylish anthology also, and a cursory reading evokes the musty odors of the assorted rejects of Kateb Yacine, Sartre, Gatti, and even Godard (the dialogue between the prostitute and Bice Parain)—not to mention the distorted echo of the négraille of *Césaire's Cahier d'un retour au pays natal,* and many others, no doubt. As a result, the novel seems cloaked with a certain stylistic ostentation which can easily surprise and actually fascinate. From this point of view, it is a greenhouse product, wholly artificial. (Sankolo's account of his adventure as a mortvivant, who is drugged and sold is a passage of virtuosity which owes a great deal to Paris and hardly anything, it seems, to Africa.) (Op. cit., 130)

It is astonishing how loath people were to criticize this novel on the grounds of its having lifted some of its material out of the works of other writers. It may be that they hesitated to make accusations which could be considered libelous.[10] Even half a dozen years after numerous articles in *Le Canard Enchaîné,*[11] *Le Figaro*, *The International Herald*, *Times Literary Supplement*, *West Africa*, *Transition*, *Research in African Literatures*, and on Page One of the daily *Times* of London had broadcast news of the borrowings, the scandal of Ouologuem's prize-winning novel has not become widely known. Most critics and even many area specialists remain impervious to the shadow cast on the book's authenticity. In a recent monograph entitled *Cultura negro africana moderna*, Alfredo Riedel appears to be unaware of the whole affair, writing as follows:

> Ouologuem's work, which is of extraordinary impact, is the product above all of a need for sincerity and pride and of the necessity to know integrally his own personality without false emotions or lies.[12]

The two most conclusive demonstrations of derivations of any significant length—and I have had personal or published reports of passages of one or several lines reminiscent of Pascal, de Maupassant, and many others—came before the public eye within several months of each other.[13] In the Fall, 1971 issue of *Research in African Literatures*, I summarized the similarities between Ouologuem and Schwarz-Bart which had induced such a response at the Vermont colloquium. In that article, I present several passages which are astonishingly similar, in which Ouologuem has paralleled, substituted for, and generally orchestrated on the rhetoric of several sections of *Le Dernier des Justes*. To give but one example, Schwarz-Bart's novel opens as follows:

> Nos yeux reçoivent la lumière d'étoiles mortes. Une biographie de mon ami Ernie tiendrait aisément dans le deuxième quart du XXe siècle; mais la véritable histoire d'Ernie Lévy commence très tôt, ver l'an mille de notre ère, dans la vieille cité anglicane de York. Plus précisément: le 11 mars 1185.[14]

With the substitution of the Blacks for the Jews, with some variations such as "such" for "stars," and with some assonantal and consonantal play of the sort practiced by Raymond Roussel (such as replacing "reçoivent" by "boivent"), Ouologuem comes as close to using as his own the words of Schwarz-Bart as one can come without overtly plagiarizing:

> Nos yeux boivent l'éclat du soleil, et, vaincus, s'étonnent de pleurer. Maschallah! oua bismillah! . . . Un récit de l'aventure sanglante de la négraille—honte aux hommes de rien!—tiendrait aisément dans la première moitié de ce siècle; mais la véritable histoire des Nègres commence beaucoup plus tôt, avec les Saïfs, en l'an 1202 de notre ère, dans l'Empire africain de Nakem, au sud du Fezzan, bien après les conquêtes d'Okba ben Nafi el Fitri.

In my article I did not accuse Ouologuem of plagiarism, for in the passages cited he has not truly plagiarized. He has borrowed and adapted some Schwarz-Bart and added a dash of Aimé Césaire, who had referred in his *Cahier d'un retour au pays natal* to the "Black men who have invented nothing." In fact, when the same diligent young man at the Vermont colloquium asked from the floor if I were accusing Ouologuem of plagiarism, I replied that I was not, that I was rather accusing him of hypocrisy and literary *mauvaise foi* in light of his frequent public statements proclaiming the authentic Africanness of his book. Despite this disclaimer and the fact that the word "plagiarism" does not appear in either my Vermont text or my *RAL* essay, I have been rebuked by several critics for having leveled plagiarism charges at a work which they contend really only imaginatively assimilates and exploits European models in a form of reverse cultural imperialism.

My brief piece published in *RAL* would probably not have attracted a great deal of attention here or abroad had it not been for the fact that the *Times Literary Supplement* and daily *Times* (London) mentioned it on May 5, 1972, on which date *TLS* published side by side a passage from *Le Devoir de violence* and a section of a 1934 novel by Graham Greene, entitled *It's a Battlefield*. The characters in the passage by Ouologuem bear different names and a few slight changes have been entered, but the lengthy passage from *Le Devoir de violence* is little more than a translation of the Greene text, sufficiently faithful that the indebtedness was recognizable even after retranslation into English by Ralph Manheim.[15] It seems to me that this does constitute plagiarism by translation, if, indeed, Ouologuem did not make use of the existing French translation published by Fayard. What's more, this discovery of a second large passage lifted from another work gave credence to growing suspicions among critics that there might be many borrowed passages quilted together to make up the bulk of this novel. Robert McDonald, writing about the Greene borrowing in *Transition*, expressed suspicion about the book in general and about several other specific passages which he felt did not ring true:

> In regard to doubts and suspicions I am unable to substantiate any other definite charges, but there are certainly at least two other important sections of the book about which I feel distinctly wary. The first of these is the section from page 150 to page 159, describing the homosexual affair between Kassoumi and the Frenchman Lambert. . . . My suspicion, then, is that the homosexual episode could very easily have been taken from one of the numerous mediocre gay novels that have flooded the American market, especially in recent years.
>
> The other passage that I feel particularly doubtful about is that from page 161 to page 163 in which Kassoumi's experiences in the Second World War are described. Again, there is nothing that particularly ties it to the character involved, and so one feels that it could have been taken from any one of dozens of post-war novels.[16]

Many critics have expressed confusion about the lack of relevance of certain sections. One section, for example, which is so incredible it should jolt any reader, is the visit to the brothel where the protagonist discovers that the girl with whom he has just had relations is his own sister! The incident would fit in better in a traditional "sous le manteau" pornographic novel of the sort with which Paris abounds. There is a major shift in tone in the novel as historical chronicle gives way to the adventures of the contemporary protagonist, and I suspect that this partial collapse of *Le Devoir de violence* is the result of reliance on inferior material. In dealing with the historical phase of his narration, Ouologuem presumably consulted literary, historical, and archival works which were better written and/or more factual than some of the recent materials which time and good taste have not yet eliminated from the scene.

After the *TLS* revelation, letters flew back and forth among critics and publishers, and the item was sufficiently newsworthy to be picked up by several other important dailies, including the Paris *Herald* and *Le Figaro*. The latter published in its weekly literary supplement of May 13 a brief item by Guy Le Clec'h summarizing the *TLS* allegations.

The only defense Yambo Ouologuem has offered, save indirectly as through remarks quoted by critics, is a reply to Le Clec'h published in the *Figaro Littéraire* of June 10, 1972. Boxed in under the heading "Polémique" are three items entitled "Le Devoir de violence" (Yambo Ouologuem), "Le Devoir de vérité" (signed B.P.), and "Le Devoir d'exactitude"

(Marie Schébéko). These consist respectively of Ouologuem's reply, a rebuttal in behalf of *Le Figaro*, and a statement by the agent representing Greene in France.

Ouologuem's remarks seem somewhat confused, even illogical, and were—I presume—composed in a state of stress. Their major contentions are (1) that use was made of work by Greene and others in order to provide the novel with several "contradictory voices" and in order that Ouologuem's African brothers not think that *he* would discredit them; and (2) that, to this end, he had placed quotation marks around the passages in his manuscript:

> Because of the explosive nature of the subject matter of my novel, *Le Devoir de violence* (torture scenes, cannibalism, insanity, legendary and historical facts, with a few winks at the thesis-stories ["récit à clés"], at racial confrontations), to be objective required that I cause to be heard, as needed, several contradictory voices reflecting the very image of the contradictory things, the prejudices, superstitions, and sensitivities inherent in the problems besetting Blacks.
>
> Thus, the passage by Mr. Graham Greene accused as plagiarism—but in fact cited in quotation marks (just as was the case with several lines from Schwarz-Bart) in my manuscript which is in the hands of my lawyer—preceded a mad scene in which a White man, disguised as the administrator Chevalier, couples a Black woman with a dog. I am a Black man. Obviously, if the facts evoked by me had been the fruit of my own imagination, my brothers in race would scarcely have forgiven me for having sullied the Blacks.[17]

Ouologuem further contends that he never attempted to disguise this technique but spoke openly of it in various lectures and interviews, particularly in the United States, but those he mentions and which I have seen make no reference, appearing to be more than a young author's intellectual "puffing" or attempts to expand the artistic scope and theoretical impact of his work:

> Under these circumstances, putting the text of Mr. Greene between quotation marks was not to act as a plagiarizer but to prevent myself from being disowned by my people as a result of considering it a literary transposition of a fact of a judicial nature. The references to Graham Greene, Kipling, and others were given openly by me to the *New York Times,* the *New Yorker,* and others, during lectures both to professors and to various Black Studies Programs. "If Graham Greene had been present at the scene here's how he might have described it." (Ibid.)

Ouologuem closes his defense with a rather lame assumption of readers' reactions and a parting *ad hominem* salvo directed at his erstwhile publisher:

> The basic question which I ask by means of these techniques and which was noticed by every intelligent reader or critic, and a fortiori by the

> members of the Renaudot jury, who are hardly illiterate, is as follows: "In a world of violence in which the 'devoir d'amour' or vocation of love has been relegated to the realm of lies, who will help the Black to get out of the straits in which he finds himself?" Certainly not the publisher of *Le Devoir de violence* with whom I am at odds and to whom I refused to give my second novel.
>
> It is less than glorious to think that we are presently engaged in a discussion involving accounts. It is not Yambo Ouologuem who has borrowed from the rich, it is the rich who have borrowed from Yambo Ouologuem by making him assume, contrary to editorial practice, the material burden of the customary thanks tendered the members of the Renaudot jury. And it is significant that this publisher should plead guilty in my name without even questioning me, and that, without the slightest claim by Mr. Graham Greene, he should withdraw my book from sale throughout the entire world. (Ibid.)

The two other inserts respond to Ouologuem's final statement. They both indicate that Greene was very upset and demanded that the book be withdrawn until that portion in question could be excised or rewritten:

> To write that Graham Greene made no claim is false. It was the request of the great British novelist that Mme Schébéko, the director of the Clairouin agency which represents Greene in France, made contact with Paul Flamand, the director of Éditions du Seuil, who in turn sent a letter of apology to Graham Greene and then took the steps he had to take in keeping with law and common sense. (B.P. Ibid.)

Ouologuem implies, then, that someone at Éditions du Seuil removed the quotation marks. This would be a very foolhardy gesture which it is difficult to imagine a reputable publisher perpetrating. Furthermore, as I have already pointed out, M. Paul Flamand denies that Seuil had any prior knowledge of the many alleged sources. One critic, who interviewed Ouologuem in the latter's Paris apartment, found the author resentful over the recent allegations:

> When I saw Yambo in his Paris flat recently he was much pre-occupied by the new attacks, and was talking somberly in terms of conspiracy. He was in particular very caustic about the whole relationship of white literary circles, especially publishers, with black writers.[18]

There ensues, in this interesting article, a passage I consider to be of the utmost significance and therefore worth quoting at length. (I do not know if the manuscript mentioned by Ouologuem is the same one allegedly left with his lawyer or an early one whence he copied his final version. It would be interesting to know how many drafts there were; I suspect there was the primitive one mentioned below and then the copy submitted to the publishers. Given the compositional technique there would be little need for an intermediary draft. Even if there are quotation marks on Ouologuem's copy of the typescript, these could have been entered after the fact and one really would have to examine the original publisher's copy to corroborate or invalidate Ouologuem's claim.):

> To demonstrate the injustice of the charges against him, he spent some time taking me through his original hand-written manuscript (in an old exercise book) of *Le Devoir de violence* showing me all the places where there had been quotation marks, if not actual mentions of his literary allusions and quotations. He gave me a fairly comprehensive run-down on all the other authors he might be accused of plagiarising, including the 16th century Portuguese explorer Lope di Pigafeta, and a modern detective story by John MacDonald (the basis of the sequence containing the asp killing), as well as traditional epic sources in Arabic, Bambara and Amharic, and even French colonial documents that he says are still in secret archives. I saw, for instance, where he had written "here ends *The Last of the Just*," a reference omitted like so many others, for whatever reason, from the published version. But it is, in truth, a fairly chaotic script, much erased and amended, with a multitude of little pieces of paper inserted and clipped into pages, some of which have been lost. And it only demonstrates what is completely apparent anyway, that the so-called plagiarism is a stylistic technique to further the purposes of the novel.
>
> Yambo compares it to the techniques of what is called the new novel, or even the work of some modern film-makers in which clips from the films of others are inserted. In a collage it is the arrangement and the juxtaposition which are important. (Ibid.)

The description of the original manuscript proves that *Le Devoir de violence* was not a composition in which inadvertent recollections of school-day readings spontaneously returned to the pen of the brilliant young man, but rather a contrived patchwork intentionally—though apparently messily—put together from various materials. If Ouologuem did not prove his own innocence by revealing this manuscript to "K. W."—for it is just as possible that the quotation marks and references were omitted in the preparation of the final draft prior to submission as omitted by the editors after receipt of such a manuscript—he did prove at least one thing: that he was aware that he was using the material he inserted into his text. It is this factor which distinguishes his text from works done spontaneously in the style of an admired author, such as the many poems by Africans at a certain period in the fifties and sixties which seemed to bear the influence of Jacques Prévert and Paul Eluard. Ouologuem claimed he had referred in various interviews to his borrowings, but these references were always vague or ambiguous and were offset by his equally fervent affirmation of the African authenticity of the work. Ouologuem came to the United States and Canada on a promotional trip in conjunction with the publication of the

American edition of *Bound to Violence. The New York Times Book Review* published a piece in which the interviewer said Ouologuem showed him many "authentic" sources, such as photographs, ancient documents, and the like. When he appeared on the "Today Show" to promote his book, Ouologuem told moderator Hugh Downs that he "wrote this book in French but followed the traditional African rhythms and the spirit of the African past." In various interviews he referred vaguely to "international models," and the like, but it is only with hindsight that these references can be construed as confessions. Representative of how he "fielded" interview questions are the answers given in an interview granted *Plexus*. Asked if there "aren't a great many things in [his] book which [he] might have identified with or expressed in the first person?" Ouologuem replied, "I would never have enjoyed writing a book in the first person. I prefer to let the systems speak and reveal themselves rather than take myself as the unique point of reference."[19] Then, when asked why he wrote *Le Devoir de violence,* the Malian replied:

> I think that one writes because of a moment when one reaches a certain density of being. . . . On the level of form, I wanted to make the epic speak, the tales of the griots, the Arab chroniclers, the oral African tradition. I had to reconstitute a form of speech filtered through a vision arising authentically from black roots. (Ibid., 136)

There were two reactions to the disclosure of Ouologuem's borrowings from other works, the immediate ones of critical disappointment and the author's self-justification and the long-range one. There was also a more concrete immediate reaction of major consequence, for subsequent to the Greene revelation, the various editions were, indeed, withdrawn from publication:

> Mr. Greene's notification [of the similarity by Robert MacDonald, who, as a devotee of Greene's works, noticed the passage in *Bound to Violence* and contacted the Englishman] came just in time to stop a shipment of 250 copies of *Bound to Violence* being distributed in Ibadan but too late to stop 3,000 copies in Nairobi, where they had been put on sale for a few weeks.
>
> The American paperback version was on the presses and the cover had been made when publication was halted.
>
> Mr. Williams Jovanovich, chairman of Harcourt, Brace, Jovanovich, the American publishers, said he had withdrawn 3,400 hardback copies of the book as soon as Mr. Greene's agent in New York had asked them to do so. (Devlin, 2)

A representative of Éditions du Seuil said that they "accepted that the passage had been borrowed and had asked M. Ouologuem to supply a new text." The *Times* quotes her as saying: "We sent him a stiff letter . . . telling him the book had been taken out of publication until this was done. So far we have not had a satisfactory reply" (Ibid.).

The long-range reaction is even more complex. It brings into question the whole notion of authenticity, literary proprietorship, the concept of genre, and the definition of art in general. In other words, once it has been established that Ouologuem did not write a book consistent with its description as given by either the author or the early book reviewers, what does one do with it? Seth Wolitz has written an eloquent if somewhat confused panegyric in defense of Ouologuem in which he raises some challenging questions. Faithful to a "new critical" stance, he would disallow any external biographical or historical explication which might tarnish our enjoyment of the work. He takes several critics to task for having termed Ouologuem and his work "unauthentic" once the source-indebtedness became known. Wolitz writes:

> Ouologuem is no longer an authentic African writer. He makes use of non-African sources and, what's worse, fails to alert the critics to his borrowings at the foot of the page. (Since when have European novelists and dramatists declared their sources?) What, should an African novelist who is making use of a *non-African* genre, a *non-African* language, be deprived of the right to draw on European models, on literary techniques and motivations *imitated* from non-African sources?[20]

Now, no one would deny Ouologuem the right to consider extra-African subjects or to "write in the style" of European writers—and the idea of footnoting the derivations which Wolitz finds repugnant did not seem to bother Ouologuem, according to K.W.'s testimony quoted above—but I still consider authenticity of vision to be the one *sine qua non* quality in a serious writer of any age or culture. There is, however, an authenticity which is *modal*! If we consider Duchamps ready-made or *objet-trouvé*, the value lies not so much in the object as in the philosophy of art which would allow one to dub an object a piece of artistic interest. Wolitz and several other panegyzers have completely missed the boat, for the notion of "authenticity" as they would vouchsafe it in Ouologuem is rationalized in terms of modern European conventions which reject old concepts of what art is. In maintaining that *Le Devoir de violence* is authentically African because it is consistent with the new novel, new-wave film, and the like, critics are merely colonizing Ouologuem's alleged authenticity. . . . We do not have, as Wolitz proverbially suggests, "new wine in old bottles," but rather old colonialism in a new critic's clothing. There remain, then, two questions of fundamental importance in this debate: (1) why did Ouologuem use the sources as he did? and (2) what are the implications of such borrowings in the context of African tradition?

The first question is conveniently asked by Wolitz: "It is, nevertheless, appropriate to ask why Ouologuem found inspiration in the novels of Greene and Schwarz-Bart" (Ibid., 134). Wolitz suggests that perhaps these two borrowings simply represent a *personal* literary creation inspired by a model and a stylistic processus to be developed (Ibid.). If Wolitz prefers to give Ouologuem the benefit of the doubt, he should find it instructive to seek the rather specific answer to his question elsewhere in Ouologuem's own writings.

Lettre à la France nègre, published very shortly after *Le Devoir de violence*, is a collection of somewhat flimsy diatribes against the racial and cultural colonialism of France. One essay, entitled "Lettre aux pisse-copie, Nègres d'écrivains célèbres," is extremely interesting with regard to the controversy over Ouologuem's alleged plagiarism; it also provides ancillary evidence to support the notion that it was, indeed, Ouologuem and not his publishers who deleted the quotation marks somewhere between the chaotic rough draft and the final edition of *Le Devoir de violence*. Furthermore, this essay and the manuscript's annotations reported by K. W. clearly establish intent to borrow and obviate the possibility of an unwitting recall of previously read material by someone with a photographic memory. As I have said, we shall consider the *implications* of borrowing in the context of African aesthetics, but with regard to the creative process used in the specific case of Ouologuem's novel, "Lettre aux pisse-copie" provides more than enough of an answer. This essay lays the grounds, as well, for my suspicion that there may be dozens, even hundreds, of sources more or less faithfully plundered by Ouologuem in his prize-winning opus.

In this essay he addresses himself to "Chère Négraille" but it is fair to assume that he is also speaking to France and the White man. Ouologuem writes: "You famous writers' Black boys, you are terribly frustrated, and castrated in your genius by the law of silence: I want you to learn, through these pages, how to proceed in order to be a "pisse-copie" and to remain white."[21] He then states that he will show his readers how to write a work in a representative vein, in this case that of the detective story: but the *modus operandi* can be applied to any type of work, and when Ouologuem describes the archetypal detective novel with "its gems of description, eroticism, and suspense, as well as the cream of the crop of its perfect crimes, the collection of their recipes. . . . " (Ibid., 167), he could very well be characterizing *Le Devoir de violence*. Furthermore, in the lists of names he suggests as sources, at least one has been connected to a passage in *Le Devoir de violence* (John MacDonald and the asp scene).

Although his syntax is ambiguous in this instance, Ouologuem seems almost confessional when he writes:

> I herewith give you, oh cancerous wretch of kitchen literature!, an unpublished gimmick which will permit you to mass produce all the works

> your boss might order. Base your work exclusively (since that's the genre we are dealing with) on the famous titles of the detective novel: the masters of the *Série Noire* (Carter Brown, James Hadley Chase, Peter Cheyney, John MacDonald, Robert Fish, Douglas Warner . . .), those of the *Série Blanche*, particularly the authors of spy novels (*The Spy Who Came in from the Cold*) or those of "sensational" crimes: Truman Capote, Hitchcok [*sic*], Simenon, Agatha Christie, Jean Bruce, and many others edited by *Fayard* and *au Masque*, either in the purple series or by Denoël (Sébastien Japrisot), or again in the Fleuve Noir or Presses Pockets. (Ibid.)

I suspect that a meticulous comparison of *Le Devoir de violence* and the books by authors mentioned in this essay would yield some interesting similarities. Ouologuem goes on to suggest in no uncertain terms how one can create acceptable books painlessly by using a compilation method not unlike the game played by the Surrealists—called "le cadavre exquis"—in which chance and multiple authorship produce surprising sentences. The following passage is devastatingly pertinent:

> Dear niggertrash, what is waiting for you here is a vast work of reading, a gigantic compilation. But such labor is not in vain. In fact, here is the magic potion of your formula. Your work as a hack, famous Black writers, will permit you—just as it permitted the surrealists—to play, as dadaists, to build your own "cadavres exquis" [exquisite corpses]. Of course, I speak allegorically. In fact, such intellectualism would be a bad idea for you. . . .
>
> For your books (such as I advise you to fabricate them henceforth) must allow you to invent, in the corridors of your imagination, A BILLION NOVELS PAINLESSLY! . . .
>
> And here is the sort of device which will give you the work fully prepared: now it's up to you to find, for your public, the sauce which will make the dish a success. (Ibid., 166–168)

Ouologuem's recipe consists of conceiving of a very general framework ("All there remains is for you to provide it with the largest accommodating framework [structures d'acceuil] with regard to its novelty—which will know no rivalry. . . . " Ibid., 169) within which one concocts a work of optimum heterogeneity and balance by introducing at will sections of suspense, eroticism, violence, humor, and the like. To be certain of success, one should draw his passages from appropriate columns of lifted materials labeled "Suspense," "Eroticism," and so on, which one has established in advance. Ouologuem even provides a sample fold-out with his essay. The would-be author then need only make minor adjustments in order for his borrowings to conform to the general framework and, *voilà*!, a completed novel. Ouologuem cautions the potential *pisse-copie* that he has one duty: "Operate under the double-calling of pedagogy and research, of flattery towards the accommodating framework, even as you retain a clear awareness of the cross-references of the plot" (Ibid., 177).

Given the laborious but unimaginative method he prescribes and the fact that *Le Devoir de violence* was conceived in student notebooks, we could go so far as to interpret the word "devoir" in the title as meaning not "duty"—the apparent sense—so much as "homework."

Now to our second question: namely, how African is the book? The fact that *Le Devoir de violence* is largely a paste-up of unoriginal material which has been appropriately adapted to fit the book's general "structure d'acceuil" does not mean that it is without significance *per se*. If it is not deeply African in its contents, it may be that one or more major African impulses were nevertheless present in the attitude of the author with regard to the notion of plagiarism—even, perhaps, unbeknownst to him—as well as in the general characteristics emerging within the larger structure of his work. In other words, I contend that while the basic contents and method of composition are not spontaneously African, Ouologuem has—in opting for an episodic structure, contrived though it might be—remained faithful to at least one fundamental African impulse found expressed in the majority of Franco-African literary works from Laye's *L'Enfant noir* to Kourouma's *Les Soleils des Indépendances*. The African writer tends, by virtue of age-old traditions of the *khawaré* or "veille poétique" and the oral folk-tale, to prefer to channel his creativity into short, self-contained episodes without undue attention to logical or smooth transitions. Within the larger "structure d'accueil" of the *khawaré* we have a variety of songs, dances, poetic chants, and musical renditions, and it was inevitable that African novels should either adopt compatible European forms like the diary, the collection of tales, and the series of salient memories neatly encapsulated in chapters, or else twist prose into an episodic structure. Examples of the former are Oyono's *Une Vie de boy* and Laye's *L'Enfant noir* and *Dramouss*; an example of the latter is *Les Soleils des Indépendances,* which has an overall structure but is textually made up of shorter entities at times resembling African fables and extended proverbs.

Thus, the collage effect which well-meaning defenders of Ouologuem would justify superficially in terms of Parisian aesthetics might better be justified in profound terms of African aesthetics. A more penetrating analysis of traditional African aesthetics leads us into another area of conjecture. Gobineau was obviously paternalistic and racist without realizing it when he said of African aesthetics that there was, no doubt, an African conception of beauty, but that it was defective compared to the "real" Graeco-Roman beauty.

Traditional African aesthetics, based as it is on a lingua-ontology quite different from the European, balks at the idea of exclusivity of artistic expression. The African artist qua craftsman has traditionally been concerned with an imitation of nature—indeed the "objective correlative" is a universal concern of the artist in all areas and times—but his approach to *mimesis* is not quite that which the Westerner's has become. We are, in Occidental aesthetics, concerned primarily with the imitation *in vacuo*, having been led to that place by Plato, Descartes, Valéry, and a host of other artists qua philosophers. We hoard these imitations of nature in libraries and art museums, paying millions of dollars not for a work of art but for a "Picasso," a "Pollock," or a "Rembrandt." Proprietorship and the urge to inscribe "fecit" after one's name are characteristic of Western art.

In the various societies called "primitive," art has maintained an efficacious function in that the artist is intimately caught up in a vital process involving art as a force and the world as things and forces, the interaction being modal. The late Janheinz Jahn has brillantly summarized African philosophy, or more accurately lingua-ontology, in his controversial book *Muntu*.[22] Suffice it to say, here, that in a world of *bantu* (human beings), *bintu* (things), *hantu* (idea of place and time), and *kuntu* (modality, such as laughter), man has a degree of dominion over things by virtue of his existential perception of them. Things are, in a sense, whatever purpose they serve, their function being conferred by man qua magician or artist. Therefore, aesthetics in such societies involves participation and the modality of the conferral process as much as it does the compositional attributes of the end product. Unlike Western art, it is meaningless in the African context to say, for instance, that a Dogon statue of a standing male figure is "better" than a Fang figure; each no doubt does precisely what it can be expected to do. As Jahn mentions, two like sculptures can represent a king and a peasant according to what the artist has dubbed them, and he can—with his power of *nommo*—redub them at will. Stripped of *nommo*—their designation and participatory essence—they are mere wood and can be discarded, left to termites, or launched on their way to end up on an art dealer's shelf in some European or American city. The so-called primitive is, indeed, concerned with an imitation of nature. He is not, however, concerned with rendering immortal imitations but rather with understanding and finding the means of expressing that which he knows to be immortal.

Even in the new literatures resulting from the linguistic and cultural overlay brought to Africa by French, English, and Portuguese colonialism, the basic lingua-ontological impulse must certainly survive. Indeed, the fact that indigenous impulses are expressed in externally imposed forms has contributed to the creation of a vigorous and unique brand of creativity in the African hybrid literatures.[23] Now, the traditional anonymity of the craftsman-artist, whose patron is not posterity but the village or the clan, makes the notion of plagiarism absolutely irrelevant. The M'zabit rug-maker in the Saharan hill town of Beni-Isguen will automatically use the town pattern when weaving his rug, and not be concerned with who invented the pattern nor with royalties. The pattern is the property of all in the community, patented only by local custom and geographical identity.

Similarly, one would scarcely accuse the Bambara sculptor of lacking originality or of stealing ideas when he makes a mask in the tribe's recognizable traditional style! If Pound's adopted imperial motto "Make It New" sums up the Western preoccupation with originality and novelty, "Make It Inevitable" might be applicable to the African attitude, which respects constancy and tradition.

The Ouologuem affair is a tragic byproduct of the cultural conflict inherent in hybrid literatures which adopt the *lingua* of another country but maintain their own *ontology* (that the conflict can be surmounted with authenticity is borne out by the works of men like Birago Diop). African critics are less nervous than Europeans about plagiarism, feeling no doubt deep in their souls that the writer is a craftsman who owes allegiance to his readership and to some pantheon or *confrérie* of past writers. In one sense, the tragedy of the Ouologuem affair lies to an equal degree in the European tradition of ownership and the quest for private immortality which would cause Mr. Greene or Western critics to care if Ouologuem has borrowed patterns and words from the British novelist. From the puristic traditional African viewpoint, to so borrow is no more spurious than to write a letter using a published book of examples as a guide or than it was for the poets of the Pléiade to use classical authors' texts for material when concocting a commissioned poem. The conflict is aggravated in the case of *Le Devoir de violence*—obviously not at all due to Ouologuem's intervention—because the book turned out to be highly successful, winning a prize which guaranteed enormous sales. Just as the traditional African barter system, prior to the introduction of a currency standard by the colonial traders, made hoarding of material wealth neither practical nor sensible, so did tradition limit the gain an artist-craftsman could achieve from his talents (true, as well, of the poets of Europe before movable type and mass media made literature a public commodity). The *mystique* which surrounds a writer in the West can only be parleyed into a fortune if it is individualized and original, and therefore the writers see to it that their individuation is protected by copyright law.

Ouologuem has committed a European faux-pas. Obviously a man of some genius, Ouologuem must have known that he was violating accepted procedure. He made the grievous error of first hiding his methods and then trying to make light of them. He has also, by calculated use of material created by others—not in the tribal tradition but in the European market place of individuation—done a disservice to his fellow African writers (whom he alternately refers to as his "frères de race" and "négraille"). Many of the writers whose impulses have led them to adopt or emulate without malice the rhythms of admired foreign writers may now find themselves accused of having used the tactics employed and promulgated by Yambo Ouologuem. Finally, Ouologuem may very well have the ability to write a great novel about Africa—entirely of his own vision—but were he to do so, it is doubtful that any publisher or reader would look upon the work without a great deal of skepticism.

NOTES

1. Yambo Ouologuem, *Le Devoir de violence* (Paris: Éditions du Seuil, 1968); British and American editions: *Bound to Violence*, translated by R. Manheim (London: Heinemann Educational Books, 1971). Yambo is the author's surname, but like the Algerian novelist Kateb Yacine he uses the reversed form of his name on his book covers.

2. "Vient de paraître," *Le Monde*, Supplément au numéro 7344, 24 août 1968, p. ii.

3. Matthieu Galey, "Un grand roman africain," *Le Monde*, Supplément au numéro 7386, 12 octobre 1968, p. i.

4. In *La Machine infernale*, which retells the Oedipus tale, the characters coincidentally speak truth; for example, when Jocasta trips over the scarf with which she will later hang herself she idiomatically exclaims: "This scarf will be the death of me"; and at one time the brooch with which Oedipus will blind himself is referred to as an "eye-catcher." Likewise, when pathological liar Thomas is fired at near the trenches, he falls down and replies that truth and fiction had become so interfused in the mind of Thomas that he had inadvertently told the truth, for he was dead.

5. Philippe Decraene, "Un Nègre à part entière," *Le Monde*, Supplément au numéro 7386, 12 octobre 1968, p. i.

6. Mbelolo ya Mpiku, "From One Mystification to Another: 'Negritude' and 'Négraille' in *Le Devoir de violence*," *Review of National Literatures*, II, 2 (Fall 1971), 142.

7. Eric Sellin, "Book Review," *French Review*, XLIII, 1 (October 1969), 64–68.

8. Extract of letter from Schwarz-Bart to Éditions du Seuil, dated August 16, 1968, quoted by Paul Flamand in letter to me dated May 9, 1972.

9. Letter to me dated July 3, 1972.

10. The great similarity in wording in the blurbs on the back covers of *Le Dernier des Justes* and *Le Devoir de violence* and the similar charges of indebtedness leveled at Schwarz-Bart's prize-winning novel a decade earlier threatened—apparently unjustifiably—to open a critical and legal Pandora's box.

11. As early as 1969, the *Canard Enchaîné* detected some lines lifted from de Maupassant.

12. Alfredo Riedel, *Cultura negro africana moderna* (Trieste: Edizioni Umana, 1973), p. 40.

13. Bernth Lindfors forwarded a good many newspaper clippings and leads he received in personal correspondence. One letter to him from Anita Kern passes on various African and European professors' unpublished assertions of derivations from Pascal, de Maupassant, Suret-Canale, and half a dozen other authors. This information reconfirms my suspicion that a great many sources are linked to *Le Devoir de violence*. I am indebted as well to the following people who either sent me clippings or supplied valuable information: M. S. Dembri, Paul Flamand, Charles R. Larson, and Wilbert Roget. Efforts to contact Ouologuem were unsuccessful.

The one Paris address I was given was an obvious and amusing coinage: 4345 rue de la Double Dissoire.

14. "Our eyes take in the light of dead stars. A biography of my friend Ernie would easily fit into the second quarter of the twentieth century; but the real story of Ernie Levy begins very early, around the year 1000 of our era, in the old Anglican city of York. More precisely: March 11, 1185."

"Our eyes drink in the dazzle of the sun, and, conquered, are amazed that they cry. *Maschallah! oua bismillah!* . . . An account of the bloody adventure of the Black rabble—shame on those men of nothingness!—would easily fit into the first half of this century; but the real story of the Blacks begins much, much earlier, with the Saïfs, in the year 1202 of our era, in the African Empire of Nakem, in the south of the Fezzan, long after the conquests of Okba ben Nafi el Fitri." (My translations.)

15. A research student in Australia, Robert McDonald, detected the derivation despite two translations (that into French and that back into English) and notified Mr. Greene, who in turn contacted his publisher, who made this wry comment: "Greene came on the telephone to me. There was a dry, old-paper feel about his voice. You could almost tear it. I immediately turned up the pages and there it was. It is remarkable how it has survived in translation." (Devlin, op. cit., p. 2.)

16. Robert McDonald, "*Bound to Violence*: A case of plagiarism," *Transition*, 41 (1972), 67–68. The pagination referred to is in the English version.

17. "Le Devoir de violence," *Figaro Littéraire*, 10 juin 1972, p. 17.

18. K. W., "In Defence of Yambo Ouologuem," *West Africa*, 21 July 1972, p. 941.

19. Translated as "An Interview with Yambo Ouologuem," in *Journal of the New African Literature and the Arts*, 9/10 (Winter/Spring, 1971), 134–135.

20. Seth I. Wolitz, "L'Art du plagiat, ou, une brève défense de Ouologuem," in *Research in African Literatures*, IV, 1 (Spring 1973), 131.

21. Yambo Ouologuem, *Lettre à la France nègre* (Paris: Éditions Edmond Nalis, copyright 1968, "achevé d'imprimer," janvier 1969), p. 166.

22. Janheinz Jahn, *Muntu: An Outline of the New African Culture* (New York: Grove Press, 1961); See also Eric Sellin, "African Art: Compositional vs. Modal Esthetics," *Yale Review*, LIX, 2 (Winter 1970), 215–227.

23. I have, here, adapted a phrase by Janet Abu-Lughod who aptly speaks of the paradox in modern Maghrebine cities as that combining "externally-stimulated urban forms with indigenous impulses, needs and problems" ("Cities Blend the Past to Face the Future," *African Report*, XVI, 6 [June 1971], 12).

8

Writing as Exploratory Surgery: Yambo Ouologuem's *Bound to Violence*

Christiane Chaulet-Achour

In 1968, when the novel *Bound to Violence* (*Le Devoir de violence*) by the Malian writer, Yambo Ouologuem, was published by Éditions du Seuil, the critics gave it an unusually warm welcome for a francophone African work of that period. Ouologuem's novel even received the Prix Renaudot. However, accusations of plagiarism quickly followed. This chapter, "Writing as Exploratory Surgery,"[1] will focus on Ouologuem's alleged plagiarism.[2] In order to evaluate the collage of texts that Ouologuem engages, I will rely upon distinctions introduced by Dominique Maingueneau, concerning the use of quotations in a text, especially his observation that "a text is not a complete and homogenous unit in which quoted utterances or inferred statements may be considered as unfortunate parasites: on the contrary, such phenomena constitute a law that functions in any discourse, and they are absolutely inseparable from it."[3] After examining Ouologuem's different borrowings, also categorizing them in order to assess them with the appropriate linguistic terminology, we will reflect upon the inferred effects of these borrowings to understand what Ouologuem's objectives may have been.

Bound to Violence: A Harlequin's Costume?

In his 1970 article, "*Le Devoir de violence* de Yambo Ouologuem est-il un chef d'oeuvre ou une mystification?" Yves Benot discussed the ideological

---

This chapter was translated from the French by Ann George. All citations from *Bound to Violence* are from the translation by Ralph Manheim.

aspects of *Bound to Violence* and the perspective it offered on African history. Though his focus differs from ours, he nevertheless wrote:

> [This novel is] an impressive anthology . . . a cursory reading evokes the musty odors of the assorted rejects of Kateb Yacine, Sartre, Gatti, and even Godard (the dialogue between the prostitute and Bice Parain)—not to mention the distorted echo of the négraille of *Césaire's Cahier d'un retour au pays natal,* and many others, no doubt. As a result, the novel seems cloaked with a certain stylistic ostentation which can easily surprise and actually fascinate. From this point of view, it is a greenhouse product, wholly artificial.[4]

Eric Sellin first disclosed in 1971 the numerous borrowings made from André Schwarz-Bart's *The Last of the Just* (1959).[5] Following in his footsteps, other critics went on to "detect" other borrowings. The sum total of this research, to which we may add the present study, informs the following analysis. We will begin by attempting to unravel a small portion of this rather fascinating textual patchwork.

Ouologuem's most spectacular borrowing is certainly his use of Schwartz-Bart's novel. In this case, Ouologuem's borrowings constitute what Maingueneau has called the *epigraphic quote;* that is, a quote that connects "the new discourse to a larger textual ensemble in order to integrate it into a series of previous textual enunciations. The intent is to demonstrate the main directions which the book has taken as a way of signaling that it belongs to a definite ensemble of other discourses" (126). In what follows, we will document Ouologuem's use of *The Last of the Just.*

From the opening of *Bound to Violence,* "The Legend of the Saifs":

> Our eyes drink the brightness of the sun and, overcome, marvel at their tears. *Mashallah! wa bismillah!* . . . To recount the bloody adventure of the niggertrash—shame to the worthless paupers!—there would be no need to go back beyond the present century; but the true history of the Blacks begins much earlier, with the Saifs, in the year 1202 of our era, in the African Empire of Nakem south of Fezzan, long after the conquests of Okba ben Nafi al-Fitri. (3)

From the opening of *The Last of the Just,* "The Legend of the Just":

> Our eyes receive the light of dead stars. My friend Ernie's biography would easily fit in the second quarter of the 20th century; but Ernie Lévy's real story begins very early on, around the year one thousand of our era, in the old Anglican city of York. More precisely: on March the 11th, 1185—the splendor of which is known—with cries of "For the glory of the world!" March the 11th, 1185: story of the Jewish community's

historic massacre with cries of "For the will of God!" called by Bishop William of Nordhouse. (3)

From *Bound to Violence:*

Then pious silence, and the griot Kutuli of cherished memory ends his tale as follows . . . (4)

From *The Last of the Just:*

Then pious commentary and the monk ends his chronicle as follows . . . (4)

From *Bound to Violence:*

The ashes of the blacks thrown in the river poison the waters for at least three years. (5)

From *The Last of the Just:*

The ashes of the Jews mix with the air that we breathe. (4)

From *Bound to Violence:*

But there is nothing unusual in this story: many others relate how terror enslaved the populations and stifled every attempt at rebellion throughout the Empire. (5)

From *The Last of the Just:*

There is nothing that remarkable in this anecdote. For the Jews, the holocaust of the tower is nothing more than a small episode in a history overloaded with martyrs. (4)

From *Bound to Violence,* introduction of Saif ben Isaac al-Heit:

Against this background of horror the destiny of Saif ben Isaac al-Heit stands out most illustriously; rising far above the common lot, it endowed the legend of the Saifs with the splendor in which the dreamers of African unity sun themselves to this day. (5)

From *The Last of the Just,* introduction of Rabbi Yom Tov Levy:

But the act of Rabbi Yom Tov Levy had a remarkable outcome; by rising above the common tragedy, it became a legend. (4)

~

From *Bound to Violence:*

To picture that renaissance of the Nakem Empire through the person of Saif, one must have heard the dismal litany of the imperial dictatorships of those days from the mouths of the elders. (5)

From *The Last of the Just:*

To understand the process of this metamorphosis, one must have come in contact with the old Jewish tradition of the Lamed-waf, a tradition which some Talmudists claim goes back to the centuries' source, in the mysterious times of the prophet. (4)

~

From *Bound to Violence:*

At this point tradition loses itself in legend, and is engulfed by it, for there are few written accounts and the versions of the elders diverge from those of the griots, which differ in turn from those of the chroniclers. "According to one version . . . in another version . . . " (6)

From *The Last of the Just:*

Here, we reach the point where history disappears into legend and is engulfed by it, for precise facts are lacking and the views of the chroniclers diverge "according to some . . . according to others . . . " (5)

~

From *Bound to Violence,* in reference to the character Saif:

The tradition of the Saif dynasty, rooted in the greatness of one man, the most pious and devout Saif ben Isaac al-Heit, who freed a slave each day . . . (6)

From *The Last of the Just,* in reference to the character Rabbi Yom Tov Levy:

At the origin of the people of Israel, there is the sacrifice of a single man, our father Abraham, who offered his son to God. At the origin of the Levy dynasty, what is found is the sacrifice of a single man, the most gentle and enlightened Rabbi Yom Tov, who cut the throat of two hundred fifty of the faithful—some say a thousand. (5–6)

From *Bound to Violence:*

How in profound displeasure, with perfumed mouth and eloquence on his tongue, Saif ben Isaac al-Heit endeavored to mobilize the energies of the fanatical people against the invader; how to that end he spreads reports of daily miracles throughout the Nakem Empire—earthquakes, the opening of tombs, resurrections of saints, fountains of milk springing up in his path, visions of archangels stepping out of the sunset, village women drawing buckets from the well and finding them full of blood; . . . in all that there is nothing out of the ordinary. (25)

From *The Last of the Just:*

How Haim endeavored to allay suspicion and was finally unmasked; what happened during his marriage ceremony and the diplomacy he used in order not to be brought back to Kiev in triumph . . . No, unless one views this as a legend, all of this could hardly be material for a historical narration. (25)

From the conclusion of *Bound to Violence:*

Often, it is true, the soul desires to dream the echo of happiness, an echo that has no past. But projected into the world, one cannot help recalling that Saif, mourned three million times, is forever born to history beneath the hot ashes of more than thirty African republics.

. . . That night, as they sought one another until the terrace was soiled with the black summits of dawn, a dust fell on the chessboard; but in that hour when the eyes of Nakem take flight in search of memories, forest and coast were fertile and hot with compassion. And such was the earth of men that the balance between air, water, and fire was no more than a game. (182)

From the conclusion of *The Last of the Just:*

Sometimes, it is true, the heart desires to die of grief. But often also, preferably in the evening, I cannot help thinking that Ernie Levy, dead six million times, is still alive, somewhere, I do not know where. . . . Yesterday, as I was trembling in despair in the middle of the street, riveted to the ground, a drop of pity fell from the sky on my face; but there was no

> breath in the air, no cloud in the sky . . . There was only a presence." (374)

Finally, it should be noted that the expressions "a prayer for him! a tear for him!" in *Bound to Violence* are taken from *The Last of the Just*. The long litany of dynasties drones out from one end to the other. Both second chapters also begin in a similar manner and then diverge.

As we have just shown, it is essentially at the beginning of *Bound to Violence* that Ouologuem inscribes his narrative within the perspective of this earlier text, marking the orientation of his narrative; the filial connection and the intentional wink can hardly pass unnoticed by an informed reader, owing to the similar network in which the two texts are enmeshed. They issue from the same publishing house (Éditions du Seuil), even the same collection; moreover, they won identical literary prizes at a nine-year interval!

It is interesting to note that, long before Ouologuem, Schwartz-Bart employed the same technique of textual collage, as the thesis of Francine Kaufmann (defended in Nanterre in 1976) attests

> The accusations of *plagiarism* brought by certain journalists against the author of *The Last of the Just* have been straight-forwardly examined: the quote which caused so much ink to flow at the time came from the writings of Madame de Sévigné. Schwarz-Bart used this quote in an anachronistic manner without giving its source. It has been easy to demonstrate that, *in this vast epic where lyricism and irony collide, the author did not deny himself a certain sense of humor and that, he also sought to mix history and myth, prefering to communicate certain ideas rather than to carry out any straight-forward or literal compilation of facts. The hero,* Ernie, for example, *appropriates numerous texts that are found elsewhere and that authentically constitute his imaginary identity.*[6]

This long quote could be applied to Ouologuem and to his novel; it would suffice to change the names, while retaining what we have emphasized above.

~

But why the choice of this particular borrowing? Why the epigraphic-quotation? Probably in order to inscribe the damnation of a people other than the Jewish people, and in order to suggest the parallels between the Jews and the Arabs in the genealogy of the African dynasty. Ouogoleum thus introduces a diachrony of subjugation: the Judaic ascendancy of the African chiefdom shows how blacks were "colonized" well before the era of European colonialism. It may be more accurate, however, to describe this ascendancy as Semitic rather than Jewish since the name of the mythic chief *Saif ben Isaac al-Heit* mixes both Jewish and Arabic elements, *Saif* meaning "the sword" and *al-Heit* meaning "life." Several passages in the novel reaffirm this conflation: "At the beginning of the black Nakem Empire, one illustrious man, our ancestor the black Jew Abraham *al-Heit,* born of a black father and of an Oriental Jewess" (6). This emphasis upon Jewish origins later resurfaces, not without a strong derisive tone: "After a brief reference to his Jewish ancestry, Saif spoke the insidious words: 'Israel is here to admonish the Church to vigilance'" (72). References to "Muslim and Jewish-Negro fetishism" are also made (73), and, later on, one finds the sentence: "And may the troubadours in Nakem sing the history of Judaism" (181).

A connection is therefore established, resulting primarily from a romantic and historical verisimilitude of situation.[7] Nevertheless, this choice is not primordial on the historical level; it is rather that the Malian novelist insists, as Bernard Mouralis has shown, upon similarities in the destiny of the Negro and the Jew, similarities "of a mental and logical order in so far as each can be regarded as the image of the other."[8] Like the European Jew of the holocaust, Senghor's negro—the black of négritude—occupies the position of victim, but only in the most superficial ways.[9] What is iconoclastic in Ouologuem's perspective is his suggestion that the violence that one exerts against the victim does not necessarily lead him to be a better person, does not lead him to redemption. As Mouralis puts it, "Ouologuem's audacity lies in his refusal of negrophobic as well as negrophile ideology. In short, his refusal to admit that there could be a *chosen or predestined people*" (88). Ouologuem himself rejects "black romanticism" as the expression of a

> miserable consciousness which speaks, which confabulates, which has created for itself a paraphernalia of verbal fictions, and which becomes delirious, precisely because, not being able to do anything, has as its only recourse the spoken word. It makes of the Black of 20th century civilization . . . a sort of mythic Jew from that very same civilization." ("La Conscience malheureuse" 124)

The *evidence quote* is "one that intervenes in the course of an argument, be it to refute, be it to defend, be it to shore up an argument" (Maingueneau 126). Ouologuem employs such quotes numerous times in his novel. In some cases, this usage is explicit, as in the following case: "That is what happened at Tillabéri-Bentia, at Granta, at Grosso, at Gagol-Gosso, and in many places mentioned in the *Tarîkh al-Fetach* and the *Tarik al-Sudan* of the Arab historians" (*Bound to Violence* 4). This form of quoting can be implicit, as one finds in passages like the following, from Jean Suret-Canale's historical study, *Afrique Noire*:

> After the siege, the assault. Ba Bemba is killed. The order is given to pillage. Everyone is captured or killed. All the captives, around 4,000, are

> assembled into a group. The colonel begins the distribution. He begins by writing in a notebook and finally gives up, saying: "Divide it up yourselves." The division takes place with arguments and blows. Then, "Let's head out!" Each European receives a woman of his choice. . . . They return in forty kilometer daily marches with these captives. The children and all those who are too tired are killed with rifle butts and bayonets. . . . The corpses are left along the side of the roads. A woman is found crouching. She is pregnant. They push her with their knees. She gives birth, still walking. They cut the umbilical cord and abandon the child without even turning around to see if it was a boy or a girl. On the same march, the men requisitioned en route to carry the millet go five days without rations, receiving fifty lashes of the whip if they take a handful of the millet that they are carrying. The infantrymen [*tirailleurs*] have so many captives that it is impossible for them to shelter and nourish everyone." (vol. 1, pp. 274–275; eyewitness account)

In *Bound to Violence,* we find the following:

> They pillage, loot, destroy everything in their path—the captives, some eight thousand of them, are herded together and the colonel, writing in his little black book, starts to apportion them. But then he gives up and shouts: 'Go on, divide 'em up.' And each white man chooses for himself more than ten black women. They return to base with captives in daily marches of twenty-five miles. The children, the sick and disabled are killed with rifle butts and bayonets, their corpses abandoned by the roadside. A woman is found squatting. Big with child. They push her, prod her with their knees. She gives birth standing up, marching. The umbilical cord is cut, the child kicked off the road, and the column marches on, heedless of the delirious whimpering mother, who, limping and staggering, finally falls a hundred yards farther on and is crushed by the crowd.
>
> Time passes; once more tornadoes send down sheets of water, roads and trails are drowned in mud. The Yame River swells and floods the low-lying plains. The Blacks requisitioned en route to carry provisions go five whole days without rations—forty lashes if one of them filches a handful of food from the twenty to fifty pounds that he carries on his bare, shaved head. The *tirailleurs*, the common soldiers, the non-coms and officers all have so many slaves they are unable to count, lodge or feed them." (27)

The faithfulness of the citation to the original text is very strong in both cases. The accumulation of historical facts functions in *Bound to Violence* as an engagement with reality, as the writer seeks to communicate to his ignorant (i.e., French) reader a historical experience of Africa. If one systematically examines the historical documents of this period, one notices that dates, names, and dynasties are rarely historically verified. What is retained is the illusion of verisimilitude rather than historic truth. This permanent or willed illusion, which is also ambiguous since it is doubtful the reader will attempt to verify all these facts, aims at progressively leading the reader toward a symbolic and metaphoric insemination: what is important is the epic of the Blacks and *not* the history of any particular dynasty: that is, the demystification of a precolonial idyllic civilization and its resistance to colonialism.

The *relic-quote,* which consists "in signalling its belonging to a discursive continuity" (Maingueneau 126), seeks to mark the place from which one speaks. The *cultural-quote*, which is very close to it, functions essentially as "a quest for tacit agreement insofar as it provokes a nearly reflexive response from the reader" (126). I will list here Ouologuem's borrowings from religious and literary texts, the former referring more directly to the cultural-quote.

The phrases in Arabic or translated from Arabic are religious formula, canonic formula:

—"*Maschallah oua bismillah!* The name of Allah on her and around her!" (*Bound to Violence* 3, 17, 47)
—"*Al'Allah!*" (4)
—"*Ouasalam!*" (23)
—"*Amin!*" (29, translated as "Amen")
—"*La illaha illahah, la illaha, illaha!*" (33)
—"*Allahou Akbar!*" (51)
—"*Allah hamdoulilai rabbi alamin!*" (65).

In the long run, the actual meaning of phrases in African languages in *Bound to Violence* matters little; rather, the narrative voice effaces itself in these citations that are drawn from oral tradition. Such phrases are inserted to signify that the linguistic milieu from which one speaks is not exclusively French or Arabic, the two forms of colonialism that are ridiculed in the text: "Amidst all this turmoil, this dissolute life with its general bastardization, its vice and corruption, the Arab conquest, which had come several centuries earlier, settled over the land like a she-dog baring her white fangs in raucous laughter" (18); or, Ouologuem writes, "Yet amid this hideous hodgepodge of tribal custom, violence, and dilettantism embedded in the pious, feudal, idle, and voluptuous life of the Muslim landowners, a few powerful families survived" (21). These phrases distinguish themselves as well in their typography since they appear in italics, thus standing out from the general composition of the text.

Certain expressions from Judeo-Christian religions undergo the same treatment, but they are much more embedded in the text, appearing more frequently and having been drawn broadly from the biblical text. First, the genealogy of the Saifs, if it is inspired by the genealogies of *The Last of the Just*, similarly imitates the form of biblical genealogies (6); second, Ouologuem's description of the arrival of Bishop Thomas de Saignac parallels the arrival of Jesus in Jerusalem as described in Matthew 21:1–11

(44); third, introductory pages from *Bound to Violence* are interwoven with numerous biblical borrowings (65–66): the creation story in Genesis 1:1–31; the temptation in the desert and the call of the disciples in Matthew 4:1–11 and 4:18–22 (but also in Luke and Mark); St. Paul's Epistle to the Galatians 3:26–29; the prologue to the Gospel of St. John 1:1–18; the apparition of Jesus to the Apostles after the Resurrection and his instructions in Jonn 20:21–23, Matthew 28:17–20, and above all, Mark 16:15–20; finally, Yves Benot has analyzed Ouologuem's representation of the missionary figure (see *Bound to Violence* 120–124). In these passages, Ouologuem compares Henry, who comes to the aid of the unfortunate, to Jesus, who brings comfort to the sick and possessed. These biblical citations cannot be passed over in silence. They are exemplary of the *cultural quote*.

Some of the more purely literary citations, probably less familiar to the majority of Ouologuem's readers, can provide surprising cultural insights. This is true, for instance, in the passage from Guy de Maupassant's *Boule de Suif* [*The Ball of Fat*]:

> Thus, two or three leagues below the town, following the course of the river toward Croisset, Dieppe . . . mariners and fishermen often picked up the swollen corpse of some German in uniform from the bottom of the river, killed by the blow of a knife or old shoe, his head crushed by a stone, or perhaps thrown into the water by a push from a bridge. The river muck buried these obscure acts of vengeance, savage but legitimate. They were unknown acts of heroism, silent assaults more perilous than the battles in broad daylight and unheralded by fame. (4–5)

In *Bound to Violence*, we find the following:

> Amid the ruins of war poor Kassoumi daydreamed under his banana tree. His eyes roamed beyond the gray leaves of the budding fruit trees to the Yame River, foul with the stench of the carcasses and skeletons which fishermen had pulled out of the river in their nets—the decomposed corpse of some German in uniform, killed by a thrust of a lance or saber, his head crushed by a stone, or thrown from a bridge. The river muck buried these obscure acts of vengeance or heroism; these silent assaults more perilous than the battles fought in broad daylight and unheralded by fame. (124)

The textually reworked quote encourages the reader to look with an amused eye upon the character Henry in order to compare him with the description of one of the nuns in the coach of *Boule de Suif.* We also discover a kinship between the portrait of a woman in "Allouma" by de Maupassant and Ouologuem's character Awa in *Bound to Violence*. The two portraits end on a similar note. In de Maupassant, we find the passage, "black women, as is well-known, are most valued in the harems where they play the role of aphrodisiacs" (134); whereas in Ouologuem, the character Chevalier exclaims to himself, "To sleep with a black woman! That's the pleasure of kings and of the gods of Olympus!" (57).

In a love scene between Awa and Chevalier, the idea of having Awa undressed by a dog seems to be a reworking of *La Maison de rendez-vous* by Alain Robbe-Grillet. Ouologuem also seems to draw from Émile Zola. During the war, Kassoumi remains alive under the ruins of a house. Eventually, he returns to Paris, terrified, famished, and approaching animality. Here, we rediscover accents of Zola, who recounts the suffering of Florent at the beginning of *Ventre de Paris*. Finally, it should be noted that the term "niggertrash" [*la négraille*], which is drawn from Aimé Césaire's *Cahier du retour au pays natal,* is cited fourteen times in the novel.

Eric Sellin, for his part, has noted Ouologuem's borrowings from Graham Greene. Bernard Mouralis has classified these borrowings into seven categories, from which we have retained the first three to differentiate the literary quotations: in the category of "occidental literary fiction" (Mouralis 1984:81), which we have just discussed, one could also include the poetry of Arthur Rimbaud and *Salammbô* by Gustave Flaubert. The second category is made up of borrowings made from African fiction written in French or English, as Hubert de Leusse has shown in his *Afrique Occidentale* (1971). Raymond Spartacus Kassoumi joins the descendants of the unfortunate assimilated Africans torn between two cultures.[10] Finally, the third category designates borrowings made from "occidental anthropological literature," especially evident in the character of Fritz Schrobénius, an obvious replica of Leo Frobenius.

At the end of this survey, in which lacunae most certainly remain, Ouologuem's narration nevertheless retains its formal integrity and originality: it has become a meaningful fiction in its own right. As Aliko Songolo wrote in 1981:

> For more than five years, Eric Sellin has never stopped repeating to all who enjoy a good scandal that *Bound to Violence* is a replica, or a near replica, of *The Last of the Just* by André Schwartz-Bart. However, he has never been able to prove that the imitating text is replaceable by the imitated text(s). Moreover, given the extreme variety of "plundered" texts, one finds oneself in a quandary when it comes to the question of determining the "true" major source of the novel: Is it a contemporary author, André Schwarz-Bart, the Bible, the Qur'an, the Arabic Chronicles, or the anonymous griot? . . . The multifunctional discourse of *Bound to Violence* leads in multiple and unexpected directions; *but it acquires in this process its own identity, which is far greater than the sum of the imitated, parodied, or violated texts.* (24)

For this reason, to merely identify Ouologuem's various sources and borrowings in *Bound to Violence* is not enough; we need to go further and ask ourselves what sort of relationships the novelist seeks to establish with the diverse texts that he employs, reinscribing them into a new narrative configuration.

> Negro art found its patent of nobility in the folklore of mercantilist spirituality, oye, oye, oye.
>
> —*Bound to Violence* (94)

Once displayed, the evidence regarding Ouologuem's alleged plagiarism tells us little about his actual work as a writer. To simply identify the weapon of a crime says little about how and why the crime was committed.

> Famous Negro writers, you are terribly frustrated and castrated in your genius by *the law of silence*: I want through these pages for you to learn how to write like a hack and to remain white. Dear niggertrash, what is waiting for you here is *a vast work of reading, a gigantic compilation.* But such labor is not in vain. In fact, here is the magic potion of your formula. Your work as a hack, famous Black writers, will permit you—just as it permitted the surrealists—to *play*, as *dadaists*, to build your own "*cadavres exquis*" [exquisite corpses]. Of course, I speak allegorically. In fact, such intellectualism would be a bad idea for you. . . . As things stand, you must of course realise that, for the likes of us, such beautiful books might as well be written in a foreign language.[11] [my emphasis] (166)

These sentences from the *Lettre à la France nègre*, which Ouologuem published several months after *Bound to Violence*, are extremely important regarding the question that confronts us. In French, to be the "negro" [*nègre*] of someone means to write literary works in the place of the one who takes credit or signs for them. The expression can be quite ambiguous. On the one hand, the already time-honored writers and writings are reduced to the *nègres* of Ouologuem who, with great alacrity, takes credit for their labor. On the other hand, he implies that, for African authors, writing in French can amount to little more than a deceptive and derisive compilation of quotes. For this reason, Yves Benot calls *Bound to Violence* a "hot-house product, wholly artificial" (130). Ouologuem's tone is always the same, in both the novel and in *Lettre:* his writing is marked by its scathing and biting sarcasm, urging the reader to revolt and rupture.

A PARODY OF THE EPIC

The dominant tonality of *Bound to Violence* is epic, which marks Ouologuem as a bard (or griot) of the collectivity and a progenitor of the collective epic tradition. He relies upon an anonymous tradition, transmitted orally, thus employing formulae like the following: "one recounts that . . . one says that . . . "[12]; or, "Yet it cannot be denied: if the memory of this past—glorious as it was—has survived, it is solely thanks to the Arab historians and to the oral tradition of the Africans, which is as follows . . . " (8). If we examine the constituent traits of the epic poem, such as they have been laid out by Mikhail Bakhtin, we may notice a certain concordance with *Bound to Violence*. According to Bakhtin, the subject of the epic poem is the "national epic past," and it has for its source a national legend, which is severed from the present of the bard by an "absolute epic distance" ("Épopée et Roman" 17).

In *Bound to Violence*, Ouologuem writes, "For at the very moment when the inexorable white man was embarking on the conquest of Africa, the chiefs of the Randigue, Gonda, Fulani, Ngodo, and certain lesser tribes promised to respect each other's independence, and to cease all raids and warfare" (21). While these clauses and other similar ones are imposed upon us, the epic tone of the novel also parodies itself, undercutting its high seriousness. The ironic tone ceaselessly transgresses the epic form of the novel as well as the epic materials employed. Sacred legend is transformed into the profane; the exemplary heroes of past epics become monstrous and bloodthirsty. Value judgments and ironic interventions by the narrator destroy the illusion of an idyllic past, of an anteriority about which one could dream. An ostensibly apologetic discourse is transformed into a polemical one. The present inscribes itself upon the past, as the narrative voice magisterially intervenes in the contemporary debate about African power:

> Whether truth or invention, the legend of Saif Isaac al-Heit still haunts Black romanticism and the political thinking of the notables in a good many republics. For his memory strikes the popular imagination. Chroniclers draw on the oral tradition to enrich his cult and through him celebrate the glorious era of the first States with their wise philosopher-king, whose history has called not only archaeology, history, and numismatics but also the natural sciences and ethnology to their highest tasks. (8)

The irony and the distance in this passage delineate not only the subjectivity of the utterance but also the ideological orientation of the utterances, which oscillate from hagiography and deference to biting and acerbic denunciation. Whenever the narrator attempts a meliorative tone, he immediately undercuts the effect by one or two pejorative terms: the rhetorical effect is increased tenfold by this detour. The accumulation of pejorative terms frequently serves to evoke a reaction from the reader to this verbal aggression.[13]

The narrator's presence is equally felt in the numerous phenomena of lexical interferences that introduce "a semantic rupture in the continuous flow of the discourse" (Maingueneau 121). The text is replete with diachronic interferences in the wordings that mix colonial discourse and biblical language: "Saif said . . . And so it came to pass. The country produced natives: the black civil servants thus recruited fed their families . . . " (*Bound to Violence* 66); there are also a number of diatopical interferences with phrases in three tongues, revealing the diversified competence of the speaker as well as his refusal of any single linguistic unity; finally, Ouologuem's text contains diaphasic interferences that mix different lexical registers.

At the beginning of chapter two of "The Night of the Giants," we find Ouologuem engaged in a totally playful and profoundly significant work of textual reconstruction. These two pages may be said to "open" contemporary African history, much like Genesis "opens" the history of humanity. Under the sign of Saif, God's equal at the beginning of creation, history is completely reconstructed. The past is rewritten; the history of colonial exploitation and those duplicitous with it is retold; but we also learn of the coming of its inheritor, Spartacus, whose brothers have names just as emblematic, John-without-land [*Jean sans terre*], René Descartes, and René Caillié. Thus, Ouologuem allows "tradition" to supplant the place of "God" in the biblical text in passages like the following: "*And the tradition relates. . . .* " Later, the signifier "tradition" will be replaced by "Saif": "*After the betrothal in the desert,*" Ouologuem writes, "*Saïf required seven centuries of history to forge a core of faithful followers among his people*" (65). This passage may also be compared to the story of Jesus's temptation in the wilderness, as told in St. Matthew 4:11 and 4:18–22, which was followed by the calling of the first four disciples. Compare the following:

Bound to Violence, three times

There was rain and there was drought: the first year.

Genesis, six times

There was evening, there was morning: the first day.

~~~

From *Bound to Violence:*

Wakoul rabbi zidni ilman!

And the tradition relates: All of you, baptized in the light of Saif Ben Isaac El Heit, you have put on Saif Ben Isaac El Heit; there is no longer any Black or Jew, you are all one in the glory of His Magnificence.
~~~

Thus it was incumbent upon the dynasty to make itself known down through the ages and in every region, in order that all men of good will might have it in their power to become children of Saif. Go, go to him, good people. (65–66)

From Paul's *Letter to the* Galatians 3:26–29:

Because you are all sons of God by faith in Jesus Christ. You are all in fact baptized in Christ: there is neither Jew nor Greek, there is neither slave nor free man, there is neither man nor woman, for you are one in Christ Jesus. But if you belong to Christ, you are in the descendency of Abraham, inheritors according to the promise.

~

From *Bound to Violence:*

Alif Minpitjè.

And there was rain and there was drought: the second year. And the tradition relates: Thus Saif ben Isaac al-Heit, descended from the luminous and sweet Saif Isaac al Heit, and scion of Nakem's thirst, had the power to enlighten. And enlighten he did, coming to dwell among us to accomplish, with the help of all, the mission of his heavenly ancestor—to fulfill the wise precept that all men should be saved and united under one leader. He will illuminate, in fact, coming to live among us in order to accomplish the mission of his celestial ancestor—this wise philosopher who desires that all men be saved and brought back under a single leader—aided by all. (66)

From the Gospel according to St. John (8, 9, 12, 14):

He was not that Light, but was sent to bear witness of that Light. That was the true Light, which lighteth every man that cometh into the world. He was in the world. . . . But as many as received him, to them gave him power to become the sons of God . . . And the Word was made flesh, and dwelt among us . . .

~

In a similar vein, Ouologuem writes, "And Saif sent the children of the people to the French mission schools and the women to the hospitals, and Saif saw that he was their lord and master"; or, "Saif said: 'May the missionaries appease the misery of the humble . . . [A]nd so it came to pass . . . " (66). Thus, in paragraph after paragraph, Ouologuem offers us a very iconoclastic rewriting in which Saif is at once God, Jesus, and the Prophet Muhammad, since he is also named "Commander of the Faithful" (118). Ouologuem willfully turns religious discourse into derision in passages like the following: “Saif says: ‘Our Father who art in heaven’ and the birds chirped in response” (117); but he also wants to show that the powers—temporal and spiritual—are in league to subject the humble to their rule. The various textual citations within this new discursive configuration take on an altogether different meaning while simultaneously retaining the preceding meaning. Moreover, Ouologuem playfully subverts a wide variety of high canonical referents, thus heightening the pleasure of the text through interference. Such transgressions add spice to the narrative, entrancing the reader in this playful *jeu des mots*.

However, the question remains: Against whom is the “violence” of Ouologuem’s textual “duty” [*le devoir*] directed? It is certainly not directed against André Schwarz-Bart, Ouologuem’s privileged creditor. If he wanted to write an epic-parody [*épopée parodique*], *The Last of the Just* no doubt offered an attractive model for him. What is more, Schwarz-Bart’s novel is rooted in the historical martyrdom of a victimized people. Such generic and historical interpretations, as satisfying as they may at first seem, may nevertheless leave us unsatisfied about the complexity of the writing itself. However, it is possible that the answers we seek can be found in the novel’s title; that is, if we define the term “duty’ [*devoir*] in a scholastic as well as moral sense.

Jean Thibaudeau has demonstrated that a text comes into being by two distinct and complementary paths. On the one hand, a text emerges from a cultural experience acquired by the writer through a process of assimilation; this experience enables him to feel that the text is uniquely his own, the expression or creation of something original. On the other hand, a text emerges from a library of real written texts: “This ‘library’ is vast but specific. In every case, it differs, depending on the individual writer, serving as a reservoir from where the writer draws his textual material, including his ‘moral’ or ‘scientific’ attitudes and techniques. His ideas about translation, adaptation, commentary, plagiarism, imitation, influence, and so on also come from this library” (“Le Roman actuel” 16–19).

In the case of Ouologuem’s *Bound to Violence*, it is surely this “library” that one reads, with one slight difference: the omission of the generally required introductory elements whenever textual citations are reported. In this light, ethically motivated accusations that Ouologuem offers us a mere compilation seem dubious: all the borrowed elements in his novel are brought into play within an autonomous system that produces highly original and new meanings. If one compares the work of Yambo Ouologuem to that of an Aïcha Lemsine, who flatly copied the pages from the translation of *In Dubious Battle* into her *Ciel de Porphyre*[14] (or, more recently, the work of Calixthe Beyala),[15] it is obvious in such cases that one is not confronted by a phenomenon of mere plagiarism. Perhaps we would do well to remember Joachim Du Bellay’s advice to the aspiring imitator:

> Before all things, it is necessary that he should know his own strength and ascertain how much his shoulders can bear; he should diligently probe the depths of his natural ability, and borrow from the authors nearest to him in both talent and sensibility. Otherwise his imitation will resemble that of a monkey.[16]

Ouologuem knows how to measure his own strength. There is within his writing a studied distance from the learned "culture," even a derisive critique of his reluctant apprenticeship, both of which demonstrate his perfect mastery of the craft. The stored "real texts" of which Thibaudeau speaks are both melted and assimilated into Ouologuem's fiction, but they are also exhibited in a game of hide-and-seek. As Michel Foucault puts it:

> [t]he imaginary does not constitute itself in opposition to the real in order to deny or compensate it; it is displayed between the signs, from book to book, in the cracks from the reeditings and within the commentaries; it is born and formed in the in-between zone of the texts. It is a library phenomenon. ("La Bibliothèque fantastique" 29)

Thus the "duty" of violence [*le devoir de violence*] is to provide readers with a subversive commentary upon the "learned" culture, to both manipulate and master it. Violence is visited upon the culture that one attempts to shatter through multiple digressions. Such digressions enlarge the dimensions of that language in the process of the work's composition.

The borrowings are so visible, even when there is a permutation and transformation, and so playful, even when the writer enjoys himself by obscuring them, that one can only speak of *Bound to Violence* in terms of a conscious and masterful undertaking. The sovereign irony within this novel underscores the imposed cultural game that Ouologuem plays and successfully dominates. Ouologuem's efforts are comparable to those of Driss Chraïba, who edited his copy of the baccalaureate examination, redirecting it to the profit of literature.[17] The colonized person sends back the parodied image of his or her culture to the colonizer. This is done in order to negate prior representations of his or her homeland; it is a gesture of revolt that seeks to crush books instead of burn them (as in the case of Sembène Ousmane and others). The fact that Ouologuem received a top literary prize for the performance of this "duty" is perhaps the crowning irony of his great accomplishment.

> In the house of our fathers, the hallways have the breadth of coffins. Let us make of our hallways limpid streets, of our blind bedrooms public squares. Let's raise up our sleeping land. Let us sew back together our shredded knowledge . . . Let's remake writing and reading. Let's build our alphabet of capital letters. Our illogical sentences will reconstruct reason. . . . [18]

This *verset pour la distribution des prix*, which is the above poem's title, was written roughly at the same time by a poet of the Maghreb. For our purposes, it can be inscribed very naturally as an accompaniment to a novel wrongly eliminated for its refusal to respect established codes.

In other words, Ouologuem's iconoclastic gesture is not merely a game: within its sphere, there dances a new understanding of Africa's past. Accusations of plagiarism have permitted the removal of this brilliant novel-essay from the field of literature, thus stifling the fundamental question that Ouologuem posed to us about Africa's past. For Ouologuem, this past was a fabric of crimes and violence, and the writer functioned as a scribe in the "archives of blood." Ouologuem therefore violated a taboo respected by all black African writers before him. As Mouralis puts it:

> One comes to wonder which, of the two elements, most preoccupies the detractors of Ouologuem: the plagiarism, the mere infraction of common right, or the ideological derivation manifest by a writer accused of having wanted to plunge Africa in despair for not taking into account, among other things, Frobenius' canonic formula: "civilized right to the marrow of the bone"?[19]

Yambo Ouologuem has disappeared today from the African literary scene after having made a stunning incursion into it. Did he listen to the exclamation of Rimbaud, who also loved to play with the words of others in order to produce his own meaning?

> The white men debark. The canon! One must submit oneself to baptism, to dress, to work.
>
> I have received the death blow in the heart. Ah! I had not foreseen it.[20]

The novel nonetheless remains with all its "retroactive power," teaching us "the unrecognized and misunderstood fecundity of the past."[21]

NOTES

1. That is an expression used by Ouologuem in his *Lettre à la France nègre*, p. 179.

2. This article is entirely reworked from a portion of my thesis (1982), edited in Algiers in 1985, under the title *Abécédaires en devenir*, pp. 425–447.

3. D. Maingueneau, *Initiation aux méthodes de l'analyse du discours*, 121. An analytical instrument preferred to the notion of intertextuality because it is truly a work of citation or quotation, a "passage from a text repeated in an explicit and literal manner in another text." On the subject of this critical field, see the recent study by Nathalie Piégay-Gros, *Introduction à l'intertextualité*.

4. Yves Benot, *"Le Devoir de violence."*

5. Eric Sellin, "Ouologuem, Kourouma, et le nouveau roman african"; "The Unknown Voice of Yambo Ouologuem"; G. Leclech, "Ouologuem n'emprunte qu'aux riches"; Aliko Songolo, "Fiction et subversion: *Le Devoir de Violence*"; Mouralis mentions the thesis of the third cycle of Kazaro Tassou, "La réception du roman sahélien par la critique de langue française," pp. 222–278, chap. 3, "*Le Devoir de Violence* face au public": Victor O. Aire, "*Le Devoir de Violence.*"

6. Kaufmann, "Compte-rendu de la soutenance," *Le Monde,* May 14, 1976.

7. J. Suret-Canale, *Afrique Noire*, pp. 70–71.

8. B. Mouralis, "Une carrefour d'écritures: *'Le Devoir de Violence'* by Y. Ouologuem," *Recherches et Travaux*, "Littératures africaines d'écriture française," University of Grenoble, UER de Lettres, Bulletin no. 27, 1984: 75–92. Here, 86.

9. S. Adotevi, *Négritude et négrologues*, p. 17.

10. "Le Récit de vie de l'assimilé," in my thesis, *Abécédaires en devenir,* pp. 298–323.

11. This commentary precedes the formula for writing thousands of detective novels using the classic genre. We have underlined the following: "Moi, Nègre, j'ai travaillé comme un Blanc, Hihi!"

12. A. Jolles, *Formes simples*, 1972. The epic poem would be a well-known form; that is to say, the result of an artistic fixation on simple forms, the saga or epic and the legend; the keywords for the saga or epic would be family, clan, and bloodline; the legend is religious.

13. Kerbrat-Orecchioni, *L'Énonciation de la subjectivité dans le langage*, p. 71. "[I]rony [is] express[ed] under the judgments of self-actualization, a judgment of self-"deactualization." She then writes concerning insults that "they stem from the pragmatics of language: they aim at placing the receiver, according to a stimulus/reponse mechanism, in a situation where one is forced to react to the verbal aggression . . . by anger or by flight" (79).

14. This plagiarism was evident at the release of the novel in 1979. See my article, "Textes, prétextes, contextes: Quelques interrogations à propos de l'intextualité," pp. 115–125.

15. Calixthe Beyala's novel, *Les Honneurs perdus,* crowned with the Grand Prix of the novel by the Académie Française, contains several borrowings on the order of plagiarism.

16. Joachim Du Bellay, *La Défense et l'Illustration de la langue française* (1549), cited by Piégay-Gros (150).

17. Driss Chraïba, *Le passé simple* (1954).

18. "Verset pour la distribution des prix," *Le Silence s'est déjà tu,* by Jamel Eddine Bencheikh (Rabat: SMER, 1981), p. 162. (The poem dates from 1973.)

19. See Mouralis, "Littératures africaines d'écriture française," (79). The expression "archives of blood" is again used in *Lettre à la France nègre* by Ouologuem.

20. Arthur Rimbaud *Une Saison en enfer*, 129. How can one *not* recognize in this text one of the sources where, as have so many others, the writer of "*Le Devoir de violence*" came to drink—without there having been any question of plagiarism?

21. Michel Butor, "La Critique et l'invention."

9

Trait d'union: Injunction and Dismemberment in Yambo Ouologuem's *Le Devoir de violence*

Christopher L. Miller

> There is no more legitimate or respectable right than that of an author over his work, the fruit of his labor.
>
> —Leopold II of Belgium

> J'écris un manifeste et je ne veux rien.
>
> —Tristan Tzara

Writing is an act normally associated with shedding light, with bringing things forward, with legitimate creation and paternity. The bond between the author and the text is God-like in that it creates supposedly *ex nihilo*, and Orphic in that it leads the object out of the darkness into the light. That juncture is the place at which the author could be said to be acting *injunctively*, in the etymological sense: to enjoin, to link, to bind. In order to make his or her object manifest, the author must bind it, chain it and drag it into the light. A negative interpretation of that relation may be particularly relevant when the international politics of literature are in question. Since it has been suggested that the situation of discourse may be more accurately represented as "the unequal relation between colonizer and colonized"[1] than as an innocent movement towards the light, the forceful, violent nature of the injunctive text, of the injunctive act of writing, takes on a new interest. Such questions are pertinent to the black African novel as a whole, and to Yambo Ouologuem's *Le Devoir de violence* in particular.

This chapter was previously published in *L'Esprit Créateur,* Vol. 23, No. 4 (Winter 1983). Reprinted with permission of *L'Esprit Créateur.*

This is a work whose composition involved the forced "bondage" or plagiarizing of other texts, and whose manifest object is to unravel myths about the African past.

The history of Africa since European conquest has been one of forced linkage, joining Africa to Europe with bonds of possession ("l'Afrique *française*") and commerce, joining African to African in order to form nations which Europe delineated. The act of cutting up Africa by tracing lines on the map (such as was done at the Conference of Berlin in 1885) is symbolic of European writing on Africa: forced redemption of raw materials, bringing an area and a people which are "stuck" in time forward onto the path of progress. Africa is thus hitched to Europe and dragged behind it ("her"), the two slouching forward in tandem. Baudelaire described a similar form of commerce among poetic objects in his "De l'idée moderne du progrès appliquée aux Beaux-Arts": the exotic, primitive world must be brought into the light by a central, therefore superior agency, namely France, so that the raw materials must be "marvelously worked and fashioned" into art.[2] The violence latent in this endeavor, the bondage which is the other side of creation's coin, is both the method and the theme of *Le Devoir de violence.*

When an African writes a novel, he or she engages in an act of "progress." The novel in black Africa is the direct result of European intervention. Written in the languages of Europe, read more widely in the West than in Africa, the African novel is nonetheless a medium in which Africans have declared their autonomy, witnessed their difference, and found their own path. But in this the myth of progress is only better served, for the novel, says Lukács, is "the art-form of virile maturity, in contrast to the normative childlikeness of the epic. . . . The novel . . . appears as something in the process of becoming."[3] As Africans write novels, they tie themselves to the course of European literature as a junior division, even as they write of their own coming into being. As the novel *enjoins* Africans to independence and freedom, it *joins* itself back to Europe through the use of language and genre. The tie that binds the novel is the same that takes it apart.

If there is a double bind in the ontology of the African novel, the work of Ouologuem is certainly not a typical case in which to study it; this is rather the exception which proves the rule. *Le Devoir de violence* cannot be held as an answer to European misconceptions about Africa (in fact it reaffirms some of these), nor as a work completely and authentically detached from that previous discourse. A more peculiar story of a novel's fate would be hard to find. Ouologuem's only novel was published in 1968, and was hailed by *Le Monde* [October 12, 1968] as a "great African novel . . . the first African novel worthy of the name." Its success snowballed, from the "Today Show" on American television to the Prix Renaudot of 1968. But the adulation began to be offset by two objections: some Africans had found the book ideologically offensive, its violence and negativism too prone to anti-African interpretations; and some critics had begun to find an excessive amount of "borrowings" (the ironic quotation marks showing that they really meant *plagiarism*). Comparison of *Le Devoir* with other texts, from the Bible to André Schwartz-Bart's *Le Dernier des justes* (1959) and Graham Greene's *It's a Battlefield* (1934), revealed a fabric of quotation, translation and incorporation, which, depending on your point of view, constituted either a freewheeling exercise in intertextuality or a cynical act of plagiarism. The ensuing *succès de scandale* was equal to the initial *succès d'estime*, until Graham Greene filed suit in the French courts, and, on the basis of a small translated passage of no significance, *Le Devoir de violence* was seized, confiscated and removed from the market. To this day the French public is enjoined from buying the novel.[4]

The question of originality and plagiarism, once posed, generates a discourse with only one axis, that of truth and falsehood, original and copy. The rocking of those questions—the preoccupation with judging Ouologuem either innocent or guilty—has precluded the reading of *Le Devoir de violence* for what it is: an assault on European assumptions about writing and creating, and a would-be refutation of the African cult of authenticity. *Le Devoir de violence*, both in its narrative method and its narrated content, posits destructive violence and theft as origin itself, and interprets cultural roots cynically, as the result of invasion and contamination. If an injunctive text is one which tells you to do something, this novel, read as an injunction, tells the reader how to look at African history, or more accurately, how to read that history as a *void*.

Before turning to that diegetic question, a few remarks on plagiarism are appropriate. What law or injunction did Ouologuem violate? Plagiarism is the violent joining of two literary bodies, from the Latin *plagiarus*, "one who abducts the child or slave of another, a kidnapper, a seducer; also . . . a literary thief" (*OED*). Someone else's text is their child or slave, over which there "is no more legitimate right" of possession (*sic*). At what particular point the many forms of legal interpenetration between texts become illicit plagiarism is a complex issue with no satisfying answer. All agree that copyright applies to form, not to "ideas"; is it therefore possible to plagiarize in translation? On the basis of such a judgment Ouologuem's novel was removed from the market. But it is equally important to point out that hardly a page of *Le Devoir* goes by without incorporating a passing reference to or an outright theft from some precursor. From the first words (which are lifted from *Le Dernier des justes*), and throughout 200 pages of the novel, *Le Devoir* is so highly refined and perverse in its manner of borrowing titles ("L'extase et l'agonie"), phrases ("Du feu. Je veux du feu . . . Je serai sauvé.") and passages from other texts, that it could not have been any simple expedient on the author's part. The interpenetration of *Le Devoir* with its precursors is a deliberate act of political-literary violence, a coup mounted against legitimacy.[5] It must be no coincidence that Ouologuem's narratological practice acts out the history that the novel recounts. As the prose of the novel plugs itself into other texts, borrowing, pillaging and violating their integrity, the characters within the story become bodies cutting and cut up, raping and raped. It is that homologous relationship that we must try to decipher.

Le Devoir de violence is concerned with the bloody history of a fictive African empire, the Nakem, and with its rulers, the Saïfs. The opening section, "La légende des Saïfs" (cf. *Le Dernier des justes*, "La légende des justes"), compresses 800 years of history into 20 pages, yet pays minute attention to the details of torture and dismemberment. This particular chronicle is in fact Ouologuem's manifesto on African history, a savage polemic directed at what he calls "Negro romanticism," at "the dreamers of the theory of African unity." The argument is this: that by the time French colonial domination arrived, it was "already too late" to take true control, for the African notables, the Saïfs, had been busy oppressing the "nigger-trash" (Ralph Manheim's translation of *la négraille*) for centuries. It is shown later in the novel that the Saïfs play the French off against the common people, making sure that Christianity and public education are aimed only at the *négraille*: "Since French law had to be made for some one, the notables made it be for the populace" (64).

The timing of this argument, appearing in 1968, when African history was struggling for academic recognition, could only increase its controversial nature. *Le Devoir de violence* appeared as an anti-manifesto of that which did not need saying. But how can a novel, a work of art, be a manifesto? There is probably a level at which any text can be seen as presenting an argument, issuing orders. Claude Abastado observes that texts written in a variety of genres have been taken as manifestoes, and suggests that the injunctive level of a text is that at which it is performative, where it perpetuates an act of "terrorism" and provokes scandal and controversy.[6] The opening section of *Le Devoir de violence* is eminently qualified to be considered a manifesto, in view of its concise and brutal argument, not to mention the scandal it provoked.

But if an argument is manifest from the beginning of *Le Devoir*, the terms on which it depends are nonetheless negative and have no substance to offer.[7] The novel exhorts the reader to view the fabric of African history in a certain way, while at the same time unraveling that fabric before the reader's eyes. The novel wants us to *know* something about its subject, while questioning how anything can be known, leaving us in limbo.

The history of Nakem has differing degrees of substance and truth, it would appear, depending on sources of knowledge and modes of expression:

the historical epistemology of non-writing culture. The various sources and modes include "narrative" (*récit*), speech, chant, "Arab historians," and "the African oral tradition." Bearing in mind that we are dealing with a genre split between a European outside form (the French language, the novel), and an African "content" or desire, "la légende des Saïfs" could be read as a working-through of Mohamadou Kane's assertion that in reading the African novel, "everything becomes clear from the moment one refers to the traditional [i.e., oral] literature." Kane also writes that "the perspective in which the author places himself" in *Le Devoir de violence* "proves to be authentically African."[8] Can this novel be wholly grounded in the oral tradition, subsumed by an authenticity it seems to scorn? The history of violence which begins to unfold has a spoken and repeated, inherited quality, and the chapters proceed with reminders such as "they say"; "it is told in the talismanic annals of the wise Elders, among the narratives of the oral tradition"; "our griots recount"; etc. At one point, the story is interrupted thusly: "There followed a pious silence, and the griot Koutouli, of precious memory, completed his gesture like this . . . ," and a quotation follows. But we did not know we were listening to the griot Koutouli; in fact the crossing of voices is so complex that no single narrator can be isolated.

In this cacophony of voices, it becomes evident that the notables, the Saïfs, effectively arrogate authenticity to themselves; but it is equally certain that their "true history" depends on their oppression of the "nothing men," *la négraille*. The gaining of any voice depends on depriving someone else of it. Thus "detaching itself from this tableau of horrors, the fate of Saïf Isaac El-Héït was of a prodigious *singularity; rising well above the common destiny*, it endowed the legend of the Saïfs with the splendor in which the dreamers of the theory of African unity still slumber" (11; emphasis mine). The Saïfs—and this original Saïf, the founder of the dynasty—are the sole principle of unity in the novel, yet they present a problem. Their origin is such that they have no single identity: The Saïf is a "fétichiste musulman et négro-juif," descended from the black Jew Abraham El-Héït, "half-caste born of a Negro father and an Oriental Jewish mother" (12). The Saïfs will exploit the prestige of this birthright, says one dissenting voice, "only for the delight of proving that their ascendance makes them superior to the Negroes" (64). The Saïfs are all things they want to be, a perverse system of masks; the source of their power is a fragmentation which creates the illusion of unity.

But from the moment the Saïfs' legitimacy is posed, the text seems to lose footing: "Ici, nous atteignons le degré critique au-delà duquel la tradition se perd dans la légende, et s'y engloutit; car les récits écrits font défaut, et les versions des Anciens divergent de celles des griots, lesquelles s'opposent à celles des chroniqueurs" (11). The Saïf dynasty is the negative principle of history which the novel makes manifest; to describe such a presence is to affront "the dreamers of the theory of African unity"; by bringing this image forward Ouologuem destroyed more than he created. The global effect is to depict the African past as a purloined, kidnapped and usurped origin, as an originary violence which precludes the autonomy of any given object, leaving only a void. The violent partisanship that runs through the novel is opposed to everything, but symmetrically counterbalanced with nothing. Like the bad boy on the beach, Ouologuem would rather kick down everyone else's sand castles than build his own. The junctures of his narrative take apart more than they put together.

On the smaller scale of immediate plot devices, sex and violence are the armatures by which human interaction proceeds through time, by which bonds are made and broken: the primal usurpation of the Saïf dynasty by Saïf El-Haram, who marries his mother and has the legitimate heir eaten alive by worms; the devouring of the sexual parts of defeated enemies; the colonial administrator whose dogs are made to have sex with an African woman. Violent atrocities destroy the barriers between one life and another; sexual intercourse, which more often than not becomes violent, is depicted as a breach in the integrity of the body; to conjoin is also to tear apart. Tambira, the mother of the protagonist Raymond-Spartacus Kassoumi, is forced to have sex with a sorcerer named Dougouli in order to gain his help for her children. Their encounter is representative of the way in which any two bodies interact in *Le Devoir de violence:*

> L'œil revlusé par le désir, les lèvres lourdes, les mains tremblantes, *ils se dévisageaient*. Les cuisses nues de Tambira se miraient dans la flaque . . .
>
> La flaque dansait devant les yeux de Tambira, fascinée, attirait, mordait furieusement ses yeux ivres; les formes tourbillonnaient toujours, s'emplumaient de violence et de luxure où sa propre ignominie était insignifiante . . . Et ce fut le néant. Plus rien que le reflet du sexe de Tambira, entrouvert au-dessus de la flaque. (148–49; emphasis mine)

Desire is at the same time the very process of revulsion. The act of looking at each other involves cutting into each other: *dévisager*, which normally means "to stare someone down," means literally to dis-figure, to deface ("Déchirer le visage de quelqu'un, défigurer"—*Grande Larousse*). Later, under the magician's curse, Tambira dies, and her body is found with "des vers rampant dans ses narines; la tête émergeait des selles, retenue par un nœud coulant. . . . " Her husband, Kassoumi, "prit une corde, écarta sans dégoût les planches, hissant le corps gluant de sa bienaimée, qu'il lava doucement. Il lui arrivait parfois, au cours de la toilette de la défunte, de lui sucer le nez, pour recracher un ver" (150–51). The head and the feces, love and putrefaction commingle; creation and destruction are so involved with each other that it becomes difficult to distinguish between them. Intercourse, even in its most positive instance (the homosexual affair between Raymond Kassoumi and a Frenchman) involves the destruction of the self, loss of "face"; "soiling of his face," "wearing away of the flesh." That process is identified as "*linking* and *opposing irremediably* the White man and him [Kassoumi]." The act of linkage and union is immediately an opposition; the identity is a difference: attraction does not occur without revulsion; love cannot be distinguished from violence.

The creator, progenitor and lover is also the kidnapper, murderer and rapist; the author is a plagiarist. As *Le Devoir de violence* recounts violence and the flowing of one body into another and into the world, the narration itself is joined to other texts in a way which *disfigures* them, violating the integrity of other literary bodies. The following resemblance was recently discovered.[9]

Le Devoir de violence:

> Parmi les décombres de la guerre, Kassoumi rêvassait sous un bananier, promenant, au-delà des feuillette grisâtres des fruits bourgeonnant, son pauvre regard sur la rive du Yamé, empestée par l'odeur saumâtre de carcasses de squelettes que les pêcheurs ramenaient souvent du fond de l'eau, dans leurs filet, *cadavre d'Allemand* décomposé *dans son uniforme, tué d'un coup de* lance ou de sabre, *la tête écrasée par une pierre* ou flanqué *à l'eau du haut d'un pont. Les vases du fleuve ensevelissaient ces vengeances obscures, sauvages, heroïsmes inconnus, attaques muettes, plus perileuses que les batailles au grand jour, sans le retentissement de la gloire.* (144)

Maupassant, *Boule de suif:*

> Cependent, à deux our trois lieus sous la ville, en suivant le cours de la rivière, vers Croisset, Dieppedale ou Biessart, les mariniers et les pêcheurs ramenaient souvent du fond de l'eau quelque *cadavre d'Allemand,* gonflé *dans son uniforme, tué d'un coup de* couteau ou de savate, l*a tête écrasée par une pierre,* ou jeté *à l'eau du haut d'un pont. Les vases du fleuve ensevelissaient ces vengeances obscures, sauvages* et légitimes, *heroïsmes inconnus, attaques muettes, plus périleuses que les batailles au grand jour et sans le retenissement de la gloire.* (Paris: Libraire de France, 1934: 7)

I have underlined the words which are identical in the two passages. A sufficiently close reading could demonstrate that the alterations of Maupassant in the Ouologuem text—the total change of context, the transplanting of the scene to Africa—produce a completely new meaning from the same words. This is the thrust of current criticism of Ouologuem.[10] Such criticism strives to redeem the kidnapper by viewing him as a creator, and the point is valid to a certain extent: the patchwork that is *Le Devoir de violence* resulted from an "original" ransacking of Western, Islamic and African literature. But that redemption should not obscure the violent nature of Ouologuem's undertaking. The precursors to this novel, as they are *bound* into their new context (cf. *Bound to Violence*, the translation by Ralph Manheim), as they are lifted and reorganized, become swollen bodies with crushed heads, both more and less than they used to be, with words added and words deleted, worms crawling out of their orifices.

The incongruously "harmonious" last section of the novel, "L'aurore," consists of a dialogue between Saïf and the European bishop Henry de Saignac, in which the double tension of the novel is clarified.

> —Vous parliez du Nakem tout à l'heure.
> —Je voulais être seul, pur.
> —Mais la solitude s'accompagne d'un sentiment de culpabilité, de complicité . . .
> —Pardon, de solidarité, rétorqua l'évêque.
> —L'home est dans l'histoire et l'histoire dans la politique. Nous sommes déchirés par la politique. Il n'y a ni solidarité ni pureté possible. (201)

Politics is interpreted negatively, as a force not of unity but of dismemberment and fragmentation: with sexual intercourse and human interactions of all kinds, ties that bind are seen by Ouologuem (here by Saïf) as forces which can tear apart. Because the body has lost its integrity, "purity" is not possible; nor is solidarity, which would require integral bodies to interact without violence. This closing section of the novel has been seen as an espousal of the Euro-Christian values of the bishop, as corrupt Africa, in the person of Saïf, reaching towards its last best hope. But the relationship between the two men is described as the sharing of a secret ("that they were the sole authentic conspirators of Nakem-Zuiko") and as an uncanny tension of attraction and repulsion: "their stares *linked* them in an *unnameable strangeness*" ("leurs regards les liaient en une indicible étrangeté," 205). The bond is one which holds the two at a certain distance from each other, in a perverse non-union.

Several pages earlier, the bishop tells a parable which comes close to naming that strangeness, the link between himself and Saïf, between Europe and Africa, and even between Ouologuem and those writers copied:

> Les Chinois ont un jeu: le trait d'union. Ils capturent deux oiseaux qu'ils attachent ensemble. Pas de trop près. Grâce à un lien mince, mais solide et long. Si long que les oiseaux, rejetés en l'air, s'envolent, montent en flèche et, se croyan libres, se grisent de battements d'ailes, de grand air, mais soudain: crac! Tiraillé . . .
>
> L'humanité est une volaille de ce genre. Nous sommes tous victimes de ce jeu; séparés, mais liés de force. (193–94)

The Chinese game describes Ouologuem's vision of the world as a whole: a forced linkage between unwilling opposites which proceed to tear each other apart. The irony of the name "trait d'union" lies in the fact that the birds will eventually "peck each other's eyes out," and that one or both will wind up dead, all because of this union. But it is well to recall that "trait d'union" also means "hyphen": "petit trait horizontal, servant de liaison notamment entre les éléments de certains composés (arc-en-ciel) . . . Fig. (mil XIXe) Personne, chose qui sert d'intermédiaire, de pont entre deux objets" (*Petit Robert*). That link, the bridge, is also a barrier; that which ties two things together is that which prevents them from ever being one. Such a link, expressed by the hyphen, accurately describes the authorship of *Le Devoir de violence*: "Ouologuem-Maupassant," "Ouologuem-Greene," or "Ouologuem-Schwartz-Bart." The political violence to which the bishop's parable obviously refers is echoed by the separation and forced linkage between the text itself and its precursors, leaving authorship, identity, and authenticity "teased" (*tiraillé*) between the two.

The implications of Ouologuem's work are different as one moves from the world within the novel to the role of the novel in the world, but on each level the force of an *injunction* is evident. Within the fictive world which the novel projects, the Nakem empire is in subservient bondage to its rulers, held on a short leash: "Dans l'attente de ce grand jour de la proche éclosion du monde où le serf est l'égal du roi, la négraille—*court lien à méchant chien!*—accepta tout" (29; emphasis mine). The "petit trait horizontal" between Saïf and *négraille* is the symbolic and real joint of a generalized injunction: political power. The populace is enjoined to efface itself before both the African notables and the incoming French. But if a false identity is forced on the *négraille* (through public education, Christianity, etc.), the Saïfs are equally false in their manner of adopting whatever identity suits their needs: the former thus become nothing, the latter everything. The bonds of power within the Nakem are bonds of violence by which bodies and identities are both made and broken—Ouologuem makes it amount to the same thing. His explanation for this comes in the tone of a credo in the last section of the novel: "Ici, ce qui importe, c'est que, toute vibrante de soumission inconditionnelle à la volonté de puissance, la violence devienne illumination prophétique, façon d'interroger et de répondre, dialogue, tension, oscillation, qui, de meutre en meutre, fasse les possibilités se répondre, se compléter, voire se contredire" (199). Violence is the language by which connections are made and therefore broken, no more apt to make sense than any other language.

Taking one step back from the pseudo-history of the Nakem, one is faced with the highly ambiguous frame in which Ouologuem placed his story. I am referring to the opening section of the novel, with its pointed scrambling of what is known in West Africa and how it is known. Here again the effect is to erase all certainties with a dispassionate cynicism, in an act of literary "terrorism." What Ouologuem wants to make clear is that nothing is clear, that history is only legend. It is here that the destruction becomes self-destruction, for the novel which follows on "La légende des Saïfs" is a product of the nothingness which has been derived, written within the "critical degree" at which nothing can be certain.

The "injunctive" nature of an author's work to which I first referred—that of binding an object and bringing it to light—is radically disturbed by Ouologuem's negativism. What is brought to light is the fact that nothing can be brought to light; that which is bound is "bound to violence," torn apart like two birds bound together. This may explain the impression shared by more than one reader of *Le Devoir de violence*, that they are reading strictly "n'importe quoi," a brilliant mish-mash.

But it is on the outermost level, that of the politics of Ouologuem's literary practice, that his novel is at its most significant. As within the novel, there is a refusal of identity, but here it is the identity of the text, the author and the genre which is negated. Ouologuem subverts the authoritative role of creator by pillaging European literature to compose "his" text. The whole notion of "text"—important not only to the legalities of copyright but also to modern criticism—is undermined, as if by sleight of hand.[11] But most importantly, Ouologuem's act violates the national and continental boundaries by which integral bodies of literature are perceived. A "corpus," whole unto itself and distinct from all others, is generally assumed in the face-off between Europe, Africa, etc. It is here where dangerous metaphors get their foot in the door, metaphors which Ouologuem explodes: for if one body is distinct from another, one can or must be different, perhaps older and therefore better. This is the root of theories such as Lukács', which projects a hierarchy according to age, between "childlikeness" and "virile maturity," between epic and novel. But *Le Devoir de violence* is written in the excrescences, the orifices and the intrusions between European and African literature, by an author without authority. Ouologuem's response to the condition of the African novel (if we can interpret his actions on such a plane) defies the rules of identity and injunction by which his work could be placed in a position of "childlikeness." Depicting all ties as destructive, Ouologuem strikes an uncompromising stance of pure negativity.

NOTES

1. Edward Said, *The World, the Text and the Critic* (Cambridge: Harvard University Press, 1983): 48.

2. *Curiosités esthétiques et l'art romantique* (Paris: Garnier, 1962): 220.

3. Georg Lukács, *The Theory of the Novel*, tr. Anna Bostock (London: Merlin Press, 1971): 71.

4. See John Erickson, "Africa Reborn: Emergence from Myth, Yambo Ouologuem: *Le Devoir de violence*," in *Nommo: African Fiction in French South of the Sahara* (York, SC: French Literature Publications Company, 1979); Matthieu Galey, "Un grand roman africain," *Le Monde* (Oct. 12, 1968); K. W., "In Defence of Yambo Ouologuem," *West Africa*, July 21, 1972; Alec Rutimirwa, "A Case of Plagiarism," *Transition* 42 (1973); Eric Sellin, "Ouologuem's Blueprint for *Le Devoir de violence*," *Research in African Literature,* Vol. 2, No. 2 (1971).

5. Ouologuem developed the logic of his subversion in a quirky book of essays innocent of literary refinement, *Lettre à la France nègre* (Paris: Edmond Nalis, 1968). Playing on the double meaning of the word *nègre* ("Negro," originally synonymous with "slave," and since the 18th century, "ghost-writer"), Ouologuem writes a "Lettre aux pisse-copies, nègres d'écrivains célèbres." For the frustration of losing the fruits of one's labor, one's writing, he proposes, "une thérapeutique dénégrifiante," which consists not in restoring wholeness to the *nègre* but in inventing a cleverer dismemberment, combining the *nègre* with the plagiarist. The new *nègre* will therefore cut and paste other novels to make his own (a chart is provided). A semblance of control is thereby returned to the formerly castrated *nègre,* but the originary character of creative thought is rendered moot. No wonder *Lettre à la France nègre* was denounced as an "all-too-real *modus operandi*" (Sellin, 120n).

6. "2. Par extension, on nomme 'manifeste' tout texte qui prend violemment position et institue, entre un émetteur et ses allocutaires, une relation injonctive flagrante . . . les circonstances historiques et la réception des textes, la manière dont ils sont entendus, lus, interprétés, entraînent des glissants de qualifications . . . " "Introduction à l'analyse des manifestes," *Littérature* 39 (October 1980): 4.

7. Wole Soyinka describes *Le Devoir* as "a fiercely partisan book on behalf of an immense historic vacuum," and points out that "the positive does not engage his [Ouologuem's] recreative attention." *Myth, Literature and the African World* (Cambridge: Cambridge University Press, 1976): 104–06.

8. "Sur les 'formes traditionnelles' du roman africain," *Revue de littérature comparée,* nos. 3/4 (July-December 1974): 549.

9. Christiane Chaulet-Achour, "Langue française et colonialisme en Algérie: De l'abécédaire à la production littéraire," Diss., University of Paris III, 1982, II, 419–43. [Revised and printed herein as "Writing as Exploratory Surgery: Yambo Ouologuem's *Bound to Violence*."]

10. See Chaulet-Achour, and Seth Wolitz, "L'Art du plagiat, ou une brève défense de Ouologuem," *Research in African Literature*, Vol. 4, No. 1 (Spring 1973): 130–34.

11. Consider the status of the passage from Greene as it finds its way, translated, into *Le Devoir*, and then, translated back into English in Ralph Manheim's translation. Greene's sentence: "Everyone is doing something different," she said, her eyes going back to the double bed and her thoughts on the pink bedspread in the other room and Jules and half a loaf is better than no bread and the lovely dead indifferent woman on the wall" (*It's a Battlefield* [London: Heinemann, 1934]: 57). Ouologuem's "plagiary": "Ils font tous quelque chose de différent," murmura-t-elle, cependent que son regard revenait au grand lit, et ses pensées vers la courtepointe rose, dans la chambre de Chevalier, puis vers Saïf" (69). Manheim's translation: "'They're all doing something different," she murmured, while her eyes returned to the big bed and her thoughts to the counterpane in Chevalier's bedroom, then to Saïf" (*Bound to Violence* [New York: Harcourt, Brace, Jovanovitch, 1971]: 56). The "identity" of the text, as in a shell game, has become a tenuous thing.

10

Yambo Ouologuem, Satirist and Pamphleteer: Irony and Revolt in *Lettre à la France nègre*

Caroline A. Mohsen

In *Lettre à la France nègre,* Yambo Ouologuem raises a number of moral, political, social, and economic issues stemming from the general feeling of discontent after the wave of independences in Africa in the beginning of the 1960s. Published in 1969 after his controversial novel *Le Devoir de violence*, *Lettre à la France nègre* is a satirical collection of essays that examine the issues tackled in *Le Devoir de violence* in fictional form. However, although the problems unveiled in *Le Devoir de violence* were mostly of social, historical, and political nature, these essays also attack the new economic problems plaguing the newly independent African nations. Ouologuem analyzes the issues of foreign aid, development, and cooperation with France, as well as the growing ties to other postindependence nations of the Third World, divulging in this process what he identifies as a growing tension in racial relations in France. He also takes a hard look at Africa's relations to the two new powers, the socialist East European block and the United States.

Lettre à la France nègre raises several important questions, both formal and ideological. Why was *Lettre à la France nègre* received as "a pamphlet in every way inferior to the novel" (Mbelolo 124)? Did the scandal following the raging debate over the charge of plagiarism[1] leveled at Ouologuem create a general feeling of disappointment that affected the reception of *Lettre à la France nègre* not only as a literary work, but as a social and political manifesto? Or does the answer to the cold and dismissive reception lie instead in the genre, style, and form of the book of essays? Is Ouologuem's problematization of visions of history and the colonial past and his scathing diatribe against the lack of political, national, and cultural identity of the postindependence African nations diminished by his use of irony, allegory, and parody as the main devices in his criticism of France and Africa, especially when the genre of satire carries with it negative connotations regarding the seriousness of the issues examined? A close reading of *Lettre à la France nègre* suggests several answers to these questions.

YAMBO OUOLOGUEM AS SATIRIST

Satire, as many have already observed, is not the highest form of literature. Yet it is unquestionably "one of the most original, challenging and memorable forms" (Highet 3). The success of Ouologuem's novelistic use of satire in *Le Devoir de violence* illustrates how gripping the genre can be when welded with confidence and mastery. "Satire," Gilbert Highet continues, "is free, easy, and direct. . . . The results have the urgency and immediacy of actual life" (3). Eschewing all conventions of seriousness of tone and formality of expression that usually characterize the essayist, Ouologuem chooses the freedom associated with the satirical pamphlet,[2] describing his tone as "humour pamphletaire" [pamphletary humor] in "asymetrical" opposition to the racist and the antiracist, the Black and the White alike (Miller 1985: 225). In doing so, Ouologuem intends not only to entertain and educate, but also to shock the reader, as any good satirist should. He luridly portrays contemporary and recognizable figures of African and French men and women in bold and vivid language. Often in a grotesque and painful manner he is funny, but ultimately he presents us with an appalling situation. Realizing that the reader will perceive *Lettre à la France nègre* as a distasteful diatribe, Ouologuem vows to offend all of his readers without discrimination. In a controversial move, he decides that all his readers are his opponents, to be pilloried without pity or distinction. Clearly Ouologuem believes that by breaking the rules of good taste and treating his readers with the contempt they deserve, the apathetic public will be embarrassed and moved to action. For the satirist in Ouologuem, social change will only result from the discomfiture of the reader reeling in horror, pain, or disgust.

In the introductory essay entitled, "BILLET OUVERT à toutes les victimes de l'anti-racisme" ("OPEN TICKET to all the victims of antiracism"), Ouologuem introduces the format of the "lettres" that follow, as well as their polemical tone. More important, Ouologuem delineates the audience of his essays. The "BILLET" is addressed to all those he designates as the victims of Charles de Gaulle's liberalism or antiracist policies, those "consciences dévorées de scrupules" [guilt-ridden consciences] (9) afraid of publicly voicing their opinions concerning the presence of blacks in France. Thus, from the very onset of this "BILLET," Ouologuem has delimited a public for *Lettre à la France nègre* constrained by good intentions, fear, or veiled racism, a lethal combination of emotions that inhibit both freedom of speech and of thought, restricting the potential reader to a liberal—therefore, according to Ouologuem, racist—framework.

Ouologuem's *Lettre* begins with definite Fanonian resonances, developing themes already treated by the Martinican writer Frantz Fanon both in *Wretched of the Earth* and *Black Skin, White Masks.* However, while Ouologuem is working with Fanonian themes, he is treating them from an infinitely more virulent stance. Like Fanon in *Black Skin, White Masks*, Ouologuem argues that there is no such thing as a specifically black problem.[3] Only human problems exist, problems that the black man—in refusing to admit any personal contribution to his fate—has "blackened." He continues: "Du jour où les Nègres accepteront de s'entendre dire des vérités désagréables, ils auront alors commencé à s'éveiller au monde" [The day niggers consent to being told disagreeable truths, their awakening to the world will have begun] (10). The black man has to take responsibility for his condition and the consequences of his actions. Only when he no longer attempts to "turn his race white" (Fanon 1968: 8–9) or turn his back on those who have not yet adopted the values of the metropolis will the "probleme noir" change from the color-specific to the neutral:

> S'il y a un problème noir en France, c'est seulement parce que depuis que les civilisés s'asseyent sur des instruments appelés chaises, ils lorgnent de leur mépris la négraille tombée, des arbres où elle vivait, sur la terre où elle ne cesse de gémir la damnation de sa peau, poursuivie par la bénédiction implacable de la déesse misère. (Ouologuem 58)
>
> [If there is such a thing as a black problem in France, it is only because recently the civilized have been sitting on instruments called chairs, and have been scornfully eyeing the niggertrash fallen from the trees where it used to live onto the ground, from where it ceaselessly laments the damnation of its skin, followed by the implacable blessing of the Goddess Misery.]

Ouologuem's sharpest criticism throughout *Lettre à la France nègre* is directed against the "évolué" who has renounced "his blackness, his jungle" (Fanon 18).

Claiming to speak for racists and antiracists alike, both the unsuspecting victims of official antiracism and "la hargne des Nègres" [the spite of niggers] (9), Ouologuem observes that any dialogue between the two groups is obstructed by the hypocrisy of what he calls a philistine negrophilia (9). He explains negrophilia as a psychological compensatory attitude that alleviates feelings of guilt toward Africans through an ostentatious love of all things African, a love without any understanding of the social, cultural, political, economic, or historical aspects of the multifaceted continent. Lemuel Johnson, in *The Devil, the Gargoyle, and the Buffoon,* identifies the same phenomenon and argues that the "Negrophilism" that began in the first decade of the twentieth century as "a creative, artistic and intelligent enterprise" degenerated after World War II into "excesses . . . [that] lacked the grinding intellect of genius" subsequently metamorphosing into an "enthusiastically silly" appreciation (95). This negrophilia is what Ouologuem alternately calls primitivism or "gauchisme de droite" [right-wing leftism] (9). Negrophilia, as a falsely liberal attitude, is founded on the one hand on the problematic identity of the African "évolué" defining himself first and foremost with regard to Europe and on the other hand on the French "one-dimensional taste for the exotic and the picturesque" (Johnson 95).

Hence, in order to speak, Ouologuem must place himself outside these parameters, without concessions to either France and whites or blacks and Africa. His objective in the essays is to cease what he fiercely terms "cette comédie du Nègre braillard, mais untouchable" [this comedy of the whining but untouchable nigger] (11) and put an end to "la mauvaise conscience" (11), the bad faith in which both blacks and whites had been forced to live.

THE "FRANCE NÈGRE," A POWERFUL ABSTRACTION

France is not the United States, "l'Amérique du *Black Power,*" nor South Africa, Ouologuem writes (11). Instead, France is a haunted place, at once inhabited by Africans and consumed by the ghostly image of Africa. By the same token, France is the ghost that haunts Africa and inhabits it. In this double position, both firmly anchored and elusive, France is an idea, an abstraction of a historical colonial past so powerful that Africans—the assimilated Africans Ouologuem addresses himself to—are using it to pose as victims and martyrs, making it into the alibi for their dependency (10).

The France Ouologuem writes to is also the France of Général de Gaulle in 1968, a year that would become, according to many, "a tragic history of ironies" (Jackson 125). That year would paralyze the nation and demonstrate the rift between de Gaulle and the younger generation, confirming to the general that his parliamentary victory in June of the same year was the result of mounting conservative concerns instead of faith in the Gaullist message (Jackson 144). Although de Gaulle was on the verge of resigning by the time *Lettre à la France nègre* was published, one must remember that this work was conceived and created during the heyday of the Gaullist mystique, at a time when de Gaulle prevailed as a symbol of national unity, acting toward the realization of French greatness in world affairs. For "once France had been extracted from her colonial problems, she had to ensure her military, political and technological independence" (Bernstein 115). The prestige of France would best be advanced by a co-operation policy, the "France-Afrique" system Ouologuem attacks in *Lettre à la France nègre* as the extension of France's "mission civilisatrice." Through the foreign policy advanced by de Gaulle in the 1960s, Africa was to be treated as a homogeneous block operating with France through bilateral structures. In maintaining the binary relation France-Africa, France also sustained an attitude of "official antiracism" that is at the very heart of "la France nègre." Official antiracism was a political project that identified and attempted to solve problems the Gaullist government considered to be specifically African. However, Ouologuem sharply notes that the roots of France's problems lay elsewhere. In addressing "la France nègre," Ouologuem makes it clear that he is also speaking to the French working class that, after May 1968, was openly disillusioned with what had become of the nation and de Gaulle's political vision.

Ouologuem's first task in *Lettre à la France nègre* is to recuperate this "France nègre" and demonstrate that it is not a homogeneous group at the basis of the French nation's internal difficulties. "France nègre" refers not only to the disparate group of Africans residing in France but also to "les gagnes-petits, la horde des gens hantés par le S.M.I.G, anonymes habitants de ce *désert français*, qui est, lui aussi, une petite Afrique" [the low-wage earners, the hordes of people haunted by the minimum wage, the anonymous inhabitants of this *French desert*, that is, in itself, a little Africa] (10). Thus, Ouologuem lays bare the truth of the matter: France's dilemma has more to do with a rapidly escalating consumer society increasingly at loss for a unified system of values after the haphazard dismantling of the colonial system than with the presence of African nationals on French soil. In fact, France has become an Africa, Ouologuem's metaphor for a state of utter confusion and humiliation. In speaking openly about a "France nègre," Ouologuem reverses the idea maintained both by France and by the bloc of newly independent nations collectively identified as "Africa" that there is such a thing as a specifically African problem.

IDENTITY AND THE PREDICAMENT OF THE POSTINDEPENDENCE AFRICANS

Ouologuem wages an attack against the identity constructed by those who leave Africa with false hopes of bettering themselves by acquiring a French education and adopting French culture and civilization. In so doing, many African expatriates believe they are purifying themselves of their savagery and immunizing themselves against the "disease" that is Africa. In order to survive in France, they must alienate themselves from their former lifestyle and sing the praises of de Gaulle and his romanticized liberalism (19–20). Addressing himself to de Gaulle, Ouologuem acerbically impersonates the newly independent nations in order to draw attention to their position:

> En faisant de ma filiation avec toi un contract librement consenti, théoriquement je pouvais m'illusionner sur ton caractère libéral. En fait tu continuais à créer une gauloiserie[4] à laquelle j'étais obligé de me prêter, pour avoir une existence physiologique et même sociale. Mon mouvement d'émancipation est resté limité au plan moral, et n'a pas en tout cas amélioré ma condition matérielle d'enfant du Général . . . (20)
>
> [In affiliating myself with you (a reference to de Gaulle) through a free and consensual contract, I could theoretically retain my illusions concerning your liberal character. In reality you continued to create a bawdy farce that I was forced to participate in, in order to possess a physiological and even social existence. My emancipation movement was limited in the moral sense, and in any case it did not improve my material condition as a child of the General.]

"Lettre au couples mixtes" [Letter to Mixed Couples] illustrates the process of emancipation through an allegory: the interracial marriage between a white woman and a black man. The practice of allegory involves doubling or reduplicating extratextual material, a previous discourse; hence it is by definition invested in what Paul de Man names a "rhetoric of temporality" (Lentriccia 293). In Ouologuem's case, we find him recuperating the past (here the metaphor of marriage between France and its colonies) while simultaneously rejecting it by unveiling its implications. In this allegory, the black man, a lesser human, will gain a higher degree of humanity only through a frightening and painful ascent into European education, his ticket to the heart of a French woman: "Temps et labeur, examens et concours ont fait que tu as su réussir à t'ouvrir le corps et le coeur d'une Gauloise, dont les ancêtres, il n'y a pas si longtemps, furent tes Romains" [Through time and labor, tests and entrance examinations, you were able to learn to succeed in opening the heart and body of a Gallic woman whose ancestors, not so long ago, were your Romans] (30). In delving into ancient European history, Ouologuem transforms traditional historical narrative to serve his allegory of contemporary history and continues his play on the words "Gaule" (Gaul), and "Gaulois" (the Gauls). The reference to Gaul is also a satirical reminder of the French civilizational mission's falsification of history in the colonial era, when every child in Africa opened his history textbook to the now infamous opening words "our ancestors the Gauls," an expression often cited in reference to the identity crisis of Africans during and after colonialism.

However, Ouologuem gives his throwback to history a strange twist, and the allegory turns to Gothic horror as the black man, with his "aspirations d'évolué" (30), becomes the aggressor in the interracial marriage, metamorphosed into the Roman attacker and legal rapist of the Sabines. This sudden reversal of the African's character in Ouologuem's allegory indicates the change in the French perception of Africans after independence. From inoffensive underdogs, Africans have come to be seen as menacing international partners, exploiting their status as ex-colonials in a vengeful effort to rob France of its standing and drain its resources. In Ouologuem's view, the interracial marriage between France and its former colonies is a loss for both. Entailing acculturation and assimilation, the relationship forces both parties into exile from their true selves. Ultimately it results in failure, unless the black man representing the African nations remains in the position of "la négraille exilée et privilégiée" [the exiled and privileged niggertrash] (34).

In "Lettre aux non-racistes" [Letter to the nonracists] ironically addressing the French as the "descendants de nos ancêtres les Gaulois" [descendants of our ancestors the Gauls] (49), Ouologuem recuperates the phrase to weave a creation myth of Africans that ironically incorporates the stereotypical descriptions of sub-Saharan Africa found in official and popular culture during the colonial era. In revealing what Johnson terms "the incongruous and the antithetical," Ouologuem, like the colonizer he mimics, is transforming Africans into a "metaphor for esthetic and ethical caricature" (Johnson 19).[5] Throughout the essay, the black man is half-human, uncivilized, and grotesque, a monkey with high aspirations. Ouologuem uses this purposefully crude and disturbing language in order to remind those "assimilé geniuses" (Johnson 91) flocking to Paris that they will never become true Frenchmen. Their downfall resides in a firm conviction in "the credo of the *mission civilisatrice*, 'nos ancêtres, les Gaulois,'" to such an extent that their naive belief "raises no crisis of allegiance, suggests no incongruity" (Johnson 91). Instead, in the repressed unconscious of the French citizen squirming under the eyes of a watchful international community, the "assimilated" remain fixed in a series of grotesque caricatures that are the very antithesis to culture and education.

Ouologuem's allegory presents his readers with several disturbing portraits of the African image in the French mind. Alternately an animal, a simpleton, a loner incapable of forming familial or social ties, recalcitrant both to education and cleanliness, the African's very being contradicts Western social values. Clearly, the French liberal who publicly heralds the liberation of his former slave can never conceive of the black man as a full-fledged individual. Ouologuem charts the progress of the black man who becomes "un type brilliant" as he plunges into the universality of French civilization. With full assimilation into French culture, after voting "oui," the "sous-developpé" no longer eats his neighbors and has acquired "des habitudes de civilisé" [the habits of the civilized] (55). All these attributes notwithstanding, the assimilated black remains uneducated in Ouologuem's book because what he has learned is a borrowed culture. "Un Nègre," concludes Ouologuem, "ce n'est pas seulement un Blanc à peau noire. Dans sa civilisation, il frise, avec ses cheveux, la crétinerie" [A nigger is not only a white with black skin. With his civilized frizzy head he's within a hair's breadth of being a cretin] (59).

In "Lettre aux femmes nègrement seules" [Letter to niggardly lonely women] the process of acculturation is examined by way of another allegory of the black man in France as a lonely woman. This allegory points to the inherent feminization of the African people by the colonial powers, a process that Ouologuem mimics and reverts to throughout *Lettre à la France nègre*. Like lonely women, the black man is a marginal by virtue of his lifestyle (97), in contrast to the Frenchman who embodies France and its dominant values. Ouologuem identifies the relationship of (French) men to women (or blacks) as colonial relationships of domination and condescension that cause solitude, silence, and self-effacement. Similarly to the "femmes nègrement seules" (97), the black man in France is passive and oppressed but resigns himself to the violence against him (98, 99, 100). The lyricism of Ouologuem here is evident, but he is clearly condemning the passive state he describes:

> Le temps s'écoule, comme à la veille de quelque armistice. Solitude, bizarrement paisible, où va se promener la mélancolie du silence, dans la vide compréhension de ce que pourrait être votre vie, peu à peu devenue interrogation calme et communément acceptée. (98)
>
> A ces heures là, le regard que l'on jette au monde . . . s'est changé à présent en un vide de lassitude, de passivité incrédule. (100)

> [Time flows as if on the eve of some armistice. A surprisingly peaceful solitude, where the melancholy of silence walks in the empty comprehension of what your life could have been, but has slowly become a calm and commonly accepted questioning.
>
> At such hours the glance one throws at the world has changed into a tired passively incredulous emptiness.]

From this passage it becomes clear that such a life, a "vie obscurément nègre" [obscurely niggardly life] disintegrates the individual and suppresses him completely, leaving him to the serenely accepted despair of the victims of consumer society (104).

WRITING AGAINST DE GAULLE AND GAULLISM

The evils of imperialism have not ended with decolonization; they have simply been recuperated by the liberalism that Général de Gaulle personifies. In "Lettre au Président de la République Française" [Letter to the

President of the French Republic] Ouologuem begins his long denunciation of Gaullist politics. He sarcastically points to France's condescending attitude that demonstrates how France still thinks of Africa as a "préhistoire," unfit yet to participate in the making of history without France's paternalistic guiding hand. In its open reception of Africans, France is merely continuing its politics of colonialism under a different guise (16). Instead of accepting the specificity of African cultures, what de Gaulle really wants is for Africa to mimic France but to remain a poor copy of the original, since the Gaullist liberals are convinced that Africa can never really become like France even "à l'heure du développement" in the most advanced stages of development (24). Ouologuem uses the stereotypical images of France and of Africa to demonstrate the impossibility and the ridicule involved in such a notion. If Africa were ever to successfully emulate the France of paintings and photographs, with its "pignons de plomb, des toits de tuiles roses, de la mer et un coin de ciel bleu, et, non loin l'onde verte où se mirent des bateaux . . . " [lead gables, pink-tiled roofs, a bit of sea and a corner of blue sky, and not too far out the green water with boats reflected in it], then there would be no difference between black and white. However, the essence of being French is in really knowing that "la présence des Nègres, dans un pareil décor, donnait aux lieux un aspect miteux et lamentable" [the presence of niggers in such a setting gave the place a shabby miserable look] (24), to the point that "la France . . . jamais ne saurait tolérer d'être nègre" [France would never tolerate being Black] (24).

In Ouologuem's view, de Gaulle has become the narrator of universal history, rewriting Africa's history so that it might one day aspire to universality. In a short sardonic fable, Ouologuem tells the story about how Africans became the children of "Mongénéral" (60).[6] In Ouologuem's tale, the indigenous emperors were exploiting the continent's riches among themselves and profiteering from a growing slave trade, which they soon shared with the invading colonizers (61–62). In such conditions, all the Whites were black emperors, and they became indistinguishable from each other. Who then are the real blacks? asks Ouologuem (63). The answer is to be found in another parable that he hastens to relate: "l'Histoire secrète de l'Indépendance de l'Empire de la Nuit" [The secret story of the independence of the empire of the night] (63). In this second fable, Africa is feminized and described as a prostitute who contributed to the downfall of the Europeans and her own because of her involvement with more than one man, causing much speculation about her political, social and ideological loyalties: "sausialistes, neutralistes positifs, neutralistes négatifs, blancs non-engagés, blancs dégagés, rouges révolutionnaires, jaunes périlleux, noirs flemmards" and "un cercle privé d'affreux-Asiatiques, le Tiers-Monde" [sausialists, positive neutralists, negative neutralists, non-engaged whites, casually disengaged whites, revolutionary reds, perilous yellows, lazy blacks (and) a private circle of ugly Asians, the Third-World]

(64–65).[7] Africa is a prostitute, her ills—spending, megalomania, verbosity, and the proletariat—are the venereal diseases plaguing those clamoring for independence but ill-prepared for it. A moral imperative demands her punishment by division into international shares. Since then, Africa has been faring much worse. "[E]lle boite. Est malade. Anémiée. Sous-alimentée. Sous développée . . . Pouvoir d'achat: nul! Les Blancs découchèrent. C'était l'indépendance. Hihi" [She limps, is ill, anemic, undernourished, underdeveloped. Power of purchase: nil! The whites spent the night elsewhere. It was independence. Heehee] (65). Ouologuem's description of the process indicates his firm belief that the former colonies were intentionally punished for gaining their independence, which resulted in their present state. As starving and subservient nations of beggars, they are led by a corrupt national bourgeois class fully aligned with the former colonialists, just as the precolonial emperors had been. Because France feared losing its former colonies at the height of the cold war, French politics of "coopération" are viewed by Ouologuem as yet another attempt to preserve France's dominion over African territories.

However, although it may appear that Ouologuem violently rejects any contact with France and is entrenching himself in a protectionist state of self-sufficiency, his position is in reality much more subtle. He realizes that cooperation is now inevitably part of history and that it had already begun in the fourteenth century at the moment of the first European contact with Africa. Yet if cooperation is the only solution, then its parameters must be redefined. No cooperation can be construed without objectivity and the shock of truths it entails for both parties, which will lead to constructive solutions. This clash of truths would force whites to relinquish deep and insidious forms of racism such as those inherent in language, an insidiousness that becomes evident in the language Ouologuem is purposely using throughout *Lettre à la France nègre*. In language, above all, the categories of black and white are pitted against each other. Blacks, however, must participate in the process and acknowledge their responsibility and accountability, instead of adopting the whining Jacobinism that has become the latest alibi of neo-colonialism.[8]

African Leaders and the Postindependence Nations

In "Lettre aux rois nègres de passage en France" [Letter to the Black Kings Transiting through France], Ouologuem scathingly criticizes the colonial mentality of the leaders of Africa. Addressing them as "Chers Blancs" [Dear Whites] (71), he considers them to be the most assimilated of all Africans as well as the most abject, since they have become slaves to a materialistic consumer culture. At independence, the stunned and confused national bourgeoisie or "les sous-developpés" [the underdeveloped] a group of imbeciles endowed only with a primitive mentality and a relentless perversity of character, become even more terrifying according to Ouologuem because they are rich (71). Ouologuem is clearly echoing Fanon's conviction that independence corners the bourgeois class and provokes its frenzied attempts to gain help from the former mother country, with often catastrophic results (*The Wretched of the Earth* 149). The ruling classes "stupidly, contemptibly," and "cynically bourgeois" (150), live in deplorable ostentation, corruption, and debt that have become a constant source of embarrassment before the international community (72).

Like Fanon, Ouologuem observes that the national bourgeoisie, the political niggertrash will never learn to govern decently, for while it loudly brays insults at colonialism, it is replacing an imperialistic rule by its own version of exploitation and deceitfully using foreign aid for its own material advancement instead of putting these valuable resources toward the development of a badly needed infrastructure (72).

Ouologuem is especially concerned by the "mariage ambigü," the "ambiguous marriage" (73) being forged with the United States, which he views as another venue for the exploitation of Africa. Ouologuem is clearly one of the very first Africans sounding the alarm of neo-colonialism. The new relations with countries other than France are seductive, but they will ultimately be disappointing. The rash new governments are blind to the similarities between colonial and postindependence foreign relations such as the new ties to the United States or socialist countries.[9] Socialist pretensions or relations with more "liberal" countries provide a superficial disguise for the fresh avenues of profiteering used by the governing classes. By way of the systems of cooperation they endorse, the African leaders are giving away the best of what their nations have to offer (74). Just as Fanon in *Wretched of the Earth* declares that the national bourgeoisie is not "engaged in production, nor in invention, nor in building, nor in labor" (149–150), Ouologuem asserts that they construct without being real builders and effectively destroy the future of their nations with their "maladresses effarantes" [horrifying blunders] (73). The African leaders' inability to govern without the innumerable technical counselors and aides provided by France, their developmental values, and colonial habits of mind are factors that effectively maintain French involvement in African affairs after decolonization and force them to advance on a path chosen for them without their consent (75).

Ouologuem pointedly criticizes the attacks against human rights that African nations have continued to propagate since the inception of the new nations. He predicts that the lifestyles of the bourgeoisie and the governing classes will soon collide with revolution. The people, Ouologuem reminds us, are well aware of the fact that preceding white colonialism, the colonialism of the black aristocracy prevailed: "Après tout quel Africain ignore qu'avant l'Homme Blanc, il y eut également le colonialisme des Notables noirs et celui de la Conquête Arabe?" [After all, what African is ignorant of the fact that preceding the white man's arrival there had been the colonialism of the black notables and that of the Arab conquest?] (90). Ouologuem thus reverses the black-white dichotomy written down in colonial and postindependence versions of African history. The agressor is not simply the white man, but also "le notable [qui] a vendu son domestique noir aux négriers" [the notable that sold his servant to the slave-traders] (90). The "Lettre aux rois nègres de passage en France" ends on an ominous note, reminding those Ouologuem calls "rois nègres" to take precautions lest they slip, fall, and break their necks! (75).

FOREIGN AID AND DEPENDENCY

In his methodology on how to differentiate blacks from whites, Ouologuem cites money, hunger, and lifestyle as the distinguishing characteristics. "Comment donc un Blanc peut-il savoir qu'il n'est pas un nègre?" [How then can a white know he's not a nigger?] is the rhetorical question that Ouologuem asks and immediately answers: the white man, "un homme développé," is superior to the black man because he does not accept gifts (52). The gift then, for Ouologuem, generates and redefines personal identity as well as that of an entire continent. Foreign aid has nefarious political, economic, and cultural implications in the relationship it creates between France and the poorer African nations. What the average Frenchman perceives as a compassionate and humane gesture on the part of his government is really a self-interested action ensuring that the poorer nations remain in servitude because they must recognize and be grateful to the donors. The gift becomes a debt in the Nietzschean sense, as it compels immediate feelings of duty that in time are transformed into a necessarily painful memory.[10] For Ouologuem, this sacrifice is a sacrifice of honor in a relationship of dominance and cultural servitude between creditor and discharged debtor. Hence, although slavery has been officially abolished, it reappears in a different guise in present-day Africa because systematic dependency is created and maintained by the flooding of the continent with foreign aid. Those who live in France, those who have been uprooted and formerly oppressed by France, as well as the leaders of African nations, are under the influence of opportunists creating the illusion of a constant need for French financial aid. They are true dependents, for, as Albert Memmi observes, the dependent is someone who believes he cannot survive otherwise and who believes in the efficiency of his provider (36).[11] Living beyond their means, seduced by the opportunity for earning free gifts, but deprived of economic and political independence (16), these dependents know that their addictions are costly, that payments must be made. Furthermore, they have lost all honor because they have ignored the fundamental basis of the gift economy, the obligation, in exchange, to give another gift of equal or superior value.

In this harangue, Ouologuem returns to his feminization of Africa and portrays the continent as a cheating, frigid, and insatiable wife. France is again in the masculine position, this time as the eventually cuckolded husband, whereas Africa, childlike and brutal, is a prostitute available to the highest bidder. Ouologuem accuses de Gaulle of having created and maintained the husband-wife relationship between France and Africa, that is, the relationship of dependency, a discreet family slavery (18) resembling what Memmi designates as a "reciprocal dependency" (23). Although some reject this relation because it no longer provides the glorious outward signs of dominance, others—the majority, in Ouologuem's opinion—continue to enjoy the moral superiority provided by their financial domination of the prostituted continent, relishing the feeling of charity gained by aiding the needy (18–19).

The Merits of *Lettre à la France nègre*

Following charges of plagiarism, Ouologuem's *Le Devoir de violence* plunged in the eyes of the literary establishment from the lofty seat of originality and authenticity, to the tainted shallow place of the quasi-criminal copy. His once enthusiastic reviewers became assiduous detractors, one commenting sourly that the "only way [*Lettre à la France nègre*] is superior to *Le Devoir de violence* is in its authenticity, for there is no reason to think that this work is not fully the product of Ouologuem's own talents and abilities!" (Sellin, "The Unknown Voice of Yambo Ouologuem" 142–143). *Lettre à la France nègre* was clearly destined for oblivion, not only because it was written by a dishonest individual who sought to trick the world into believing he was a great writer, but also because the discrepancy between the novel and the essays "was so great" ("The Unknown Voice" 143). Although interest in *Le Devoir de violence* subsisted and grew over the years, little mention was made of the book of essays that followed, other than to reveal it as a possible blueprint to the infamous novel.[12] Perhaps *Lettre à la France nègre*, because of its tone and because it reminded critics of all that was disappointing in *Le Devoir de violence,* remains inscribed in the annals of literary history with Sellin's crushing commentary: "a collection of flimsy diatribes against the racial and cultural colonization of France" ("The Unknown Voice" 156), nothing more than "persiflage or pathetic irony" ("Ouologuem's Blueprint" 120). Although

Sellin's assessment of Ouologuem's diatribes is admittedly influenced by his frustration with the preceding novel, and he warns the uninitiated reader about admiring Ouologuem's tone of "sheer vitriol and righteous indignation" ("Ouologuem's Blueprint" 120), I maintain that Ouologuem's critics have too long been caught up with issues of formulas, blueprints, and brain-picking and have neglected the real ideological value of his satirical essays. Through the devices of irony and paradox and in privileging a satire of realism, Ouologuem institutes himself violently as an agent of change. Not only is he in a formalist revolt against the forms that African literature has had to adapt itself to, he is also in an ideological revolt achieved by a constant defamiliarization of the reader effected through his use of language and the fracturing and negation of any possibility of stable identity.

Abiola Irele writes that "the essential force of African literature" is "its reference to the historical and the experiential" (1990: 11) as it has "grown out of the rupture created within . . . indigenous history and way of life by the colonial experience" (27). African literature, in its early works, focused on realist historical reconstruction in order to come to terms with the legacy of colonialism and a fractured history. In the disillusionment of the postindependence era, historical engagement becomes even more meaningful as history provides the links between colonialism and the state of present-day politics. Yambo Ouologuem's *Lettre à la France nègre* stems from this dissatisfaction, and in his case, the problem of history goes beyond redeeming or annihilating the past, as he challenges the very authority of past histories. He authorizes himself to do so because he recognizes that every history is an authored text, a mode of discourse both culturally conditioned and ideologically motivated. By withdrawing the scientific authority history has abrogated itself,[13] Ouologuem treats history as a text made up of words, always, necessarily an authored fiction that can be destabilized and rewritten.

CONCLUSION

Lettre à la France nègre is about modern-day African rulers and pseudo-intellectuals as well as about the average French citizen confronted with a new relationship to Africa and Africans. History, however, repeats itself. For Ouologuem, it is clearly related to language, and he goes to great lengths to unveil various types of racism, both French and African. Ouologuem's tone is self-derogatory, crude, and often calumniating because he is attempting to illustrate how language mediates the way in which we see the past and the traditions that inform the present. In "Post-Colonial Allegory and the Transformation of History," Stephen Slemon argues that "history, like fiction requires an act of reading before it can have meaning," something Ouologuem is himself keenly aware of. Slemon adds that "[t]he "point for postcolonial allegory is that historical material must be *read*, and read in *adjacency* to a fictional reenactment of it" (160). *Lettre à la France nègre* provides both historical material and the fictionality that comes with the exaggeration and distortion of satire.

Lettre à la France nègre is built upon Ouologuem's understanding of the provisional and discursive nature of history built into the literary text, so that history is approachable only in its connection to fictionality. The book of essays can be read as a fictionalized or personalized take on the racial relations and the political and cultural ties between France and its former colonies. While it parodies, mimics, allegorizes, and inflates events, personalities, and actions, the work also serves to demonstrate how the concurrent discourses from heterogeneous sources actualize the relationship between Africa and France. At the same time, it illustrates that relationships to history can only be textual, partial practices, fictions that refer to other fictions, texts that point to other texts. The historical narrative is viewed as a complex structure especially built to show a carefully selected part of the past. In other words, in parodying various discourses, Ouologuem shows that the historian's language is not a transparent passive medium through which we can see the past, nor does it aim to represent the past. Rather, the numerous sources of history available in the book of essays show that we do not look at the past through language but from a vantage point provided by it.

Replete with crude language, sadism, and a gory view of present-day racial relations, Ouologuem's *Lettre à la France nègre* unveils what is at the basis of any construction of history, namely, violence. Violence, finally, is a duty, what is necessary to reconstruct a fragmented identity and history. As a literary text, Ouologuem's book of essays wrenches itself violently away from what has previously been written in African literature. As a historical text, it distances itself from previous official versions of events and violates them in order to destroy the links between colonialism and textuality.

"Decolonization," Frantz Fanon writes in *The Wretched of the Earth*, "is always a violent phenomenon"; that is, it responds to violence with violence and effects a tabula rasa calling for change from the bottom up (35). It is also a historical process that is effected in complete disorder. In this sense, *Lettre à la France nègre* could be read as a fictional application of the precepts Fanon calls for in *The Wretched of the Earth*. By allowing the "history of pillage" (51)—a pillage both African and Western—to resurface, Ouologuem is also attempting to bring into existence what Fanon announces should follow: namely the "history of decolonization" (51). In *Lettre à la France nègre*, finally, there is no recuperable system.

But the interrogation of already inscribed ones can act as a kind of antisystem that resists European master narratives of history as well as romantic African myths of origin. In maintaining itself as an allegory, this satire is not redeeming or annihilating previous histories; it is only displacing history as a concept and opening up the past as text to other readings of it and to the violent and imaginative revisionism necessary to nationalism.

NOTES

1. Christopher Miller notes in *Blank Darkness* that the "succès de scandale" Ouologuem attained with the publication of *Le Devoir de violence* "was proportional to the initial succès d'estime" (219). Many critics focused on the issue of plagiarism itself, such as Sellin (1971, 1976), Randall (1990, 1991), Frazer (1992), and Lack (1995).

2. In associating himself with pamphlet literature, Ouologuem is necessarily situating himself in the not-so-distant French tradition of political pamphleteering of the likes of Paul Nizan, Georges Bernanos, and Louis-Ferdinand Céline, who typically used the genre in the 1930s as a forum for personal opinion permitting a violent outpouring of personal hatred of perfidious vituperation. Ouologuem's *Lettre à la France nègre* differs, however, in his association of humor with bitter ideological tension, producing a more readable text.

3. Fanon writes in *Black Skin, White Masks* that "there is no black problem. Or, at any rate, if there is one it concerns the whites only accidentally" (29).

4. This is only one of Ouologuem's play on the words *Gaule* (Gaul): *gauloiserie,* which refers to Gallic or bawdy humor (to tell a *gauloiserie* is to tell a bawdy story or a ribald joke); the adjective *gaulois* (Gallic, which he also uses later in the feminine *gauloise* in reference to an archetypal Frenchwoman), and finally combining all the above meanings with the name *de Gaulle* that, taken euphonically and understood in the context of this play on words, results in the combination of the meaning "from Gaul" as well a sarcastic reference to what Ouologuem perceives as de Gaulle's aim to represent the French character, or de Gaulle as the epitome of being French.

5. Johnson's book, published in 1969, the year after *Lettre à la France nègre*, shows the dehumanization of the black man throughout the history of Western culture and civilization. A more recent examination of the topic is Christopher Miller's *Blank Darkness* (1985). The introduction to his more recent book (1990) also sheds light on how Africans are portrayed in anthropological discourse.

6. In his sarcastic use of the term *Mongénéral* [Mygeneral], Ouologuem is referring to the long-standing devotion of Africans to de Gaulle even while his popularity with the French public was failing. De Gaulle is seen in this sense as the protective father of the new African nations and their citizens (especially at the time of de Gaulle's France-Afrique project), which, in turn, are referred to by Ouologuem as the "children of the general."

7. Ouologuem skillfully uses the meanings of color codes in effect throughout history: each color mentioned corresponds to one of the human races but also to the flags used in wartime: the white flag is used universally for truce; the black in early times was a symbol for piracy; the red symbolizes mutiny or revolution; and the yellow is a sign of infectious diseases.

8. The "Jacobinisme" Ouologuem speaks of alludes to the Jacobins in French history, the political club of the French revolution. Formed in 1789, the club was named after the monastery of the Jacobins where it met. The members were mainly bourgeois and sought to limit the power of the king, and during the ascendancy of Robespierre, they instituted the Reign of Terror, which they used not only against counterrevolutionaries but also against their former allies. Ouologuem could be accusing the bourgeois blacks in France of instituting a similar reign of terror, where no one could accuse them of irresponsibility and corruption without being in turn accused of racism. However, in a typical double-edged fashion, Ouologuem could also be alluding to the African Jacobins of Freetown, the slaves recaptured by those opposing the slave trade and freed. Lacking a homogeneous culture, they were fully assimilated into Western culture and alienated from their own by the English government that introduced a deliberate policy of turning them into a homogeneous Christian community. In a second sense, Jacobin is used by Ouologuem in the same manner as "assimilé" or "évolué," to denote alienation and the belief in a French claim to universality.

9. Ouologuem is clearly criticizing a core-periphery world order as well as what Richard Sklar in "The Colonial Imprint on African Political Thought" identifies as "a theory of social class that is derived from the experience and study of early capitalist development in Europe, vanguard elitism, be it left and Leninist or right and corporatist" (21). Ouologuem is against emulating Western forms of government because he senses that they are an imposition, an importation, and do not stem from the needs of African countries.

10. In *The Genealogy of Morals*, Fredrich Nietzsche writes that the measure of the powerful state is the extent of its humanitarian giving without personal injury and the necessity of repayment. When the creditor benevolently discharges his debtor of the obligation of repayment, the truly terrifying moment of the gift-giving process has arrived. Ultimately, the debtor owes a wholesale sacrifice to his creditor. Only the powerful and the sovereign can promise, give, and forgive.

11. In "International Assistance and International Capitalism: Supportive or Counterproductive?" S. K. B. Asante comments on the necessarily negative impact of international assistance and foreign capitalism upon the economic growth and well-being of African nations. He contends that imports have retarded or even halted development as well as any economically effective "structural reorganization in recipient nations" (250). That is what Ouologuem clearly implies. Ouologuem also alludes to a point Asante develops extensively, the fact that "aid tends to be concentrated in the modern more efficient sectors of society or prestigious and easily identifiable projects rather than on those which serve the real development interests of the country concerned" (260). Asante adds that foreign aid was often tied to specific goods that could only be purchased from the donor country.

12. Such is the contention of Eric Sellin in "Ouologuem's Blueprint for *Le Devoir de violence*." Later, more meticulous analyses, such as that of Thomas Hale in the chapter dedicated to Ouologuem in *Scribe, Griot, and Novelist*, offer little more than a smiling passing comment on the book of essays. "One does not need to go very far, though," writes Hale, "to discover that Ouologuem is hardly obscure . . . when he proposes to his reader a highly amusing system of plagiarism in *Lettre à la France nègre*" (138).

13. History has attempted to position itself within the sciences since the Enlightenment, and especially the nineteenth century was saluted as the century of history, in which the historian must ideally disappear from the text and allow the events to tell themselves.

11

Pornography, or the Politics of Misbehaving? A Feminist Reading of the Voices of Yambo Ouologuem

Ann Elizabeth Willey

Most readers of Yambo Ouologuem are concerned with the novel *Le Devoir de violence*. Indeed, reams of discourse have been dedicated to this novel; as early as 1972, shortly after it was awarded the Prix Renaudot, *Le Devoir de violence* was at the center of hotly contested debates that have not subsided to this day. And yet in the voluminous and quite thorough scholarship on Yambo Ouologuem, whether celebratory or castigating, very little has been said about Ouologuem's two other major pieces of prose, *Lettre à la France nègre* and *Les Milles et une bibles du sexe.*[1] This chapter will ask of these two lesser-known works the kinds of questions usually posed in reference to *Le Devoir de violence*. In particular, I wonder if these two works can shed some new light on the question of how we can or should receive Ouologuem's troubling corpus.[2] Ouologuem is usually read as engaging in a "politics of misbehavior," but this has been challenged by some readers, particularly those who are concerned with questions raised from feminist standpoints.[3] I suggest that although *Le Devoir de violence* can indeed be read convincingly as a subversive text, when it is looked at in conjunction with *Lettre à la France nègre* and *Les Milles et une bibles du sexe,* this recuperation of Ouologuem is much harder to effect. An extension of the feminist critique to these other two texts seriously weakens any representation of Ouologuem's work as subversive.

Short of Chinua Achebe's *Things Fall Apart*, Yambo Ouologuem's novel *Le Devoir de violence* may be one of the most written-about novels in African literature, but for very different reasons. Whereas Achebe's novel is celebrated as a foundational text in African literature, Ouologuem's novel is infamous for committing a host of sins. Rather than establishing a canon, Ouologuem's novel departs radically from the norms that had shaped the francophone African canon prior to its publication. It is very definitely not a book that had truck with négritude, unless you read it as a scathing critique of the same. It is not lyrically nostalgic like Cheikh Hamidou Kane's *L'Aventure ambiguë*, nor is it a mildly ironic, subtly critical realistic novel bent on exposing the contradictions of the civilizing mission like *Une vie de Boy* or almost any of Mongo Beti's novels. Ouologuem's vitriolic, pugnacious, and scatological version of African history as one of corruption, sadism, and hypocrisy outraged many African readers. Its flagrant plagiarism added fuel to the critical fire. Since its early scandal-ridden appearance on the scene, however, *Le Devoir de violence* has come to mean many different things.

Indeed, the scholarship surrounding *Le Devoir de violence* largely seeks to recoup this objectionable, disruptive text from the early attacks made against it on several fronts. Many have argued that, in fact, this novel was exactly what francophone African literature needed in the late 1960s to counterbalance what were increasingly obvious as the shortfalls of a novelistic tradition shaped by orthodoxies of négritude. In this vein, Wole Soyinka claims *Le Devoir de violence* as a corrective to the types of history posited by Kane's *L'Aventure ambiguë,* calling *Le Devoir de violence* "a studied repudiation of historical blinkers" (100). Kwame Anthony Appiah similarly claims that *Le Devoir de violence* is primarily a work of political critique aimed at contemporary Africa. Appiah describes it as a novel that "seeks to delegitimate the forms of the realist African novel, in part, surely, because what it sought to naturalize was a nationalism that, by 1968, had plainly failed" (150).[4]

Not only is *Le Devoir de violence* read as a critique of foregoing political and literary traditions, its plagiaristic mode is often read as a profoundly subtle and disruptive commentary on the dynamics of colonial discourse and postcolonial relations. Critics such as Aliko Songolo, Jonathan Ngaté, and Christopher Miller respond more directly to the charges of plagiarism and always in such a way as to recoup the plagiarism as a critical statement on discursive relations of power. They argue that Ouologuem's plagiarism is an attempt to disrupt the unidirectional flow of discourse posited by the colonialist enterprise. Miller refers to the novel as "a brazen act of trifling with the idols of literary creation, respecting the taboos of neither the African nor the European literary establishment" (1985: 218), which Ouologuem does in order to look the Africanist tradition in its eye and "disfigure it in his own fashion" (238).[5] Aliko Songolo goes even further in claiming for this novel subversive techniques and goals:

> Cette technique, que je nommerai la technique de la subversion, fait violence non seulement à tout ce que le roman africain représentait avant 1968, mais encore à la notion acquise du rôle social et politique de la tradition d'une part, et d'autre part à la notion de propriété littéraire.[6] (1981: 25)

Ngaté combines these readings and calls the text "a radical invitation to conspiratorial misbehavior" and again later places the novel firmly in a context of "a politics of misbehavior which [is] shaping the African novel" (44, 58). The readings of Ngaté, Miller, and Songolo that emphasize Ouologuem's use and misuse of European literary conventions, his flouting of the laws of patriarchy, all agree: Ouologuem's misbehaving is a politically subversive act that works to undermine the hegemony of colonial discourse about Africa. And these are convincing ways to read Ouologuem's novel. From a feminist standpoint, though, the prospect of men misbehaving is not always a heartening thought.

In an essay that examines the representation of rape in Ouologuem's *Le Devoir de* violence, Eileen Julien, in fact, points out that though Ouologuem's text is radically critical of the hierarchy inherent in European colonialism, it does not challenge hierarchical gender relations; in fact, on a textual level, it reinscribes female passivity.[7] If we extend Julien's argument to the reception of Ouoluguem's novel, what we see is, I think, that the defenses of *Le Devoir* depend on reading literary discourse and political disourse as analagous, or metaphors for each other. We see Ouologuem's rejection of European literary norms as a type of rebellion against European political hegemony. Plagiarism becomes guerrilla warfare. And yet, this tropological slide covers over the other norms that Ouologuem leaves in place, most notably unequal gender relations. What happens to "the politics of misbehavior" if we unlink the concepts of the violence of colonial discourse, the violence of Ouologuem's textual practice against that discourse, and the violence against women in Ouologuem's discourse? An awareness of how this third term underpins the first two throughout Ouologuem's work, I argue, seriously challenges the easy metaphorical substitution of plagiarism for radical politics. The transgressions against the European-derived, patriarchically inflected laws of authority and authorship are only subversive in a masculine context. What many claim for Ouologuem—that he is making a call for a new humanism (*pace* Appiah), that he is representing the disenfranchised of Africa (*pace* Fatunde),[8] or even that he posits brutality as part of the human condition (*pace* Julien and Thomas Hale)—begs the question of who is acknowledged as human, disenfranchised, or even brutalized, in Ouologuem's work.

Ouologuem's *Lettre à la France nègre* and *Les Mille et une bibles du sexe* are less well known and certainly less often discussed, though both were published within a year of *Le Devoir de violence*. In 1968, the same year *Le Devoir de violence* appeared, Ouologuem published a collection of satiric essays called *Lettre à la France nègre*. This series of "letters" comprise highly sarcastic attacks on the French and French culture, wherein Ouologuem takes a great deal of pleasure in turning both French and

African pieties on their heads. One letter, for example, examines the well-known lament of the négritude poets concerning the negative associations of blackness in the French language. Ouologuem starts off by quoting the famous examples of whiteness as purity, truth, light, and so on, but then goes on to show how whiteness has also been used in the French language to imply things that are not nearly so savory, such as the idea of insubstantial and insincere speech known as blandishments; the treatment of treating symptoms that mask a much more serious underlying disease, known as "un traitement qui ne fait que blanchir" (40); or similarly, the craftiness used in exculpating criminals, referred to as "un bon avocat peut blanchir un criminel" (40). Although this essay is in part a chastisement aimed at the négritude poets for their too simplistic critique of the French language, the letter ends with the observation that France is not nearly as "white" as it would like to think itself either. Ouologuem concludes with the question, "la France est-elle nègre ou pas?" to which he poses the answer, "consulter le Bottin alphabétique, pour voir si y figure l'Afrique des banlieues . . ." (46). This is the type of playful and yet pointed reversal that Ouologuem's critics celebrate in reading *Le Devoir de violence*.

Lettre à la France nègre contains one letter in particular that critics of Ouologuem's work, most notably Christopher Miller and James Olney, have identified as central to a reading of Ouologuem's literary politics. Ouologuem's "Lettre aux pisse-copie Nègres d'écrivains célèbres" is a long exegesis on how the black writer in French is in some ways always a "ghostwriter." Miller points out that one meaning of the word *nègre* in French is "ghostwriter"; thus, for the black writer to write in French is always to write as a *nègre*—that is, necessarily as someone writing in a language of which she or he cannot claim ownership. Ouologuem tells the black writer not to despair but instead to relish his anonymity, to leave the task of thinking to others, and instead to get rich by producing mass quantities of hackneyed but lucrative detective fiction quickly and simply by combining elements of already published fiction. In the middle of this essay, he provides a pull-out chart with several passages from popular detective novels conveniently excerpted and classified, complete with plot schematics and possible combinations for effective fiction.

Certainly, his *Lettre à la France nègre* seems to be a nonfiction version of the defense that others have posed in his stead. In his evenhanded attacks on the discourse that promotes both a sense of African victimhood and thus a loss of subjectivity and conversely a sense of French superiority that is both hypocritical and dependent on the presence of African wealth, Ouologuem plays into a reading of his work as subversive or an invitation to misbehavior. The how-to fold-out chart outlining the mechanics of plagiarism is the pinnacle of his exploding of these myths. The excoriating letters to those who would forget their investment in perpetuating the racist tropes of colonialism frame a call to wholesale plunder of French literature that will lead to handsome remuneration for the black writer, even if he cannot take credit for "the white work of thinking" (166). How better to live up to the "radical politics of misbehavior" than to publish a "how-to" book for plagiarists? Ouologuem's *Lettre à la France nègre* fits well into the pattern that would have us read his narratives as an invitation to misbehavior for the purposes of dramatizing the violence-fraught relationship that Africans have to writing in French.

However, even in this work, women are invoked and silenced simultaneously, much as they are *Le Devoir de violence*. In the sometimes very personal essays in which Ouologuem invokes his own childhood or tries to explain the motives for African men in marrying Frenchwomen, women, either European or African, are invoked only as symbols, not subjects. In the first letter, Ouologuem invokes the common image of Africa as a women who has prostituted herself to Europe to explain the neo-colonial context. He uses this image again in the fourth letter through an extended parable about "Binta," a woman who disfigures herself in a vain attempt to become more desirable to the white lovers who eventually abandon her—this is his metaphor for cultural colonialism and the arrival of independence. The seventh letter, titled "Lettre aux femmes nègrement seules" (Letter to blackly alone women") begins with the claim "Femmes seules, vous êtes comme les Nègres, dès lors même que votre état vous tient à l'écart de la vie, reléguées dans la société marginale des groupes minoritaires" (97).[9] From here, Ouologuem goes on to explain how women who remain alone become too interiorized and thus make orphans of themselves, and then he asserts that this is why African women in Europe will not marry African men. Whereas African men who marry European women are seeking a promise of acceptance, African women are shown simply as rejecting African men because of mental maladjustment. The status of woman is explicitly one of silence; she is unable to voice or act on her desires.[10]

Ouologuem's other major piece of writing is *Les Milles et une bibles du sexe* (1969), a collection of erotic, or more accurately, pornographic,[11] short-stories that Ouologuem claims are culled from a thousand such stories handed to him by a Parisian aristocrat named "Utto Rodolph" for his editing. What follows is a series of "poker confessions" of four sexual adventurers whose exploits range from the relatively mild scene of mutual masturbation on a subway train to the outrageous orgies of hundreds of couples each trying to outdo the other in the preposterousness of their sexual appetites. The structure of this collection would seem to follow the program laid out in his "Lettre aux pisse-copies nègres d'écrivains célèbres": Ouologuem hides behind a pen name, the position of the ghostwriter, and engages in producing a series of stories that fall under one of the more formulaic genres of writing, the pornographic short story. Can this pornography also be recouped as part of a politics of misbehavior? Can we claim it as a commentary on the social, political, and discursive relations between France and the ex-colonies that invites subversion?

In his introduction, Ouologuem claims this position for himself and this work. He claims that Utto Rudolph came to him because certain aspects of *Le Devoir de violence* suggested that Ouologuem would be an appropriate editor for a collection of "erotic confessions." Ouologuem writes:

> But I do not intend to specialize in this area. This is my first and last effort. I have taken it upon myself to present this thousand and one bibles of sex partly because it was the erotic aspects of my first novel that caused several African countries to close their borders to *Bound to Violence*. In the eyes of the irresponsible and uncultivated heads of state, I was, for having dared to say that the black man makes love, a sell-out to a racist France, which amuses itself by watching a black man strip other black people of their identities and customs as black people. So be it.[12]

Echoing the defenses made on his behalf by critics like Appiah and Soyinka, Ouologuem poses this collection as a political statement aimed at the heads of state in Africa who would keep him from treating African subjects as wholly human.

Critics have been willing in part to accept Ouologuem's own positioning of this text as a political response to the objections launched at *Le Devoir de violence*. James Olney, for example, reads *Les Milles et une bibles du sexe* as a somewhat raunchy retort to the claims that Ouologuem's goal is the perpetuation of the colonialist stereotypes of the barbaric African. The Europeans of *Les Milles et une bibles du sexe* are more savage in their customs than the worst of the Saifs, and indeed some of the most objectionable scenes in *Le Devoir de violence* are repeated here, translated into a European context.[13] Olney points out:

> The erotic adventures in *Les Milles et une bibles du sexe*—and this fact of setting reflects, I think, significantly on actions in *Le Devoir de Violence*, which is located almost entirely in Africa—take place, for the most part, in France and the participants, again for the most part (when they are not dogs or other dumb beasts), are French." (225)

Olney ascribes a political motive to Ouologuem's translation of the more egregious scenes in *Le Devoir de violence* to a French setting. As Olney says at another point in his reading, Ouologuem is generous in his distributions of vices, neglecting neither the Africans nor the Europeans that he writes about (211). Although Miller (1985) gives Ouologuem much less credit for this collection, (he argues that *Les milles et une bibles du sexe* is a much less original work [245], which ironically would suggest its appropriateness as an example in Ouologuem's exercises in mass-production of formulaic literature), he follows some of the same lines of argument as Olney, suggesting that Ouologuem's appropriation of sexual discourse about Europe presents itself as a political act.[14]

Although this positioning of *Les Mille et une bibles du sexe* works into the common reading of his corpus as subversive, critics feel compelled to recoup the one story in the collection that takes place in Africa. The narrator himself displays the same desire: this is the only story which the narrator prefaces with an apology for its content. During the interminable Parisian adventures of the main characters, they arrive one night at an orgy, accompanied by three Liberians. The proprietor of the club they wish to enter will not admit the Liberians. The main character threatens the owner, and eventually they all enter, but the mood has been sullied and they quickly retire. The Liberians, rich businessmen, offer the four Parisians round-trip tickets to Africa as a thank you for their efforts on behalf of the Africans. Ouologuem interrupts the collection of stories to report in his own editorial voice:

> I must somewhat naively declare that I was sorry to see Africa mixed up in this business. I had wished, for form's sake, that Utto Rudolph would have chosen another type of story—a less collective exoticism, perhaps, so problematic did it seem. The leisurely activity of the safari; does it give the traveler anything more than a little local color? One of the confessees wrote on page 732 'Safaris are another thing altogether. They have the refined sex appeal of a hunt with hounds." I had to rewrite the opening of this confession. To reread it. And still I was not satisfied: it lacked the psychological dimension of eroticism. (275)

What follows is a conversation between Ouologuem and the couple who had submitted this particular story in which he pushes them to explain the connection between safaris and eroticism. The wife compares a safari to a bullfight—an elaborately staged dance that, by implication, always ends in blood. She says later though, that she finds the unequal contest between man and beast unnerving. Her husband identifies this aspect as precisely the root of eroticism. The wife explains:

> W: It's about the male being seen. A reflection of his masculine power. Of his superiority over the female.
> H (to his wife): Exactly.
> W: What do you mean "Exactly"?
> H: Sexual love is very violent.
> YO: And so the Safari . . .
> H: It is beautiful . . . the woman on safari is very sweet/soft.

YO: She gives the feeling of being a victim?
H: She is seductive, fascinating. (276–277)

The characters clearly lay out for us the erotic appeal of unequal relations of power that are doubly displayed in the erotic/exotic safari. As is so often the case in colonialist discourse, the white man claims his power over a feminized landscape. This is not substantially different from the position that the pornographer takes in relation to the female body. In this passage, for example, the wife's objections to the coupling of power and sexuality as a particularly male phenomenon are ignored as the two men agree on the seductiveness of creating victims.

The adventures of our Parisian foursome begin in Liberia with very little "action" whatsoever. The first four pages of this episode are given over instead to a description of the African landscape, the evils of neocolonialism, the interethnic conflicts that bedevil the West Coast, and the abundance of natural resources available. The foursome then decide to travel to Kenya, where they amuse themselves by going on a safari with an African guide who agrees to chaperone them only with great reservations and insists that they do not carry weapons. After driving quite a bit, they decide to stop and make love in the bush while the guard does his best not to look on, but instead looks after the car. When the two couples are surprised making love in the bush by a lion, they soothe him, as Miller points out, by continuing their natural way of being by continuing to have sex. The African guide then masturbates the lion to distraction, tosses a gourd down the lion's throat, and causes it to choke to death. Everyone flees the scene in terror, but the guide calmly returns and rifles through the Europeans' goods, appropriating for himself a cigarette that he proceeds to smoke in an attitude of (postcoital) satisfaction.

This story is indeed fraught with the usual tropes of colonial discourse, from the worried, nagging, effeminate African guide to the naturalness of sex in the African landscape. But to read this scene as Miller and Olney do as one where the African is on a par with the bestial lion (they are, after all, sex partners in a sense here) begs the question of who is fooled by the colonialist trope. Although one could read the African guide as equal to the lion, all one part of the African landscape, one could also read this story as suggesting how the Europeans, in their own misguided projections of what is "natural" on to this landscape, are lulled into unreason, at which point they can be taken advantage of. The sly little ending of this story indeed suggests that the African will have the last laugh while Europeans breathlessly watch what they think is an African moving in his own natural state. This echoes the dynamics of the first reviewers calling *Le Devoir de violence* "the first truly African novel," suggesting that what they were seeing was the perversions of their own projections. Meanwhile,

Ouologuem, having tamed the lion of colonialist discourse, will take his prize money and laugh all the way to the bank.

All three of these texts then, can be read as participating in the "invitation to a politics of misbehavior," an attempt to subvert colonialist discourse. But what I think is at stake in reading Ouologuem as inviting his reader to participate in a politics of misbehavior is a certain construction of the relationship of the discourses of politics and sexuality. If we read these two as being metaphorically related, we can read his stories of rape, torture, and maimed female bodies as a metaphorical representation of Africa under colonialism or in Ouologuem's terms, of man's propensity to mistreat man. Certainly, this is a common trope in Africanist discourse, both in the works of apologists for colonialism who wish to tame Africa and also in the works of those who fight against colonialism in the name of Mother Africa. What happens though, if we read the relationship between discourses of politics and sexuality as being metonymically related in Ouologuem? What if politics and sexuality are not mutually substitutable but instead have been naturalized as such? What happens to Ouologuem's politics of misbehavior if we question this apparent similarity between politics and sex?

The long-standing connection between rhetorics of gender and rhetorics of colonialism do indeed underlie all three of these texts. When discussing *Les Mille et une bible du sexe,* Ouologuem's critics all point out the disingenuous, at the least, if not frankly tongue in cheek, remark that this collection of pornography was in part the result of a sense of pique on Ouologuem's behalf at *Le Devoir de violence* having been banned in several African countries because, he claims, of its lascivious nature. What few have mentioned is that earlier in the same introduction, Ouologuem sarcastically remarks that he sought the prior approval of the Renaudot Prize jury for this collection. If indeed Ouologuem's African critics are sliding from political objections to sexual objections, his comments suggest a reversal with regard to the jury of the Prix Renaudot where he implies a political intent in his sexual writing. Where Ouologuem posits that African leaders use sex to hide their anxieties about his politics, Ouologuem suggests that the European literary establishment is so wrapped up in his sexual discourse that they fail to perceive the politics of an African describing European sex. As this reversal shows, Ouologuem, along the same lines as his critics, posits another type of misbehavior (in this case sexual rather than literary) as a substitution for political misbehavior.

On one level, Ouologuem's pornography is the perfect fictional working out of his claims in the "lettre aux pisse-copies nègres d'écrivains célèbres." The reams of formulaic prose stitched together under a pen name in a genre that has historically proven lucrative works as an example of how to succeed as an African writer writing in French. The display of

European degradation similarly works as a response to the charges that Ouologuem degrades Africa through his portrayal of African atrocities in *Le Devoir de violence*. He is indeed generous with his libel. The subtly ironic nod toward the literary establishment found in his introduction, when he claims to have gotten the prior approval of the Prix Renaudot jury for his salacious undertaking, begs the reader to see Europeans as too occupied with the abstract concern for the French patriarchy (in the case of plagiarism) to be able to see Ouologuem's manipulations of French discourse as a power move. And yet all these readings ignore the trail of maimed and mutilated female bodies that literally litter the paths of Ouologuem's work. In using pornography to turn the tables on the European piety of the plagiarism debacle, Ouologuem cannot, as his defenders suggest, come out the good guy. In order to subvert the paradigms of colonial discourse in its claim to white male authority over Africa, Ouologuem simply reverses the claim by reinscribing African male control over white sexuality. Ouologuem does not subvert the trope; he simply claims the right to be on top. This metaphoric substitution depends on our acceptance of a naturalized relationship between sexuality and politics as both exemplifying male power.

In rethinking the connections we draw between discourses of sexuality and politics, it is useful, I think, to fall back on Paul de Man's distinctions between metaphor and metonym. Although the political discourse of and about Africa has often used a gendered metaphor for the position of Africa (a landscape raped, the Mother Africa that has been abused/abandoned, and the resulting metaphor of the process of colonization as an emasculation of African people), it is possible, even necessary, to reread the connections between gender and politics in Africa as being metonymically connected. In defining metaphor and metonymy, de Man refers to a choice of rhetorical figures as being motivated by "necessary links" or "perchance":

> a distinction that corresponds to the difference between metaphor and metonymy, necessity and chance being a legitimate way to distinguish between analogy and contiguity. The inference of identity and totality that is constitutive of metaphor is lacking in the purely relational metonymic contact: an element of truth is involved in taking Achilles for a lion but none in taking Mr. Ford for a motor car. (14)

To susbstitute sexuality for politics assumes that there is an element of truth in decribing sex as a form of colonization instead of seeing the brutalization of women as an effect of the colonial discourse that Ouologuem would subvert. His texts taken together, then, reinscribe an essential part of the discursive system he would challenge.

Ouologuem does seem to recognize this paradox in *Le Devoir de violence,* but only in limited ways, as Eileen Julien points out. Julien argues that Ouologuem establishes a metonymic relationship between rape and "sickness of political relations": "Rape is represented then not as an isolated, gratuitous instance of violence that can be read metaphorically. . . . It is portrayed rather metonymically, as a quintessential act of violence in a context of rampant abuse" (161). However, in his textual silencing of the women who are subjected to rape, Ouologuem replicates the objectification of women that he thematically depends on as indicating an abusive and intolerable climate.

Though rarer than the metaphoric use cited above, a metonymic understanding of the association of gender power and political power is present in some Africanist discourse but is rarely highlighted. For example, in Ama Ata Aidoo's "For Whom Things Did Not Change," the narrator quite consciously questions the metaphoric relations of political hierarchies as gendered when he questions the metaphorical import of what it means to be a black man who cooks for a white man and then poses the question of what it means to be black man cooking for another black man. To read this metaphorically brings up issues of neo-colonialism that reinscribe the association of masculine identity and political power. But to read it metonymically would be to identify the axis along which this particular trope operates and ask what it means to be a black woman cooking for anybody. The black woman's body is erased and naturalized as part of the landscape in the metaphorical tropological system that equates cooking with the loss of political power. Similarly, in Ouologuem's African pornographic story, the African guide who exploits the perverted European notions of nature and sexuality as a trope for Africa does so in a truly male display of the matador: he masturbates as he watches the lion die. As the European recounters of this story argue to the narrator, sexuality is defined as the display of male power over a victim, either a woman or an animal.

To read Yambo Ouologuem's objectification of European women as politically subversive (the role that he himself claims for this collection of stories in the preface, wherein he situates this text as a response in kind to the political reaction to *Le Devoir de violence*) begs the question of what is being subverted. Without the discursive gloss provided by *Lettre à la France nègre*, the pornography of Yambo Ouologuem feels less like a subversion of European hegemony than a restatement of the ultimately nihilistic view presented by *Le Devoir de violence*: that brutality is the human condition. The coupling of exoticism and eroticism, both dependent on an objectification of the "other," is nowhere challenged. Objectifying women to make the point that Europe objectifies Africa writes women out of the picture.

To read Yambo Ouologuem's texts as engaging in a conspiratorial invitation to misbehavior raises the question of to whom this invitation is extended. The metaphorical relationship between plagiarism and political independence, between displaying the depravity of French pornography and staking a claim for social and cultural freedom of/in Africa, depends on reading the relationship between political and sexual discourses along the metaphorical axis of substitution. If we instead ask how these two are related syntagmatically, we are instead confronted with Ouologuem's displacement of political and cultural frustrations onto the bodies of women, white and black, who like the bull in a bullfight find their ultimate fulfillment through their eventual annihilation in a bloody display of male superiority. We can resist this metaphorical reading, though, by recasting the relationship between politics and gender as metonymy. If we understand metonymy as a chance relationship, we can uncouple political and sexual oppressions as naturally or necessarily linked. To read the oppression of women as not linked to political oppression opens up new possibilities for thinking through the position of women vis-à-vis both personal and political violence against their persons. In particular, we can take a look at the tendency of postcolonial discourse to silence women either in the heavily masculine discourse typical of nationalist movements or in the falsely universalized appeals to a "a new humanism," both of which subsume the particular experiences of women to "larger" concerns. To read political and sexual oppression in a metaphoric relation, that is, as analogous, in Ouologuem's body of work serves to naturalize the oppression of women. The subversion of the laws of patriarchy in writing via plagiarism may be enough to kill the father. You may displace him, you may be able to sleep with the mother through pornography, but you will never hear what she has to say about it.

NOTES

1. An earlier version of this chapter was presented at the 23rd Annual African Literature Association Conference, Michigan State University, April 16–20, 1997.

2. The two exceptions to this are Christopher Miller, *Blank Darkness,* and James Olney, *Tell Me Africa.*

3. I am thinking here of Eileen Julien's essay, "Rape, Repression, and Narrative Form in *Le Devoir de violence* and *Le Vie et demie,*" which will be discussed at length later in the chapter.

4. Appiah goes on to assert that Ouologuem's text ends up promoting a "new humanism" in the name of the downtrodden and oppressed "niggertrash," representative of both the slaves of former times and those who currently suffer under a vast array of African dictators. Although I agree with Appiah's argument that the novel delegitimates the naturalizing tendencies of nationalism, I do not find the extension of this argument to the promotion of a "new humanism" to be convincing. Nihilism does not erect new postive values to replace those that it discredits.

5. Thomas Hale has shown very thoroughly the great extent to which Ouologuem uses African traditions of many types, especially oral epics and Arabic langauge historians of West and Sahelian Africa. See *Scribe, Griot, and Novelist,* 135–159.

6. "This technique, which I will call the technique of subversion, does violence not only to everything that the African novel represented before 1968, but also, on one hand, to the acquired notions of the political and social roles of tradition, and on the other hand, to the notions of literary propriety." Translation mine.

7. This is a summary of Julien's essay cited in note 3.

8. Later in his essay, Fatunde goes on to question the ideological ramification of Ouologuem's portrayal because the narrative displays the misery of the working class without ever suggesting that the working class responds to the violence wrought against them. In Ouologuem's *Bound to Violence,* they are, Fatunde argues, merely passive victims suffering from an ahistorical and eternal violence against them, and thus Ouologuem's narrative ultimately ends up supporting the exploitative status quo and those who benefit from it. In a response to this type of reading of *Bound to Violence*, Christopher Wise argues that a more careful reading of the novel based in the traditions of Sufism show Ouologuem to be a strident critic of a practice of Islam that has worked to support exploitative governments and tyrants at the expense of both the poor and the true nature of Islam. Thus, Wise argues, we can read Ouologuem as truly speaking up for the liberation of the oppressed—their liberation from secular authorities and secularized Islam used to support those illegitimate authorities. See Wise, "Qur'anic Heremeneutics, Sufism, and *Le Devoir de Violence*: Yambo Ouologuem as Marabout Novelist."

9. "Women alone, you are like Negros in that your status holds you on the outside of life, relegated to the marginal society of minority groups." Translation mine.

10. This echoes a similar distinction made by Fanon in *Black Skins, White Masks*. In her essay, "The Nigger of the Narcissist: History, Sexuality and Intertextuality in Maryse Condé's *Heremakhonon,*" Susan Andrade has shown how Fanon attributes to black men an understandable, if lamentable, motivation in seeking partners of a different race, whereas his discussion of black women who seek partners of a different race claims that they are motivated purely and simply by self-hatred.

11. The difference between pornography and eroticism is indeed a difficult one to draw with any convincing certainty. Here, I refer back to Ouologuem's own definition of pornography as something that lacks the "psychological dimension" of eroticism. The story of the African safari that I discuss in more length below is singled out by Ouologuem as lacking this depth.

12. This text has not been translated in its entirety: short sections of it are translated by both Olney and Miller. This passage and all that follow are my translations, with reference to the parts that Olney and Miller have translated elsewhere. P. 18.

13. Particularly significant in this regard is the use of a scene where a woman is subjected to cunnilingus performed by a dog. It is a scene of this type that raised the most vociferous objections to *Le Devoir de violence*.

14. Miller goes on to argue that Ouologuem is ultimately less successful at disrupting European discourse in this story because he gets caught up in the "trap of libertinism" (245), whereby the act of promoting Africans as equally sexual and free subjects as Europeans recreates the act of reducing them to purely sexual objects.

Part 3

Historical Reconsiderations: Islamic-Sahelian Influences in Ouologuem's Writings

12

Rewriting the Songhay Past in Yambo Ouologuem's *Le Devoir de violence*

Thomas A. Hale

If we begin by comparing the context in which the modern African writer functions with those of the writers of the *Tarîkh es-Soudan* and the *Tarîkh el-Fettâch*,[1] we find many differences. The scribe who writes in Arabic to record events for the political and intellectual elite or for his own family and the griot who recounts the past for those who seek to legitimize their station in society communicate to immediate, relatively small audiences—although, in the long run, indirectly their words reach much larger groups. The writer using a European language, however, can be read almost immediately by an international audience that includes both Africans educated in Western-style schools and non-African readers worldwide. But he or she may not enjoy the direct relationship with the audience that some scribes and bards could claim.

If the portraits of the rulers produced by the scribes and griots depended to some extent on their relationship with their different audiences, how, then, will the modern African author, formed by both African and Western cultures, interpret the same events? What meaning can the *askias* and the Songhay empire provide to African society five centuries after the demise of the Songhay empire? How will the writer convey his message to both the literate elite in Africa and the non-African audience whose view of the continent has been formed by texts as diverse as *Heart of Darkness* and *Tarzan?*

This chapter was previously published in *Scribe, Griot, and Novelist: Narrative Interpreters of the Songhay Empire* (Gainesville: University of Florida Press, 1990). Reprinted with permission of the University of Florida Press.

It is difficult to formulate an all-encompassing answer based on the works of each African writer because texts constitute individual, often rather personal, responses to the question of what the African past means to people today. Chinua Achebe replied to *Heart of Darkness* (1902) with *Things Fall Apart* (1958), the most widely read novel in English by a Black African. The debate among Conrad specialists that Achebe generated with his essays about the Polish-born writer, however, pales in comparison with the outcry over Yambo Ouologuem's contribution to the dialogue between Africa and the West. Ouologuem's view of African history differs markedly in tone and in theme from anything written to date by African authors.

There are many reasons why *Le Devoir de violence* became the most controversial novel ever written by an African writer. One cause of the stir was the author's emphasis on sex, violence, and, quite often, a synergistic combination of both of these themes. Another was the extent to which Ouologuem borrowed from European writers, among them André Schwarz-Bart, Graham Greene, and Guy de Maupassant. Some readers discovered that Ouologuem had modeled his novel on *The Last of the Just* by Schwarz-Bart and had lifted passages, with only minor modifications, from Greene's *It's a Battlefield* and other works by well-known Western novelists. Finally, critics from all parts of the world questioned the novelist's interpretation of African history from written and oral materials.

My focus here is not so much on the matter of how and what Ouologuem borrowed and modified from European literary sources. Instead, I am more interested in his use of African material and the message he seeks to convey about the past and its impact upon the present. By comparing, then, *Le Devoir de violence* to the Arabic chronicles and the oral tradition, I shall attempt to place the novel in a new literary and historical context that is more firmly linked to the past than anyone has been willing to admit. Just as the scribes' description of Askia Mohammed marked a shift in values associated with the spread of Islam to the elite, and the griot's portrait affirmed the importance of the original, more deeply rooted set of beliefs, so, in *Le Devoir de violence*, we shall find Ouologuem promoting, through his reading of the past, yet another interpretation of social relationships that contrasts sharply with those of the other narrators.

Ouologuem wrote *Le Devoir de violence* in Paris during the mid-1960s while studying philosophy, literature, sociology, and English. According to one account of how he came to create the novel, an editor at Seuil asked him to write an African version of *The Last of the Just* by André Schwarz-Bart (1959), a fictional history of a Jewish family from the early medieval period to the present. Whatever the case, Ouologuem produced a sweeping portrait of the imaginary West African empire of Nakem from the thirteenth century to 1947. Composed in a variety of styles, the narrative offers a veritable catalog of sexual activities. When Seuil published the book in France in 1968, critics hailed it as the true African novel. The keepers of the Renaudot, France's second most prestigious literary prize, selected the work as that year's winner. The novel appealed, it seemed, to Europe's long-standing image of Africa, a continent seen as inhabited by libidinous and violent savages. When *Le Devoir de violence* appeared as *Bound to Violence* in the United States, the *New York Times* listed it as one of the seven most significant novels of 1971. But after its initial publication in Paris, and well before the debate over plagiarism began to catch the attention of a wider audience, some critics argued that Ouologuem was inventing a history that had nothing to do with reality. J. Mbelolo ya Mpiku questioned Ouologuem's view of the Sahelian Middle Ages. More recently, Sandra Barkan has argued that the novel, especially the opening chapter entitled "La Légende des Saifs," may be considered as a pseudohistorical screen behind which lies a complex discussion of good and evil based on both biblical and Dogon sources. Derek Wright, in the latest attack against the historicity of the novel, comments that "the story which we are reading raises reflexive doubts about its own authenticity. Ouologuem's counterfictions—the Semitic origin of the Saifs, the cunning manipulative control of the colonists by the colonized, and the ruling caste's restrictions of a French education to the serf class—are all either of doubtful authenticity or deliberately and grossly unhistorical" (93).

Until now, however, no one has attempted to penetrate the forest of names, places, and events cited in the novel in order to see if, in fact, there is any foundation for what the author portrays. One does not need go very far, though, to discover that Ouologuem is hardly obscure, both when he proposes to his reader a highly amusing system of plagiarism, as in *Lettre à la France nègre*, published in 1968, or when his narrator mentions on the second page of *Le Devoir de violence* that some of the events described come from the *Tarîkh el-Fettâch* and the *Tarîkh es-Soudan*. Is Ouologuem, then, simply retelling or reinterpreting the story of the Songhay empire? The answer appears at first to be ambiguous.

Links Between the Novel and the Songhay Empire

At first, Ouologuem's tipoff to the reader appears almost too obvious. In the barrage of names and places in the early pages of the novel, one finds it difficult to identify clearly the Songhay empire. On the first page, we discover the sixteenth-century kingdom of Nakem (an anagram for Kanem) near Lake Chad, south of the southwestern Libyan region of Fezzan in what is today western Chad. But the names of the people and places that quickly follow take us west toward the broad area controlled at one time or another by the Mali and Songhay empires. The narrator partially anagrammatizes the names of many ethnic groups, families of groups, and places in the Sahel. Thus we find the Randé, which may be read as the Mandé, a large collection of peoples descended from the Mali empire that was partially absorbed by the Songhay. The mountains of the Goro Foto Zinko recall the Fouta Toro of Senegal. Among the ethnic groups that populate the area the narrator lists the Radingues, a variant for Mandingue, and the Gondaites, which we may substitute for the Songhay. Ouologuem anagrams his own Dogon people into the Ngodos, but leaves the Peulh (also known as the Fulbe or Fulani) with their original name. The river Yamé on whose bank much of the action takes place appears at first to echo the name of the capital of Niger, Niamey, located on the left bank of the Niger River. But the Yamé is an actual river, a tributary of the Niger and the only permanent watercourse in the Dogon homeland of the novelist.

The region covered by these ethnic groups includes a vast area of the West African Sahel and might well refer us to the empires of Mali, Songhay, or some smaller political unit. But the next clue on the third page brings us closer to a geographic reality. The capital of the empire of Nakem is Tillabéri-Bentia, a term that Ouologuem appears to have come across in Jean Boulnois and Boubou Hama's 1954 study, *L'Empire de Gao*. Boulnois and Hama refer to the area of Tillabéri and Bentia as the heartland of the empire. It lies between present-day Tillabéri, a provincial town 110 kilometers upriver from the capital of Niger, Niamey, and Bentia, an island 60 kilometers downriver from Gao in eastern Mali. Some scholars see Bentia as the modern site of Koukiya, which was the capital of the Songhay long before the empire reached its peak (Hunwick 4–5). Two other place names localize further the area of the empire in the region of eastern Mali and western Niger: Grosso and Gagol-Gosso. Grosso, an apparent partial anagram for Dosso, is a major crossroads town about 140 kilometers southeast of Niamey and the seat of the best known of the chiefs of the Zarma. As recorded in the griot epics,[2] the Zarma, led by Mali Bero and Yefarma Issaka, came to the aid of the retreating Songhay. The chief's title is the Zarmakoy or Djermakoye of Dosso, and the name of the current ruler is Abdou Aouta. The other local reference is to the Gagol-Gosso, a Ouologuem variant for the Dallol Boss ("Valley of the Tamarind Trees" in Songhay), the dry riverbed 107 kilometers east of Niamey that leads from the Aïr mountains south into the Niger River and where, as in the oral version, Yerfarma Issaka learned of the Arma invasion.

Although Ouologuem attempts to generalize his portrait of the empire of Nakem with brief references to the Zulu-speaking peoples of South Africa and the Masai from East Africa, it is evident from the geographical and ethnic references just cited that he is focusing on West Africa, and on that part of the Sahel that was the heartland of the Songhay empire. By the end of the second text page, his narrative gives historical weight to the account by citing his two principal sources: "That is what happened at Tillabéri-Benita, at Granta, at Grosso, at Gagol-Gosso, and in many places mentioned in the *Tarîkh al-Fetach* and the *Tarîkh al-Sudan* of the Arab historians" (4).

The error in attributing these texts to Arab authors appears of little consequence next to the great credibility that the narrator manages to attach to his account by referring to early written sources. When questioned about the accuracy of his portraits of bloodthirsty and corrupt rulers during interviews in France and this country, Ouologuem offered as evidence copies of the two chronicles. But he was not simply transposing into fictional form a reality described in the chronicles. He was, instead, reinterpreting that portrayal to advance his own thesis about the nature of Sahelian societies today. To understand more clearly his use of the past, we need to look more closely at how Ouologuem drew on the written and oral traditions.

SONNI ALI BER AND ASKIA MOHAMMED, MODELS OF EVIL AND GOOD

The descriptions of the rulers of the Songhay empire in the chronicles offer models for some of the people and events Ouologuem describes in the opening chapter of the novel. For example, in the first few pages we find a basic opposition between the bad leader, Saif Moshe Gabbai of Honaine, and the good sovereign, Saif Isaac al-Heit. Ouologuem has patterned the first on Sonni Ali Ber and, in a far more detailed way, modeled the second on Askia Mohammed. In the novel, Saif Moshe Gabbai of Honaine appears as a violent ruler who did not hesitate to kill children. In a biblical tone, the narrator informs us:

> It came to pass that one day in the year 1420 Saif Moshe Gabbai of Honaine—after hearing the words of a soothsayer who predicted that he would be overthrown by a child to be born during the coming year in Tillabéri-Benita, capital of the Nakem Empire—ceased to ignore the strange cravings of pregnant women. He consigned all newborn babies to the red death and lined up their shrunken heads along the wall of his antechamber. (5)

For the European reader, Saif Moshe's suppression of male children echoes the story of Moses. But if the biblical tale motif provides an obvious parallel, the Timbuktu chronicles offer more direct and widely known evidence of a Sahelian ruler's mistreatment of children. In the *Tarîkh el-Fettâch*, Sonni Ali Ber had the fetus torn from the womb of a mother, forced a woman to grind up her baby in a mortar, and wanted to kill a crying baby.

Ouologuem was obviously familiar with both stories of foreign origin. His extensive background in Western culture provided information on the biblical tale. The tales of Sonni Ali Ber and his successors came from both his reading of the chronicles and, in all probability, from the oral tradition in the Dogon area, a region over which the Songhay maintained control for many generations. If Saif Moshe's hatred of children resonates in many cultures, it is nevertheless likely that the Dogon remember particularly well both his historical model, Sonni Ali Ber, and the successor who attempted to convert them to Islam, Askia Mohammed. The evidence for the relationship between these two rulers and the Dogon comes from Askia Mohammed's correspondence with the North African scholar al-Maghili. After overthrowing the Sonni dynasty, Askia Mohammed reported that in some of the lands he entered to repair the havoc wrought by his predecessor and to free slaves, adherence to Islam was superficial, and that some peoples still relied upon foxes for guidance. Hunwick's reading of al-Maghili's ruling is that these people

> must be fought, their men killed, their women and children enslaved and their property seized. Their priests may be immolated, if necessary. This severe judgement appears to concern a specific ethnic group—their practice of a fox cult suggests the Dogon—who have been adjured to abandon their polytheistic practices, have refused to do so and are therefore deserving of having a jihad launched against them. (123)

Hunwick is probably correct. The Dogon were, indeed, one of the peoples most resistant to the spread of Islam. Germaine Dieterlen, a French scholar who has devoted a lifetime to the study of the Dogon, argues that the most important reason for their migration from the west to settle in the Bandiagara cliffs area was a collective refusal to convert to Islam in the twelfth century (9).

Scholarship on the Dogon has focused primarily on their language, mythology, social structure, and belief system. Although I have not yet encountered information from the Dogon oral tradition concerning Sonni Ali Ber, it would be hard to imagine that their collective memory has erased all traces of the man who spent nearly all of his time on expeditions to conquer peoples living inside the bend of the Niger River. Today, Songhay, Dogon, and Peulh communities share the Douentza region on the northeastern limit of the Dogon country. This area of Mali includes the Hombori mountains, an island of Songhay once governed by Askia Mohammed.

In the Arabic chronicles, Sonni Ali Ber does not limit his violent tendencies to children. In the novel, the narrator attributes to Saif Moshe

Gabbai of Honaine Sonni Ali Ber's bloody reputation when he declares ironically, "In that age of feudalism, large communities of slaves celebrated the justice of their overlords by forced labor and by looking on inert as multitudes of their brothers, smeared with the blood of butchered children and of disemboweled expectant mothers, were immured alive" (5).

THE CHRONICLES AS SOURCES OF SEX, VIOLENCE, AND DECADENCE FOR THE NOVELIST

The reader of the chronicles discovers that the history of the empire, under both the Songhay rulers and their Moroccan-controlled successors after 1591, contains numerous murders, immurings, poisonings, and torture—events that are hardly different from what we find in the European Middle Ages. For three reasons, however, the violence in the novel, compared to what we read in the chronicles, appears greatly magnified. First, Ouologuem has compressed time considerably, reducing many generations and hundreds of pages of the chronicles into his twenty-three-page first chapter. Second, he has drawn mainly from the pattern of incidents describing sex and violence. Finally, his narrator recounts these events in an ironic tone that distances the reader from the events portrayed. The following description of some of Saif Isaac al-Heit's successors typifies this narrative technique:

> On April 20, 1532, on a night as soft as a cloak of moist satin, Saif al-Haram, performing his conjugal "duty" with his four step-mothers seriatim and all together, had the imprudent weakness to overindulge and in the very midst of his dutiful delights gave up the ghost . . . The next day his raven-eyed minister Al Hadj Abd al-Hassana, having established a stripling boy and Hawa, the most beautiful of Saif's stepmothers in his bed, was stung by an asp which he was caressing in the belief that he was holding something else, opened his mouth wide three times and died . . . His successor was Holongo, "a horrible biped with the brutal expression of a buffalo," humped in front and back; after a reign of two years, moaning in enviable torment, he died in the arms of a courtesan Aiosha, who strangled him as he was crying out in ecstasy. His successor was Saif Ali, a pederast with pious airs, as vicious as a red donkey, who succumbed six months later to the sin of gluttony, leaving the crown to Saif Jibril, Ali's younger brother, who, slain by the sin of indiscretion, was replaced by Saif Yussufi, one of the sons of Ramina (mother of Saif al-Haram, got with child by her son at the cost of great effort). An albino notorious for his ugliness, he was twice felled by one of his wife's admirers; the third time—at last!—much to his amazement, he was carried off by an ill wind, ceding his place to Saif Medioni of Mostanagem, who was recalled to God ten days later, torn to pieces, so it is said, by the contrary angels of Mercy and Justice. (16)

In the context of the activities described, Saif al-Haram's name appears charged with irony. In Arabic, the word "haram" can mean either "sacred" or "prohibited, unlawful," depending on the length of the second vowel (Qazi 19).

If Ouologuem has drawn on the chronicles in a broad sense for Saif Moshe Gabbai of Honaine and the violence associated with his successors, his portrait of Saif Isaac al-Heit leaves little doubt that he is following the medieval written sources regarding Askia Mohammed. Aside from the change in name, there is a relatively small difference between the itineraries of the real and the fictional ruler. Both Askia Mohammed and Saif Isaac al-Heit recognize, correspond with, and sometimes meet well-known representatives of Islam: the Egyptian scholar es Soyouti; the North African scholar al-Maghili; Chamharouch of the race of genies; and the prince of Mecca, Moulay El Abbas. Where the written tradition reports that Askia Mohammed defeated Chî Bâro, nephew of Sonni Ali Ber, Ouologuem's Saif Isaac defeats Saif Moshe, who flees south. Moulay El Abbas proclaims both the real and the fictional character as the eleventh caliph of the Sudan. Although this sequence represents a reversal and minor modification in the events of Askia Mohammed's life (he overthrew Sonni Ali Ber first and then went to Mecca, while Saif Isaac al-Heit merely received a message from Mecca about his promotion and then went on to defeat Moshe), there is no doubt about the line between the medieval and the modern characters.

Ouologuem maintains the image from the chronicles of Askia Mohammed as a pious and good man who freed a slave each day. But piety does not preclude military power. His Saif, like Askia Mohammed, fights the enemies of Islam throughout the Sahel. Here Ouologuem's narrator, like the griot, conflates the link to Mecca with the many battles Askia Mohammed fought.

> Terrible in battle, he defeated the Berbers, the Moors, and the Tuareg, recognized the Sheikh Mohammed ben Abd-al-Karim al-Meghili, the Sheikh Shamharouk of the race of the Jinn, and the Hassanid Sherif Mulai al-Abbas, Prince of Mecca: God hold them all in His compassion. In Bengazi he fought the enemies of the Imam Abu Bakr ben Omar al-Yemani, in Tripoli he destroyed the usurpers who were plotting to assassinate the Qadi Abd-al-Qahir ben al-Fizan, and one day when he was staying with Beni Tsa'aleb in the province of Algiers, the Sheikh Abd-ar-Raman al-Tsa'albi brought him the prophecy of Imam Mahmud, Grand Sherif of Mecca: "There will come a new Saif who will quench the thirst of the men of the Nakem Empire: thou, Issac al-Heit, art that man, thou art the first, for thou art the water and the salt and the bread, thou art holy and wilt be caliph." (7)

In the oral version by Nouhou Malio, we saw Askia Mohammed fight many battles to convert peoples to Islam so that he could earn the right to go to Mecca. In the chronicles . . . Askia Mohammed is supposed to have carried out only one jihad, or holy war—against the Mossi after his return to Mecca. Although the battles and enemies are different, the notion of the ruler as a defender of Islam matches closely in all three versions.

Ouologuem takes pains to change some of the dates in the chronicles' version of the past. Where the scribes place Askia Mohammed's death in 1538, Ouologuem's "mild and just emperor" Saif Isaac al-Heit dies in 1498, leaving three sons. Ouologuem continues, however, to draw on some of these successors' adventures. For example, in the long excerpt just cited, Saif al-Haram takes his father's wives and concubines in a wild orgy. His model, Askia Moussa, as recorded in the chronicles, had violated the sanctity of his father's wives and concubines first by refusing to allow them to go home after the death of their man and then forcing them to parade before him completely naked. In appendix II of the *Tarîkh el-Fettâch*, another version of the events suggests that Askia Moussa "kept aside for himself several wives of his father and cohabited with them" (339–40). This act by Moussa prompted Askia Mohammed's vengeance cited earlier, in which Moussa falls off his horse and finds himself naked on the ground. In the *Tarîkh el-Fettâch* the incident appears in the following terms:

> They say that . . . Askia Mohammed asked God not to let him die before having exposed the private parts of Moussa. And God granted this wish, for one day, while Askia Moussa was riding on horseback past the market square in Gao and was spurring his mount, the horse threw him on the ground, one of his feet caught in the strap of a stirrup, his clothes fell back over his head, the waistband of his pants broke, his private parts were exposed, and all the people who were at the market could see them as he was dragged by the frightened, fleeing horse. (340)

Ouologuem changes the place from the market to the palace and embroiders somewhat on the scene in his version of the same incident.

> Then the Emperor Saif al-Haram, the wicked brother and accursed son—God's malediction upon him!—returned from a war against the Fulani escorted by twelve thousand Tukulör slaves to Tillabéri-Benita, the capital, where the people, crushed beneath the sun, were waiting at the gates. His horse pranced majestically as he saluted the frantic crowd. To his right, notables, chiefs of various provinces, court dignitaries, to his left, women, children, and old men, behind him the army flanked by long rows of slaves with shackled ankles. A triumphal homecoming; his victories seemed to have washed away his taint.
>
> Entering the courtyard of his palace in full pomp, he was about to alight from his horse to greet his wives, who were at the same time his stepmothers, when suddenly—such be the fate of those who curse Thee!—his horse shied; in his fall he tore the short trousers of his blue tunic, exposing his nether regions to the crowd in the manner of Adam at his birth. (9)

In Ouologuem's portrayal, the narrator emphasizes the distance between the ruler and the masses while reminding the reader of the moral decay associated with Askia Moussa's reign. Ouologuem's modification of this one incident reflects, in microcosm, the fact that he does not simply report the past, but instead offers his readers an interpretive, creative image. In the following passage, the narrator distances himself from any claim of historical accuracy. His style, typical of Ouologuem's complex narrative voice, shifts from the objectivity of the historian to the solemn oratory of the elders before ending with the irreverence of the young generation.

> At this point tradition loses itself in legend, for there are few written accounts and the versions of the elders diverge from those of the griots, which differ in turn from those of the chroniclers . . . When the Immortal One makes the sun—diamond of the house of his Power—set, then, along with the tales of the oral tradition, the elders intone the famous epic (the value of which some contest, because they deny Saif's Jewish descent, insisting that he was a plain ordinary nigger) written by Mahmud Meknud Trare, a descendant of griot ancestors and himself a griot of the present-day African Republic of Nakem-Ziuko, which is all that remains of the ancient Nakem Empire. (6)

Christopher Miller is quite correct in his view that Ouologuem is using this passage "as a device for problematizing history" (*Blank Darkness* 231). The distance the narrator establishes between his account and his sources discredits both the sources and the values they represent. The striking comparison between the evil Moshe and the good Isaac, lifted straight from the chronicles, provides Ouologuem with a convenient opportunity to question the value system of both men, leaders of an aristocracy that depends for its existence on the fealty of captive masses. By questioning history, Ouologuem establishes the basis for what Miller terms the "fragmentation and mythification" of the past (231). In so doing, Ouologuem's sardonic narrator addresses both his audiences: Europeans, with their image of a violent and savage continent, and Africans, who see in Askia Mohammed the pinnacle of a Sahelian civilization. Finally, for those of his readers who see Sahelian history from a Dogon perspective, the demystifying portrayals of the powerful Songhay rulers must generate smiles of recognition.

> Whether truth or invention, the legend of Saif Isaac al-Heit still haunts Black romanticism and the political thinking of the notables in a good many republics. . . . Chroniclers draw on the oral tradition to enrich his cult and through him celebrate the glorious era of the first States with their wise philosopher-king, whose history has called not only archeology, history, and numismatics but also the natural sciences and ethnology to their highest tasks. (8)

Ouologuem's narrator mocks the older generation of African and Caribbean writers who re-created the African past in the poetry of négritude. Here one is reminded of the line in Aimé Césaire's long poem, *Cahier d'un retour au pays natal*, where the narrator refers to the golden age of West Africa—"No, we've never been Amazons of the king of Dahomey, nor princes of Ghana with eight hundred camels, nor wise men in Timbuktu under Askia the Great" (61)—to emphasize the fact that those sent to the New World were of captive rather than of noble origin. But Ouologuem also criticizes the tendency among African leaders to identify with the great rulers of the past. The best-known example was Guinean President Sékou Touré's claim of descent from the last great rebel against the French in the nineteenth century, Samory Touré. In the novelist's own country, the first president of Mali, Modibo Keita, made much of his clan link with Sundiata Keita, the founder of the Mali empire. Modibo Keita was deposed in a coup d'état in 1968, the year *Le Devoir de violence* was published in France. Seen in the broader context of relations between the rulers and the masses in the novel, the passage announces Ouologuem's basic message. In spite of colonialism and independence, some African countries are still governed by an elite that purports to have roots going back to the Middle Ages and whose values vary little no matter whether the ruler is the evil Sonni Ali Ber/Moshe Gabbi of Honaine, the good Askia Mohammed/Saif al-Heit, or one of their twentieth-century successors.

THE DYNASTY AND THE JEWS: TRACES OF THE DIASPORA IN THE SAHEL

In addition to the general pattern of violence that marks human relations and the modeling of two early characters on actual medieval rulers, Ouologuem has borrowed other bits and pieces of information from the chronicles. For example, in the passage cited earlier from page 6, we learned that both the written and oral traditions of Nakem report that the rulers have some Jewish ancestry, although the elders contest the notion. The narrator/chronicler provides additional information on this surprising bit of genealogy.

> The Lord—holy is His Name!—showed us the mercy of bringing forth, at the beginning of the black Nakem empire, one illustrious man, our ancestor the black Jew Abraham al-Heit, born of a black father and an Oriental Jewess from Kenanan (Canaan), descended from Jews of Cyrenaica and Tuat; it is believed that she was carried to Nakem by a secondary migration that followed the itinerary of Cornelius Balbus. (6)

The idea that Jews may be related to these rulers may astonish both European and African rulers. Sandra Barkan sees this as an imaginary use by Ouologuem of Maurice Delafosse's now-discounted theory of the origin of the Fulani people. But if Ouologuem had read Delafosse, he was also familiar with the accounts of Jews in the chronicles. A *Tarîkh el-Fettâch* narrator relates a story told to him by the father of one of his contemporaries, who received the story from his grandfather, that Tendirma, a city 90 kilometers upriver from Timbuktu, was once populated by Jews. They built wells in the area to provide water for their irrigated vegetable gardens. We learn too that at the time of the Jews in the region, "there reigned seven princes descending from the king of the Jews," each having control over certain wells, each leading twelve thousand horsemen and an uncounted number of foot soldiers (120).

The legend of the Jews of Tendirma, passed on from generation to generation and finally recorded in the *Tarîkh el-Fettâch,* was confirmed by A. Bonnel de Mézières in October 1913. Approximately 90 kilometers southwest of Timbuktu, in the area of Lake Fati, between the Niger and a dead branch of the river at Goundam, he found traces of what he called the "Beni-Israël": a variety of pottery shards, fields, a cemetery, tumuli, and wells (128–31). The wells were 40 to 60 cubits (forearms) deep, built of masonry, and lined with a concretelike material.

The reference by the novel's narrator to a secondary migration south from the area of "Tuat" accords with two probable scenarios to explain the existence of the Jewish community in the Tendirma region. The first is that they may have been the southernmost of Jewish peoples who lived in North Africa well before the arrival of the Muslims. They came with the Phoenicians to found Carthage in 814 B.C. and much later migrated northward into Spain as well as southwest into Morocco and directly south into the Sahara. This would account for the vague, legendary outlines of the community in the *Tarîkh el-Fettâch.*

The second is that they were late-fifteenth-century refugees from Algeria. At that time there was considerable scholarly debate in North Africa about the status of Jews. Al-Maghili, who visited Gao in 1498, was one of the leading anti-Jewish theologians of the region. The massacre of the Jews sometime in the 1480s in Tamantit, a town in the Tuwat Oasis area of central Algeria, 1,100 kilometers north of Gao, is generally imputed not only to al-Maghili's inflamatory prose and poetry but also to his more direct actions, such as offering a reward of seven mithqals for every Jew killed. Hunwick, in his edition of the al-Maghili/Askia Mohammed letters, provides details on this little-known chapter in the history of an ethnic group that people many corners of Africa (33–39).

By his reference to the Jews, Ouologuem's narrator addresses, then, both European Africanists, with their early and sometimes erroneous interpretations of Sahelian cultural history, and his African readers who may not be aware of the role Jewish communities in the region played in the trans-Saharan trade between the Songhay empire and North Africa. Ouologuem's portrayal of the rulers of Nakem as of partly Jewish origin is plausible from the history of the region and emphasizes once again the complex nature of ethnicity among the peoples there.

This link with Jews invites interpretations that stress both the higher status of a people with such a long and richly documented past as well as identification with the suffering that they have undergone. For example, Miller argues that Ouologuem uses this bit of ethnic information about the Jewish presence in the Sahel not simply for local color but also so that the rulers of Nakem can "exploit the prestige of this birthright to lord it over the *négraille*" (231). French African literature critic Bernard Mouralis, in another analysis of the novel, draws on comments by Ouologuem made in a broader context in 1976 to offer a comparison between the oppressed situation of Blacks and Jews (Ouologuem's comments are in quotation marks):

> The audacity of Ouologuem resides in his refusal of both the negrophobic ideology and the negrophilic ideology. In brief, in this visceral refusal to admit that there may be a chosen people, either by predestination or because the exceptional amount of violence which they have suffered through the ages allowed them to be viewed as exemplary victims.
>
> The death of violence and racism assumes at the same time the death of the myth to which Africa tries to attach itself: Negritude and "negro romanticism," the expression of this "unfortunate conscience which speaks, fabulates . . . and which has made of the Black of 20th century civilization a kind of mythic Jew of this same civilization . . . The writer is Jew, Black, unhappy conscience, drama, and, at the same time, desire for authenticity." (Mouralis 1986: 74)

POLITICAL REVISIONISM AND THE NOVELIST: OUOLOGUEM'S USE OF THE NINETEENTH-CENTURY MODIFICATIONS OF THE *TARÎKH EL-FETTÂCH*

Ouologuem compresses the early history of the empire, including his interpretation of Sonni Ali Ber and Askia Mohammed, into a single introductory chapter entitled "The Legend of the Saifs." In his next chapter, Ouologuem's narrators skips forward to the nineteenth century. The rapid trip through the Middle Ages in the first chapter slows down so that the narrator can dwell on the momentous events surrounding the encounter between African and the West. But Ouologuem does not, however, abandon his Arabic-language sources at this point. Indeed, at the end of the first chapter, his narrator announced, as we saw earlier, the coming of the twelfth caliph of the Sudan in the nineteenth century. Ouologuem has simply adopted for his own novelistic purposes the nineteenth-century modification to the *Tarîkh el-Fettâch* by the Fulani leader Sékou Amadou.

> Had the Imam Mahmud, grand sherif of Mecca, not predicted that in the thirteenth century of the Hegira a caliph would come from Tekur? And was this caliph not Saif ben Isaac al-Heit, whose mother, "that the commandments of the Eternal One might be fulfilled," had arranged to bring him into the world and baptize him in Tekrur on the date foreseen by the prophecy and the legend? (23)

The narrator's use of the term *arranged* stands as a subtle hint that Ouologuem was aware of the manipulation of the *Tarîkh el-Fettâch* centuries after it was written. But the prophecy invented by Sékou Amadou in the nineteenth century and written into manuscripts of the *Tarîkh el-Fettâch* serves as a convenient device for Ouologuem to bind the Middle Ages to the modern era. It also allows him to broaden his discussion about the relationship between the rulers and their subjects. In the wake of Saif ben Isaac al-Heit's surrender to the French in 1900, the narrator reports: "The Empire was pacified, broken up into several zones which the Whites divided. Saved from slavery, the niggertrash welcomed the white man with joy, hoping he would make them forget the mighty Saif's meticulously organized cruelty" (31).

By drawing upon medieval sources, Ouologuem is able to establish clearly at the outset of the novel the Machiavellian nature of the rulers of Nakem. For the remainder of the narrative, the masses and their representatives become pawns in the game of power played out between the aristocracy of Nakem and the French. From chapter 3, "The Night of the Giants," which recounts in great detail the life of a slave couple at the Saif's palace in the early twentieth century, to the election of one of their sons, Raymond-Spartacus Kassoumi, as a representative of the colony of Nakem-Zuiko in the French Parliament after World War II, the narrator never lets us forget the power of the ruling aristocracy over those of captive origin.

Robert Arnaud, in his 1912 study on French policy in Muslim Africa, offers numerous examples of how the aristocracy and the Muslim clerics maintained power over most of francophone West Africa (21–37). The family of Kassoumi seems to fit Arnaud's portrayal of the situation. It is significant that the wife in the slave couple, mother of those who will be controlled by the rulers, is named Tambira, which means in Songhay "the slave of the princes" (Olivier de Sardan 352). "For Saif ben Isaac al-Heit, the task of subjecting the educated niggertrash was completed. But the master of Tillabéri-Bentia knew that it is easier to subjugate a people than to hold it down" (167). For this reason, the ruler smothers dissent among the elite in order to maintain the influence of his aristocracy over the puppet candidate of the French, the architect Kassoumi. "Kassoumi had miscalculated: armed with his degrees and the support of France, he had expected to become his old master's master, when in reality the slave owed his election exclusively to the torch of Saif, more radiant than ever after a momentary lapse" (167).

MANIPULATION OF THE FRENCH BY AFRICAN RULERS

Although critics have contested Ouologuem's view of the relationship among the traditional leaders, the Muslim elite, and the colonial powers, a more recent generation of Africanist historians has begun to support the notion that the French were often manipulated, at least until just after World War II, when the novel ends. Although the French played different clans and ethnic groups against each other, both the French and their subjects sought to maintain their positions by a variety of devices. At the turn of the century, the French colonial administration in West Africa became increasingly concerned about subversion organized by the social and religious elite. After one incident involving the Sultan of Zinder in eastern Niger, Robert Arnaud was sent to investigate. Harrison reports that Arnaud "confirmed the alliance between the aristocracy and the marabouts against the colonial authorities who had liberated their slaves" (47). After reviewing several decades of monographs from the Centre des Hautes Études d'Administration Musulmane in France, Harrison adds that these studies "reinforced suspicions that the clerical castes in the southern Saharan areas had taken the French for a ride in posing as men of peace harassed by the warrior aristocracies of the desert edge" (196).

In western Niger, an obvious example of such manipulation by an aristocratic family appears in the rise of the *Zarmakoy* of Dosso, the best known of the rulers among the Zarma. Up until a century ago, there were many local *zarmakoy*, or rulers of Zarma populations in that part of the country. When the French arrived in Dosso in 1898, *Zarmakoy* Attikou was apparently too busy to deal with his European visitors because his attention was needed for more pressing matters, among them the conflicts with the Tuareg and the Fulani. He delegated the task of negotiating with the French to one of the princes in the ruling family, Aouta. As Pearl Robinson has shown in her research on traditional chiefs in Niger, Aouta began to work closely with the visitors, and eventually expanded considerably his family's power base by his ability to deal with the newly arrived colonial power. Where authority had once been shared among several families on a rotating basis, the family of *Zarmakoy* Attikou began to play a more prominent role after contact with the French. Although members of his family have since World War II played a variety of key roles in the government of Niger, their early relationship with the French has sometimes worked against them.

If the impact of France on parts of Africa today is unmistakable, French-style dress, food, and automobiles as well as education and systems of administration cannot obscure the fact that some nobles of the past managed to strengthen their position thanks in part to their ability to deal with the French. Today, however, there is a rising class of people who are not of noble origin, citizens who are able to climb the social ladder because of their inborn talent in business, academia, and other fields. But Finn Fuglestad, in his 1983 study of the history of Niger from 1850 to 1960, which was based to a great extent on archival material, concludes that the traditional social structure has not changed very much as a result of the relatively recent and brief impact of France on a society and a set of values that has existed for many hundreds of years. Olivier de Sardan's extensive research, founded almost entirely on interviews conducted in rural contexts, confirms Fuglestad's conclusions.

From these scholars' perspectives, which matches that of Ouologuem in the novel, the French appear as latecomers in the region's long history. The Songhay have a proverb that conveys what they see as the ephemeral nature of European contact in Africa: "The white man comes and goes like the morning mist on the Niger River." The French came, conquered, and then transferred political power a few generations later, leaving the traditional social structure largely intact and, in some cases, considerably strengthened.

Ouologuem's lurid portrayal of the ruling aristocracy's lifestyle and power seems, nevertheless, so exaggerated that one may wonder if he is simply pandering to European stereotypes of Africa. At the most superficial level, given his interest in producing soft-core pornography, there appears little doubt that one of his audiences is the European reader more interested in sex than history. But the chronicles, especially the *Tarîkh es-Soudan*, provide numerous references to decadence in the empire as the source of the Songhay defeat at the hands of the Moroccan force. In the portrayal of events after the battle of Tondibi, for instance, we find descriptions of wine drinking, sodomy, adultery, incest, and venereal disease (al-'Said 223–25). Ouologuem has drawn on these accounts to reach, at a deeper level, another kind of reader sensitive to his concern about what he sees as decadence in Africa today.

THE MULTIPLE VOICES OF OUOLOGUEM'S NARRATOR

The impact of Ouologuem's thesis stems not simply from the social differences that he portrays and from his reliance on sex and violence, but from the tone of the narrative and, above all, from the diverse styles he employs. His multivocal narrator ranges from passages that reflect the epic—"That the Holy Bibles of the missionaries would be burned as the wind blowing from the Yamé fanned the flames" (46); to the stereotypical dialogue of the love story between Tambira and Kassoumi—"'Look, Tambira,' he stammered, "'it can't go on like this'" (41); and the surrealistic ravings of the drugged Sankolo, sold into slavery—"'My body is floating. My legs are pedaling. My arms are thrashing. But it's not me. I feel good. An Angel is carrying me'" (103).

The many forms of the oral tradition Ouologuem might have drawn from appear to be subsumed under a more general narrative voice simply labeled "legend" or "the tradition." On the first page the narrator includes them among his sources: "What is more interesting, when the elders, notables, and griots, peering wide-eyed into the bitter deserts, speak of that Empire . . . " (3–4).

But here as in later references, parts of the narrative attributed to griots do not stand out from those forms that echo the chronicle tradition. For example, the passage cited earlier mentions the Jewish heritage of the Saifs, information reportedly contained in an oral epic written down by a modern griot. But the text begins with an apostrophe to the Lord, a form associated more with the chronicles than the oral tradition: "The Lord—Holy is His Name!—showed us the mercy of bringing forth, at the beginning of the black Nakem Empire, one illustrious man . . . " (6). There are other reference to griots—"The griot Kutuli of cherished memory ends his tale as follows" (4). Ouologuem's use of the oral tradition, then, may be seen less as a matter of form than of content. Both the oral tradition and its written counterpart recount the past. Neither may be accurate. Each may influence or blend with the other.

The narrative form that really sustains Ouologuem's story, often in the parodic mode, remains the exclamatory and pious phrasing of the chronicles with their frequent asides to God: "His reign was just and glorious (God keep his soul)" (8); "On the twelfth day of Ramadan the worms began to eat him alive and on the twentieth day of the same month he died . . . A prayer for him" (9); and, finally, "*Mashallah! wa bismillah!* The name of Allah upon them and around them!" (17).

This style, seen on nearly every page, enables Ouologuem to maintain a unity of tone that deflates the values of the aristocracy. As the narrator concludes the first chapter, he announces Ouologuem's thesis in that bitter, sardonic tone:

> But to Nakem the colonial powers came too late, for with the help of the local notables a colonial overlord had established himself long since, and that colonial overlord was none other than Saif. All unsuspecting, the European conquerors played into his hands. Call it technical assistance. At that early date! So be it! Thy work be sanctified, O Lord. And exalted. (24)

THE ATTACK AGAINST ISLAM AND THE SOCIAL HIERARCHY

The fundamental difference between Ouologuem's twentieth-century fictional vision of the Askias and their empire and those found in the other versions we have explored, oral and written, appears to be the novelist's frontal attack on the structure of society and its leadership. Unlike the accounts by the scribes and the narratives by the griots, both of which were designed to legitimize the social structure, Ouologuem sets out to illustrate the way in which the nobility exploits and manipulates the lower classes. His novel stands as a modern reply to what he sees as religious and social values expressed in the chronicles, echoed in the oral tradition, and perpetuated today. The Guinean historian Lansine Kaba draws the same conclusion as the novelist when he comments that "Islam under the Askias (1493–1592) became an ideology of domination which helped the clerics to institutionalize the methods by which they had access to power as an ideology of the status quo" (255). As African literature critic Aliko Songolo points out in his perceptive essay "Fiction et Subversion: *Le Devoir de violence*," the novelist thus seeks to supplant both the oral tradition and written history by presenting a narrator who is "the sum of all possible knowledge about the Empire of Nakem" (26).

Beyond the author's critique of his own society, however, the novel, by its composition, offers another message, this time for the West. Just as Ouologuem has drawn on African written sources for his narrative, embellishing and compressing events to convey more directly his criticism of the aristocracy portrayed in those texts, he has also borrowed from the Western literary tradition for the structure and some of the scenes in the novel. One may attach many meanings to his use of Western sources: weakness, creativity, or simply an acute sense of mischievousness. But his borrowings, followed by a bold revelation of his methodology in *Lettre à la France nègre* (1968), may be seen on one level as another form of social criticism. Here, however, the target is not the people portrayed in works by Greene, Maupassant, Schwarz-Bart, and others, but the Western literary establishment. By violating the rules of the game controlled by the West, and by playing to the prejudices of readers whose understanding of Africa was formed by a variety of negative images, Ouologuem deliberately attacked a part of the production system over which non-Western writers have little or no influence. As Mouralis suggests, "*Le Devoir de violence* is perhaps only a game" (1986: 64).

Ouologuem seeks to give an air of authenticity to his novel in both the formal and the thematic sense by drawing upon African and European texts to compose his narrative. But in the case of the African accounts, he makes no effort to camouflage his sources, for they are referred to directly in the text. He waited for six months after the novel was published before announcing his method of plagiarism from the European novels that provide both structure and a variety of formal devices. One may interpret the difference in his approaches to the two traditions that nourish his verbal art in many ways. It might be suggested that Ouologuem is demonstrating, at bottom, a sense of honesty and attachment to Africa, reflected in his concern for the future of the continent. This sentiment would appear to be the opposite of what comes from his manipulation of the European sources and his subsequent self-exposure in *Lettre à la France nègre*.

This difference in Ouologuem's approach to his sources may be more clearly appreciated by viewing the novel in the broader context of the dialogue between Africa and the West. By drawing in different ways on his diverse material, African and Western, for the composition of *Le Devoir de violence*, Ouologuem has expanded the terms of the dialogue between north and south. He engages several Western audiences, from those who appreciate the pornographic scenes to the literati who were fooled by his borrowings and, finally, the intellectuals who consider themselves knowledgeable about the relationship between Africa and the West. At the same time, however, he addresses Africans of the diaspora in order to demystify the present by revealing the ties with the past. As the African critic A. H. Ohaegbu argues, "Ouologuem is not less 'committed' than his predecessors . . . who have unequivocally denounced colonial oppression. But the difference is that his own commitment is more internally oriented, and therefore more critical of the African himself than of the white man who has hitherto appeared in the African novel as the black man's permanent oppressor" (132–33).

Violence and Humanity

Ouologuem's reinterpretation of the African past from the Songhay empire generates a reevaluation that, for some critics, points to a paradoxical "humanization" of African cultures. Africans, Ouologuem seems to say, can be as violent and corrupt as peoples from any other part of the world. But if, to reach the various audiences just described, Ouologuem appears to exaggerate these negative qualities, he is swift to place them in a larger context. To the question of whether Africans are fundamentally more violent than the rest of the world, Ouologuem once replied sardonically:

> I would like to think that Africa excels in everything. For example, in the novel, the Black leader kills by using snakes. But, unfortunately, after the Hundred Years War, Stalin, the Inquisition, Hiroshima, Nagasaki, et cetera, I am afraid that we poor Blacks, underdeveloped Africans . . . I believe violence is part of the human being. (interview with Hugh Downs on the *Today* show, National Broadcasting Corporation, March 18, 1971)

Violence is part of the human condition, suggests Ouologuem, but Africans will never catch up with the rest of the world in developing the kinds of murderous devices that the West has recently demonstrated. For the Malian novelist, to deny the violence of Africa's history and to ignore the reality of the Sahelian social hierarchy is to misunderstand both the past and its impact on the present.

Ouologuem's negative interpretation of Askia Mohammed and the social structure of the Songhay empire, pinnacle of millennia of Sahelian civilization and source of values for so many different people in the centuries to follow, contrasts sharply with the more positive readings we find in historical studies such as Adam Konaré Ba's analysis of Sonni Ali Ber (1977). The discussion that Ouologuem generated among Africans and Europeans, however, has propelled the debate over the African past to a new level where, it seems, scholars feel a greater independence from both the colonial prejudices of Europe and the defensive responses of Africans.

CONCLUSION

For Yambo Ouologuem, the prose narrative that he composed in French and published as a novel in 1968, based on so many diverse African and European sources, has generated two kinds of discourse. One is retrospective, in the sense that he refers us back to the chronicles and the keepers of the oral tradition, and the other is prospective, for he has generated, and participated in, a wide-ranging literary, historical, and legal debate over the form and content of his novel. *Le Devoir de violence*, now out of print in the original French, continues to live in English translation as a text that stands at the nexus of the contact between Africa and the West. For Ouologuem, as well as for the scribes and griots, the medium, a Western literary form into which the author has blended a variety of verbal modes, conveyed effectively his critical attitude toward the social and cultural order portrayed in the chronicles and the oral tradition. His borrowings from Western sources written originally in French and English, as well as from African manuscripts penned in Arabic and, finally, in a less clearly defined way, from the omnipresent oral tradition, represents the most complex use of "literacies" by any African author today.

NOTES

1. The *Tarîkh es-Soudan* and the *Tarîkh el-Fettâch* are early histories of Sahelian West Africa, written in Arabic. They date from the 16th and 17th centuries, recounting the exploits of Askia Mohammed. See Hale's longer study, *Scribe, Griot, and Novelist* [editor's note].

2. Hale includes a lengthy transcription of Nouhou Malia's oral rendition of "The Epic of Askia Mohammed" in his *Scribe, Griot, and Novelist.*

13

Qur'anic Hermeneutics, Sufism, and *Le Devoir de violence*: Yambo Ouologuem as Marabout Novelist

Christopher Wise

> Moses said to his servant: "I will journey on until I reach the land where the two seas meet, though I may march for ages."
>
> —Qur'an 18:60

Introduction

In *Scribe, Griot, and Novelist* (1990), Thomas Hale has described Yambo Ouologuem's novel *Le Devoir de violence* (1968), later published in English as *Bound to Violence* (1971), as "the most controversial novel ever written by an African writer" (137). The reasons for the many controversies surrounding this novel are well-known in France and throughout Africa, and they are increasingly becoming known throughout North America, especially since the publication of Hale's landmark study, as well as the publication of recent critical commentaries like Christopher L. Miller's *Blank Darkness: Africanist Discourse in French* (1985) and Kwame Anthony Appiah's *In My Father's House: Africa in the Philosophy of Culture* (1992). Far from waning or finding resolution, nearly three decades since Ouologuem's novel was first published in Paris, the literary debates regarding *Le Devoir de violence* have never been more significant or provocative.

This chapter was previously published in *Religion and Literature,* Vol. 28, No. 1 (Spring 1996). Reprinted with permission of *Religion and Literature.*

Thus far, critical discussion of *Le Devoir de violence* has centered on at least two main issues (though there are many others): First, numerous critics have discussed the controversy surrounding charges that Ouologuem plagiarized lengthy passages from Graham Greene's *It's a Battlefield* (1934), André Schwartz-Bart's *Le Dernier des justes* (1959), and numerous other literary texts. While the novel gained widespread acclaim almost immediately, winning the Prix Renaudot in 1968, in the ensuing years the novel's "derivative" nature was increasingly debated, especially after the *Times Literary Supplement* demonstrated Ouologuem's heavy reliance on Graham Greene. As Christopher Miller has put it, the French literary establishment at last came to feel that it had been thoroughly "duped" by Ouologuem (219). Besides Seth I. Wolitz, who has argued that the language of Ouologuem's novel is actually much more "original" and creative than Greene's earlier work (which Wolitz accuses of banality), Miller has upped the ante in these discussions by performing a poststructuralist reading of *Le Devoir de violence*, suggesting that Ouologuem's "highly refined and perverse" method of intentionally stealing from other well-known sources functions as a deliberate deconstruction of European literary conventions.

Secondly, *Le Devoir de violence* offended many African critics by its (un)timely reminder that Africans (especially African Muslims), along with their European colonizers, were at least in part responsible for the trans-Atlantic slave trade, as well as the violent epoch of history which occurred following the arrival of the Portuguese, French, and others in West Africa. In other words, Ouologuem's novel seemed to pander to the West's desire to extricate itself from its more primary responsibility for the slave trade and for Africa's long-standing and systematic underdevelopment. Following on the heels of encomiastic and "romanticized" novels like *Things Fall Apart,* Ouologuem's novel was, not surprisingly, celebrated for restoring "an historical dimension" and "candor" to African literature, which presumably was then deluded by prevailing mythical accounts of life in precolonial Africa. Since then, commentators like Hale, Sandra Barkan, J. Mbelolo ya Mpiku, and others have sought to demonstrate the unreliability of much of Ouologuem's account, its distortion of basic historical facts and its own quasi-mythical historiography. While many commentators today generally agree that Ouologuem's depiction of precolonial life and violence is both "polemical and exaggerated" (Hale 176), few seem to question the flawed assumption that the novel's most basic thesis is that "violence remains an inevitable element of the human condition" (Hale 177), or that "the French were already too late" in exploiting the always-already exploited people of the Western Sudan (Miller 1985: 229). In this sense, even those who attack the warm reception of the novel for its so-called "candor" and "honesty" nevertheless tend to buy into the logic that Ouologuem's novel indeed seeks to demonstrate how outrageous cruelty and horrific violence are to some extent unavoidable aspects of the human experience. The latest discussion of the way in which *Le Devoir de violence* functions as an intervention in debates about precolonial African history, and the uses/abuses of the past in postcolonial nation-building, occurs in Appiah's *In My Father's House*. Appealing to a redefined concept of Pan-Africanity, Appiah appropriates Ouologuem's novel to suggest the emergence of a new transnational consciousness, based in a more "universal" ethics of human suffering (152). As we shall see, however, all of these arguments are predicated upon the erroneous assumption, contiguous with the earliest reception of *Le Devoir de violence* in France, that Ouologuem promotes a largely nihilistic (if not high modernist) philosophy of "maturity"—as opposed to the "childishness" of, say, the early Achebe, Camara Laye, Cheikh Hamidou Kane, and others—able to fathom and at last embrace the unavoidable cruelty of human history.

Other notable foci of recent critical thought on *Le Devoir de violence* include discussion of Ouologuem's parody of Leo Frobenius and Western anthropology in general, especially in Christopher Miller's later and more polemical study *Theories of Africans: Francophone Literature and Anthropology in Africa* (1990); African "aesthetics" and their relation to postmodernism debates, especially in Appiah; and, in Hale's *Scribe, Griot, and Novelist*, Ouologuem's creative appropriation and subversion of the *Tarikh el-Fettach* and the *Tarik es-Soudan*, sixteenth- and seventeenth-century historical accounts, written in Arabic, of the medieval Sahelian empires of Ghana (700–1200 A.D.), Mali (1200–1500 A.D.), and Songhay (1350–1600 A.D.), as well as the largely unrecorded oral epics of various griots in Niger, Mali, and elsewhere in the Western Sudan, especially Nouhou Malio of Saga, Niger.[1] Besides demonstrating the complexity and wealth of *Le Devoir de violence*'s literary sources, Hale's study bears out George Lang's pertinent observation in his essay "Through a Prism Darkly" that, with its mixture of Arabic/Islamic, French, and Sahelian cultural influences, West African society today may provide us with "an exemplary metaphor for interactions on the global scale" (307). However, Lang also rightly observes that Western ignorance of Islam's extensive impact on Sahelian culture has tended to produce a skewed view of the literature of West Africa, especially in Christopher Miller's Derridean reading of Ouologuem, which Lang argues reflects a "blatant Western stereotyping of Islam" (301).

Similarly, in his "Introduction" to *Faces of Islam in African Culture* (1991), Kenneth Harrow laments the way in which the topic of Islam is routinely ignored in nearly all critical discussions of African literature (19n). While Harrow and Lang both advocate that we reevaluate Islam's role in shaping contemporary African culture, they also seem unaware of the profoundly theological nature of Ouologuem's novel, which I will argue here reflects a deeply religious sensibility that is only comprehensible when refracted through the lens of Qur'anic hermeneutics and Sufism. Lang, for example, terms Ouologuem an "apostate" (300), while Harrow characterizes *Le Devoir de violence* as a novel that pessimistically attests to "the loss of traditional beliefs" (13). Other notable scholars such as David Robinson, Mybe B. Cham, and Edris Makward also accept the overly simplistic notion that *Le Devoir de violence* represents a "particularly negative" (Robinson 1991: 124–125) and "caustic savaging" of the Islamic faith (Cham 183). Paradoxically, Marxist critic (and Nigerian playwright) Tunde Fatunde rejects Ouologuem's novel precisely because it reflects a theological worldview which Fatunde finds unacceptable (115–116). In the following essay, I will seek to problematize Fatunde's narrowly ideological dismissal of *Le Devoir de violence* because of its unavoidable religious dimensions, but I will also build upon Fatunde's argument that Ouologuem's novel offers a uniquely Muslim perspective rather than a nihilistic or anti-Islamic one.

More precisely, if *Le Devoir de violence*'s critique of Islam seems "exaggerated and polemical" (Hale 176), as well as "sweeping and superficial" (Makward 188), it is at least in part because Sufi literature in its very essence seeks to antagonize, parody, and undermine institutionalized and more "profane" (or secularized) forms of Islam. In this sense, ignorance of the basic tenets of Sufism—better defined as "true" Islam rather than largely Western-based notions of mysticism as something peripheral or existing on the margins—has led many Euro-American critics like Miller to overemphasize the "nihilistic" dimensions of the novel, divorced from their basis in religious belief. The inherent oppositionality of Sufism, an emphatically secret and esoteric inner tribunal that seeks to protect and chastise Islam but *from within* Islam, has often led to such misunderstandings by Western critics and orientalists, as Sufi authority Indries Shah has observed, who commonly mistake parody, irreverence, and criticism for anti-Muslim sentiment (39).

In demonstrating the Islamic dimensions of *Le Devoir de violence*, my argument will not coincidentally parallel recent commentaries on Salman Rushdie's *The Satanic Verses* that have located Rushdie's novel within the context of both the literature of Sufism and traditional Qur'anic hermeneutics, especially in Timothy Brennan's *Salman Rushdie and The Third World* (1989) and in Michael M. K. Fischer and Mehdi Abedi's *Debating Muslims: Dialogues in Postmodernity and Tradition* (1990). In fact, if the "fundamentalist" reaction against *The Satanic Verses* has been more virulent throughout the Islamic world than the reaction against *Le Devoir de violence*, it is not because Ouologuem's novel is any less relevant to problems of Islam today, nor because *Le Devoir de violence* is any less unequivocal in its critique of secular Islam.

However, Ouologuem's novel differs from Rushdie's in at least one significant way: Whereas *The Satanic Verses* is driven by a post-Fanonian or post-revolutionary aesthetics (which is to say, a post-oedipal aesthetics), an approach which Brennan characterizes by employing the Gramscian concept of *positive contaminatio* (48), Ouologuem's *Le Devoir de violence* exhibits a more profound indifference to the West, to Fanonian (or "Manichean") aesthetics, to Oedipus altogether. Like the "posthumous" Ouologuem today,[2] the real Ouologuem who "no longer needs the West" (Hale 169), the Ouologuem of *Le Devoir de violence* does not oppose Westernized nihilism (or Nietzschean high modernism) over and against a primoridially corrupt Islam, but rather he opposes the "heart" of Islam (or Sufism) against a secularized form of Islam in an effort to renew Islam from within it.

OUOLOGUEM IN THE POSTMODERN

> The notion of the text as an unending process of meaning has been extended to the extreme in much of contemporary critical theory, especially in the work of Barthes and Derrida. The *text* has become, in fact, as divine an object, as authoritative a source of meaning—indeed the very field of existence itself—as was the Torah for the Rabbis. Whether called *Text* or *Écriture*, the text today is the Holy Scripture for its critics, or perhaps we should say "worshipers." As Barthes plainly puts it in his *The Pleasure of the Text*, a work which expresses this attitude as none other, "The text is a fetish object, and *this fetish desires me*."
>
> "In fact," says Barthes, "there really is no 'me' independent of the text; 'I' is itself a plurality of other texts." Nothing exists outside the text, says Derrida.
>
> —Susan Handelman, *The Slayers of Moses* (79–80)

> It is only in the invisible world of the Realm (*fi ghaybi' l-malakut*) that the value of the lights of the hearts and of the innermost centers of being (*anwar al-qulub wa' l-asrar*) is known, just as the lights of the sky do not manifest themselves except in the visible world of the Kingdom (*shahadatu 'l-mulk*).
>
> —Ibn 'Ata'illah, *Sufi Aphorisms* (58)

> Every verse of the Qur'an has an outside and an inside.
>
> —Muhammed, *the hadith*

In *Postmodernism and Islam: Predicament and Promise* (1992), Akbar S. Ahmed attempts to account for the hostile reception of recent critical theory in the Islamic world, where philosophers like Lyotard, Baudrillard, Barthes, Derrida, and others are commonly equated with "destruction, anarchy, and Americanization" (28). For many Muslims, Ahmed observes, Western theory subverts "the faith and piety which [lie] at the core of their world view," especially those theories celebrating groundless freeplay and "purely" lucid irony (5–6). Ahmed's comments regarding the cultural irrelevance and imperializing tendencies of Western theory have been widely echoed by many postcolonial theorists. While Islam obviously does not lend itself to any easy, overly homogenizing description, Muslim (and Sufi) approaches to both the Qur'an and secular literature contradict poststructuralist "hermeneutics" in many far-reaching ways, especially Derrida's widely imitated "worship" of the text as a divine object, to quote Susan Handelman.[3] Before focusing our attention directly on Ouologuem's novel, it may therefore be instructive to briefly survey the potential distortions and misunderstandings that may arise when a strictly secular approach is adopted in reading an emphatically Muslim novel.[4] In so doing, I will propose that a textual methodology sensitive to Qur'anic hermeneutics and Sufism may provide a more accurate account of *Le Devoir de Violence*'s meaning. By "meaning" I hereby intend both a logocentric and hermeneutic concept, an interpretive bias that is by no means abandoned in Islamic and Sufi discourse for a purely syntactic or linguistic one.

Of course, I refer mainly to Christopher Miller's widely-quoted chapter "Dis-figuring Narrative: Plagiarism and Dismemberment in Yambo Ouologuem's *Le Devoir de violence*," from his book *Blank Darkness*. As we will see, by borrowing extensively from Derrida, especially the long essay "Plato's Pharmacy" from *Dissemination* (1981), Miller distorts Ouologuem's novel so that it may be coherently appropriated by Western academics with the least possible reference to Islam. However, from a Muslim or Sufi perspective, perhaps the most significant effect of this interpretive strategy may be that, by relying exclusively on Derrida, Miller tends to arrogate the novel's entire meaning to the sphere of human understanding alone, wholly divorced from theology. While Islam has its own "grammatology," or its own theory of the trace, as in Derrida (or, as in the more properly Rabbinic notion of "divine sparks" of meaning),[5] from its earliest days to the present Muslims have systematically rejected interpretive approaches emphasizing lucid freeplay or polysemous ambiguity, specifically Jewish hermeneutic orientations stressing humankind's sole responsibility for ascertaining the meaning of a text, be it sacred or profane.[6] For example, while rabbinical approaches have maintained that "The Torah is not in Heaven" but revealed to each new generation (Handelman 40), Muslims have always emphasized oral recitation of the Qur'an, evoking not its written transcription or "dead letter" but rather the primordial Qur'an in the Seventh Heaven, "the preserved tablet" [*lawh mah fuz*] (Abedi and Fischer 108). Indeed, the word *qur'an* itself means "oral recitation" rather than a *mus-haf* or a "written text" (97). Hence, as Kristina Nelson rightly observes in her study *The Art of Reciting the Qur'an* (1985), "it's not the Qur'an unless it is heard" (xiv).[7]

The Islamic insistence on the Qur'an's orality, or on the priority of the oral word over the written word, is fundamental to any understanding of Muslim literature and of the attitudes which shape it. For example, when Raymond-Spartacus Kassoumi of *Le Devoir de violence* rejects the French academic system, he does so in part because he feels himself to be "living amidst the dead carcasses of words" (137), an attitude echoed in the Qur'anic analogy of scribal exegetes as "donkeys laden with books" (62:5).[8] In short, the Derridean attack on logocentrism runs antithetical to the most basic tenets of Islam, without which one may not fully comprehend Ouologuem's novel. As Abedi and Fischer have put it, from early on, "Muslims have been as ambivalent about writing as was Plato" (100). The unavoidable logocentric basis of Islam, a belief system which posits not simply a binary opposition between oral *Text* and written *text* (in a Derridean sense), but rather a more primordial opposition between the imperfect text (*mus-haf*) and its ineffable or "prelinguistic" Other, is equally fundamental to Sufism's separation of the esoteric realm from the exoteric one, a realm without which the "Real" Islam (which is to say, Sufism, or Islam's "heart") would be unable to critique its mirror-image in the fallen and "real" world.[9]

Because Miller uncritically accepts the poststructuralist dogma that "there is nothing outside the text" (Derrida *Of Grammatology* 158), or because he endorses a largely hypostatic and fetishized concept of textuality, his reading of Ouologuem is deaf to how *Le Devoir de violence* may be answering its own questions, instead of "ours" in the West. In effect, the chapter, "Dis-figuring Narrative," becomes enmeshed in a purely exoteric reading of *Le Devoir de violence*, unconsciously replicating the fallen "hermeneutics" of Saif and Bishop Henry, the novel's arch-villains, for whom horrific murder and violence are only "a manner of questioning and answering" (173), a profane "dialogue" that is "no more than a game" (182).[10] Similarly, Miller (1985) characterizes even graphic descriptions of extreme physical pain and torture as narrative sophistries on Ouologuem's part (128), a playful "assault on European assumptions about writing and originality" (219). Miller asserts that "*Le Devoir de violence*, both in its narrative method and in its narrative content, posits destructive violence and theft as origin itself" (219): all this in a cleverly subversive attempt to "spoil the distinction between text and copy" (228). Hence, "Dis-figuring Narrative" ends by congratulating Ouologuem for his "triumphantly hopeless gesture" of seeking to violate "the rules of European logic" (245), a curious tribute, to be sure.

In opposition to Miller's insistence that *Le Devoir de violence* posits "theft as origin" (222), or that Ouologuem, in his filial desire to "break away and negate" the West, becomes hopelessly entrapped in European literary obsessions (218), it may be worth observing that, from its earliest days to the present, Islamic literary theory [*Balaghah*] has necessarily preoccupied itself with questions of originality, imitation, and plagiarism (Sharif 1032), issues which early literary scholar Ibn Sallam (d. 231/845), for example, once defined as "the foundation" of any legitimate literary criticism (1033).[11] In other words, Western literature hardly has a monopoly on questions of originality and plagiarism, a point that Derrida acknowledges but that Miller elides.[12] More importantly, however, if Ouologuem's novel "assaults" European (i.e., Miller's) assumptions about originality, it is not because *Le Devoir de violence* posits theft as origin, as Miller argues, but because the Sufi bias which permeates the novel supports a characteristically logocentric dialectic between inside and outside, the movement from the greater *jihad* (or "holy war") to the lesser one.[13] To quote Lings, "Sufism is nothing if not a movement of return, an ebb" (28).[14] The return of which Miller speaks therefore signifies not a return to a scene of primordial theft and violence, but rather a return to that inner Realm of lights wherein the possibility of freedom—the unbinding of the *négraille* or "wretched of the earth"—may triumph. As we will more fully explore, the novel's most basic thesis turns on one question alone: Those who are "bound" must be set free; those who are oppressed must find respite.

Ouologuem's Sufistic and traditional "logocentricism" is perhaps best encapsulated in a brief passage from *Le Devoir de violence*, alluded to above, which describes Raymond-Spartacus Kassoumi's response to the Parisian literary scene:

> And so, taking refuge beneath the dead tree of academic complacency, a mage of knowledge without hearth or home, living admidst the dead carcasses of words, Raymond Kassoumi, after a period of apery in which he took on the accent of a Paris wise guy, gave himself up to literary drivel, turning his learning into a demagogic ventriloquism and sinking under its weight. (137)

In the Qur'an "the good word" is compared to a good tree while the "evil word" is compared to an evil tree, "torn out of the earth and shorn of all its roots."[15] The "dead tree" of academic detachment and serenity, under which Kassoumi momentarily takes refuge, diametrically opposes the true and living tree of "the good word" (or God himself),[16] which implicitly provides Kassoumi with his true "roots" and sense of well-being (137). Similarly, the "mage of knowledge without hearth or home" may be contrasted with the Sufi doctrine that Islam itself is the one true "Abode of Peace" [*Dar-as-Salam*], a *nonviolent* refuge of "wholeness, soundness, faultlessness" (Shah 57–58). Additionally, for Sufis, the Kaaba or "House of God" (literally, the "cube") resides at the heart of Makkah and, more importantly, symbolizes the center of man's being (Lings 37). In this sense, Islam is the "knowledge *with* hearth and home" [*feu et lieu*], the possibility of a Logos-centered consciousness that opposes the "dead carcasses of words" which Kassoumi rejects.[17]

By ignoring the Islamic elements of Ouologuem's novel, Miller's deconstructive reading of *Le Devoir de violence* therefore buries (or "sinks") it under the weight of a theoretically dazzling, but finally deadening, academic complacency, condemning Ouologuem to play the role of ventriloquist (or "ghostwriter"), who may only speak through the bad wood/word of literary dummies. Hence, if Ouologuem deliberately plagiarizes from a variety of literary sources, both European and African, it does not necessarily follow that *Le Devoir de violence* posits "theft as origin" in an effort to assault "European" notions of originality and plagiarism. Nor is Miller entirely correct in his assertion (with Wole Soyinka) that "'the positive does not engage [Ouologuem's] re-creative attention'" (233), and that "[t]he violent partisanship [of *Le Devoir de violence*] is opposed to everything and symmetrically counterbalanced by nothing." What is missing from Miller's account are the unavoidably theological and utopian dimensions of the novel, specifically the hope held out by Ouologuem that the "men of nothing" [*hommes de rien*],[18] or the scorned *négraille*, may yet be unbound.

Paradoxically, we may say then that *Le Devoir de violence* offers a vision of human existence in which the oppressed seem wholly static and powerless, crippled indefinitely by a false and purely exoteric form of Islam (but also French colonialism), yet one that nevertheless maintains the possibility of their ultimate emancipation from bondage. The utopian is preserved by Ouologuem in the realm of the esoteric, the secret hearth where the Hidden Treasure resides, which neither moths nor rust may corrupt,[19] and which may not be corroded by the outward world of "unreal" forms, those profane "signs on the horizons" (Lings 81–82). It is in this sense that Ouologuem as marabout novelist may be said to embody "two centers of consciousness," as Lings puts it (14), even a non-Western and pre-capitalist form of "schizophrenia," which may be historically characteristic of Islam as it has been practiced throughout West Africa.[20]

In a widely influential reading of *Le Devoir de violence,* Kwame Anthony Appiah emphasizes the more affirmative dimensions of Ouologuem's novel, which for Miller simply do not exist. Appiah describes *Le Devoir de violence* as a "novel of delegitimation rejecting the Western imperium . . . but also rejecting the nationalist project of the postcolonial national bourgeoisie" (152). But Appiah is aware that Ouologuem's novel, like the larger project of "delegitimation" itself, is based in an unavoidably *ethical* (but also "universal") "appeal to a certain simple respect for human suffering, a fundamental revolt against the endless misery of the last thirty years." Though compelling, especially in its hopeful suggestion that a new

Pan-Africanity may be on the horizon, like the defunct Pan-Africanisms of the past, Appiah's reading of the novel errs in underestimating the ongoing significance of Islam (as well as African religion in general), which provides the historically specific basis of Ouologuem's "universal" ethical appeal, and which has been a proven obstacle to all previous secular appeals to Pan-African unity. In other words, Appiah overdramatizes the extrinsic and theoretical *effects* of Ouologuem's novel because they seem to fit his own theses about an emerging Pan-African and transnational consciousness.

However, the misery which Ouologuem address in *Le Devoir de violence* is much older and deeper than Appiah will allow. For example, Appiah argues that Ouologuem's Nakem kingdom is a mere "fabrication" (157), for the sake of critiquing political developments in postcolonial Africa over *the last thirty years* (151). However, when one considers that Ouologuem's novel was first published in 1968, the mathematics of Appiah's argument seem suspect. Like Miller, Appiah tends to focus not so much on *Le Devoir de violence*'s essential meaning but rather its implications for current academic literary debates. Nevertheless, Appiah's appropriation of Ouologuem's novel is much more deliberate than Miller's. Appiah therefore succumbs to what he himself calls a "temptation" peculiar to many African writers today, which is "to celebrate and endorse those identities that seem at the moment to offer the best hope of advancing our other goals, and to *keep silent about the lies and the myths*" [my emphasis] (178). Though a Muslim reader would obviously take exception to any characterization of his/her belief system in such terms, Appiah's careful bracketing off of Islam's relevance to Ouologuem's novel seems applicable (151).

For example, Appiah overemphasizes the thematic significance of Ouologuem's iconoclastic attack on Roots (i.e., Leo Frobenius, *négritude*, the commodification of African art, encomiastic literature, Euro-American "negromania"), while Ouologuem's more primary concern with the sins of secular Islam is dismissed by Appiah as a red herring (151). If Ouologuem's savaging of Roots is indeed compelling (perhaps one of the most fascinating aspects of the novel from a postmodern perspective), its motivations cannot be fully explained without reference to Islam, as Appiah attempts. In other words, the derisive scorn with which Ouologuem describes precolonial African religious art, what he repeatedly labels "native idols" (76) and "old wood" (85), obviously resonates with widely-held Muslim attitudes towards representational art of all sorts, a prejudice supported by the Biblical and Qur'anic injunction against graven images. In this sense, Ouologuem attacks two separate avatars of idolatry: the *precolonial,* in which the religious object is originally valued as a tribal fetish, and the *(post)colonial*, in which the religious object is allegorically resemiotized as a commodity fetish. Unlike Achebe then, whose novels are often empowered by the "call to the ancestors" scorned in *Le Devoir de violence*, Ouologuem can well afford to dismiss pre-colonial and "native" African religious art because such a gesture in no way undermines the ultimate ground from which he speaks. In fact, Islam itself is often said to begin precisely at the moment Abraham smashes the pagan idols in his father's house, an act replicated upon Muhammad's triumphant return to Makkah. Ouologuem's iconoclastic smashing of idols, be they the idols of French literature or pre-colonial African culture, cannot then be divorced from its basis in Islam, despite the inventiveness of prevailing academic approaches.

THE GOSPEL ACCORDING TO YAMBO OUOLOGUEM

> The Spirit of the Lord is upon me: because the Lord hath annointed me to preach good tidings unto the meek: he hath sent me to bind up the broken hearted, to proclaim liberty to the captives, and the opening of the prison to them that are bound.
>
> —Isaiah 61:1

> The Spirit of the Lord is upon me, because he hath annointed me to preach the gospel to the poor, he hath sent me to heal the broken hearted, to preach deliverance to the captives, and recovery of sight to the blind, to set at liberty them that are bruised.
>
> —Luke 4:18

> We sent forth Jesus, the son of Mary, confirming the Torah already revealed, and gave him the Gospel, in which there is guidance and light, corroborating what was revealed before it in the Torah, a guide and an admonition to the righteous.
>
> —Qur'an 5:46

> . . . In anticipation of the great and not too distant day when a world would dawn in which a serf would be the equal of a king, the nigger-trash—dogs that bite, leash them tight!—accepted whatever came their way. Forgive us, O Lord. *Amba, koubo oumo agoum.*[21]
>
> —Ouologuem, *Le Devoir de violence* (22)

In *Scribe, Griot, and Novelist* Thomas Hale states that Ouologuem's "return" to the Muslim faith signals "a rediscovery of a belief system that he had abandoned"; however, Hale's suggestion that there may be two Ouologuems, the early apostate novelist versus the pious marabout of today, does not really do justice to the more affirmative and theological dimensions of *Le Devoir de violence*. In other words, if a *marabout* is a spiritual leader who seeks to negate the oppressive materialism of a profane and exoteric form of Islam (Harrow, "Camara Laye," 287), particularly through appealing to an inner realm of harmony and nonviolence [*Dar-as-salam*], the two Ouologuems implied by Hale's reading may be said to already (and simultaneously) co-habit the pages of *Le Devoir de violence*. Like the "apostate" Ouologuem then, the more traditional marabout's spirited attack on secular Islam is *not* motivated by spleen but by charity, one's ethical obligation to end the suffering of the oppressed, to unbind those who are held captive.

Though Ouologuem rejects the "dead letter" of Western academe, the more fundamental targets of his literary assault in *Le Devoir de violence* may be the Arabic chronicles of West African history, the *Tarîkh el-Fettach* and the *Tarîkh es Soudan*.[22] In other words, *Le Devoir de violence* seeks to challenge "scribal" (and profane) accounts of precolonial, secular history, such as Seku Amadu's notorious alteration of the *Tarîkh el-Fettach*, which Robinson calls "the most ambitious forgery in African history" (Hale 51).[23] As marabout-novelist, Ouologuem desires to help the oppressed, or the *négraille*, by correcting earlier and false "corrections" of West African history that once empowered evil and purely secular Muslim regimes. However, far from being a unique gesture, Ouologuem's subversive literary strategy is characteristic of Sufi poetic traditions which flourish throughout West Africa, especially the Sufi Quadriya, Tijaniya, and Mourides (Lang 301–302), as well as Sufi poetic traditions throughout the greater Islamic world.

In the opening pages of *Le Devoir de violence*, the religious and ethical theme of the novel is announced: "Our eyes drink the sun's glare, and conquered, surprise themselves weeping" ["*Nos yeux boivent l'éclat du soleil, et, vaincus, s'étonnent de pleurer,*" (90)] (Miller 1985: 229). This curious and seemingly opaque beginning is immediately followed by the Arabic exclamation,"*Maschallah! oua bismillah!*" a commonplace phrase throughout the Arabic-speaking world but forbidding to the Western reader. Most commentators on Ouologuem simply ignore the novel's opening, which is largely incomprehensible without reference to Islam. Though crucial to *Le Devoir de violence*'s principal theme, the initial effect of these deliberately obscure sentences is that a protective veil [*al-hijab*] is cast over the novel's meaning, a narrative strategy that is commensurate with postcolonial literature in general,[24] and with Sufi poetics in particular.[25] For an educated, Arabic speaker/reader, however, Ouologuem's references would seem neither obscure nor particularly forbidding, especially his invocation of the *Bismillah* [literally, "In the name of God"], which is the opening line of every sura (but one) in the Qur'an. Similarly, Ouologuem includes "*Maschallah!*" [literally "Whatever God wills"], a word which commonly expresses awe, or a sense of wonder, but also "submission" (i.e., Islam).

More importantly, perhaps, the novel's opening sentences may be clarified with reference to the story of Hagar, especially the legendary (and

Biblical) account of her expulsion by Abraham. It will be remembered that, because of the jealousy of Sarah (who feared for the inheritance of Isaac, her own son), Hagar and Ishmael were cast into the wilderness with only a few figs and a leather skin of water (Esin 18). When both mother and child were nearly dead from thirst, water miraculously appeared at the feet of Ishmael, traditionally, at the source of the well of Zamzam where Muslim pilgrims continue to draw consecrated water. The rite of Sa'y, during the Hajj to Makkah, commemorates Hagar's desperate search for water, which is a moment of primordial significance for Muslims. As told in the Torah, at the moment of her deepest despair, "God opened Hagar's eyes, and she saw a well of water" (Genesis 21:19).[26] The Biblical emphasis on God's role in opening Hagar's eyes is reiterated in the traditional Islamic account wherein the angel Gabriel directs Hagar to the well's source. For this reason, during the conclusion of the Sa'y rites, the pilgrim reads a prayer on the steps of Al-Marwah in hopes that God will "bestow true vision" upon him/her (Kamal 64), like Hagar in the wilderness.

In Ouologuem's opening sentence, the eyes which drink in the sun's glare are accordingly "conquered" [*vaincus*] by the sun, or by the God who is "light of the Heavens and Earth" (24:35).[27] Here, Ouologuem echoes the Qur'anic passage, "[t]heir sight overtaketh Him not, but He overtaketh their sight, and He is the All-Pervading, All-Prevailing, the Infinitely Aware" (6:103). If God "overtakes" or defeats all human efforts to see Him, however, our tears of compassion, like those of Hagar for her dying child, finally enable us to *see* Him; or, as Lings puts it, evoking the writings of Sufi Abd al Karim al-Jili, "[o]nly the Eye of Water [the eye of mercy and compassion] can see water [the source of life/the well of Zamzam]" (71). Ouologuem's opening sentence suggests that *Le Devoir de violence* itself cannot be understood unless read in the right spirit, or with "the Eye of Water" leading to the Heart. The novel's beginning sentence may therefore be paraphrased as follows, "Our eyes that lead to the Heart, where the inner and outer worlds meet, drink in the power of God: we are utterly defeated by the encounter, but we are amazed to find that our tears enable us to both see and be seen by God." More specifically, our tears of compassion should be for the "men of nothing" [*hommes de rien*] (3), or the *négraille*, who are never far from "the eyes of the all-powerful (and just) God" (12) ["*sous le regard de Dieu tout puissant (et juste)*" (18)] throughout Ouologuem's narrative. The expression "*Maschallah!*" in the second sentence signifies both awe and submission ["it is how God wills"], as we have already seen, but it is also commonly stated to ward off the Evil Eye, or "the Eye of Ice" (Lings 71), which cannot reach the Heart. Hence, when Al Hadj Ali Gakore, a minor character in the novel, questions the viciousness of Saif ben Isaac al-Heit's caliphate, Ouologuem tells us that "all hearts were struck with ice" (45), refusing to heed his appeal to true religion. Both Arabic expressions "*Maschallah!*" and "*Bismillah*" ["In the name of God"] are uttered at exactly the beginning of the novel (by the narrator) and at the end of the novel (by Saif), polemically signifying the vast distance between their sacred and profane meanings.[28]

Ouologuem's affirmation of Sufism, which is to say the "heart" of Islam, is stated more explicitly in his description of Saif ben Isaac al-Heit's wholly cynical appropriation of Islam (but also Sufism) "to hold down the people and exploit them" (22). Earlier, Imam Mahmud, Grand Sherif of Makkah, prophesied the coming of a Caliph to Nakem who would deliver the oppressed from their bondage, a messianic "gospel" that provides the novel's moral center and its most basic theme: In the words of Al Hadj Ali Gakore, the good news that, "at the coming of a new caliph, blood and tears would vanish from the world . . . [And] servants and masters, now equal, would devote themselves in common to the service of God" (46). However, Saif ben Isaac al-Heit successfully co-opts even this utopian prophecy as a "principle of *spiritual advancement*" to aid in further exploiting the *négraille* [Ouologuem's emphasis] (22). In other words, because the people receive *mere* spiritual comfort from Islam, rather than spiritual and material benefit, there is no real spiritual benefit either. If purely exoteric learning for the Sufi leads to inappropriate behavior,[29] true esoteric knowledge invariably leads to ethically sound and humane behavior: a value summed up in Khwaja 'Abdullah Anjari's injunction that the Sufi adherent must "strive to become a man and one who knows pain" (218). This point is dramatically reiterated by Ouologuem when he states that Raymond-Spartacus Kassoumi's quest was *not* for a self-gratifying experience of ecstasy, a common misconception about Sufism in the West (Danner and Lings ii), but rather for "the profound meaning of his own destruction" (156). No matter how vicious and gratuitous Ouologuem's descriptions of violence may appear, they are not then "symmetrically counterbalanced with nothing," as Miller puts it (233), but are instead denounced from a radically utopian and theological perspective implicit in Ouologuem's lamentation for the "lost mystical content" of true Islam: "Religion, whose soul had been vomited by the clergy of Nakem, became a deliberately confused mumbling about human dignity [under Saif]," Ouologuem tells us, "a learned mystification. *Losing its mystical content, it became a means of action, a political weapon*" [my emphasis] (23).

The overriding and recurring point made throughout *Le Devoir de violence* is that the Islam of the Saifs, modeled on rulers of Sahelian society from the Songhay Empire to the present, profanely (even satanically) parodies true Islam, which is why Ouologuem as marabout-novelist, like any good Sufi poet, irreverently parodies the still more irreverent parody of the Saifs. We are told, for example, that infibulation (or female "circumcision") was a rarity in Nakem before the demonic reign of the Saifs, who mandate such practices to increase their power (48). Similarly, the Hajj to Makkah, made by one of Saif al-Haram's ministers, degenerates to failed political maneuvering by a scheming and cruel rogue (10). Additionally, the exoteric "wisdom" of Nakem's Arab universities, established upon wealth from the slave-trade, is parodied by Ouologuem as a form of learned idiocy, an "obtuse theology" benefiting only cats, toads, and insects (17–18). Meanwhile, Sufi or true wisdom, what Ouologuem calls "the sacred union of knowledge and morality," goes unheeded (20).

In his "Introduction" to *Faces of Islam in African Literature*, Harrow borrows from Clifford Geertz's anthropological study *Islam Observed* (1968), particularly Geertz's discussion of *maxzen* complexes in Muslim sub-Saharan Africa, or popular belief in the "royal assumption of sacred power assured through descent in the Prophet's line," to demonstrate how *Le Devoir de violence* parodies "an Islam [that is] portrayed solely as an institution" (6).[30] Besides Harrow, Hale also historicizes and provides many of the literary contexts for Ouologuem's critique of the *maxzen* complex in *Le Devoir de violence* (148). What only need be added here is that greater clarity may be gained into Ouologuem's critique of *maxzen* cults in Sahelian society by demonstrating how it is informed by Sufism, particularly the Sufi doctrine of the chain [*silsilah*], which provides the axiological basis for Ouologuem's demonization of the Saifs (but also the French colonizers). In *What Is Sufism?* Lings states that "[e]very Sufi order [*tariqah*] is descended from the Prophet . . . [Hence] initiation into a *tariqah* means attachment to a particular chain" (38). This spiritual chain (or "life-line") invariably leads back to Muhammad, who is said to reside at the "center point" of human perfection, an exemplary "incarnation of the Revealed Book" (33). In *Le Devoir de violence*, Ouologuem diametrically opposes the Sufi doctrine of the chain against the fallen *maxzen* cults of the Saifs that prevail in the soulless, exoteric realm.

Throughout the novel, the various Saifs perversely play at being the Messiah (23), the "First Man" (7), the "wise philosopher-king" (8), as well as "the water, salt, and bread" of Nakem (7). Ouologuem's parody of the Saifs' claims to messianic status is relentlessly consistent, if not redundant. In the imagery with which the various tyrants are described, each successive Saif joins with his predecessor to form a demonic chain of Evil Incarnate, a succession of profane embodiments of the anti-Prophet (but also Anti-Christ) in the exoteric realm. We are told, for example, that the Saifs seem to have been "born of a serpent" (17), that their national holiday commemorates *"the fire of the vipers of the supernatural"* [Ouologuem's emphasis]" (11). Far from being on the side of the exploiters then, as Tunde Fatunde has charged (and as many commentators have implied), Ouologuem takes great pains to show us how the reign of the "viper-spawned" Saifs may actually be "guided by the invisible breath of Satan"

(11). It may therefore be Iblis himself, or at least his temporal avatar, who is the unnamed (but odorous) villain "at the center of it all" in the novel's conclusion (173). The philosophy expounded in the final pages of *Le Devoir de violence*, commonly attributed to Ouologuem (his resignation to violence's inevitability, for example), in fact culminates his description of a wholly satanic universe, a world unconditionally given over to violence, murder, and "the will to power."

In case we think that the French colonizers like Bishop Henri are somehow less culpable than the Saifs, advocates of "*le devoir d'amour*," as Barkan puts it (106–107), Ouologuem shows us how a unifying bond inextricably links the old regime with the new, a bond [*lien*] based in *both* exploiters' unfounded claims to divinely sanctioned privileges over the *négraille*. Following the brutal murder of an ally to Bishop Henri, for example, Saif cautions Henri to forget about crimes not his own: "I wouldn't pass judgment if I were you," he states. "For the Church [i.e., the French colonial regime] with its hierarchy and its credo might well be charged with hypocrisy: 'The first will be the last'" (72). Here, Ouologuem develops a conceit that may unlock the novel's deeper meaning:

> *[T]he mystery of Israel resides in its refusal to accept the Gospel* . . . Israel is here to admonish the Church to vigilance . . . Vigilance toward the idea of the 'remnant.' . . . [T]his "remnant," present in the Old Testament, recurs in the New Testament and in the Church. It is a bond between the Old Testament and the New, it marks their unity and is the unifying bond between the pre-Christian Church and the post-Christian Church . . . Missionary activity among the people of Nakem—fetish, Moslem, and black Jewish—confronts the Church with the question—a question that has lost none of its timeliness—of its justification and existence. [my emphasis] (72–73)

Like the previous Saifs, Saif ben Isaac al-Heit purports to be of Jewish ancestry, descendant of the black Jew Abraham al-Heit (6), which aids him in further exploiting his subjects in Nakem. Saif's (and Ouologuem's) profane conceit collapses Israel, or Judaism, with the order of the Muslim tyrants of Nakem, beginning in the year 1202, but *not* with the arrival of Islam itself in the Western Sudan (3). In other words, Ouologuem's so-called "savaging" of Islam is historically specific to a form of Islam that emerges in West Africa nearly *five hundred years* after the arrival of the first Muslims in the area. Moreover, if the Saif's caliphate mimics authentic Islam, the religion of the French Catholic powers in Nakem similarly mimics true religion for Ouologuem. The antagonistic relationship between Saif's secularized Islamic regime and Sufism (or true Islam) directly parallels the discordant relationship between Bishop Henri's secularized Catholic regime and the true inner church (or, perhaps, the *ekklesia*).

"The mystery of Israel," which is to say the mystery of the Saifs' tyrannical reign (but also the mystery of Henri's French colonial regime), consists largely in its "*refusal to accept the gospel*" (72). In the Book of Isaiah, and in the Gospel of Luke, the "good news" (or gospel) proclaimed, first by the Prophet Isaiah and later by the Prophet Jesus, informs us that those who are "bound" or "held captive" shall be set free, and that those who are broken-hearted shall be healed. Repeatedly (and even militantly), the Qur'an reaffirms this gospel of liberation, or the declaration that "God has promised the faithful the Garden" in the Torah, the Gospel, and the Qur'an (9:111). In Ouologuem's articulation of this theme, embedded in the form of a prophetic message that comes from faraway Makkah, the good news is proclaimed that a "new world" may be on the horizon, a world in which "serf will be equal of a king" (22). However, this gospel is brutally suppressed by the Saifs because its egalitarian utopianism denies the privilege upon which their oppressive order (as well as the French colonial rule) is founded. For example, when Al Hadj Ali Gakore, who has been to Makkah, dares to proclaim this gospel to Saif's face, not only is he murdered for his efforts, but Saif immediately confiscates all the missionaries' Bibles (as well as their *Lives of Jesus*), burning them by the hundreds (46–47). Besides being linked in their denial of the gospel, *both* the Saifs and the French are linked in the "idea of the 'remnant'" [*reste*] (72), or in their separate claims to racial superiority over the "serfs" whom they exploit. In other words, if the Saifs believe they are entitled to oppress Nakem's populace because of their privileged status as Black Jews, the French preserve this long-standing tradition through their own bogus claims to racial superiority as whites.

CONCLUSION

Le Devoir de violence's quintessentially Muslim but also "ecumenical"[31] message transcends the concerns of Mali, Niger, and Africa itself, as well as the concerns of a more narrowly defined Pan-Africanity (like Appiah's). While the oft-repeated assertion that Islam is a "color-blind" religion may be problematic in a historical sense, the egalitarian thrust of Islam, which forms the basis of ethical appeals like Ouologuem's (but also El Hajj Malik El-Shabazz's, Warith Deen Muhammad's, and others), is nevertheless indisputable.[32] If *Le Devoir de violence* is among the most important African novels yet written, its significance must therefore be measured not simply by its literary sophistication, as Miller attempts, but rather by its profoundly human concern for those in pain, especially for the victims of racial prejudice: the *négraille*, or "niggertrash." Like the Sufi mystic then, Ouologuem as marabout-novelist professes or *submits* to "the religion of love,"[33] the exact opposite of the "unconditional surrender to the will to power" (173), stigmatized throughout the pages of *Le Devoir de violence*.

The current critical consensus that Ouologuem teaches us that violence is an inevitable aspect of human experience must therefore be challenged, especially by delineating *Le Devoir de violence*'s unavoidably Islamic dimensions: Islam, in this sense, may be defined as the "Abode of Peace" [*Dar as-Salam*], a utopian and pre-linguistic site that is altogether *beyond* violence. Obviously, such an approach militates against the anti-religious thrust of much contemporary criticism and prevailing stereotypes of Islam in the West. But these are perhaps still more reasons to reevaluate the growing significance of Ouologuem's novel.

NOTES

1. Hale includes in *Scribe, Griot, and Novelist* a lengthy transcription of *The Epic of Askia Mohammed* in the Zarma dialect of the Songhay language as well as a linear translation in English, recorded in two separate sessions with Nouhou Malio in the early 1980s (178–291).

2. In *Scribe, Griot, and Novelist*, Hale reports that at the 1989 African Literature Association gathering in Dakar, Ouologuem's name was erroneously listed among deceased writers to be honored during a moment of silence (168).

3. Besides Handelman, see Jürgen Habermas's reading of Judaic elements in the writings of Derrida in *The Philosophical Dicourse of Modernity*, especially Habermas's discussion of Handelman (406–407 footnote).

4. This is not to say, however, that Qur'anic hermeneutics and poetics may not be complemented by deconstruction, poststructuralism, and the like, as Fischer and Abedi plainly demonstrate in their chapters "Qur'anic Dialogics" (95–149) and "Fear of *Différance*" (150–221) from *Debating Muslims*. The question is rather one of accent and emphasis, or sensitivity to Muslim approaches, which, throughout history, have defined themselves precisely in opposition to purely textual orientations. For more on Derrida and Islam, see Abdelkebir Khatibi's *Maghreb pluriel*.

5. See Abedi and Fischer's discussion of the *bismillah*, the Islamic tradition which asserts that the entire universe is "contained in the dot of the Arabic *b* [ب] of the *bismillah*" (147–148).

6. See Abedi and Fischer's comments on the differences between Jewish and Muslim hermeneutics (462ft). It may be worth noting that Christians are also criticized by Muslims, but for their proleptic *refusal* of interpretative play, (rather than overindulging in wordplay like the Jews), or because they do not sufficiently "wrestle with God" like Israel (or Jacob)—a consequence of their worship of Christ as incarnate God or archetype [*ta'wil*] (147).

7. Also, see William A. Graham, "*Qur'an* as Spoken Word" (30–33).

8. The full passage from the Qur'an reads as follows: "Those to whom the burden of the Torah was entrusted and yet refused to bear it are like a donkey laden with books. Wretched is the example of those who deny God's revelations. God does not guide the wrongdoers" (62:5).

9. Lings demonstrates the inherent logocentric bias of Islam in his suggestion that the *Shahadah* (or, the most basic profession of faith and the first pillar of Islam, "There is no God but God") is commonly interpreted by Sufis to mean that "there is no reality but the Reality" (69).

10. While Qur'anic hermeneutics are also a "game" of sorts, they must nevertheless be defined as a "*profoundly ethical structure* [that is] insistent upon debate (*bahth, mubahatha*) and dialogue (*jadal*), adjustable to the level of knowledge of each person, and open to the educative process of those more knowledgeable" [my emphasis] (Abedi and Fischer 100).

11. In *A History of Muslim Philosophy, Vol. II* (1966), M. M. Sharif defines *Balaghah* as "the whole field of literary appreciation, analysis, judgment, and comparison on the practical as well as the theoretical side" (1031). In addition to Ibn Sallam, Al-Amidt (d. 371/981) discusses problems of origin and plagiarism extensively in his *Muwazanah*. Sharif states that Al-Amidt's study "gives one of the best practical accounts of the phenomenon of plagiarism, which greatly occupies the attention of [Muslim] critics, permeates a good deal of their comparative studies, and to some extent colors their judgment of literary values" (1037).

12. See Derrida's observation that Plato's "god Theth [no doubt] had several faces, belonged to several eras, lived in several homes" (*Dissemination* 86).

13. Such a movement is commonly signified in Sufi discourse by employing the term *hijra* ("removal" or "withdrawal"). In its historical sense, *hijra* refers to the migration of the early Muslim community to Al-Medina due to religious persecution faced in Makkah. As Al-Hajj 'Umar Tal has put it, "*hijra* is of two kinds, the greater and the lesser" (Martin 89). In a more general sense, *hijra* can refer to an exoteric strategy allowing the Muslim community to retreat as a self-protective measure; in the esoteric and Sufistic sense, however, *hijra* refers to an "internal, personal 'migration' . . . [or a] disassociation from worldly things" (89). *Hijra* in the latter sense is considered to be of greater significance.

14. According to Lings, Sufis claim that their entire belief system may be summed up in the following sura (2:156): "We belong to God and to Him we shall return" (Lings 28).

15. The full Qur'anic sura reads as follows: "Do you not see how God compares a good word to a good tree? Its root is firm and its branches are in the sky; it yields its fruit in every season by God's leave. God speaks in parables to men so that they may take heed. But an evil word is like an evil tree torn out of the earth and shorn of all its roots" (14:25).

16. "Profundity is a flat outwardness," Lings observes. "Sufism's dismissal of it is expressed in the words of the Qur'an: 'Say Allah, then leave them to their idle talk' (6:91). The name Allah is . . . the good word which the Qur'an likens to a good tree. Idle or profane talk, that is, flat outward talk, is the bad word which the Qur'an likens to a bad tree sprawling uprooted across the ground for lack of firm foundation" (92).

17. In Sufi discourse, Muhammad himself functions as the "personification of the center" (Lings 38). Lings states "In [Muhammad] the lost perfection is remanifested." Perfection is therefore the "goal" of the Sufi mystic (Harrow, "Camera Layer," 293), that is to say, *al-fana* or "extinction, evanescence; the extinction of the individuality of the Essence in the state of union" (Danner and Lings 73).

18. Ralph Manheim translates the phrase "hommes de rien" (*Le Devoir de violence* 9) as "worthless paupers" in the opening pages of the English translation (*Bound to Violence* 3).

19. The Hadith in question reads, "I was the Hidden Treasure and wished to be known and so I created the world" (see Lings 23).

20. See, for example, Brad G. Martin's historical account of Al-Hajj 'Umar Tall's difficulties in serving as both military leader and Sufi *shaykh* in the Western Sudan (specifically Guinea, Senegal, and Mali) in *Muslim Brotherhoods in Nineteenth-Century Africa* (68–98). Martin argues that 'Umar's conflicting duties

as both religious and secular authority may have led to a form of "schizophrenia" that resulted in 'Umar's eventual fall from power and suicide (94).

21. The phrase "*Amba, kouba oumo agoum*" is Dogon for "God, I grovel at Your feet, begging for mercy from you." It may be worth noting that there are at least seven distinct dialects of the Dogon language. This particular phrase originates in the Bandiagara dialect of Dogon; that is, the village where Ouologuem was born.

22. In *Scribe, Griot, and Novelist*, Hale fortuitously employs the term "scribe" rather than "chronicler" to describe the authors of the *Tarîkh el-Fettach* and the *Tarîkh es-Soudan*, a term originally referring to Palestinian scholars of Jewish law [*sophers*] (30), and which indeed dramatizes the way in which such texts, from a Sufi perspective, may violate the logocentric spirit of Islam; or, as Harrow more simply puts it, "Sufism stands in opposition to Muslim legalism" ("Camera Laye" 265).

23. Seku Amadu was an early nineteenth-century Caliph (of Fulbe descent) whose forgery of the *Tarîkh el-Fettach* has been well-documented. See Robinson, "An Approach to Islam in West African History" (113–114).

24. Bill Ashcroft, Gareth Griffiths, and Helen Tiffin, in their section "Untranslated Words" from *The Empire Writes Back*, observe that "the choice of leaving words untranslated in postcolonial texts is a political act, because while translation is not inadmissible in itself, glossing gives the translated word, and thus the 'receptor' culture, the higher status" (66).

25. For example, many suras in the Qur'an refer to a semantic veil that cloaks the text's sacred or interior meaning, prohibiting access to unbelievers (i.e., "We have cast veils over their hearts lest they understand Our words, and made them hard of hearing" (18:57).

26. The Qur'an does not directly refer to this incident or to Hagar, though the Hadith tradition speaks of both (Torrey 84). Abu Ja'far Muhammad ibn Jarir al-Tabari, early Islamic historian and author of the *Tarîkh al-umum wa al-muluk* [*History of Peoples and Kings*], also retells the story of Hagar, drawing directly from the Biblical account in Genesis, which he regarded as divinely inspired (Parrinder 172). In the Islamic context then, the story of Hagar is drawn from a variety of sources, but not the Qur'an. There is, however, one reference to Zamzam in the Qur'an (2:158), the sanctification of the well following Muhammad's return to Makkah when some charged that Zamzam's sacred status was derived from pagan idolatry (Kamal 61).

27. The doctrine of divine light, or "the light of Muhammad" [*al-Nur al-Muhammadiya*] is a prominent feature of Tidjaniya Sufism in West Africa (Martin 96).

28. In a strictly "exoteric" sense, *maschallah* and *bismillah* can also amount to little more than trite or vulgar expressions, depending upon tone, context, and other considerations, as in Saif's usage (181).

29. Ibn 'Abbad of Ronda states that "exoteric learning is diametrically opposed to Mystic Truth. It leads to inappropriate behavior" (67).

30. While for Harrow, Ouologuem's attack on *maxzen* cults "testifies to the metabolic vitality of Islam," he nevertheless argues that *Le Devoir de violence*'s ultimately "pessimistic" theme may be characterized as "the loss of traditional beliefs," even "the death of God" (13).

31. I am borrowing from Indries Shah's employment of this term in *The Elephant in the Dark: Christianity, Islam, and the Sufis*, by which he means its original Greek sense, "belonging to the whole world" (7).

32. The Qur'an states, for example, that "The believers are a band of brothers. Make peace among your brothers and fear God, so that you may be shown mercy"

(49:10). There are also hadith in which Muhammad states, for example, that "People are equal like the tooth of a weaver's comb; no superiority of the White over the Black or the Arab over the non-Arab" (Gardet 59).

33. One of the most beloved and widely quoted passages of Sufi literature is Ibn 'Arabi's poem "Bewilderment, Love, Madness," which reads: "I profess the religion of love; / Wherever its caravan turns along the way, / that is the belief, / the faith I keep."

Part 4

Interviews: Yambo Ouologuem Today

14

In Search of Yambo Ouologuem

Christopher Wise

Yambo Ouologuem, the Malian author of *Le Devoir de violence* and other literary works, has not been interviewed in nearly three decades. In fact, his doings have been shrouded in mystery ever since he "disappeared" from the West, in effect turning his back on literature. Like Arthur Rimbaud, J. D. Salinger, and others, Ouologuem has become an enigma for many, a mysterious figure as well as a highly respected author. The reasons for Ouologuem's silence are complex and will perhaps never be fully known. It is certain, however, that Ouologuem has blamed the publishers of *Le Devoir de violence* for plagiarism controversies that followed the novel's appearance in 1968.[1] In the early 1970s, Ouologuem claimed that numerous unauthorized deletions had been made in his manuscript, specifically references to Graham Greene's *It's a Battlefield*, André Schwartz-Bart's *Le Dernier des justes*, and other sources. Rather than acknowledging these revisions, the novel's publishers simply disavowed all responsibility and placed the onus entirely upon Ouologuem.[2] Nevertheless, Ouologuem's refusal to write cannot be easily attributed to any ancient grudges he might bear toward the French literary establishment. What complicates matters is Ouologuem's wholehearted return to Islam, the faith of his childhood. In the mid-1970s, Ouologuem returned to Mali, where he is now widely known as a devout marabout, or Muslim holy man.[3] However, as I have argued elsewhere,[4] even the writings of Ouologuem's

This chapter was previously published in *Research in African Literatures,* Vol. 29, No. 2 (Summer 1998). Reprinted with permission of *Research in African Literatures.*

"apostate" period cannot be fully understood without reference to Islam, specifically Tidjaniya Sufism as it has historically been practiced throughout West Africa.

During a year's residency at the Université de Ouagadougou in Burkina Faso, I sought to find Ouologuem and conduct an interview with him, for I hoped to better understand the reasons for his "conversion" to Islam and his rejection of literature. It seemed for a time that my wishes would not be fulfilled. Repeatedly, I was warned that Ouologuem would refuse to see me, or anyone else from the West. Gaoussou Mariko, the U.S. Cultural Affairs Assistant in Bamako, informed me that "Yambo's current state of mind may cause him to be reluctant to meeting [sic] and talking with people." Among my colleagues at the Université de Ouagadougou, I'd also heard many strange rumors and tales. Some claimed that Ouologuem was a great genius—even the "African Joyce"—while others insisted that he was a shameful plagiarist and dangerous lunatic.

My break came during a conference at the Université de Ouagadougou on the literatures of the Sahel, when I delivered a paper on Islam and *Bound to Violence*. In the audience that day happened to be a French professor named Nicole Vinciléoni, who had lived in West Africa for some twenty-five years. After my presentation, Professor Vinciléoni invited me to dinner at her home in Ouagadougou, along with another colleague and friend of mine, Ute Fendler. Professor Vinciléoni told me that she liked my paper in one very important regard: I had suggested that the conflicting demands of secular and religious life among West African Muslims created a kind of "schizophrenia" that could be traced at least as far back as al-Hajj Umar Tall, a thesis that I had first come across in Brad G. Martin's now-classic study, *Muslim Brotherhoods in Nineteenth-Century Africa* (1976). What I had suggested in my presentation was that this non-Western form of "schizophrenia" could be observed in Ouologuem's *Bound to Violence*, although most occidental critics tended to misread Ouologuem's disassociative (or "esoteric") critique of Islam as a blanket dismissal. Professor Vinciléoni had observed such "schizophrenia" often, which for her was not a pejorative term but rather an inadequate, Greek word for an experience little known or understood in the Western world. Since Ouologuem lived in the Sévaré-Mopti area, which was a highly venerated seat for West African Islam, and since Ouologuem had reputedly become a devout Muslim, possibly even a marabout, she recommended that I get in touch with the main religious leaders of the Mosquée Riméibé at Sévaré. If these men felt that Ouologuem should meet with me, it would be difficult for him to refuse an interview.

Professor Vinciléoni also told me that there lived in Ouagadougou a certain al-Hajj Sékou Tall, a well-known local figure and an immediate descendant of al-Hajj Umar Tall, the Peul conqueror and great Sufi *sheikh* who had brought Tidjaniya Islam to the Dogon country—with many prayers and great bloodshed. Through al-Hajj Sékou Tall, it was possible that I could secure an introduction to Ouologuem, or at least to the religious leaders of Sévaré. As it turned out, the husband of Ute Fendler, my German friend who had accompanied me to Professor Vinciléoni's house, was well acquainted with the son of Tall Sékou (or "Sékou Tall," as the name would appear in the West). Jean-Claude Naba, Ute's husband and fellow professor at the Université de Ouagadougou, had once attended school with Tall's son and could probably introduce me to Tall.

In January 1997, Jean-Claude and I drove to Tall's house in one of the older sections of Ouagadougou. After introducing me to Tall's family, including two of Tall's wives, Jean-Claude quietly explained that I was editing a book on Yambo Ouologuem, and that I'd like to include a recent interview and other updated, biographical information. We were concerned, however, because of stories we'd heard about Ouologuem's strange behavior. While Jean-Claude spoke, Tall sat back in his chair, patiently stroking his closely cropped head. He was eighty years old, as I'd found out from Jean-Claude, though he seemed as healthy as a man in his early sixties. In a country where the life expectancy is less than forty years, I was amazed by his vigor and obvious good health. When I got to know him better, I found out that he had some twenty children between four wives. "I saw Yambo four years ago," Tall told us. "At the funeral of his father, Boukary. Yambo's father and I were schoolmates in Bandiagara."

"How did he seem?" Jean-Claude asked. "At the time of the funeral?"

"He's fine. He's not crazy like these people say. It's true that Yambo's a quiet man, but he's not mad. In fact, he teaches French at a lycée in Sévaré."

"So he's not mad?" I said.

"No," Tall said. "He's a religious man, a devout man."

"Is it true he's become a marabout?"

"No, he's a militant, like myself. A marabout teaches the Quran to children. Yambo is serious about his religion, but he's not a marabout. A marabout has a particular job." In his free hand, Tall clutched a white, intricately woven prayer cap along with a handsome, silver-handled cane. He was a big man with thin, gangly limbs from under his black robe. It was clear that he wanted to say something further but wasn't sure how to begin. "If you like," he said, "I can send my son Mountaga with you. He can introduce you to Yambo on my behalf." When he saw my response, Tall became even more thoughtful. Then he began to tell us that there had been a recent death in his family. One of his brothers, who had been chief at Bandiagara in the Dogon country, had recently died. For a long time, it was believed that Sékou Tall himself, as direct heir of al-Hajj Umar Tall, would be appointed as new chief. However, an older brother had been found, which meant that Tall was now officially second-in-line to become chief at Bandiagara.

Much of this history, Tall told us with a deliberate end, for he had decided to accompany me to Mali himself, along with his son Mountaga, so that he could formally greet his older brother, the recently appointed chief of Bandiagara. First, we would attend to the business of meeting Yambo Ouologuem, Tall said, and then we'd drive on to Bandiagara. What remained now was to work out the details of our journey.

Because of the excruciating heat that would come to the Sahel after February, our trip to Mali could not be delayed for long. One practical problem was transportation. My own Toyota station wagon worked well within the city of Ouagadougou, but it was not made for trips to the bush (as I had found out the hard way). What we needed was a four-wheel-drive, or "*quatre-quatre*," which would no doubt quadruple my costs. However, there was a friend of mine, an American named Robert Hans, who worked for the World Bank, and who was willing to take us in his Jeep Cherokee. Besides Tall and his son Mountaga, we had arranged for Robert's driver to accompany us, a Liberian political refugee named James Wade. Due to our late start, we planned to spend the first night in Ouahigouya, Tall's "hometown" of sorts, and then we would drive into Sévaré the next morning.

As the African bush blurred outside the car window, Tall's son Mountaga explained to me the many complicated alliances wherein his father had come to be heir-apparent to the chiefdom of Bandiagara, as well as the "first Muslim" in Ouahigouya. According to Mountaga, Sékou Tall was the great-grandson of al-Hajj Umar Tall; grandson of Aguibou Tall, builder of the palace at Bandiagara; and son of Alpha Makí Tall. Mountaga also informed me that the chief at Bandiagara was in reality chief of the entire Dogon people. At first, this seemed confusing to me given the rather obvious fact that Sékou Tall was himself Peul (or Fulani) and not Dogon. In other words, I couldn't figure out why a Peul was to be appointed chief of the Dogon people. The more Mountaga spoke, however, I gradually began to realize what I should have known from the start: Tall was himself descendant of the very Saifs criticized in Ouologuem's novel, the so-called "black Jews" who, according to Ouologuem, shamefully exploited the teachings of Islam to oppress the masses of Nakem, or the more "primitive" Dogon.

Later, when I asked Tall if it was true that the Peul were Jews, I saw that my use of the word "Jew" had been indiscreet, acceptable only because I was a foreigner. What Tall preferred to say was that the Peul originally came from Palestine, which avoided the more distasteful allusion to Jews. "It is said that the Peul are a white stream in a land of black water,"

Tall said, "a black stream in a land of white water." The Dogon people that I spoke with in Mali did not take such a lyrical view of things, but the mysterious origins of the Peul turned out to be a favorite topic of Tall's, who was obviously proud of his ancestry.

Still, what I had not fully understood before speaking with Mountaga was that Yambo Ouologuem's grandfather, Umar Karambé Ouologuem—who was of course Dogon—had conspired with the family of al-Hajj Umar Tall to subdue the Dogon country on behalf of the Peul. In fact, this is how Sékou Tall and Boukary Ouologuem, Yambo's father, had come to be childhood friends. For, unlike the vast majority of Malians, Yambo Ouologuem was no *lumpenproletariat*, or poor subaltern, but rather one of the wealthiest and most highly educated men in Mali. However, if Ouologuem came from an elite, aristocratic caste, I saw now that it was because his family had sided with the Peul in ruling over the Dogon people.

From Sékou Tall, I also learned that Ouologuem came from a long line of Tidjaniya Muslims, the very form of Sufism imported by al-Hajj Umar Tall. Sékou Tall himself was a practicing Tidjaniya Muslim, though he preferred not to talk about it, except to say that it was dangerous to discuss such things. Although Yambo Ouologuem would not have been directly exposed to Sufi teachings as a child—since, as Tall pointed out, Sufi teachings are certainly *not* matters for children—Yambo's ancestors on both sides of his family were among the most prominent Tidjaniya Muslims in the region. In other words, for Tall, Yambo Ouologuem was in some sense "born" a Tidjaniya Muslim.

The more I learned about Ouologuem's prominent family, the better I understood Tall's earlier insistence that Yambo Ouologuem was no marabout. For Tall, a marabout taught the Quran to young children and was supported by his pupils who begged for alms on his behalf. In many Dogon villages today, Mountaga explained, Muslim children as young as four years old commonly leave their parents to follow a marabout for several years, until they have sufficiently mastered the Quran. A child's time with a marabout is determined by his ability to orally recite the Quran from memory. In this way, the marabout can devote his life to religion and to the study of the Quran. Because Yambo Ouologuem came from a wealthy family and because he was freed from the necessity of taking on pupils, this disqualified him in Tall's eyes from being a marabout. In Sévaré, however, others told me that there were marabouts who did not take on pupils, whose wealth made it possible for them to be freed from this obligation. Despite Tall's reservations, the consensus in Sévaré was that Ouologuem was most definitely a marabout. However, as I was soon to learn, Tall was mistaken about Ouologuem in other ways as well.

For, when we finally arrived in Sévaré the next afternoon and began to search for Ouologuem in earnest, Tall was clearly astounded at the reports we heard: at the Mosquée Riméibé, an ancient imam named Pâte-Touré, who was nearly blind and almost toothless, told us that Ouologuem was indeed a marabout but a very dangerous one, a man who walked the hardest of paths. He had become an expert in the Quran, in the Arab language, and in Muslim literature. As the old imam fingered his rosary, Sékou Tall leaned forward in his chair, his mouth agape at the accounts of Ouologuem's doings. As it turned out, Ouologuem not only did *not* teach at the French school, but his hatred of the French was such that he sent his own children to the Arab-language school in Sévaré. At present, he occupied a government post at a *maison de jeunesse*, which required very little of him. This was necessary, the old imam told us, because Yambo did not have many lucid days; in fact, in the eyes of most, Ouologuem was quite mad. Though reluctant to use such terms himself, Pâte-Touré insisted that Yambo's was a special case, a man who had been "touched" by Allah.

The old man told us about the incident, recorded by Thomas Hale in *Scribe, Griot, and Novelist*, when Ouologuem threw rocks at two French tourists who had attempted to photograph the inside of the Mosquée Riméibé. This incident had a quasi-legendary status in Sévaré, and we were to hear several different versions of it during our stay. But there were other incidents as well. Not long ago, Ouologuem had provoked a quarrel at the public courthouse, exhibiting such rage that many fled in terror. On the streets, he might approach a Muslim brother and began expounding upon the most esoteric of questions regarding quranic law, the hadith, dress codes, and other arcane religious matters. While his discourses were often brilliant, he tolerated absolutely no interruptions or contradictions. If his monologues were ever interrupted, he would break off, as if deeply affronted, and then go abruptly about his business.

One incident in particular seemed to bother the old imam. Before prayers one Friday, he had met Ouologuem on his way to the mosque. Under one arm, Yambo had carried a worn edition of the Quran. When the old imam extended his right hand in greeting, Ouologuem declined to shake hands, claiming that he had not yet performed his ablutions. In refusing to shake hands, Ouologuem implied that he was unclean, yet his right hand rested upon his Quran. For Pâte-Touré, no other conclusion was possible: it was not Yambo Ouologuem who was unclean but he himself. Given the saintly demeanor of the old man, such an inference seemed not only highly insulting but comical. It upset Sékou Tall so much he got up from his chair and began pacing the room.

"I can only warn you to be cautious," Pâte-Touré said. "There is a precedent. Two other Americans came before you, and Yambo hid himself in the mosque for two days. I wish you the best of luck in your venture but you must use extreme care. May God's blessing and peace be with you."

We dropped off Sékou Tall and Mountaga at the home of their relatives, and Robert and I took a room at the Hotel Oasis in Sévaré, as it turned out, across from a large piece of property that was owned and managed by Ouologuem. Tall planned on meeting with Ouologuem's uncle that evening, the former mayor of Sévaré, al-Hajj Timbely Umar, to arrange the introduction. From the hotel patron and his son, I heard more stories about Ouologuem, his religious fervor, his wealthy father, and his eccentric behavior. The patron, however, insisted that the best way to meet Ouologuem was not through his uncle, whom Ouologuem distrusted, but through his mother. "Yambo will do anything his mother says," the patron told us. "He listens absolutely to his mother." I declined his offer to take me "vite-vite" to meet Ouologuem's mother, but walked over to Ouologuem's property, where I saw many small gardens and little straw shacks. From the people I had spoken with so far, including Tall's acquaintances in Sévaré, the blind imam, and now the patron and his son, I could only conclude that the majority of people here believed Ouologuem to be a religious fanatic and near lunatic. The word that I heard repeatedly in connection with Ouologuem was "le fou," or madman, yet all agreed that he was the most highly educated person in Mali and a truly great man. "They really treated him very badly over there," the patron said. "You see, the French did this to him."

That night, al-Hajj Timbely Umar came to pay his respects to Sékou Tall as we all sat in the courtyard of Tall's relatives in Sévaré. Timbely was accompanied by nearly a dozen elegantly dressed men, who encircled him as if part of a royal entourage. Timbely himself wore a white *bou-bou* with gold trimming and a white prayer cap. His face was truly remarkable, one of the wisest-looking men I'd ever seen. After Tall and Timbely exchanged greetings, Robert and I were introduced. I explained to Timbely that I was editing a collection of essays on his nephew, Yambo Ouologuem, and I'd like to speak with him. I did not want to disturb him if he truly wished to be left alone, but I wanted to be sure that he was aware of this opportunity to air his views. Timbely listened patiently to my explanation, his hands resting on a scepterlike cane. At last, he told me that he was happy I'd come and that in actuality he'd been anticipating my visit.

"I will do what I can to help you," he said, "but you must know that Yambo has not been himself lately, especially since the death of his father," Timbely paused, carefully searching for the right words. "Life has lost its flavor for Yambo. You might say that he has become disgusted with the business of living. He has rejected all things worldly and spends his time reciting the Quran and praying. He has even built a small mosque in the courtyard of his house. For a long time, all of us have waited for a change to come to him."

One of Timbely's nephews described Yambo's current state of being. As before, we heard of Ouologuem's dislike of the French and apparently for whites in general. We also heard once again that he had difficulty conversing in any meaningful sense: he often lectured on Islam—sometimes brilliantly, sometimes incoherently—but he rarely engaged others in true dialogue. On the streets, Ouologuem at times greeted his friends, but he might just as likely ignore them altogether. One evening, when a group of lycée students, both boys and girls, happened to study together under a streetlight, Ouologuem grew so enraged at the impropriety of this gathering that he grabbed a stick and smashed the streetlight into pieces. He also regularly lectured the Muslim mothers of Sévaré who allowed their daughters to expose their hair outside their veils or who wore any kind of decorative mesh. For the second time, I heard a story about Ouologuem's refusal to accept his government pension, much to the chagrin of his family. Because Ouologuem believed the present Malian government and president to be corrupt, he refused to accept any money from them whatsoever.

"After the death of Yambo's father," Timbely added, "we all gathered at the mosque to read the Quran. It is customary for the son to make a sacrifice on such occasions, and so Yambo came to the mosque carrying several large books, all written in the Arab language. He wanted us to spend the next few weeks reading these books and studying them with him. We agreed to recite the Quran with him, but we refused to even look at the other books. There were so many of them, we would have been reading books for the next two years."

That evening, as friends and relatives described Yambo's behavior, many laughed at his eccentricity, but their laughter seemed indulgent, not ridiculing. If Ouologuem was "fou," he was apparently functioning well enough, living on the inheritance from his father, taking care of his immediate family, and practicing his highly idiosyncratic Islam. When I tried to thank Timbely for helping me, he only shrugged and said that he considered it his duty. Above all, he wanted to help Yambo get over his bitterness. "He speaks often of a certain French publisher and his years in France," Timbely said. "We are not sure here what happened there, but it was obviously something terrible." I explained the best I could the controversies surrounding *Bound to Violence*, how many had accused Ouologuem of plagiarism. I could see, however, that the details of this controversy did not really interest those present: for most, it was simply another example of French irresponsibility toward Africans, but in this case Yambo was the victim. "The important thing is that you have come," Timbely said. "We will attend to Yambo tomorrow."

During breakfast the next morning, Robert and I reviewed Timbely's plan for meeting Ouologuem. First, Timbely and Sékou Tall would go alone to greet him on the pretext that Tall wanted to express condolences over the death of Yambo's father. (This confused me somewhat since, in Ouagadougou, Tall had originally told me that he'd personally attended the funeral of Boukary Ouologuem.) After sufficient time passed, Robert and I would then casually join them and, in the company of Timbely, Tall, and others, Ouologuem would most likely be on his best behavior. Timbely also warned us to hide Robert's Jeep Cherokee, which still bore the decals of Coopération Française, the French organization from which Robert had purchased the vehicle. If Yambo saw the decals and believed we were French, it was certain he would have nothing to do with us.

When we arrived at our predetermined meeting place, a complication arose when it turned out that Ouologuem was not at home but making a tour of Sévaré. Tall and I were content to await his return, but Robert grew frustrated and insisted that we drive to the mosque to find him. "Listen, Tall will sit around here chewing kola-nuts all morning," he told me. "Then we'll never get anywhere. Believe me, it's like this at my office. You've got to push these guys at times, or you'll never get anything done." We argued the question for awhile, but Tall himself had no objections to Robert's plan, so we all climbed into the Jeep and began searching for Ouologuem. At last, we found him at the public courthouse, where he'd gone to photocopy some old documents. These documents, we learned later, were letters written by some Frenchmen during Mali's colonial period. Ouologuem wanted them preserved in the public archives as a testament to France's crimes in Sévaré. For now, we carefully hid the Jeep behind a tree, while Tall and Timbely approached Ouologuem on the front steps of the courthouse. A few minutes later, Umar Sow, one of Tall's nephews, motioned for us to come.

Ouologuem never saw our approach because his back faced us, and he was deeply engrossed in conversation with Tall and Timbely. He wore a sky-blue *bou-bou* with a white scarf, white slippers, and a white prayer cap. His arms dramatically flailed about as he spoke, the packet of letters clutched in one hand. He immediately noted our presence but did not break off his speech. When Timbely introduced us, he irritably shook our hands but did not allow the flow of his lecture to be interrupted, an energetic clarification of the different orders of Muslim religious leaders. However, his speech became faster and angrier, his eyes glaringly fastened upon his uncle. As he spoke, I became transfixed by his face, which seemed to me profoundly ugly, not unlike a bust I'd once seen of Socrates, the dog-faced philosopher, or perhaps Danton. His cheeks were round and enormous, and they were set in an intense if not bellicose grimace. I lost his train of thought and only caught up again when he made a heated reference to Judas Ischariot, all the while glowering at his uncle.

Timbely only smiled serenely, and soon we all sat upon metal chairs, brought out by the judge and his secretaries, as Ouologuem continued his discussion of the Muslim laity. I asked him if I could record his voice, but he refused and said, "No, this is not an interview. I came to the courthouse to visit my friends, that is all. Besides, these things can be used against me. I have been exploited before." Nevertheless, his friends repeatedly encouraged him to speak with me or at least to look at the list of questions I'd prepared. In the large circle of his elders and friends, I began to feel sorry for Ouologuem, who had clearly been ambushed by all of us. After awhile, however, he warmed to the idea of being interviewed and even seemed to enjoy the attention he was receiving. He spoke freely on a wide range of subjects, though he never directly answered any of my questions. In fact, he spoke for about three hours altogether. During this time, I listened attentively, wondering how I could possibly remember everything he'd said. Later, after going over my notes with Robert, Sékou Tall, and Mountaga, we all agreed upon the basics of what we'd heard.

However, it was difficult to follow Ouologuem's reasoning since his speech was filled with references to his private dreams, prayers, and religious experiences. He also spoke in parables, analogies, and riddles, insisting that the Greek syllogism was vastly inferior to the paradox in its communicative power. His reading in Muslim literature clearly exceeded that of everyone present, who deferred entirely to him in these matters. Often, he built upon a subtle network of allusions from the Quran and the hadith, which he seemed to assume—erroneously—was shared knowledge by all those present. Repeatedly, he insisted that God speaks through dreams, that the future can be known if we are attentive to our dreams. At times, whenever the subject of French colonialism drifted into his speech, he grew angry all over again, leaning forward in his chair, his voice nearly shouting in rage. His energy was intense, perhaps manic, and when he broke off into a sudden joke, dispelling his previous acrimony, our relief was immense. After one of his jokes, Ouologuem would often slap hands with the judge, with whom he was on very good terms.

Perhaps Ouologuem's most important revelation was that former president Moctar Oul Dada had once offered him a position as minister of education in Mauritania, clearly no job for a "fou." Three times Ouologuem had been asked to journey from Mali to Mauritania to completely reform its educational system. The first two times, Ouologuem had refused the offer, leery of the intent of Mauritania's Arab-led government, whose policies toward blacks have historically verged on the genocidal. Given the fact that Mauritania banned slavery as recently as 1980, Ouologuem was rightly cautious about Dada's offer. However, the third time, Ouologuem had been visited at his house by the ambassador of Mauritania in Mali and by Mali's ambassador in Nouakchott. This time, Ouologuem accepted the offer, contingent upon an interim period of several months, so that he might have time for prayer and reflection. However, for reasons that were never clear to me, Ouologuem had not yet assumed this position, apparently as a result of certain political complications that had later developed. The challenges he would confront there would arise chiefly from his desire to synthesize the requirements of a thoroughly modern and yet thoroughly Quranic education. He was inclined to accept the position, he told us, because of his desire to end the suffering of his brothers in Mauritania, that is, black Muslims who have historically been oppressed and enslaved by Arab Muslims.

At no point was Ouologuem willing to discuss his writings, and even questions related to literature seemed to irritate him. "I will leave that for you smart ones, the professors," he told me. "I am not a 'smart' man, thanks be to Allah, and 'smart' subjects do not interest me." When I mentioned the name of Wole Soyinka, Ouologuem would not let me finish my sentence. "Another 'smart' one," he said. "An intellectual."

Many of his most hostile remarks were directed at the publishing industry and its many prizes, like the Nobel Prize given to Soyinka. He saw such prizes as a way of controlling African writers and the kind of literature they produced. Ouologuem's criticism, however, was not so much directed against Soyinka as against the publishing industry at large and the way in which Africa's best minds were routinely exploited by faraway presses and the demands of a foreign readership. In his own case, *Bound to Violence* had been published before he'd even signed a contract and after numerous unauthorized changes had been made on his manuscript. The most famous editorial change was, of course, his editor's deletion of quotation marks in passages later labeled as "plagiarized," a fact never denied by his publisher. Ouologuem also claimed that his novel had been translated into English without his consent. If neo-colonization was to be fought, Ouologuem said, the book industry itself would have to be entirely restructured. One place to start was the prize system with its seductive but pernicious cash awards. On an even more critical note, Ouologuem spoke harshly of Léopold Sédar Senghor, "the most French" of African writers and "a black man who wished that his skin was white."

In fact, one of Ouologuem's greatest fears seemed to be that he would be turned into a "petit Senghor," a Malian curiosity like the mosque at Djenné or any other tourist attraction. The scorn that Ouologuem heaped upon Senghor echoed a common attitude about the Senegalese throughout the Dogon country. Whereas the Senegalese abused the Dogon as "primitives," the local Dogon (as well as Peul, Malinké, and others) ridiculed the Senegalese as French "bootlickers" and self-hating blacks. In any event, almost everyone present seemed to share Ouologuem's sentiments about Senghor, or they were at least amused by his rapid-fire monologue. When I asked him his views on the Salman Rushdie affair, Ouologuem refused to comment (as he did with any of my direct questions), but it was clear he'd given the matter a great deal of thought. His friend, the judge, seemed particularly upset that Ouologuem would not respond to my question, and he informed us that they had been discussing Rushdie only a day ago. However, Ouologuem steadfastly refused to comment, except to say that his remarks would probably be misunderstood and used against him. In fact, Ouologuem returned to his invective against Senghor, and to the amusement of all, he began to ridicule négritude, especially its reception in the United States. At this point, it dawned on me that Ouologuem believed I was myself an African American in some remote way, a suspicion that was later confirmed when he confided that he'd foreseen this visit in a dream.

It was evident that the situation of the African American, especially in the United States, incessantly occupied his attention and even formed a private obsession with him. He spoke at length of his time in the United States, his appreciation of Malcolm X, his meetings with Cassius Clay, and his participation in the formation of black studies programs at several American universities. When Robert asked him which states he visited, Ouologuem again refused to answer directly, but he finally laughed and said, "In any case, I was not in any pious state." Unexpectedly, he blurted out, "You know, we Africans cannot be held accountable for the actions of our brothers over there. This is a fallacy. Many would disagree with me, of course, and I have heard it said that if your goat destroys your neighbor's garden, you are responsible for the damage. Still, these Africans who are causing so much trouble are not Muslims." Like Senghor and all advocates of négritude, he said, blacks in the United States are too obsessed with skin color. "They have been infected by too many poisonous ideas. In Islam, however, there is no color." Here, Ouologuem cited two or three hadith wherein it is said that people of all colors are equal in God's eyes.

"Blacks in America must repent," he insisted. "Until they do so, they will continue to live in their own private hell, and this has nothing to do with us in Africa." Here, Ouologuem claimed that his own problem, as well as that of his fellow Malians, was hardly a question of skin color but rather imperialism. With the arrival of the French in Mali, the plight of his fellow Dogon was more closely akin to that of the American Indian, "a new spaghetti Western" in Africa. Above all, he feared that an extraordinarily rich culture and its many ancient customs could be destroyed in favor of the most vulgar technological innovations—all in the name of modernization and "progress." Later, I was to learn how serious he was about this when I discovered that, much to the frustration of his wife and mother, Ouologuem refused to allow electricity to be installed at his house in Sévaré. Ouologuem also refused to have his photograph taken by me, citing the biblical injunction against graven images. Timbely, Tall, and everyone present expressed their outrage at Ouologuem's refusal and even pleaded with him to change his mind. I also reminded him that I'd seen a movie theater across from the Mosquée Riméibé, but he would not budge. The Quran tolerated no equivocation on this issue, he said. In fact, this was one of the most defining features of Islam, as opposed to more infidel variants of Ibrahimic religion. As for the movie theater, this was a fault of the local Muslim community, much to be regretted.

By now, Robert and some of the others had wandered off, and only a few of us remained. As our discussion wound down, Umar Timbely spoke at length, though he had previously said little. Whatever rancor Ouologuem harbored for his uncle for "betraying" him, he evidently held him in great esteem and was sufficiently respectful to him, not unlike a young man in the presence of his father. Indeed, it was difficult not to be slightly in awe of Timbely, who had all the trappings of a great king. "We are all happy that you have come this far to see Yambo," Timbely said, "and I believe that you will be fair to him, for I can see by your face that you are an honest and just man. That is all we ask really, that you be fair. Yambo has been treated poorly in the past. He has been exploited and misrepresented. It is only right that he receive justice at last."

At the words of his uncle, Yambo's defiant attitude seemed to dissipate, and he relaxed for the first time that morning. He thanked his uncle for his words, and I promised to do my best to be fair to Yambo. In the meantime, Robert had returned, and he was obviously anxious to be on the road. In fact, throughout the interview, Robert had buried himself in a recent issue of *The Economist*, especially during moments in which Ouologuem discussed his private dreams. It was evident that Ouologuem did not know what to make of this American, with his short trousers, CD walkman, and two-day beard stubble. Tall also seemed disturbed, attempting to cajole Robert by informing everyone that he was "le frère de Clinton." Robert disavowed Tall's remark with a shrug and said, "I can't be Clinton's brother. Clinton's a Christian, and I'm a Jew."

If he'd intended to shock everyone, he enjoyed one of his greatest successes. However, there were more surprises in store for us, for in the interim he had instructed his driver to bring the Jeep Cherokee around. When we left together from the courthouse, James stood directly in front of the Coopération Française decal until the moment Yambo turned the corner. At that point, James had been told to step aside and reveal the decal. Later, Robert told me that he'd merely wanted to "get a rise" out of Ouologuem to see if he couldn't "turn Yambo into Rambo." Not surprisingly, Ouologuem was distressed when he saw the French decal, until we were able to assure him that Robert had only purchased his vehicle from the French and that he was indeed a real American.

Afterwards, we were all exhilarated at our great success. Those who knew Yambo were amazed that he'd spoken at such length. Umar Timbely told me that we'd caught Yambo on a good day, when he'd been at his absolute best. Our luck had been extraordinary: He had been lucid, funny, sharp-witted, and entirely coherent. It was true that there had been moments of great intensity, when we all sensed his tremendous anger, but the presence of Timbely, Tall, and the others seemed to have a calming effect upon him. In retrospect, I questioned the local consensus that Ouologuem was mad, which seemed to me entirely too severe a judgment upon him. Sékou Tall also assured me that, in his own estimation, Ouologuem was no madman. "He's a disappointed man," Tall said. "But he's not any madder than the rest of us." In parting, I left a copy of my interview questions with Umar Sow, one of Tall's nephews. Mountaga informed me that Yambo would pray about this matter during our journey to Bandiagara. On our return trip through Sévaré, he would decide whether or not to speak with me any further.

In Bandiagara, we lost Sékou Tall, who had insisted upon returning to Ouagadougou a day early and taking Mountaga with him. Our parting had not been on the best of terms, so when we returned to Sévaré, there were a few awkward moments when I tried to explain to Tall's relatives what had happened: either Tall had confused our original return dates, or I had somehow misunderstood him. At the moment, Robert was back at the hotel in Mopti, down with a serious upset stomach, so I'd only brought James with me to the house of Tall's relatives. Umar Sow, Tall's oldest nephew, heard me out, and then he walked me over to the house of al-Hajj Umar Timbely, Ouologuem's uncle. There, I explained all over again what had happened with Sékou Tall.

In his own house, which seemed like a palace with its complex of buildings, courtyards, and labyrinthine corridors, Timbely's stature was even further enhanced, and I realized now that he was a man of incredible, even extravagant, wealth. When a friend stopped by, Timbely introduced me as "the one who had come to bring about the change in Yambo." In fact, Timbely was quite excited about what had transpired in my absence. "Yambo came to see me twice," he said. Timbely repeated the word "twice" as if this was a fact of remarkable significance. "The first time, he was furious that I'd dared to bring a Jew into his presence. He told me that this was unforgivable. But he returned the next day, and he was very happy this time. He wanted to know when you were coming back. It is certain he will see you again."

Immediately, we sent out James and a nephew of Timbely's to see if Ouologuem wouldn't come by. They'd been instructed to tell Yambo that I was leaving in the morning and that I wanted to say farewell. In the interim, we discussed the student strike in Ouagadougou, and President

Blaise Camparoré's recent amendment to the Burkinabè constitution.[5] Our conversation was interrupted, however, when James and Timbely's nephew returned with news of Yambo. "You must come quick," James said. "He wants you to come to his house." I saw that James was flustered, even radiant, after speaking with Ouologuem. I quickly bid farewell to Timbely and followed James to Ouologuem's house. James smiled broadly and could not contain his excitement. "I didn't know what your mission was," he said. "Robert told me to stay out of it. It was only tonight that I finally understood. But now I've spoken with Yambo, and I can see that he's a great man, a blessed man." James stopped walking for a moment, and then he exploded in laughter. "But, of course, this guy's completely mad."

"What do you mean?" I said.

"His English is good. This guy speaks better English than people in Liberia. He told me that he wouldn't come to his uncle's house because his uncle is a member of a certain political party in this country that's been exploiting him for the past thirty-three years. He said, 'The reason I don't pay any attention to them is because I consider them to be very insignificant. They think that what they are doing is great, but what they are doing is very simple and worthless, and that's why I don't even question them. They think that I'm a fool, but they are the fools. He's sitting over there calling me. Go and tell Christopher that I'm not going to that house.'"

"Tell me exactly what happened," I said. "What did he say when you approached him?"

"He was coming back from a funeral and had been praying all afternoon. When he saw me, he said in English, 'Where is Christopher's friend? The one with the short trousers?'

"'He's not feeling well,' James told him. 'He has an upset stomach.'

"'His sins will see him through. He's very insolent.'

"'No, he's only joking around,'" I told him. "'He likes to joke. He's not really insolent.'

"'He's a Jew,' he said. 'And you were trying to play smart. I saw you at the car. You went to the car to cover up that sign. What are you trying to hide? Coopération Française? You see, they have bought you. And they reduce you. You have sold your dignity. Just as they have killed Thomas Sankara and taken his body to Wall Street.'"[6]

"He spoke of Sankara?" I asked.

"Yes, he said the body of Thomas Sankara has been taken to Wall Street. So, I asked him, 'Why Wall Street? Why not Paris?'

"'Blaise Camporé will account for that,' he said. 'He will explain why they didn't take his body to Paris and instead to Wall Street. Blaise Campaoré will explain that when the time comes. It's just a matter of time. But you Liberians,' he said, 'from the day of your independence, you have been killing one another. And you will continue to kill one another because you have abused your identity. When the Americans realized they were very wicked in dealing with blacks, they decided to export them, to get rid of the rejects. That is what 'Liberia' means. It comes from a latin word meaning 'the condemned ones,' the ones who were condemned by the whites. They had to find a place for these rejects, and they chose Liberia.'" At this James began to laugh all over again and assured me what a brilliant man Yambo was. "'But the whites made one mistake,' he said. 'They should've left everything with the blacks, but they decided to run things themselves. If they'd done this, today there would be no blacks in America. Instead of giving black Americans the chance to administer their own affairs, they interfered, and today they regret it.'

"'They got a lot of blacks over in the United States who don't know the direction of their lives, and they are condemned to hell. These blacks say they admire me, they admire my books, but I care nothing for them because they have forgotten their brothers, the suffering masses in Africa. They have sold their dignity. If they really admired me, they would come to Africa and join me for what I have fasted the past ten years, and for what I'm still fasting. I am fasting because I want to see black people everywhere freed from their oppression.'"

By now, we'd arrived at Ouologuem's house, where I was to hear much of what James told me repeated. For the moment, I was too astonished to know how to respond. We knocked on Ouologuem's gate and were greeted by his mother, an ancient, veiled woman who had some trouble with the heavy chains upon the metal posts. The old woman informed us that, unfortunately, Yambo could not speak with us that evening because he was in mourning and occupied with his nightly prayers. We persisted, however, insisting that it was Yambo who had sent for us. "I'm leaving early tomorrow morning," I told her. "I have an important message for him." Finally, she relented and went to get her son. Ouologuem greeted us but refused to shake hands, as he had already performed his ablutions. Our presence did not seem to make him happy, but his mother offered us chairs while he himself sat upon a huge, felled tree limb. It was completely dark now, except for the light of the moon and stars. Ouologuem's courtyard had a wild, unkempt look with scraggly bushes and vegetation everywhere. We were also introduced to Ouologuem's grandmother, who sat in complete darkness further under the house's awnings.

"I will speak with you tonight at your insistence," he said, "but it would be better if I said nothing." He spoke in English now, and James had been right about his mastery of the language, which was total. "You must know that you are in grave danger," he said. "You and the Liberian are in grave danger here. There are people who would like to kill you. I refused to speak with you because I wanted to protect you. For now, I shall pray for you." From where I sat on a short-legged, metal chair, Ouologuem seemed larger than he actually was, his face, scarf, and prayer cap illuminated by moonlight. "It has been four years now since I saw you in a dream," he said, rubbing his eyes. "I dreamed that a Jew would bring me a Liberian and an African-American." Here, he stopped and looked me over: the fact that I did not seem to be black disturbed him, but only slightly. "These things that I know are hard for you to understand, I realize this. I have the authority to speak the way I want to speak, but if I decide to talk to people like you, I must put things in simpler terms. Still, it would be better if I said nothing at all.

"Silence is always better, you see. This is why I refuse to answer your questions. We speak too much, myself included. Jesus was a silent man. Muhammad was a silent man too. We forget this with all our books and radios. We drown ourselves in meaningless noise. But, if you are able to be silent, you will see that it is much better than speaking." He paused for a moment and placed both hands on his knees. He seemed tired now, as if indeed the effort to speak exhausted him. "I have seen Jesus more than fifty times," he said. "I have spoken with him and with the Prophet. The angels too, including Gabriel, and they're mostly silent. You must be very careful with people who speak a lot. They think that they know a lot, but they really know nothing." Ouologuem himself fell into silence at this point, as if listening for the sound of the wind blowing through the trees.

It was James who finally spoke. "You are truly a blessed man," he said softly. "God has truly blessed you."

"I am not a blessed man," Yambo insisted. "Far from it. I am simply a man who is seeking God's blessing."

"But you have knowledge," James said, "and knowledge is power."

"No, knowledge is not power. When you are blessed by God, then you acquire wisdom. And when you acquire wisdom, then you have power. Knowledge in itself is not power. You see, God has allowed me to journey to the very frontiers of the human mind. I have seen them unfold before my eyes." With this Ouologuem swept his hand over his head, urging us to look up at the stars. "The world we live in is truly magnificent," he said. "In Allah, all things are possible if we are only open to them."

There was another long moment of silence, until Ouologuem's mother cleared her throat, signaling for him to dismiss us. "If there's just one message you have," I said quickly, "if there was just one thing you'd like to say to black people in America, what is it?" I'm not sure why I asked such a question, but I said the first thing that came to mind.

"Go back to America and tell my black brothers that I've been fasting for the last ten years on their behalf. I've been fasting so that they'll come back to Africa. Tell them to come back to help ease our suffering, and Allah will be merciful. That is the first thing you must say. Then you may tell them that I am now preparing to take over the leadership of the educational system in Mauritania, where blacks suffer more than anywhere on earth. I hope to help establish there a truly Islamic government that will administer to the total affairs of Mauritanians, including Arabs. The worst enemies for blacks right now are racist Arabs, Arabs who have been satanically blessed with oil and who are now funding the Jews and apartheid-type governments everywhere. It is the Arabs who are sponsoring all these organizations that are against blacks, and who invest their money in Switzerland, America, and South Africa. Many have tried to stop me in this, but I am not so easily defeated. The French have tried to stop me. Even the CIA has offered me a few million dollars. The CIA has already done what it could to me, and they think they have defeated me, but they are mistaken. That is all I have to say."

Ouologuem arose from where he sat, preparing to dismiss us. He again apologized for not shaking our hands and told us that it was time for his evening prayers, that we had detained him long enough. He disappeared into the darkness of his courtyard, and we were led to the gate by his mother.

That night I had many questions for James about his long walk with Ouologuem while I waited at Timbely's house. Though it had not been possible to record Ouologuem's words, James's short-range memory was excellent—in fact, far better than mine—so I recorded our conversation back at the hotel, as we told Robert about our adventure. Robert was feeling slightly better though his face was quite pale. When James and I had finished speaking, Robert sat up in his bed and laughed. "Yambo's a nutcase," he said. "A paranoid schizophrenic, and what's worse, an anti-Semite. Seriously, the guy could benefit from medication. He might not be able to talk to Jesus all that often, but he could function better." When James repeated that Ouologuem was fine, Robert said, "You don't think he's all that mad because you talk to Jesus all the time. That's the way it is with you religious types."

"Yes," James said simply. "This man is blessed. He said a lot of good things. He's right about blacks in America too. Africa is the place they come from, but blacks over there don't come and help us. Our brothers in America do not care for us. When we are together, they treat us worse than white men do, as if we are inferior to them. If you look around at all these programs in Africa, the majority of Americans who come are white. Why? With the Peace Corps, even the white ladies are willing to go to the villages and teach our people, but blacks are not willing to come. The problem is that we do not love one another."

"Look, it's hard for *all* Americans here," Robert said. "Things are so different in Africa you don't know what the hell's going on half the time.

It's even harder for blacks who have to adjust to this place and then deal with all this bullshit about being 'African American.' Most blacks in the United States don't have a clue what goes on in Africa. They've got enough problems of their own."

James listened carefully, but he was far from convinced. I remembered then that he'd lost a child and his wife had lost an arm before they'd fled Liberia as political refugees. Sometime later, James had converted to an anti-Catholic, charismatic form of Christianity, some import from the United States. "Okay," James said, "there is truth in what you say, but Yambo is still right. When I was at a refugee camp in Côte d'Ivoire, a brother of Michael Jackson came to sing for us. He came there, and he stood on a bench. Everyone wanted to see this Jackson hero. We were all suffering, and we were glad this guy came to help us. So we listened, and he said, 'You know, I gotta tell you, America is a useless country. America got itself involved in the Middle East thing, in the Gulf War, wasting billions of dollars when they got you here suffering.' So we all looked at one another and said, 'This guy is mad.' There were many highly educated people among the group, some professors, and they too said, 'This guy is mad.' 'You know, when I get back to America,' he said, 'I'm gonna get to Congress and do something for you.' I tell you," James said. "We wanted to stone him. This useless guy came, and he made a lot of promises. Then he left, doing nothing."

"What was he supposed to do?" Robert said. "Save Africa all by himself? Believe me, it can't be done. It's not possible. You know, I'm not a religious person, but I believe very strongly that God helps those who help themselves. There are many Jews in the United States like myself who have been very successful. But no one helped me. No one gave me a job or cut me a break. My belief is that countries are successful and that people prosper or suffer as a result of their capability to help themselves or not help themselves."

"Yes," said James. "You are right about that. Now you are speaking from the Bible." Both James and Robert were somewhat surprised when I told them that the saying "God helps those who help themselves" did not come from the Bible but was coined by Benjamin Franklin. Robert, in particular, was amused by this, which made him feel all the better about being an American. He was currently in the process of securing an entry visa to the United States for James, and he was certain that once James arrived in America, he'd feel exactly the same way he did.

My search for Yambo Ouologuem had ended. Back in Ouagadougou, I met several more times with Sékou Tall and Mountaga, both of whom insisted that Ouologuem was no madman. Tall promised to write me a piece for my book, offering his own perspective on Ouologuem's current doings. Mountaga only nodded serenely and said that Yambo was "dur" (or "hard in his faith"), and that was all. He was one of the "hard ones," not unlike his own father. As for the books Yambo had written some years ago, Mountaga said, these were all literary questions, and so they had of course ceased to interest him.

NOTES

1. See K. W.'s (Kaye Whiteman) "In Defence of Yambo Ouologuem," *West Africa*, July 21, 1972. In an interview with Ouologuem, Whiteman reports the following:

> To demonstrate the injustice of the charges against him, he spent some time taking me through his original hand-written manuscript (in an old exercise book) of *Le Devoir de violence* showing me all the places where there had been quotation marks, if not actual mentions of his literary allusions and quotations . . . I saw, for instance, where he had written "here ends *The Last of the Just*," a reference omitted like so many others, for whatever reason, from the published version. (941)

2. The altogether strident response of Ouologuem's publisher is documented in B. P., "Le Devoir de vérité," *Figaro littéraire*, June 10, 1972.

3. See Thomas Hale, *Scribe, Griot, and Novelist: Narrative Interpreters of the Songhay Empire* (Gainesville: University of Florida Press), 1990: 169.

4. Christopher Wise, "Qur'anic Hermeneutics, Sufism, and *Le Devoir de violence*: Yambo Ouologuem as Marabout Novelist," *Religion and Literature*, Vol. 28, No. 1 (Spring 1996): 85–112.

5. In January 1997, Blaise Campaoré altered Burkina Faso's constitution in regard to limitations on the terms of the president. As things stood now, Camporé could be president for the rest of his life.

6. Thomas Sankara, the former president of Burkina Faso, was assassinated by a gang of thugs during a coup d'état in Burkina Faso in 1987. Afterwards, Blaise Campaoré, who claimed to be ill with malaria at the time, took over the country's leadership.

15

Yambo Ouologuem Among the Tidjaniya

Christopher Wise

Several months after my visit with Yambo Ouologuem, I had the opportunity to return to Mali, this time accompanied only by Mountaga Tall. From Mountaga, I had discovered that Ouologuem had written two (possibly more) books on Tidjaniya Islam, which might be available at certain Quranic book vendors in Mali. These books were written in Arabic, Mountaga informed me, although at least one had been translated into French. Whether or not I would be allowed to purchase these books was another question, but I was determined to find them, if at all possible. More importantly, there was still much I did not understand about my previous visit with Ouologuem that I hoped to learn, specifically regarding the religious sect to which he belonged.

After a hard day of travel, Mountaga and I arrived in Sévaré-Mopti on a wet night at the height of the rainy season. Two hours after we arrived in Sévaré, on the same road we'd taken in from Djenné, there was a fatal car accident at a bridge outside Sévaré in which four people perished, including a child and two high-ranking government officials. One of those officials was Yirafin Fomba, the president of the tribunal in Sévaré, and one of Ouologuem's closest friends. It was Fomba, whom I referred to in my interview as "the judge" and who had so warmly encouraged Ouologuem to respond to my questions. Our visit coincided with this incident, which left the village in a state of shocked bewilderment. For the moment, it did not seem discreet to call on Ouologuem, but I decided to pay my respects to al-Hajj Umar Timbely, his uncle. That morning, Timbely and those in Sévaré had only recently learned the news of Fomba's death, whose body lay as yet unburied in the very courthouse where I'd first spoken with Ouologuem. Along with those who had been killed in the car accident, another member of Ouologuem's family had died the day before in Bandiagara, and so Timbely was somewhat flustered when I arrived, making preparations to visit all these corpses on the same day. As we spoke, the old man packed his bag for the trip to Bandiagara immediately following our meeting. We exchanged greetings and discussed recent politics in France. Since time was limited, I came straight to the point and asked Timbely about the existence of recent books written by his nephew on Tidjaniya Islam.

In Bamako, Mountaga and I had spoken with a Dogon man named al-Hajj Issa Ongoïba, who owned a quranic bookstore and, like Sékou Tall, had been a close friend of Yambo's father, Boukary Ouologuem. Al-Hajj Ongoïba confirmed the existence of at least one of these books, written in Arabic and entitled *Islam and Society*. Another book, which Mountaga knew of, described the history of the Tidjaniya rosary, involving the controversy between orthodox and Umarian Tidjaniya. Ongoïba had read the first book himself, he told us, and highly recommended it. Unfortunately, it had been published some five to ten years earlier and was no longer widely available. Occasionally, Ongoïba had requests for it, but he had not seen it in some time. The subject matter of this book, he had informed us, involved the proper behavior of Muslims in the contemporary world.

Timbely denied point-blank that he'd ever heard of any such books written by Ouologuem. He went on to add that Yambo was far too involved with his books and that he'd be better off if he did not spend so much time with them. He repeated the story he'd once told me about Yambo carting out an armload of books following the death of his father, Boukary. Though clearly distracted by the day's events, Timbely seemed frankly exasperated with some of Yambo's more recent behavior. Evidently, the "great change" that he'd hoped to come to his nephew had proven illusory, for Yambo still enervated and embarrassed the old man. "The problem with Yambo is that he's an intellectual and a fanatic at the same time," he said. "This is what makes such a terrible mix. Only last Friday, he continued to pray on the floor of the mosque, long after the imam had dismissed everyone. It's not normal," Timbely said, irritably. "C'est pas normale."

I asked after the health of Yambo's mother, who, according to Sékou Tall, had been ill during the last pilgrimage to the grotto of al-Hajj Umar Tall. She was better now, Timbely informed me, much better. As for Yambo, he'd come by since my visit and had said that he was not happy about the way the interview had occurred, but he accepted it out of respect for his uncle. It was purely out of this respect, Timbely assured us, that Yambo had agreed to see me a second time. Later, however, when Mountaga chanced upon Ouologuem at the home of a mutual acquaintance in Sévaré, Yambo told him that he'd received me at his house last February only because of his dream, the dream that had predicted our visit. He asked Mountaga if he'd come alone this time, and when Mountaga informed him that he'd brought "the professor" with him, Yambo thanked us for our discretion in not calling upon him.

According to most historians, al-Hajj Umar Tall was born in 1794 at the Toucouleur village of Alwar, in the territory of Podor (now northern Senegal). However, if you ask people today in Bandiagara or anywhere nearby in the *pays Dogon* whether al-Hajj Umar Tall continues to live two hundred years later, what they will probably say is that he "disappeared"—without really admitting the possibility of his death. The distinction is a fine one, but it is important. A young Dogon guide I met put it this way: "I have not been taught that al-Hajj Umar is dead, and I have not been taught that he is alive. He disappeared." This is not to say that the ghost of al-Hajj Umar Tall has been spied upon the escarpments, as if he were a sort of Sahelian Elvis Presley, but that Tidjaniya Muslims believe that al-Hajj Umar Tall departed life without having experienced death, not unlike Elijah with his chariot of fire. No one claims to have seen al-Hajj Umar Tall today, although it is widely believed that he appears to his followers in their dreams and in their prayers. He is regarded as a great saint or holy man who may intercede on behalf of those who pray to him for health, prosperity, children, and so on. Those who make the pilgrimage to the grotto where he disappeared commonly sacrifice a *mouton* or other animal to ensure that their prayers will be heard. The meat is then distributed to the Dogon of Deguembéré, who are guardians of the grotto.

It is partly al-Hajj Umar Tall's status as saintly "intercessor" that makes Tidjaniya Islam in West Africa an unorthodox inflection of the faith, but it would be erroneous to conclude that the Tidjaniya are not "real" Muslims—as one might say, for instance, of the American cult led by Louis Farrakhan, the Nation of Islam. Whereas Arab Muslims have tended to reject any notion whatsoever of a saintly intercessor, West African Muslims have tended to be more flexible in their approach to this issue; however, there can be no question of the theological integrity of Tidjaniya Islam as an "authentic" variant of the Islamic faith. Tidjaniya Muslims are highly sophisticated in their approach to religious doctrine, and they harbor absolutely no inferiority complexes about the value of their religion as compared to Arab, or "Mekkan," Islam. If anything, the Tidjaniya I spoke with looked down upon their Arab brethren, whose historically racist behavior toward blacks had served to diminish their status as "true" Muslims.

What intrigued me, however, was the delicate relationship between the Toucouleur Tidjaniya (the descendants of al-Hajj Umar Tall and his Peul followers) and local Dogon Tidjaniya like Ouologuem as well as the less privileged Dogon Muslims who lived in the escarpments. I was also interested in the Tall family's role throughout the history of the *pays Dogon*: To what extent did the Talls' reign, from the time of al-Hajj Umar Tall to the present, parallel that of the Saifs, described in Ouologuem's novel? To what extent did Ouologuem's ancestors collaborate with the Tall family in subduing the *pays Dogon* in the name of Islam? I remembered a remark made by Ouologuem in the early 1970s—a remark that is mostly ignored by his Euro-American readers today—that *Le Devoir de violence* recounted the history of those closest to him: "It took me a lot of courage to write this book," Ouologuem once stated, "which is about oppressors *who were my own family* [my emphasis]" (Kuehl 312). In my conversations with local Dogon, it was clear that many were deeply ambivalent about al-Hajj Umar Tall's importance as either a great saint or historical figure. This ambivalence gave way to obvious disdain in the case of some of Tall's reigning descendants particularly King Aguibou Tall of the late nineteenth century, who first cut a deal with the French. The treaty between Aguibou Tall and Colonel Louis Archinard in 1893 had led not only to the establishment of French authority in the *pays Dogon* but had also resulted in the subjugation of the Dogon people to Toucouleur rule, specifically to the descendants of the first Saif of Bandiagara, al-Hajj Umar Tall.

It must be remembered that the Dogon people, who are of Mandinka origin, first became a distinct ethnic group when they refused to convert to Islam, absconding from their kin and spilling into northern Mali, near Ségou, Mopti, and the escarpments near Bandiagara. Besides this historical aversion to Islam, the Dogon people's identity today is shaped by their pride in having always remained a *peace-loving* community. Rather than engaging in violent conflict with Arab Muslims, who sought to win Mandinka converts by the sword, the Dogon and their cousins the Bozo preferred to flee altogether, not to soil their hands with the blood even of those they despised. These two defining features of the Dogon, their resistance to Islam and their hatred of violent conflict, are, of course, defining features of Ouologuem's novel, *Le Devoir de violence*.[1] "Violence is the way of knowing how to play the game of the other and outplaying him," Ouologuem once remarked. "If I had a taste for this kind of game I think I would not have written the novel" (Kuehl 314). It is therefore doubly ironic that, although the Dogon originally fled to the escarpments of northern Mali to avoid converting to Arabian Islam, they were nonetheless unable to resist al-Hajj Umar Tall and the Toucouleur Tidjaniya. Today, what you might hear from a Dogon Muslim, but not from a Toucouleur, is that al-Hajj Umar Tall won his first disciples among the Dogon by threatening to kill all those who did not convert. When it became apparent that the

Dogon were not particularly interested in al-Hajj Umar Tall's good news from Makkah, he vowed to cut throats on a massive scale if they did not start showing up for prayers at the Grand Mosque.

Much of this was recounted to me by a young Dogon man named Mamadou Kansaye, who ran the local auberge, and a cluster of his friends as we sat near the banks of the Idiwal in Bandiagara. Kansaye and his friends repeatedly insisted that the Dogon were fiercely proud of their own legends that had nothing to do with al-Hajj Umar Tall; that is, for Kansaye, Toucouleur rule in Bandiagara was a vestige of traditions that were now obsolete, eroding in the face of sweeping changes that had come to the *pays Dogon*. Having no Arabic or French, the Dogon had originally succumbed to the Toucouleurs, who had functioned as intermediaries for them with the French colonizers. But now that television and electricity had come along, the old life would soon be finished, Kansaye believed. Holdouts like Yambo, who refused to allow electricity in his home, were few and far between. In any case, the Dogon had their own chiefs, one young man added, and plenty of young people now spoke French. Many of those who had converted to Islam secretly preserved their animist beliefs, remaining Muslims and pagans at the same time—if that was at all possible.

The next morning, however, when a delegation of Toucouleur Tidjaniya came for me at the auberge, Kansaye and his Dogon friends no longer seemed so bold. The chief of Bandiagara, Mountaga's namesake, had granted permission for me to visit the grotto of al-Hajj Umar Tall, and this in itself seemed extraordinary to the cluster of Dogon men who watched us drive off. I too began to get uneasy, at last realizing that the grotto was no mere tourist site but Tidjaniya holy ground, the golgotha of al-Hajj Umar Tall.

Mountaga introduced me to the chauffeur and to Amadou Diana Seck, the man who had been appointed to serve as my guide. There was a moment of awkwardness about my Christian name, but Mountaga quickly testified that he had seen me purchase both the Quran and the hadith at a book vendor in Bamako, which somehow seemed to even things out. Seck spoke in Fulfulde, as Mountaga translated into French for me, starting at the very beginning, when al-Hajj Umar Tall was born in Senegal over two hundred years ago. As he spoke, Seck absently fondled his black-beaded rosary, his other hand braced against the dashboard for support. The same storm that had killed Yirafin Fomba had washed out the main bridge on the road connecting Bandiagara and Mopti. The *pays Dogon* was flooded with rich brown water that made the drive to Deguembéré difficult, if not perilous. We were often jostled about as Seck told his story.

As it turned out, my guide was the direct descendant of Umar Almada Seck, al-Hajj Umar Tall's personal griot and scribe. It was Seck who had taken dictation from al-Hajj Umar Tall, transcribing the poems that Tidjaniya today recite in hopes of evoking an image of the Prophet. These poems, if uttered by the pure of heart—that is, by adepts who have been utterly disciplined in their submission—may summon an apparition of Muhammad and even speak with him under ideal circumstances. I was thus privileged to be accompanied by Mountaga Tall, al-Hajj Umar Tall's direct heir and descendant, as well as Amadou Diana Seck, the descendant of his most trusted companion and griot. When I learned of the Tidjaniya practice of evoking the Prophet's image, I questioned Seck about Ouologuem's remarks that he had often spoken with Muhammad, Jesus, and the angel Gabriel. Seck was not particularly surprised to learn that Yambo was involved in such forms of prayer, but he said that Yambo's practice of speaking with the Prophet Jesus was not common. He refused to say more but seemed pleased by my curiosity.

"To be 'Tidjaniya' means to be a *simple* Muslim," Seck began, "a Muslim as described in the Quran. We are the slaves of God, and we do everything that the Quran commands of us. The mother of al-Hajj was just such a Muslim, and so she prayed to God for a gifted child, a son blessed in submission. Two hundred years ago, al-Hajj was born at Alwar, near Podor, and even as a child he was feared for his great gifts and his great mind. While attending quranic school, even his masters feared him and did not know what to do with him. Once, when all the other boys went to fetch wood for the nightly fire, al-Hajj stayed seated upon the floor. After reproaching him for his laziness, his master was astonished to find that a pile of wood lay at the feet of al-Hajj, though the boy had never once moved from his spot. Another time, when sent to beg for food with the other boys, al-Hajj's eating bowl was miraculously replenished with food. Thus, al-Hajj was sent away by his master, who grew afraid of him.

"For years al-Hajj traveled about the Western Sudan, absorbing all he could and learning at all the great quranic schools and universities. At last, he realized it was time for him to visit the great holy sites of Islam and to make a pilgrimage to Makkah. With a band of followers, al-Hajj traveled across the Sudan to Al-Medina and the Holy City. When he arrived at Makkah, he found above the city gates a sign that read, 'ALL WHO ENTER HERE, NO MATTER HOW GREAT IN LEARNING, WILL FIND SOMEONE MORE KNOWLEDGEABLE IN ISLAM THAN HIMSELF.' However, after speaking with religious leaders at Makkah, al-Hajj found that this was not true in his own case. In Africa, he had already learned more about Islam than the wisest of those at Makkah. He found that the knowledge of Islam in Africa was stronger, more developed, than what he found in the Arab world.

"After many adventures, al-Hajj journeyed to the tomb of the Prophet in Al-Medina, where he composed his most famous poem, the *Safinatou*. In the *Safinatou* of al-Hajj Umar, the ninety-nine names of God are recorded, all but the hidden name of God that is known only to the saints. For all who recite this poem with a pure heart, living according to the prescriptions of the Quran, it is possible to evoke an image of the Prophet. One may even speak with the Prophet's spiritual body, his double. This in itself is of course insignificant, but it is a sign and a gift to the individual who is faithful."

At this point, Mountaga interrupted Seck's story to remind me that Yambo had spoken of the one hundred names of God during our meeting back in February. There are one hundred beads on the rosaries of both the Quadriya and the Tidjaniya (both Umarian and orthodox), the difference consisting only in the division of the beads. This was the subject of one of Yambo's Arab-language books. Each bead represents one of the names of God, ninety-nine of which are known. The one-hundredth bead, which resides at the center of the rosary, represents the hidden name of God, a name known to al-Hajj Umar Tall and other great saints. The secret name is in some way related to the number nineteen, but it is quite difficult to attain. Only those who obey God's rules, do not partake of what is forbidden, and live in a state of sanctification may discover the secret name. Mountaga himself did not know the name, but he aspired to its knowledge. If he could learn to practice Islam perfectly, he could find it. In fact, *anyone* could find it. What irked Yambo, however, was that some charlatan-marabouts pretended that they possessed this secret knowledge, and they used it to make themselves rich.

As Mountaga spoke, Seck smiled from the front seat. I was not sure how much of Mountaga's French he could follow, but he occasionally nodded in agreement. Not long afterward, our vehicle nearly slid off the embankment into a rushing stream of brown water. Seck braced himself from the passenger seat and resumed speaking. "It was not long after composing this poem that Mohamed al-Ghâli, the present *sheikh* of the Tidjaniya from the order of Amed El Tidjaniya, appointed al-Hajj Umar to be sheikh of the Tidjaniya in the land of the blacks. One night, both Mohamed al-Ghâli and al-Hajj Umar shared the same dream, even at the same moment. In their dream, the Prophet Muhammad appeared to both al-Ghâli and al-Hajj Umar, instructing them that al-Ghâli should renounce his title as Tidjaniya sheikh, passing on his baton to al-Hajj Umar. Along with the baton, al-Ghâli entrusted al-Hajj with other sacred relics, including a lock of hair from the Prophet's head. Both agreed that al-Hajj should return to the land of the blacks, spreading Tidjaniya Islam throughout the Western Sudan. Islam was there already, of course, but it needed purification. This was the start of the Islamic Empire of al-Hajj

Tall Umar, which extended from his homeland in Senegal as far as northern Nigeria."

When we arrived at Deguembéré, the village chief was not immediately available, or at least this is what I was told by Mountaga and Seck. The grotto could not be visited without the permission of the local Dogon chief, even with the prior consent of the present Tidjaniya *sheikh* and Toucouleur chief of Bandiagara, al-Hajj Mountaga Tall (Mountaga's uncle). While awaiting the Dogon chief's return, Seck laid a blanket upon the ground and continued his narrative of the life of al-Hajj Umar Tall. This time, however, he spoke of Islam more generally, the history of its development, and the life of the Prophet. I wasn't sure what Mountaga had told Seck, if there had been some misunderstanding about my reasons for wanting to see the grotto, but I realized now that Seck was attempting to convert me to Islam. Perhaps it was not comprehensible to Mountaga and Seck that one might visit this site for purely "academic" reasons rather than religious ones? How much of the misunderstanding was my own fault, I am not sure. But it was clear now that I was being proselytized, that whatever my professional motives for coming here, they would try and make a Muslim of me whether I liked it or not. If I was interested in al-Hajj Umar Tall and Tidjaniya Islam—if I had journeyed such a vast distance to this holy place—there could only be some greater design that had shaped my steps. I began to feel that I had made a terrible mistake.

At last I saw a stooped-over figure approach from the village. The chief carried a staff to support himself and wore a Dogon hunter's cap. Not far from where we sat, a stream ran quietly along the base of the escarpment, 50 feet from the natural, rock-hewn stairway that led up to the grotto. Seck rolled up his mat as we now walked toward the stream to perform ablutions before climbing the grotto. We took off our shoes at the stairway and walked barefoot to the stream. At the water's edge, we knelt to wash our faces, arms, and feet. I was not sure what would be required of me or how I would respond. Despite my respect for Islam, I had no intention of converting that day. At this point, I just wanted to get through the visit without compromising myself or misleading my friends. In the end, I was allowed to climb the grotto but not to enter inside it or see the precise spot where al-Hajj Umar Tall stepped off into eternity.

While Seck, Mountaga, and the others prayed inside the grotto, I sat outside staring down into the valley. It was a magnificent spot, rivaled only in natural beauty by places like the Grand Canyon and Joshua Tree National Park. It was not difficult to imagine the dread that must have filled al-Hajj Umar Tall and his three sons when the army of the Macina

Peul spilled into the valley below them. For there was no escape possible: the escarpment shot straight up, like a cliff at Monument Valley that could be surrounded on all sides. When confronted with the ultimatum of the Macina Peul, that al-Hajj Umar Tall and his sons must surrender and become slaves of the Quadriya, the Tall family chose death—suicide, according to the historians. The sons of al-Hajj Umar Tall were found dead in a ditch that is now filled with water. As for al-Hajj Umar Tall himself, the Tidjaniya claim his body was never recovered.

The more I learned about Tidjaniya religious practices, the more convinced I became that the Yambo Ouologuem of today could not simply be dismissed as a "madman." Seck's reference to the Tidjaniya prayer technique of evoking the Prophet's image had only served to confirm this impression for me. Later, Mountaga offered to introduce me to one of his older brothers, to whom he deferred in such matters, Mohamed Abdoulaye Maïga. Among those members of the Tall family that I had so far encountered, Maïga appeared to live in the most modern of circumstances, working as an orderly at a nearby hospital. We ate lunch together before Mountaga explained the reasons for our visit. When the conversation turned to Sufi mysticism, Maïga's wife turned off the television and left the room.

"There are those that say Yambo is mad," I told him. "I know that in the *Safinatou* and other poems of al-Hajj, an image of the Prophet can be evoked. But Yambo claimed that he also spoke with Jesus and the angel Gabriel. What I want to know is if these prayer practices are shared among Tidjaniya Muslims, or if they are strictly Yambo's own doings? Could they be a sign of his madness?"

Maïga grew thoughtful. "Everything Yambo has told you is entirely possible," he said, "but only for those who are disciplined in Islam. What's curious is that he would tell you these things in the first place."

"Yambo told him he'd foreseen his visit in a dream," Mountaga said. "When I saw him in Sévaré this time, he told me that he'd only agreed to see the professor because of his dream."

"The part about Jesus is what is strange," Maïga said. "It may be that Yambo told you this because you are white [*nasara*], from the Occident. He may have thought that you'd be more inclined to listen. I cannot really say for sure, but I can say that there is nothing extraordinary about his conversations with Jesus and the Angel Gabriel. These practices are by no means 'signs of his madness,' as you say.

"What you must know is that there are certain sounds that exist, pure sounds that have been passed down through the centuries. These sounds have no real meaning in themselves. They are devoid of sense, you might say. Their number is very limited."

"Are they sounds from the Quran?" I asked. "Because of Arabic's status as revealed language?"

"No, it's not like that. It has nothing to do with the Arab language. You will find these sounds in the Quran, but they are much older than the time of Muhammad. They originate beyond the founding of Christianity, even Judaism. The Egyptians taught these sounds to the Jews, who passed them down in their turn. They are sounds only, not words as such. So you will find them in the Quran, but unrelated to its meaning. I cannot tell you what these sounds are, but if you would like to attend a prayer meeting with me, you may learn them yourself."

I explained that my plane for the United States would be leaving within the week. "Dommage," Maïga said. "You would profit from the knowledge of these sounds, but only if you uttered them with a pure heart. If uttered by the person disciplined in Islam, one may evoke images of the dead, even conversing with the dead. But you must know that this only occurs after one lives a faultless life for many years. One must be disciplined by prayer, living as the Quran instructs. God loves all people the same, of course, but those who follow his commandments receive higher favors. If such a person utters these sounds, he can gain access to the archive wherein the totality of human history resides.

"This archive contains everything that has ever happened and that will happen in history, the past as well as the future. Everything that has ever occurred and that ever will occur exists within this archive. Everyone who has ever lived or who will ever live also exists within this archive. I mean their psychic bodies, of course, our *doubles*. Not our physical bodies. For example, when Muhammad took his night journey to Jerusalem, it was his double that traveled such a distance, not his body limited within the plane of the physical. When the *Safinatou* of al-Hajj Umar Tall is performed, it is his double that is brought forth from this archive.

"When these sounds are uttered, they evoke the psychic bodies of those who have already lived, not only the Prophet's. One can therefore freely converse with the dead. For obvious reasons, it is preferable to speak with the Prophet, but if Yambo so desired he could summon the double of Jesus as well. This would be a personal matter. Additionally, one may visit the future as well as the past, events that have already happened and that will happen at a later point. One can see them in one's mind-eye. Thus it was that Yambo 'foresaw' your visit in a dream. It would therefore be erroneous to conclude that Yambo is a 'madman' or to feel pity for him. Those that call him 'mad,' I mean those in Bandiagara and Sévaré, are terrified of him. They fear and avoid him, not for his great learning, but because of his mystical knowledge. Indeed, he is a dangerous man with great powers. Even fools can see this."

Before leaving Mali, I had one more opportunity to locate the Arab-language books written by Ouologuem. At a book vendor in Mopti, along the banks of the Niger River, I spent an afternoon waiting for M. Mamoudou Keita, a "commerçant de livres coranique," who was reputed to be close to the Ouologuem family. My bush taxi to Bobo-Dioulasso was scheduled to depart in the late afternoon, so my window of opportunity was limited. A young man, who was Keita's assistant, informed me that he knew of these books but was not authorized to sell them to me. He would not confirm whether or not they were on the premises. Only M. Keita could give this permission. I waited for several hours but Keita never showed up. A man whom I believed to be Keita arrived after lunch, speaking briefly with his assistant in Fulfulde, before departing at once.

In the end, I let the matter drop, as the hour for my car's departure approached. If these books do exist, it is likely they would be short texts like pamphlets, of no more than one hundred pages, like many similar French-Arabic books on Islam that one sees in such stalls. Not many editions would have been printed, and their circulation would have been restricted to Tidjaniya initiates. That Ouologuem himself continues to write is certain, as he himself had informed me in February 1997, alluding to poems he had written on the Palestinian resistance.

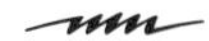

What bearing my experiences in Mali would have upon how I read *Le Devoir de violence* in the future was difficult to ascertain. However, I grew more convinced than that Ouologuem's writing is inextricably connected to the world of Islam, specifically Tidjaniya Islam as it is practiced in the Sahel. His writing is centered in Muslim concerns from the first words of *Le Devoir de violence*. As a writer, Yambo Ouologuem therefore belongs more in the company of authors like Cheikh Hamidou Kane, Tayyib Salih, and Amadou Hampâté Bâ rather than French authors such as the Marquis de Sade, Michel Foucault, and Jacques Derrida. If we are willing to approach Ouologuem on such terms, the gap between the young author of *Le Devoir de violence* and the devout (if slightly eccentric) Muslim of today may not seem so wide after all. In other words, our understanding of Ouologuem should be grounded within the historical realities of daily life in West Africa, the distinct cultural practices that form the lifeworld of Muslims like Ouologuem.

Bellingham, Washington
September 24, 1997

NOTE

1. See my article, "Quranic Hermeneutics, Sufism, and *Le Devoir de violence*: Yambo Ouologuem as Marabout Novelist." Also, see Linda Kuehl, "Yambo Ouologuem on Violence, Truth, and Black History."

16

Interview with al-Hajj Sékou Tall

Christopher Wise

The following interview was conducted in the home of al-Hajj Sékou Tall on July 8, 1997, in Ouagadougou, Burkina Faso. Present at the interview were Sékou Tall, Mountaga Tall, Michel Tinguiri, and me. Tinguiri, a translation student at the University of Ouagadougou, helped me transcribe the contents of this interview. To some questions, Tall had already prepared written statements; to others he responded more informally. Before responding to my questions, which I had dropped off a week earlier, Tall opened our discussion with the following remarks:

S. TALL: Before we begin our inquiry on Mr. Yambo Ouologuem, I would like to invoke certain names, literary works, and places that are inextricably bound to our subject. What are they? "The Dogon country, Bandiagara and its escarpments, Kaani, Kambari, Sangha, Nagabana, Ouologuem, Yambo, Karambé, Sévaré (Sewa Waaré), Macina, Sékou Amadou, Hamdallaye, Deguembéré, Tidjaniya, Quadrya, etc."—to mention only a few. However, the most important names are al-Hajj Umar Tall and Yambo (Amadou) Ouologuem. Why do I say this? Umar was born around 1794 at Alwar, a small village in the territory of Podor [Senegal], the child of Saïdou and Adama Tall and a descendant of marabouts. He was given the name "Kodda Adama Aysé" because he was the youngest son among six other children. His mother was known by all as a model of virtue, so she

---

This interview was translated from the French by Christopher Wise.

was called "Sokhna" out of respect. Umar grew into a highly gifted child, strongly inclined toward spiritual matters. Thus, he memorized the Quran when he was only nine years old, toured Mauritania, then attended the university at Cayor, and finally went to Guinea to study quranic hermeneutics and mysticism. His studies in Islam culminated in a series of voyages to many diverse places and countries.

At thirty-three years old, having mastered all known manners of studying Islam in the western Sudan, he began a pilgrimage to the holy places of the faith. Umar left for Makkah in 1826, passing through Macina, Sokoto, Fezzan, and Egypt. At Al-Medina, he met Sheikh Mohammed al-Ghâli, Caliph of the Tidjaniya, who appointed him the Caliph of "Bilad es Sudan," the land of the blacks. Thus, Umar visited Jerusalem and Damas, growing richer in experiences of all sorts. In 1831, he decided to return to the land of his birth. He returned to Fouta-Toro in 1846. His desire to promote Islam throughout his homeland [jihad] led to the establishment of an immense Muslim empire stretching from Senegal to Macina. Al-Hajj Umar Tall stayed at Hamdallahi between 1862 and 1863. However, the Macina Peul revolted against him in 1863, laying siege to the town until February 1864.

By a miracle, he escaped, fleeing towards the escarpments of Bandiagara in the Dogon country, where he disappeared at the grotto of Déguembéré. The Macina Peul and colonial historians claim that al-Hajj Umar Tall perished at Deguembéré in an explosion that shook the grotto, but his followers maintain that he is alive to this day.

With the increasing emancipation of various territories and peoples globally and after more than a century of degrading submissions and frustrations, Africa at last broke free from the shackles of colonialism. Now Africans began to assert their right to independence in literary works that violently denounced their former colonizers. What motivated many writers of this period was their desire to demonstrate Africa's unique identity, which had been scorned and humiliated, when not nearly destroyed, during the colonial period. Africa was at last becoming aware of itself.

In *God's Bits of Wood* (1960), Sembene Ousmane—docker, writer, and filmmaker—denounced the corruption and mediocrity of those African chiefs who had once sided with the colonizers. The search for African dignity similarly inspired Ferdinand Oyono in *The Old Negro* and *The Medal*. In *The Poor Christ of Bomba*, *Mission to Kola,* and *The Miraculous King*, Mongo Beti also depicted how traditional African society became degraded by the rise of urbanization and the influence of European civilization.

If African novelists contested colonial society, they also sought to demonstrate the importance of our traditional African heroes from the past. The strong need to identify with such prestigious historical figures and significant events may explain the success of a literature defined by its epic retellings, chronicles, stories, and legends that exalted the cult of heroes.

Such novels aimed at restoring cherished memories of the past, providing Africans with an authentic witness of the value of a culture that had been ridiculed and scorned for many years. Such impulses are apparent in novels like Cheikh Hamidou Kane's *Ambiguous Adventure* and Bernard B. Dadie's *Climbié*.

It is thus alongside these literary works, with an anguish expressed in such a compelling style, that one novel in particular has endured through the years, that of the Dogon, Yambo (Amadou) Ouologuem. With an amazing virtuosity, *Bound to Violence* offers us the spectacle of an Africa that is utterly delirious, a hypocritical Africa that is seething with evil and fearful demons, a land where the most grotesque and cynical rulers abound.

WISE: Many readers and even critics of *Bound to Violence* understand very little of life in Mali, at Sévaré-Mopti, Bandiagara, and so on. I hope you can supply us with lots of details. First, before our trip to Sévaré, what did you know about Yambo Ouologuem? Can you describe your relation to Yambo and his father?

S. TALL: Before our trip to Sévaré, I was aware of several bonds that existed between the Tall and Ouologuem families, some secular, some religious, some personal. Time and history have united us within a single garment of destiny. Yambo Ouologuem, baptized as "Amadou" at his birth, is the child of Boukary Yambo Ouologuem, a Malian professor and former student at the École Normale des Instituteurs of Katibougou, about fifty kilometers from Bamako. During his professional career, Yambo's father served as director of the normal school in Sévaré [14 kilometers from Mopti], which later was renamed the Lycée Hammadoun Dicko (after an important Malian figure). Boukary Ouologuem was considered a "light among lights" by his countrymen and the pride of the Dogon people.

A childhood companion and longtime schoolmate, Boukary Yambo Ouologuem has always been my friend and brother, and he remains so even now after his death, for "death is only the beginning of Immortality." The mother of Yambo Ouologuem is named Aïssata Umar Karambé. Thus, Yambo Amadou Ouologuem comes from a family of animists on the side of his paternal grandparents, from whom he received the name "Yambo." He also comes from a family of Muslims on the side of his maternal grandparents, as a descendant of Umar Karambé, the father of Aïssata, his mother. Moreover, he bears the name of his maternal uncle, Amadou Umar Karambé, a Malian army colonel. So, you see, Yambo Amadou Ouologuem is both a homonym for "Yambo," the name of his paternal grandfather, and for "Amadou," the name of his maternal uncle.

WISE: Can you tell us more about your family and the importance of your family in Bandiagara and in Sévaré?

S. TALL: For the Tall family, Sévaré and Bandiagara are two towns that have marked our history and our lives. Sévaré is connected to Hamdallaye, the religious capital of the theocratic Empire of Sékou Amadou, father of Amadou Sékou, who was killed at Hamdallaye in the battle of the Macina Peul, united with the Kounta [Peul], against the Toucouleurs of al-Hajj Umar. It is at Hamdallaye that Sékou Amadou is buried. Hamdallaye is to the Macina Peul what Déguembéré is to the both Toucouleurs and the Dogon, disciples of al-Hajj Umar. Bandiagara was the capital of the Toucouleur kingdom of al-Hajj Umar. It was also the capital of the Macina kingdom during the reign of Aguibou Tall, the sixth son of al-Hajj Umar. This last son was named king of Macina by Colonel Archinard. He reigned there from 1893 to 1907. It was during King Aguibou Tall's reign, supported by Captain Desenave, that the conquest of the Mossi country [now Burkina Faso] was begun, under the command of officers Voulet and Chanoines, Loury and Lejariel, etc.

WISE: In Europe and the United States, it's been written that Yambo Ouologuem is the descendant of Malian "kings," that he comes from a royal family possessing "vast territories." Is this true?

S. TALL: The Ouologuem family constitutes one of the principal grand families among the Dogon people in the escarpments of Bandiagara in Mali. The Dogon, who originated from Egypt during the time of the pharaohs, are a people who are partly animist. Sangha, their sanctuary, is regularly visited by tourists from all over the world. It has given birth to many philosophical and sociological books, such as those by the well-known professor Griaule (see *Dieu d'Eau*). However, most Dogon are Muslims. If Yambo Ouologuem is a prince, descending from his paternal grandfather Yambo, who was an important Dogon patriarch, he also comes from a family of Muslims, descending from his maternal grandfather Umar Karambé, who was not only a well-versed scholar of Islam but, more importantly, one of the greatest muezzins at the Grand Mosque of Bandiagara.

WISE: Can you tell us more about the religion of Yambo Ouologuem and his family?

S. TALL: The maternal grandfather of Yambo (Umar Karambé) was both a well-versed scholar of Islam and a great muezzin. And so, Yambo Ouologuem and his father Boukary Yambo are Muslims. Why Tidjaniya Islam, and what is Tidjaniya Islam? The militantism of the Ouologuem family of the Tidjaniya "sect" originates from the teachings of al-Hajj Umar at Déguembéré in the escarpments of Bandiagara. When a coalition of the Kounta and the Macina Peul, all militants of the combined Quadriya sect of Damas in Irak, forced al-Hajj Umar to take refuge in the grotto at the escarpment of Deguembéré, al-Hajj commanded his nephew and war-chief Tidjani Amadou to seek reinforcements among the Dogon of Kambari, in the Dogon region, and of Kaani, another Dogon region. The Dogon came in thousands to help al-Hajj Umar. Known and respected for their legendary hospitality, the Dogon selflessly responded to the call of the stranger, lending their support to al-Hajj in his time of need.

When the Dogon army arrived at Deguembéré with Tidjani Amadou, they found that al-Hajj Umar had disappeared, leaving with the chief of Deguembéré some relics of the caliphate of the Tidjaniya, now to be passed on to his nephew: the scepter that you saw as well as his prayer rug and rosary. The Dogon army also found that three children of al-Hajj Umar had been assassinated by the enemy: Haady, Mahin, and Maki. Their bodies, laying at the entrance to the grotto where their father had disappeared, were carried back to Bandiagara to be buried. Their tomb [was] the most important of those established in the sepulcher of the Kings of the Toucouleurs [sedentary Peul] of the family of al-Hajj Umar Tall at Bandiagara.

The Ouologuem family and Tall family are thus united in Islam.

WISE: Does Yambo regularly perform the pilgrimage of al-Hajj Tall Umar? Like many others, does he too believe that al-Hajj Tall Umar is still alive?

S. TALL: Al-Hajj Umar has been, is presently, and will always remain important for Yambo and his parents, who all adore him and swear only by God, Muhammad, and him. Each year, on the twelfth of February or in March depending on the circumstances, a large pilgrimage reunites the militants of the Tidjaniya at Deguembéré, surrounding the grotto where al-Hajj Umar disappeared. No matter how busy he is, Yambo always finds time to participate in the pilgrimage. This year, on March 20, 1997, 1,200 militants of the Tidjaniya came from Senegal, Côte de'Ivoire, Niger, Guinea, Mali, and Burkina to reunite, pray, and honor their saint with fervor, devotion, and humility. Like all militants among the Tidjaniya, Yambo believes that al-Hajj Umar, the very same hero of old, continues to live to this day. Yambo is prepared to passionately defend his faith in al-Hajj Umar.

WISE: Is it true that Yambo Ouologuem has written books on Tidjaniya Islam? Are you familiar with the titles and subjects of these books on Islam?

S. TALL: I'm not aware of any such writings by him. I do know that he has "devoured" the sixty verses of the Quran, and that he speaks with great gusto and true authority upon all literature written in Arabic on the Quran and the hadith. He will not hesitate to correct any Muslim who is in error, no matter whether he is Arab, Black, or of any other origin. Nor will Yambo hesitate to instruct all those who are misinformed about the Quran, the hadith, prayer rituals, or Islamic mysticism. A man with his knowledge and talents is, of course, more than capable of writing such critical commentaries upon Islam.

WISE: How are Tidjaniya Muslims like Yambo different from "orthodox" Muslims? What religious practices make them unique?

S. TALL: Yambo Ouologuem is a Muslim of the Tidjaniya sect. From a religious point of view, the Tidjaniya are different from the Quadriya sect. The Tidjaniya support Cheikh Amhed al-Tidjaniya. It was from the order of this great saint that al-Hajj Umar was given the title of caliph, under the protection of Cheikh Mohamed al-Ghali, whom I mentioned earlier. The Quadriya support their great saint, Sheikh Abdel Kader Gelani. The difference between the two resides in their rosaries. The orthodox Tidjaniya pray with a rosary of eleven beads. The Umarian Tidjaniya pray with a rosary of twelve beads. Both are impregnated with a mystical practice called "Sayfi." The Quadriya pray with a rosary of one hundred beads. The main difference between the rosaries of these three camps consists in the fact that the rosary of the Quadriya, that of the one hundred beads, is wholly continuous. The rosaries of the Tidjaniya, on the other hand, are broken into distinct groupings of eleven beads (those of the Tidjaniya) and twelve beads (those of the Umarian Tidjaniya). While the beads of the Tidjaniya rosaries move through our fingers, we also say a special communal prayer, which is called the "Salatoul fatiya."

WISE: What do you most remember about our meeting with Yambo Ouologuem? Do you recall what he said about the Twaregs, the Arabs, and so on? For me, it was an extraordinary meeting, but it's hard for me to recall everything he said.

S. TALL: He talked on and on [laughter]. What I most recall about our meeting with Yambo were a few unusual things that he said, but also his humor. Yambo is truly a master of humor. Concerning the Twaregs, he told us that the sultan of the Twaregs had once amassed a large supply of arms, which he hid away with the intention of fighting against the regime of Modibo Keita [Mali's first president]. Thus it was that Colonel Diby Sylla, a very audacious and aggressive soldier like all the Bobo, an ethnic group well-known for its bravery and audacity in battle, offered to President Keita to go and destroy this rebellious sultan of the Twaregs. Modibo hesitated for a moment, but he finally agreed because of Diby's ferocious determination to go and take on this undisciplined sultan. When Diby Sylla at last found himself face to face with the sultan, he questioned him about his hidden supply of weapons. The Sultan denied everything, of course, calling Diby's charges "pure conjecture." Angrily, Diby said to the Sultan, "You are a Muslim, and I am an animist. I hate lies like all men of my race. But, you, you are a Muslim, a white-man, and a liar." He executed him on the spot and recovered all the hidden arms, thus bringing an end to this racist rebellion.

WISE: Don't you think that Yambo himself has become somewhat racist? After everything that happened to him in France?

S. TALL: Yambo was badly disappointed by the French, so now he tends to hate everything connected with white people. He doesn't want to speak with any whites now, even after his travels in Europe, Asia, and America, where he lectured on several occasions upon a wide array of subjects. His aversion for whites, it is said, comes from the treachery of the publisher of *Le Devoir de violence*. He won't even allow this subject to be mentioned in his presence. From the moment it appeared, his book *Le Devoir de violence* caused much controversy and many hostile reactions. It was said that Yambo quoted Shakespeare, the English writer, in his book. He then discovered that his publisher had deleted the quotation marks at some earlier time. This act made Yambo an object of derision in the eyes of the entire world. He was deeply affected by this betrayal, and he still suffers from the slanderous actions of his publisher. Today, he refuses all offers to speak at conferences and debates or to contribute written articles anywhere. He continues to serve [as an educator], but he refuses to accept remuneration. Actually, Yambo is neither a racist nor an anti-Semite. He is a philosopher and a humanist. He believes that man is both a perfectible and peace-loving being, and he continues to uphold the equality of all races.

WISE: What do you recall of his remarks about other African writers?

S. TALL: He was disappointed in Léopold Senghor, who, he said, had failed to appreciate the beauty and virtues of the black woman or to properly sing her praises. He criticized Senghor for divorcing his African wife and then marrying a white woman for the money. [Laughter]. He didn't get along very well with Amadou Hampâté Bâ either. This resulted from his having espoused certain ideas on oral literature to Bâ when they once worked together on a project, and Bâ rejected his ideas and approach to this question.

WISE: Can you say more about Yambo's relationship with Bâ?

S. TALL: Amadou Hampâté Bâ and Yambo are both from the same village. They come from Bandiagara, and so they have worked together on oral literature, as well as many other subjects and themes. On the outside, Amadou Hampâté had published two books that did not please Yambo, *Amkoullel: L'enfant peul* [Paris: Babel, 1991] and a second book. This was because Amadou Hampâté told of things that weren't really true and because they had at one time developed their ideas together, in common accord. They are from the same village, and so they have a similar way of understanding the world. But Amadou deviated from what they had agreed upon in their private discussions and in their work together. Yambo was disappointed in Amadou and was unhappy with his writings. This is what he told us. Bâ failed to include what Yambo told him in his book [*Amkoullel: L'enfant peul*]. In other words, there are explanations of certain things in this book that they had once agreed upon together, and that Yambo had himself contributed, but Bâ left them out. Instead, Bâ described things that are not true. He misled his reader. He wrote according to his own ideas, rather than those of the townsmen. He wrote for himself, but not for the people of Bandiagara, whom he disregarded. So there was a disagreement between them. Yambo and Bâ disagreed on what had been said earlier.

WISE: You were once a friend of Bâ's?

S. TALL: Hampâté is from Bandiagara. It was my father, the chief of Bandiagara, who first sent him to the colonial school. When the white man came, the commandant in the time of the whites, we called him the *résident.* He said to bring the village children to enroll in the whites' school. At that time, Amadou Hampâté Bâ was a student of my uncle's, Cerno Bokar Salif. Hampâté wrote a book about my uncle entitled *Le Sage de Bandiagara*. He was his [Bâ's] master. Thus Hampâté was a student of Bokar Salif Tall. Then there was also Alfa Ali, who was his big brother. Their slave, the slave of their family, brought both of them, the big brother and the little brother, Amadou Hampâté, to the house of my father. My father told the messenger of the *resident* that they could not send both brothers to the school. They would only send the youngest brother and allow the other boy to return home. He said that the two of them should not be sent together because, later, they would both turn against us. Thus, at that time, it was believed that when you went off to the white man's school, you became wicked; you were lost.

My father, the chief of Bandiagara, said to the messenger: "You can bring my own son instead of the eldest brother, whose name is Madâni (and who is my [Sékou Tall's] eldest brother), and Amadou Hampâté. So go and give these two boys to the *resident,* and you can say to him that if he wants to take Amadou as a student, he must also take Madâni. They must go together or neither of them will go." The white man asked Madâni, "Do you want to go to the school?" He replied, "I don't want to go to the school." The white man asked, "Why?" and he said, "Because the white man pisses while he's standing up. The white man drinks alcohol. The white man doesn't pray. That's why I don't like the white man." So the messenger said, "Okay, step aside." And then he asked Amadou Hampâté, "Do you want to go to the school?" Hampâté said, "Yes, I want to go to the school." Then the white man said, "Why?" He said, "So I can come back and properly beat the slave who brought us here." Since my father, the chief of Bandiagara, had already said, "If you take one, you must take the other," they took both of them off to the white man's school. When they sent the sons of the chief of Djenné to the school, at that time there was another school for the sons of slaves, [but] the sons of the chief were taken and placed in a special school that was only for the sons of the chief. This school was at Djenné. There was also a school at Kaye and afterwards a school was built at Fédherbe, that one called the slaves' school.

Before his death, every time Hampâté saw me, he called me his brother. Everytime he saw me, he said, "20,000 CFA," and then he gave the money to me, saying to me, "Because of your father." Thus, all that he wrote, every time he wrote something, he sent me a copy with a letter.

TINGUIRI: You've said that Amadou Hampâté Bâ wrote things that don't really reflect reality as you know it. However, Amadou Hampâté Bâ is considered one of the greatest defenders of African culture.

S. TALL: Ah, yes, you are right. When you say something in Africa to a white man, he often misses the humor because he's too busy taking notes. Well, Bâ wrote much, it's true. He had a terrific mind. He knew many things. Only, he exaggerated sometimes [laughs]. He was always saying things like "I'm the one." That's what I didn't like. He would say, "'I did this,' or 'I did that.' 'I said this,' or 'I said that.'" But, of course, we knew him well. I myself have participated in conferences on Bâ.

WISE: What do you remember of Yambo Ouologuem's remarks about black Americans?

S. TALL: He spoke of Muhammad Ali, the American boxer and his one-time friend. Besides Ali, he doesn't believe that black Americans really care for Africa. However, he has every confidence in Muhammad Ali. As for the others, if they really cared about Africa, they would come here to learn more about it. You can't just stay in America and then go around telling everyone what is and isn't "African." He said that they still have a complex because they rarely bother to come here. He wishes that more would come, like Alex Haley, the author of *Roots*, who came to search for his ancestors. Take yourself, for instance, you weren't familiar with Africa, and so you decided to come and see it. Now you have seen certain things. When you go back to America, you will speak about what you have seen, and people will have to believe you.

WISE: Is there anything else that stands out to you about our visit with Yambo?

S. TALL: I remember someone asked him why he didn't build a retirement home for his old father, and he said, "I am bound to inherit all that is my father's. If I had built such a house for him, after his death, it would have become a burden to me. Anyway, I prefer for my father to live under my own roof. I didn't want to put him away in some retirement home."

Then, someone else asked him, "Do you admire the skyscrapers of America?" and he said, "The Dogon live up in the escarpments. These are higher, more powerful, and more solid than skyscrapers. Why should I admire these skyscrapers more than what we have right here in the Dogon country? Buildings that are more ancient and more solid?"

WISE: Can you discuss the offer that Moctar Oul Dada, the former president of Mauritania, once made to Yambo Ouologuem? Is he really going to become Minister of Education in Mauritania?

S. TALL: Yambo has taken a hard look at Mauritania, and he's convinced that this country must be helped: that is, it must be given proper advice so that it can achieve progress and stability. He's been to several conferences there, and he has a deep affinity for Mauritanian culture. He has found in this country all the essential elements of a truly Islamic society, the sort of society to which he's thoroughly and passionately committed. After his experiences there and after thinking these matters over, Yambo has grown more firm than ever in his desire to go to Mauritania and help its people and leaders. He is wholly committed to the development of Mauritanian culture, to enhancing the progress of its political, economic, and social life. I can't affirm that Yambo will become Minister of Education in Mauritania. However, after hearing him declare his friendship and solidarity with the Mauritanian people and its leaders, I can verify that if there was an offer to that effect, he would gladly accept it.

WISE: Yambo told me that the United States, specifically the CIA, has sought to block him from becoming Mauritania's Minister of Education. This seems a little hard for me to believe.

S. TALL: If he said it, then it must have happened. He never lies. Really, he doesn't even know how to lie. He doesn't know how. He will tell you exactly what he thinks [laughter]. There are aides from the United States who have come to Mauritania. The United States has given aid there in the past. Now that we all know Yambo's intentions, the CIA can no longer be against him. He has been to Mauritania. He has traveled all over Mauritania, everywhere. He believes that they are a good people, and he has had many relations with its president [Moctar Oul Dada]. He wants to help reform the country. He has the ability to do so, if people will listen to him. So if they give him the opportunity, I'm sure he'll go.

WISE: There are those who say that Yambo Ouologuem is "mad." It was evident to me that he remains a man of extraordinary intelligence, but he is also a man of paradox. He is quite complicated.

M. TALL: It's Islam that's done that to him.

S. TALL: [laughing]. Yambo is no madman. He is far from being mad. He is a visionary. His principles are such that he is compelled to act whenever he sees any moral defect in his society. He acts the same way everywhere, whether he is in a mosque, at a holy site, or walking the streets. Men like Yambo are often considered "mad" because their highly moral vision of the world clashes with those who have little education or cultural background.

Bibliography

Abastado, Claude. "Introduction à l'analyse des manifestes." *Littérature,* vol. 39 (October 1980).

Abu-Lughod, Janet. "Cities Blend the Past to Face the Future." *African Report,* vol. 16, no. 6 (June 1971): 12.

Abun-Nasr, Jamil M. *The Tidjaniyya: A Sufi Order in the Modern World.* London: Oxford University Press, 1965.

Achebe, Chinua. *Things Fall Apart.* Portsmouth, N.H.: Heinemann Educational Books, 1958.

Achiriga, Jingiri J. *La Révolte des romanciers noirs de langue française.* Sherbrooke, Quebec: Editions Nadman, 1978.

Adotevi, Stanislas Spero K. *Négritude et négrologues.* Paris: Union Generale d'Éditions, 1972.

Ahmed, Akbar S. *Postmodernism and Islam: Predicament and Promise.* New York: Routledge, 1992.

Aidoo, Ama Ata. "For Whom Things Did Not Change." *No Sweetness Here.* 1970. New York: Feminist Press at the City University of New York, 1995. Pp. 8–29.

Aire, Victor O. "Le Devoir de violence." In *Dictionnaire des oeuvres littéraires négro-africaines de langue française des origines a 1978.* Sous la direction de Ambroise Kom. Sherbrooke, Quebec: Editions Naaman. Paris: Agence de Cooperation Culturelle et Technique, 1983.

Aizenberg, Edna. "Historical Subversion and Violence of Representation in García Marquez and Ouologuem." *PMLA*, Vol. 107, No. 5 (October 1992): 1235–1252.

Andrade, Susan. "The Nigger of the Narcissist: History, Sexuality and Intertextuality in Maryse Condé's *Heremakhonon.*" *Callaloo,* vol. 16, no. 1 (1993): 213–226.

Ansari, Khwaja 'Abdullah. *Intimate Conversations (Munajat).* Trans. by W. M. Thackston, Jr. New York: Paulist Press, 1978.

Appiah, Kwame Anthony. *In My Father's House: Africa in the Philosophy of Culture.* New York and Oxford: Oxford University Press, 1992.

Arnaud, Robert. *L'Islam et la politique musulmane française en Afrique occidentale française.* Paris: Comité de l'Afrique Française, 1912.

Asante, S. K. B. "International Assistance and International Capitalism: Supportive or Counterproductive?" In *African Independence: The First Twenty-Five Years,* Gwendolyn M. Carter and Patrick O'Meara (eds.). Bloomington: Indiana University Press, 1985. Pp. 249–274.

Ashcroft, Bill, Gareth Griffiths, and Helen Tiffin. *The Empire Writes Back: Theory and Practice in Post-colonial Literatures.* New York and London: Routledge, 1989.

Ba, Adam Konaré. *Sonni Ali Ber.* Études Nigériennes no. 40. Niamey: Institut de Recherches en Science Humanines, 1977.

Bâ, Amadou Hampaté. *Vie et enseignement de Tierno Bokar: Le sage de Bandiagara.* Paris: Seuil, 1980.

Bakhtin, Mikhail. "Épopée et Roman." *Recherches Internationales,* No. 76 (1973).

Barkan, Sandra. "*Le Devoir de violence*: A Non-History." In *Interdisciplinary Dimensions of African Literature,* Kofi Anyidoho, Abioseh M. Porter, Daniel Racine, and Janice Spleth (eds.). Washington, D.C.: Three Continents Press, 1985. Pp. 101–112.

Baudelaire, Charles. *Curiosités esthétiques et l'art romantique.* Paris: Garnier, 1962.

Benot, Yves. "*Le Devoir de violence* de Yambo Ouologuem est-il un chef d'oeuvre ou une mystification?" *La Pensée,* No. 149 (January-February 1970): 127–131.

Bernstein, Serge. "De Gaulle and Gaullism in the Fifth Republic." In *De Gaulle and Twentieth Century France,* John Horne and Hugh Gough (eds.). London: Edward Arnold, 1994. Pp. 109–124.

Beverley, John. *Against Literature.* Minneapolis: University of Minnesota Press, 1993.

Boulnois, Jean, and Boubou Hama. *L'Empire de Gao: Histoire, coutumes et magie.* Paris: Adrien-Maisonneuve, 1954.

Bouygues, Claude. "Yambo Ouologuem, ou le silence des canons." *Canadian Journal of African Studies/Revue Canadienne des Études Africaines* Vol. 25, No. 1 (1991): 1–11.

B. P. "Le Devoir de vérité, *Figaro littéraire,* June 10, 1972.

Breitman, George. *The Last Year of Malcolm X: The Evolution of a Revolutionary.* New York: Pathfinder Press, 1988.

Brennan, Timothy. *Salman Rushdie and the Third World.* New York: St. Martin Press, 1989.

Brenner, Louis. *West African Sufi: The Religious Heritage and Spiritual Search of Cerno Bokar Salif Tal.* London: Hurst, 1984.

Bu-Buakei, Jabbi. "Influence and Originality in African Writing." *African Literature Today,* Vol. 10 (1979): 106–123.

Butor, Michel. "La critique et l'invention." In *Répertoire III.* Paris: Éditions de Minuit, 1968.

Césaire, Aimé. *Cahier d'un retour au pays natal.* In *Aimé Césaire: The Collected Poetry,* trans. by Clayton Eshleman and Annette Smith. Berkeley: University of California Press, 1983.

Cham, Mybe B. "Islam in Senegalese Literature and Film." In *Faces of Islam in African Literature,* Kenneth W. Harrow (ed.). Portsmouth, N.H.: Heinemann Educational Books, 1991. Pp. 163–186.

Chaulet-Achour, Christiane. *Abécédaires en devenir.* Algers: Éditions de l'ENAP, 1985.

———. "Langue française et colonialisme en Algérie: De l'abécédaire à la production littéraire." Diss., University of Paris III, 1982, vol. 2: 419–443.

———. "Textes, prétextes, contextes: Quelques interrogations à propos de l'intertextualité." *Langues et Littératures*, Revue de l'Institut des Langues Étrangères de l'Université d'Alger, No. 5 (1993): 115–125.

Chipman, John. *French Power in Africa*. Cambridge: Basil Blackwell, 1989.

Chraibi, Driss. *Le passé simple*. Paris: Denoel, 1954.

Clifford, James. *The Predicament of Culture: Twentieth-Century Ethnography, Literature, and Art*. Cambridge, Mass.: Harvard University Press, 1988.

Coulon, Christian. *Le Marabout et le Prince: Islam et pourvoir au Sénégal*. Paris: Pedone, 1981.

Dabla, Séwanou. *Nouvelles écritures africaines: Romanciers de la seconde génération*. Paris: Éditions L'Harmattan, 1986.

Danner, Victor, and Martin Lings. "Preface." In Ibn 'Ata'illah's *Sufi Aphorisms (Kitab al-Hikam)*. Leiden: E. J. Brill, 1973. Pp. xi–xiii.

Dathorne, O. R. *African Literature in the Twentieth Century*, Minneapolis: University of Minnesota, 1974.

Decraene, Philippe. "Un Nègre à part entière." *Le Monde*, Supplément au numéro 7386, October 12, 1968: 1.

Delafosse, Maurice. *Les nègres*. Paris: Editions Rieder, 1927.

———. *Les civilisations negro-africaines*. Paris: Librairie Stock, 1925.

———. *L'ame negre*. Paris: Payot, 1922.

———. *Les noirs de l'Afrique*. Paris: Payot, 1922.

de Man, Paul. *Rhetoric of Romanticism*. New York: Columbia University Press, 1984.

de Maupassant, Guy. "Allouma," *Short Stories of the Tragedy and Comedy of Life*, Vol. 4. New York and London: M. Walter Dunne, 1903.

Derrida, Jacques. *Dissemination*. Trans. by Barbara Johnson. Chicago: University of Chicago Press, 1981.

———. *Of Grammatology*. Trans. by Gayatri Chakravorty Spivak. Baltimore: Johns Hopkins University Press, 1974.

Devlin, Tim. "Echoes of Graham Greene Halt Prizewinning Book." *The Times* (London), May 5, 1972: 1.

Dieterlen, Germaine. *Le Titre d'honneur des Arou: Dogon, Mali*. Paris: Société des Africanistes, 1982.

Dunton, Chris. "'Wheyting Be Dat?' The Treatment of Homosexuality in African Literature." *Research in African Literature* Vol. 20, No. 3 (Fall 1989): 422–448.

Eagleton, Terry. *Literary Theory*. Oxford: Blackwell, 1983.

Egejuru, Phanuel Akubueze. *Towards African Literary Independence: A Dialogue with Contemporary African Writers*. Westport, Conn.: Greenwood Press, 1980.

Elaho, Raymond O. "Le Devoir d'amour dans le devoir de violence de Yambo Ouologuem." *L'Afrique littéraire et artistique*, Vol. 56 (1979): 65–69.

Erickson, John. "Africa Reborn: Emergence from Myth, Yambo Ouologuem: *Le Devoir de violence*." In *Nommo: African Fiction in French South of the Sahara*. York, S.C.: French Literature Publications, 1979.

Es-Sa'di, Abderrahman ben Abdallah ben 'Imran ben 'Amir. *Tarîkh es-Soudan*. Trans. by O. Houdas. Paris: École des Languages Orientales Vivants, 1898–1900; 2nd ed., Paris: Adrien-Maisonneuve, 1964.

Esin, Emel. *Mecca the Blessed/Madinah the Radiant*. New York: Crown Publishers, 1963.

Faik, Sully. "Yambo Ouologuem: *Le Devoir de violence*, Prix Renaudot 1968." *Congo-Afrique*, Vol. 9, No. 32 (1969): 91–101.

Fanon, Frantz. *Black Skin, White Masks*. Trans. by Charles Lam Markmann. New York: Grove Weidenfeld, 1968.

———. *Les Damnés de la terre*, Paris: Maspero, 1973.

———. *Peau Noir, Masques Blancs*. Paris: Seuil, 1952.

———. *The Wretched of the Earth*. Trans. by Constance Farrington. New York: Grove Press, 1963.

Fatunde, Tunde. "Images of Working People in Two African Novels: Ouologuem and Iyayi," *Marxism and African Literature*, Georg M. Gugelberger (ed.). Trenton, N.J.: African World Press, 1985. Pp. 110–117.

Fischer, Michael M. J., and Mehdi Abedi. *Debating Muslims: Cultural Dialogues in Postmodernity and Tradition*. Madison: University of Wisconsin Press, 1990.

Flamand, Paul. "Letter to the Editor." *Research in African Literatures*, Vol. 2, No. 2 (1971): 116.

Fleischmann, Ulrich. "Violence dans l'histoire et dans l'utopie: Evolution d'un theme dans le roman africain." *Franzosisch-Heute* (Frankfurt am Main, Germany) No. 2 (June 1982): 93–103.

Foucault, Michel. "La Bibliothèque fantastique." In *Travail de Flaubert*. Paris: Le Seuil, Points, 1983.

Françon, André. *La Propriété littéraire et artistique*. Paris: PUF, 1970.

Frazer, Robert. "*Two Thousand Seasons*: Literary Ancestry and Text." In *Critical Perspectives on Ayi Kwei Armah,* Derek Weight (ed.). Washington, D.C.: Three Continents Press, 1992. Pp. 298–314.

Frobenius, Leo. *Histoire de la civilisation africaine*. Traduit par H. Back et D. Ermont. Paris: Gallimard, 1936.

Fuglestad, Finn. *A History of Niger: 1850–1960*. Cambridge: Cambridge University Press, 1983.

Galey, Matthieu. "Un grand roman africain." *Le Monde*, Supplement au numéro 7386, 12 Octobre: i.

Gardet, Louis. *La Cité musulmane, vie sociale et politique*. Paris: Librairie J. Vrin, 1954.

Geertz, Clifford. *Islam Observed*. Chicago: University of Chicago Press, 1968.

Gérard, Albert. "Littérature francophone d'Afrique: Le temps de la releve." *Revue Nouvelle*, Vol. 49 (1969): 198–204.

———. "Historical Origins and Literary Destiny of Negritude," *Diogenes*, No. 48 (1964): 14–38.

Graham, William A. "Qur'an as Spoken Word: An Islamic Contribution to the Understanding of Scripture." In *Approaches to Islam in Religious Studies*, Richard C. Martin (ed.). Tucson: University of Arizona Press, 1985. Pp. 23–40.

Greene, Graham. *It's a Battlefield*. London: Heinemann, 1934.

Habermas, Jürgen. *The Philosophical Discourse of Modernity*. Cambridge, Mass.: MIT Press, 1991.

Hale, Thomas. *Scribe, Griot, and Novelist: Narrative Interpreters of hte Songhay Empire*. Gainesville: University of Florida Press, 1990.

Handelman, Susan A. *The Slayers of Moses: The Emergence of Rabbinic Interpretation in Modern Literary Theory*. Albany, N.Y.: SUNY Press, 1982.

Harrison, Christopher. *France and Islam in West Africa: 1860–1960*. Cambridge: Cambridge University Press, 1988.

Harrow, Kenneth. "Camara Laye, Cheikh Hamidou Kane, and Tayeb Salib: Three Sufi Authors." In *Faces of Islam in African Literature,* Kenneth W. Harrow (ed.). Portsmouth, N.H.: Heinemann Educational Books, 1991. Pp. 261–297.

———. “Introduction: Islam(s) in African Literature.” In *Faces of Islam in African Literature*, Kenneth W. Harrow (ed.). Portsmouth, N.H.: Heinemann Educational Books, 1991. Pp. 3–20.

Highet, Gilbert. *The Anatomy of Satire*. Princeton: Princeton University Press, 1962.

Huggan, Graham. “Anthropology and Other Frauds.” *Comparative Literature*, Vol. 46, No. 2 (Spring 1994): 113–128.

Hunwick, John O. *Shari'a in Songhay: The Replies of al-Maghili to the Questions of Askia al-Hajj Muhammad*. New York: Oxford Univerity Press, 1985.

Ibn ‘Abbad of Ronda. *Ibn ‘Abbad of Ronda: Letters on the Sufi Path*, trans. by John Renard. New York: Paulist Press, 1986.

Ibn ‘Ata'illah. *Sufi Aphorisms* (*Kitab al-Hikam*). Leiden: E. J. Brill, 1973.

“An Interview With Yambo Ouologuem.” *Journal of New African Literature and the Arts*, Vols. 9–10 (Winter/Spring 1971): 134–138.

“Interview: Yambo Ouologuem.” *Cultural Events in Africa*, No. 61 (1969): 2.

Irele, Abiola. *The African Experience in Literature and Ideology*. Bloomington: Indiana University Press, 1990.

———. “Negritude and Black Cultural Nationalism.” *Journal of Modern African Studies*, Vol. 4 (1965): 321–348.

———. “Negritude Literature and Ideology,” *Journal of Modern African Studies*, Vol. 4 (1965): 499–526.

Iyayi, Festus. *Violence*. London: Longman, Drumbeat, 1979.

Jackson, Julian. “De Gaulle and May 1968.” In *De Gaulle and Twentieth Century France*. John Horne and Hugh Gough (eds.). London: Edward Arnold, 1994. Pp. 125–146.

Jahn, Janheinz. *Muntu: An Outline of the New African Culture*. New York: Grove Press, 1961.

Johnson, Lemuel. *The Devil, the Gargoyle, and the Buffoon: The Negro as Metaphor in Western Literature*. Port Washington, N.Y.: Kennikat Press, 1969.

Jolles, A. *Formes Simples*. Paris: Le Seuil, 1972.

Julien, Eileen. “Rape, Repression, and Narrative Form in *Le Devoir de violence* and *La Vie et demie*.” In *Rape and Representation*, Lynn A. Higgins and Brenda R. Silver (ed.). New York: Columbia University Press, 1991. Pp. 160–181.

Kaba, Lansine. “The Pen, the Sword, and the Crown: Islam and Revolution in Songhay Reconsidered: 1464–1493.” *Journal of African History*, Vol. 25 (1984): 241–256.

Kamal, Ahmad. *The Sacred Journey: Being Pilgrimage to Makkah*. New York: Duell, Sloan, and Pearce, 1961.

Kane, Mohamadou. “Roman africain et traditions,” Diss., University of Lille, 1978.

———. “Sur les ‘formes traditionnelles’ du roman africain.” *Revue de littérature comparée*, Nos. 3–4 (July-December 1974): 536–568.

Kâti, Mahmoud. *Tarîkh el-Fettâch ou chronique du chercheur pour servir à l'histoire des villes, des armées et des principaux personnages du Tekrour*. Trans. by O. Houdas and M. Delafosse. Paris: Ernest Leroux, 1913.

Kaufmann, Francine. “Compte-rendu de la soutenance,” *Le Monde*, May 14, 1976.

Kerbrat-Orecchioni, C. *L'énonciation de la subjectivité dans le langage*. Paris: Colin, 1980.

Kersteloot, Lylian. *Les Ecrivains noirs de langue française: Naissance d'une littérature*. Brussels: Editions de l'Université de Bruxelles, 1963.

Khatibi, Abdelkebir. *Maghreb pluriel.* Paris: Éditions Denoël, 1983.

Kohn, Ingeborg M. "Satire in African Letters: Black Appraisals of White Ethnologists in the Works of Ferdinand Oyono, Tchicaya U'Tam'si and Yambo Ouologuem." *Studies in Twentieth Century Literature*, Vol. 4, No. 2 (Spring 1980): 213–227.

Kuehl, Linda. "Yambo Ouologuem on Violence, Truth, and Black History." *Commonweal,* June 11, 1971: 311–314.

K. W. (Kaye Whiteman) "In Defence of Yambo Ouologuem." *West Africa*, No. 2875, July 21, 1972: 939–941.

Lack, Roland-François. "'La littérature de Martial': Plagiarism as Figure in Sade, Lautréamont, Ouologuem, and Sony Labou Tansi." *Romantic Review*, Vol. 86, No. 4 (1995): 681–696.

Lang, George. "Text, Identity, and Difference: Yambo Ouologuem's *Le Devoir de violence* and Ayi Kwei Armah's *Two Thousand Seasons.*" *Comparative Literature Studies,* Vol. 24, No. 4 (1987): 387–402.

———. "Through a Prism Darkly: 'Orientalism' in European-Language African Writing." In *Faces of Islam in African Literature*, Kenneth W. Harrow (ed.). Portsmouth, N.H.: Heinemann Educational Books, 1991. Pp. 299–311.

Lanotte, Jacques. "Un Renaudot africain: *Le Devoir de violence.*" *Culture et Développement*, Vol. 1 (1969): 670–676.

Le Carvennec, Ernest. "La Prise du récit dans *Le Devoir de violence* de Yambo Ouologuem." In *Récit et historie*, Jean Bessière (ed.). Paris: Presses Universitaires de France, 1984: 159–175.

Leclech, G. "Ouologuem n'emprunte qu'aux riches." *Le Figaro Littéraire*, Vol. 1356, 13 mai 1972: 15.

Lentriccia, Frank. *After the New Criticism.* Chicago: University of Chicago Press, 1980.

Leusse, Hubert de. *Afrique Occidentale: Heurs et malheurs d'une rencontre: Les romanciers du pay noir.* Paris: Ed. de l'Orante, 1971.

Lings, Martin. *What Is Sufism?* Berkeley and Los Angeles: University of California Press, 1975.

Lukács, Georg. *The Theory of the Novel.* Trans. by Anna Bostock. London: Merlin Press, 1971.

Lusebrink, Hans-Jurgen. "De l'incontournabilité de la fiction dans la connaisance historique: Questionnements theoriques à partir de romans historiques contemporains d'Alejo Carpentier, de "Yambo Ouologuem et d'Ousmane Sembene." *Neohelicon: Acta Comparationis Litterarum Universarum* (Amsterdam: The Netherlands), Vol. 16, No. 2 (1989): 107–128.

Maes-Jelinek, Hena. "Yambo Ouologuem." *African Literature Today*, Vol. 164 (1970): 54–55.

Maiangwa, Yusufu. "The Duty of Violence in Yambo Ouologuem's *Bound to Violence.*" In *New West African Literature*, Kolawole Obunbesan (ed.). London: Heinemann, 1979. Pp. 70–79.

Maingueneau, D. *Initiation aux méthods de l'analyse du discours.* Paris: Hachette Université, 1976.

Makward, Edris. "Women, Tradition, and Religion in Sembène Ousmane's Work." In *Faces of Islam in African Literature*, ed. Kenneth W. Harrow (ed.). Portsmouth, N.H.: Heinemann Educational Books, 1991: Pp. 187–200.

Martin, Brad G. *Muslim Brotherhoods in Nineteenth-Century Africa.* Cambridge: Cambridge University Press, 1976.

Maupassant, Guy de. *Boule de Suif.* Paris: Societe d'Editions Litteraires et Artistiques, 1902.

Mbelolo, J. Mpiku ya. "From One Mystification to Another: 'Négritude' and 'Négraille' in *Le Devoir de violence*." *Review of National Literatures* Vol. 2, no. 2 (Fall 1971): 124–147.

McDonald, Robert. "*Bound to Violence*: A case of plagiarism." *Transition,* Vol. 41 (1972): 67–68.

Memmi, Albert. *Dependence: A Sketch for a Portrait of the Dependent.* Trans. by Philip A. Facey. Boston: Beacon Press, 1984.

Miller, Christopher L. *Blank Darkness: Africanist Discourse in French.* Chicago: University of Chicago Press, 1985. Pp. 216–245.

———. *Theories of Africans: Francophone Literature and Anthropology in Africa.* Chicago: University of Chicago Press, 1990.

———. "Trait d'union: Injunction and Dismemberment in Yambo Ouologuem's *Le Devoir de violence*." *L'Ésprit Createur,* Vol. 23, No. 4 (Winter 1983): 62–73.

Moore, Gerald. "The Debate on Existence in African Literature," *Présence Africaine*, Vol. 81 (1972).

———. "Towards Realism in French African Writing," *Journal of Modern African Studies*, Vol. 1 (1963): 61–73.

Mouralis, Bernard. "Une Carrefour d'écritures: *Le Devoir de violence* by Yambo Ouologuem," *Recherches et Travaux,* "Littératures africaines d'écriture française," University of Grenoble, UER de Lettres, Bulletin No. 27 (1984): 75–92.

———. "Littératures africaines d'écriture française." Université de Grenoble, UER de Lettres, Bulletin No. 27, 1984. Pp. 75–92.

———. "La réception du roman sahélien par la critique de langue française." Paris III, La Sorbonne Nouvelle, 1981.

Mudimbe, Valentin. *Invention of Africa.* Chicago: University of Chicago Press, 1988.

Nelson, Kristina. *The Art of Reciting the Qur'an.* Austin: University of Texas Press, 1985.

Ngaté, Jonathan. *Francophone African Fiction: Reading a Literary Tradition.* Trenton, N.J.: Africa World Press, 1988.

Nicholls, J. A. "Towards a Camusian Reading of *Le Devoir de violence*." *Australian Journal of French Studies,* Vol. 28, No. 2 (May-August 1991): 211–219.

Nietzsche, Friedrich. *Basic Writings of Nietzsche.* New York: Random House, 1968.

Nwoga, Donatus I. "Plagiarism and Authentic Creativity in West Africa." *Research in African Literature,* Vol. 6, No. 1 (1975): 32–39.

Obiechina, E. N. "*Bound to Violence*" (review). *Okike: An African Journal of New Writing*, Vol. 1, No. 3, 1972: 53.

Ohaegbu, A. E. "An Approach to Ouologuem's *Le Devoir de violence*." *African Literature Today,* Vol. 10 (1979): 124–133.

Olivier de Sardan, Jean-Pierre. *Concepts et Conceptions songhay-zarma.* Paris: Nubia, 1982.

Olney, James. *Tell Me Africa: An Approach to African Literature.* Princeton: Princeton University Press, 1973.

Oloruntimehin, B. O. *The Segu Tukulor Empire.* London: Longman Group Limited, 1972.

Ouologuem, Yambo. *Bound to Violence.* Trans. by Ralph Mannheim London: Heinemann Educational Books, 1971. New York: Harcourt, Brace, Jovanovich, 1971.

———. "La conscience malheureuse." *Nouvelle poésie négro-africaine, Poésie I*, Nos. 43–45 (January-June 1976): 124.
———. *Le Devoir de violence*. Paris: Éditions du Seuil, 1968.
———. *Lettre à la France nègre*. Paris: Éditions Edmond Nalis, 1968.
——— (under the pseudonym Utto Rodolph). *Les Milles et une bibles de sexe*. Paris: Editions du Dauphin, 1969.
———. "A Mon Mari" *Presence Africaine*, Vol. 57 (1966): 95.
———. "Le Devoir de violence." *Figaro litléraire*, 10 June 1972.
Parrinder, Geoffrey. *Jesus in the Qur'an*. New York: Oxford University Press, 1977.
Philipson, Robert. "Chess and Sex in *Le Devoir de violence*," *Callaloo: A Journal of African-American and African Arts and Letters*, Vol. 12, No. 1 (Winter 1989): 216–232.
Piégay-Gros, Nathalie. *Introduction à l'intertextualité*. Paris: Dunod, 1996.
Prescott, Peter S. "Wanderers in Disaster." *Newsweek*, March 29, 1971: 100.
Qazi, M. A. *A Concise Dictionary of Islamic Terms*. Chicago: Qazi Publications, 1979.
Randall, Marilyn. "Appropriate(d) Discourse: Plagiarism and Decolonization." *New Literary History: A Journal of Theory and Interpretation*, Vol. 22, No. 3 (Summer 1991): 525–541.
———. "Le Presuppose d'originalité et l'art du plagiat: Lecture pragmatique." *Voix et Images: Littérature Quebecoise*, Vol. 15, No. 2 (Winter 1990): 196–208.
Riedel, Alfredo. *Cultura negro africana moderna*. Trieste: Edizioni Umana, 1973.
Rimbaud, Arthur. *Une Saison en enfer*. Paris: Coll. Poésie/Gallimard, 1984.
Robinson, David. "An Approach to Islam in West African History." In *Faces of Islam in African Literature*, Kenneth W. Harrow (ed.). Portsmouth, N.H.: Heinemann Educational Books, 1991: Pp. 107–130.
———. *The Holy War of Umar Tall*. New York: Oxford University Press, 1985.
Rushdie, Salman. *The Satanic Verses*. New York: Viking, 1988.
Rutimirwa, Alec. "A Case of Plagiarism." *Transition*, Vol. 42 (1973): 8–9.
al-'Sadi, 'Abd al-Rahman ibn 'Abd Allah. *Tarîkh es-Soudan*, edit. par O. Houdas, avec la collaboration de Edm. Benoist. Paris: E. Leroux, 1898–1900.
Said, Edward. *The World, the Text and the Critic*. Cambridge: Harvard University Press, 1983.
Saint-Martin, Yves. "Un fils d'El Hadj Omar: Agibou, roi du Dinguiray et du Macina (1843?–1907?)." *Cahier d'Études Africaines*, Vol. 8 (1968).
Schikora, Rosemary G. "Outfoxing the Fox: Game Strategy in *Le Devoir de violence*." *Perspectives on Contemporary Literature*, No. 6 (1980): 72–79.
Schwarz-Bart, André. *Le Dernier des justes*. Paris: Editions du Seuil, 1959.
Sellin, Eric. "Book Review: *Bound to Violence*," *French Review* 43, no. 1 (October 1969): 64–68.
———. "African Art: Compositional vs. Modal Esthetics." *Yale Review*, Vol. 59, No. 2 (Winter 1970): 215–227.
———. "Ouologuem's Blueprint for *Le Devoir de violence*." *Research in African Literature*, Vol. 2, No. 2 (1971): 117–120.
———. "Ouologuem, Kourouma, et le nouveau roman africain." In *Littératures ultramarines de langue française: Genèse et jeunesse*, Thomas H. Geno and Roy Julow (eds.). Sherbrooke, Quebec: Naaman, 1974. Pp. 35–50.
———. "The Unknown Voice of Yambo Ouologuem." *Yale French Studies*, Vol. 53 (1976): 137–162.

Semujanga, Josias. "Le Genre comme procès axiologigue et esthetique: Élements pour l'enseignment du roman africain." *Tangence*, Vol. 49 (December 1995): 94–111.

———. "De l'histoire à sa metaphore dans *Le Devoir de violence* de Yambo Ouologuem." *Études Françaises* (Montreal, Canada), Vol. 31, No. 1 (Summer 1995): 71–83.

Scott, Walter Sir. *Minstrelsy of the Scottish Border, with his introductions, additions, and notes*. Endinburgh: A. & C. Black, 1873.

Shah, Indries. *The Elephant in the Dark: Christianity, Islam, and the Sufis*. London: Octagon Press, 1974.

Sharif, M. M. *A History of Muslim Philosophy, Volume II*. Wiesbaden: Otto Harrassowitz, 1966.

Skurnik, Walter A. E. "Léopold Sédar Senghor and African Socialism." *Journal of Modern African Studies*, Vol. 3 (1965), 349–450.

Sklar, Richard L. "The Colonial Imprint on African Political Thought." *African Independence: The First Twenty-Five Years,* Gwendolyn M. Carter and Patrick O'Meara (eds.). Bloomington: Indiana University Press, 1985. 1–30.

Slemon, Stephen. "Post-Colonial Allegory and the Transformation of History." *Journal of Commonwealth Literature*. Vol. 23, No. 1 (1988): 157–181.

"Something *New* Out of Africa?" *Times Literary Supplement*, May 5, 1972: 525.

Songolo, Aliko. "Fiction et Subversion: *Le Devoir de violence*." *Présence Africaine,* Vol. 120 (1981): 17–34.

———. "The Writer, The Audience and the Critic's Responsibility: The Case of *Bound to Violence*." In *Artist and Audience: African Literature as a Shared Experience*, Richard Priebe and Thomas A. Hale (eds.). Washington, D.C.: Three Continents Press, 1979. Pp. 126–140.

Soyinka, Wole. *Myth, Literature, and the African World*. Cambridge: Cambridge University Press, 1976. Pp. 104–106.

Spivak, Gayatri Chakravorty. *In Other Worlds: Essays in Cultural Politics*. New York: Routledge, 1988.

Strobbe, Nicolas. "Instituting the Imaginary Subject Colonial: *Men in the Sun* and *Bound to Violence*." *Southern Review: Literary and Interdisciplinary Essays* (Churchhill, Victoria, Australia [SoRA]), Vol. 27, No. 4 (December 1994): 459–474.

Suret-Canale, J. *Afrique Noire*, Vol. 1, Paris: Éditions Sociales, 1958.

Tassou, Kazaro. "*Le Devoir de violence* face au public." Chapter 3, "La réception du roman sahélien par la critique de langue française," thèse de III cycle, Paris III, La Sorbonne Nouvelle, 1991. Pp. 222–278.

Thibaudeau, J. "Le roman actuel: Flaubert et Lautrémont," In *Interventions: Socialisme, avant-garde, littérature*. Paris: Éditions Sociales, 1972. Pp. 16–19.

Torrey, Charles Cutler. *The Jewish Foundation of Islam*. New York: Ktav Publishing House, 1967.

Trimingham, J. Spencer. *A History of Islam in West Africa*. London, Glasgow, and New York: Oxford University Press, 1962.

Trotsky, Leon. *Literature and Revolution*. New York: Monthly Review Press, 1974.

United States Congress, House Committee on Foreign Affairs, Subcommittee on Human Rights and International Organizations. *Human Rights in the Maghreb and Mauritania*, June 19, 1991. Washington, D.C.: U.S. Government Printing Office, 1991.

"Vient de paraître." *Le Monde* (Supplément au numéro 7344), 24 août 1968: ii.

Vignal, Daniel. "L'homophilie dans le roman négro-africain d'expression anglaise et française." *Peuples Noirs, Peuples Africains,* Vol. 33 (May-June 1983): 63–81.

Watkins, Mel. "Talk with Yambo Ouoluguem," *New York Times Book Review,* March 7, 1971, p. 7.

Welch, Claude E., Jr. "Yambo Ouologuem and His Times: Aspects of Literature of Violence." In *Commentaries on a Creative Encounter: Proceedings of a Conference on the Culture and Literature of Francophone Africa.* Albany: African-American Institute, 1988. Pp. 47–51.

Wise, Christopher. "In Search of Yambo Ouologuem." *Research in African Literature,* Vol. 29, No. 2 (Summer 1998): 159–182.

———. "Qur'anic Hermeneutics, Sufism, and *Le Devoir de violence*: Yambo Ouologuem as Marabout Novelist." *Religion and Literature,* Vol. 28, No. 1 (Spring 1996): 85–112.

———. "Yambo Ouologuem dans le postmoderne: Les débats littéraires sur *Le Devoir de violence* depuis 1985." *Littératures du Sahel,* Joseph Paré, Sanou Salaka, and Christopher Wise (eds.). Bellingham, Wash.: CamNexus/Kola Tree Press, 1998. Pp. 117–122.

Woddis, Jack. *New Theories of Revolution.* New York: International Publishers, 1972.

Wolitz, Seth I. "L'Art du plagiat, ou une brève défense de Ouologuem." *Research in African Literature,* Vol. 4, No. 1 (Spring 1973): 130–134.

Wright, Derek. "Orality in the African Historical Novel: Yambo Ouologuem's *Bound to Violence* and Ayi Kwei Armah's *Two Thousand Seasons.*" *Journal of Commonwealth Literature,* Vol. 23, No. 1 (1988): 90–101.

Zhang, Longxi. *The Tao and the Logos: Literary Hermeneutics, East and West.* Durham, N.C.: Duke University Press, 1992.

Zoghby, Samir M. "Blacks and Arabs: Past and Present." *Current Bibliography on African Affairs,* Vol. 3, No. 5 (May 1970): 5–22.

Zupancic, Metka. "Problem plagiata pri Yambu Ouologuemu." In *Bajt Drago,* Frane Jerman and Janko Moder (eds.). Iz zgodovine prevajanja na Slovenskem. Ljubljana: Drustvo slovenskih knjizevnih prevajalcev, 1982. Pp. 385–391.

The Contributors

KWAME ANTHONY APPIAH teaches at Harvard University. He is the author of *In My Father's House: Africa in the Philosophy of Culture.*

CHRISTIANE CHAULET-ACHOUR teaches at the University of Caen in France. She has written and edited many studies of African literature, including *Myriam Ben* and *Contes algériens.*

CHRIS DUNTON teaches at the University of the North-West in South Africa. He has written numerous articles on African literature.

TUNDE FATUNDE teaches at the University of Ife, Nigeria. He is the author of numerous plays and works of literary criticism.

THOMAS A. HALE teaches African literature in the Departments of French and Comparative Literature at the Pennsylvania State University. Past president of the African Literature Association, he was also a Fulbright senior lecturer at the University of Niamey in Niger. He is the author of *Scribe, Griot, Novelist: Narrative Interpreters of the Songhay Empire.*

CHRISTOPHER L. MILLER teaches in the Department of French and Program in African and African-American Studies at Yale University. He is the author of *Blank Darkness: Africanist Discourse in French and Theories of Africans: Francophone Literature and Anthropology in Africa.*

CAROLINE A. MOHSEN teaches at Pennsylvania State University in the Department of Comparative Literature.

J. MBELOLO YA MPIKU lives in the Democratic Republic of the Congo.

ERIC SELLIN teaches African literatures at Temple University in Philadelphia. He has written many studies on African literature.

WOLE SOYINKA presently teaches at Emory University in Atlanta, Georgia. He is the author of numerous books and a previous winner of the Nobel Prize in literature.

ANN ELIZABETH WILLEY teaches African Literatures at the University of Louisville in Kentucky. She is presently a Fulbright senior lecturer at the University of Ouagadougou in Burkina Faso.

CHRISTOPHER WISE teaches global literatures at Western Washington University in Bellingham. In 1996–1997, he was a Fulbright senior lecturer at the University of Ouagadougou in Burkina Faso.

Index

About the Book

From the appearance of *Bound to Violence* in the late 1960s, Yambo Ouologuem has been one of Africa's most controversial writers. For some critics, the young Malian signaled an entirely new direction for African letters: a fiercely courageous postindependence literature. For others, his novel revealed too much, bringing to light horrors many preferred to ignore. Today Ouologuem is credited with delivering the final death-blow to Senghorian négritude, thus clearing the way for a more honest literature divested of the longing for a false African past.

This book gathers the most important essays on Ouologuem from critics on three continents. Wise also includes his recent interviews with the reclusive author and a companion essay on Ouologuem's present life among the Tidjaniya Muslims of northern Mali.

Christopher Wise is assistant professor of English at Western Washington University, where he teaches global literary studies. His research interests focus on Sahelian literature and postcolonial theory.